UNTAMED

VAMPIRE AWAKENINGS
BOOK 3

BRENDA K DAVIES

Untamed
Vampire Awakenings Book 3

Cover Art and Design: Christian Bentulan
Formatting: Jamie Davis

To all the fans, you are all amazing and without you, I couldn't do any of this. To my husband for always being there. To Leslie for her continued hard work and to ebook launch for their amazing cover work!

CHAPTER ONE

ETHAN FELT like he was trying to squeeze himself into a space the size of a high school locker as he kept his arms close to his sides in an attempt to avoid bumping into anyone around him. It was bad enough hearing the human's heartbeats and smelling the blood flowing through their veins, but the thought of touching one of them made his skin crawl.

He'd been crazy to make this trip though he'd fed almost double what he normally did before leaving home to curb the ever-present hunger within him. Being this close to so many humans strained his control and tried his patience. That nagging voice inside him, the one wanting to taste every single one of these people, begged to be obeyed. He was afraid of what might happen if he didn't get away from this crowd soon.

Sliding his sunglasses into place, he stepped out of the airport and into the bright light of the day. The heat was like a slap in the face after the cool air inside the airport, and it caused him to inhale sharply. Adjusting the bag in his hand, he scanned the crowd of people swarming around him. *Ants*, he thought. Annoying ants he would prefer to stomp, but he gritted his teeth and concentrated on keeping his desire to become a blood-sucking terminator under control. He'd never been a fan of people; however, being enclosed within three different flying tin cans for almost a day, had frayed his nerves and shortened his already low tolerance for the creatures.

He couldn't believe he'd let Isabelle talk him into this, but getting away from his siblings for a month and vacationing in paradise had seemed a lot more appealing before he stepped onto the first airplane. He glanced around the crowd again, searching for two familiar dark heads, but he didn't see them amongst the crush of people.

Inhaling, he took in the familiar and pleasant aroma of the tangy ocean air. After a shower, a change of clothes, some blood, and a few drinks, he'd be back to looking forward to spending the next month with his sister and brother-in-law in Bermuda again.

He stepped away from a young girl who brushed his arm and smiled flirtatiously at him. Normally, he would at least return the smile; now he stared relentlessly back until she blushed and hurried away. The last thing he needed was some human thinking was interested in them. He may have embarrassed the girl, but she didn't know just how close he was to the edge, how close she'd come to being the one who finally eased the insistent call for blood flowing through his system.

A small squeal alerted him to Isabelle before he spotted her. He turned just in time to catch her as she flung herself into his arms. A small grunt escaped him, but he dropped his bag and wrapped his arm around her waist as she laughed loudly. "I'm so glad you came!" she cried.

Relief filled him as he lifted her off the ground and hugged her back. It had been almost six months since she and Stefan left home, a week after their bond was completed. Until now, he hadn't realized just how much he'd missed her, even if she was a pain in his ass.

"I'm glad I did too," he replied honestly as he placed her back on the ground.

Her violet eyes twinkled in the sunlight shining on her as she grinned up at him. The golden highlights in her deep brown hair were more vibrant and blonder than the last time he'd seen her. She was tanner too, and freckles now dotted the bridge of her slender nose.

"Did you have a good flight?" she asked.

"A few of them." He wasn't about to tell her he'd been tempted to eat the tourists more than a few times during the trip. He loved Issy, she was his best friend and the sibling he was closest to, but there were things he didn't share, not even with her.

She laughed as she took a step back from him. Her eyes focused on his right arm and she slapped her hand against the tattoo there. "What is this?"

"That, dear sis, is what most refer to as a tattoo," he teased.

She rolled her eyes at him. "I know that, but when did you get it?"

"Three months ago."

"Why? You've never shown an interest in tattoos before."

Ethan glanced at the intricate black flames curling up from his wrist to the middle of his bicep. A black phoenix, on his upper bicep, rose from the top of the flames with its wings spread wide. He wasn't about to tell her the real reason he'd gotten the tattoo, so he just shrugged and retrieved his bag. "Boredom," he answered absently.

"Boredom?" she inquired in a disbelieving tone.

"What can I say? I've had no one to entertain me since you left home."

His words had the effect he'd been hoping for as she

laughed and slipped her arm through his. "I'm sure you've had plenty of people keeping you entertained with the mob living there."

"Yes, but no one quite as fun as you."

"I *do* have to agree with that," she said and flashed a smile. "You should see the house Stefan rented for us, it's beautiful!"

His gaze traveled past her to the large and powerful vampire standing beyond her shoulder. Stefan's onyx eyes focused on Isabelle before he turned to look at Ethan. His black hair curled around his face, easing the austerity of his high cheekbones and the narrow bridge of his nose. Ethan was never quite sure what to make of the guy; he'd always been a bit arrogant, and more than a little overprotective when it came to Isabelle. But he made Isabelle happy, and in the end, that was the most important thing.

"Stefan," he greeted.

"Ethan." Stefan smiled at him as he extended his hand. "It's good to see you."

"You also." Ethan realized those words were true as they shook hands. Stefan had become easier going and more approachable after he completed his bond with Isabelle, but Ethan had never really considered him a friend. He was family though.

"Is this all you have for luggage?" Isabelle inquired.

Ethan turned his attention back to his sister. "I travel light."

"Apparently. Too bad mom and dad couldn't come with you." He was used to her abrupt changes in conversation, so he wasn't thrown off by it now.

"They have enough going on with that devious horde their raising."

Isabelle laughed as she tugged him into the crowd. "I can't wait to see them again. I've missed them and everyone else *so* much."

"They've missed you too," he told her as Stefan parted the crowd before them. "I know they're looking forward to you returning home next month."

"Me too, but we've had an amazing trip. I loved Rome; I think it was my favorite. You *have* to see it one day. Maybe the next time we go, you can come with us. Australia too, you would *love* it there. Aiden would probably get himself killed swimming with the sharks, but I'm pretty sure that's where he belongs."

"You think he belongs in Australia or inside a shark?" Ethan was unable to keep the humor from his voice as he asked the question.

"Australia," she said with a laugh. "But there were a few times I would have liked to feed him to a shark."

"Me too," Ethan agreed.

Ethan couldn't help but smile as she started to ramble on again about all the places she and Stefan had visited over the last six months. It amazed him how much she'd changed from the girl who once never left home because she was determined not to find her mate. That girl had been content with her life, but the woman on his arm radiated joy and seemed to glow as she bounced along beside him.

Stefan stopped beside a blue Jeep and opened the passenger side door. Isabelle released his arm, kissed Stefan on the cheek, and jumped into the passenger seat. Stefan smiled at her as he closed her door and walked around to open the hatch door. They stepped aside as the door swung out toward them.

"She's missed you guys," Stefan told him as Ethan placed his bag inside.

"We've missed her too," Ethan said as he closed the door. "She seems happy though."

"She is, but she became a lot happier after you agreed to

join us here. She can't wait for Ian and Aiden to arrive in two weeks."

"You're in for some trouble then," Ethan told him with a grin.

"Looking forward to it."

Ethan realized Stefan seemed to mean that. He'd never been entirely sure what Stefan thought about all of them. It was obvious how he felt about Isabelle, but he'd always thought Stefan found them to be the annoying family unit he would have to put up with to be with Issy. He was beginning to think maybe he'd misjudged him.

Ethan walked around the side of the SUV and opened the back door. Isabelle turned in the front seat, propped her hands on the shoulder of the chair, and continued talking about their travels without missing a beat. Stefan pulled onto the road and drove cautiously down the clustered streets winding through the island.

Ethan sat back in his seat to watch all the yellow, blue, orange, and green colored houses they passed. People walked the streets and rode their bikes down the sidewalks as they explored the sites or went about their day. The aqua-colored ocean shimmered in and out between the buildings lining the waterfront as they drove onward. Boats of all makes and sizes dipped and swayed on the calm sea. The people strolling the beach, splashing in the water or fishing, reminded him of a postcard of paradise.

He'd never been more than a couple of hundred miles away from home; being here now seemed almost unreal as he took in the pink sandy beaches and the numerous bikini-clad bodies. He may not enjoy being near the humans in those suits, but he wasn't above admiring the bodies wearing them.

The further they drove, the more into vacation mode he became. After a shower, he might check out one of these beaches. He wasn't like Ian and Aiden, he didn't chase after girls or go to clubs often, but he was going to be here for a few weeks, and the idea of a vacation hook-up was appealing. This trip was already out of character for him; he might as well completely enjoy himself while here. He just hoped there was another sane, female vampire on the island, but then again, if she wasn't a killer then he didn't care if she was entirely sane.

The last woman he was seeing hadn't been the type he would bring home to his mom, or anywhere near his family for that matter. In fact, she'd treaded the fine line between becoming a brutal killer and maintaining her control as a vampire. He was ashamed by the fact he completely understood how she felt, that he found the line exciting too, and enjoyed walking it with her. Hell, he'd walked it his entire life, and finally found someone who understood him and the madness lurking just beneath the surface. Not to mention the wildness within her was something irresistible and fascinating to him in bed.

Until the day she'd crossed the line. His murderous urges were something he was growing tired of struggling with, and though he was tempted to go over the edge with her, and finally give into the clamoring demands of his body for blood and death, he knew he couldn't. He had his family to think of, his siblings would know if he killed someone, and he couldn't bring himself to let them down in such a way. He was the one they all looked up to even though he was the one who deserved their admiration the least.

If they knew what he truly was, there would be no admiration from them; there would only be revulsion and horror.

But then they would never know the depravity lurking within him, not if he had anything to say about it. However, there were some days when he found the lure of blood and death almost impossible to resist. Some days it took all he had not to walk out of his home, slaughter the first human he came across, and finally ease the constant driving pressure within him to feed.

He'd been dealing with it for as long as he could remember. High school was an endless battle for him, but he managed to get himself through it. The intensity of the urge to kill had increased steadily since he'd reached maturity though. If it continued, he didn't know how he could maintain his control for eternity. He was beginning to think he would welcome death over that bleak prospect.

So, he stayed away from the temptation of humans as often as possible. The five women he'd been with since he'd lost his virginity at sixteen were all vampires, and women he knew he couldn't accidentally injure. Women who were as indifferent to him as he was to them.

The last woman was the first time he'd stayed with someone for any significant amount of time. It wasn't because he cared for her but because of the enticing immorality thriving within her. There were nights he relished in the agony and devastation she unleashed on him with her claws, chains, and even a whip that had flayed his skin open more times than he could count. He'd deserved everything she did to him, but it still wasn't enough to drown the depravity within him.

The only things they didn't use to hurt each other were their fangs. He'd never exchanged blood with another vampire, and he never would unless that vampire was his mate. With the way he was heading, he highly doubted he'd ever find his mate though, and God help her if she turned out to be a human. He may maul her to death before he ever had a chance to establish any bond with her.

Part of the reason he'd agreed to come here was because he hoped a change of scenery would help him deal with what was inside him. That maybe if he were somewhere else, it would all ease a little. It didn't seem very likely, but he was willing to try anything. So, when Isabelle suggested this trip he didn't immediately shoot her down. Surprisingly, he'd found himself accepting her offer, even though he knew it was going to suck to be around people for such an extended period during the flights.

Stefan made a turn and drove up a hill winding through some of the most colorful homes he'd ever seen. At the top of the hill, they pulled into the driveway of a large, sunshine yellow house overlooking the harbor below it.

"You can see the ocean from every room," Isabelle said as she jumped out of the front seat before Stefan had the Jeep in park. Stefan shook his head and scowled at her as he shifted into park and turned the vehicle off.

Isabelle took Ethan's arm when he climbed out and pulled him toward the house. She unlocked the front door and flung it open to reveal an open floor plan that made his eyebrows shoot into his hairline. White tile floors gleamed in the sunlight spilling through the wall of windows across the way. The three sofas within the massive, sunken living room were also white and centered around a circular glass coffee table with golden legs. Above the couch pushed against the wall was a painting of the ocean at sunset. The assorted hues of the paintings were the only vibrant colors within the room.

To his left was a kitchen about half the size of the living room and filled with new, stainless steel appliances. Blue marble countertops ran beneath the numerous white cabinets, and an island was in the center of the kitchen. A breakfast bar with four stools lined up along its counter divided the two rooms.

He descended the two steps to the massive living room and placed his bag down on the floor. Isabelle's sandals tapped on the floor as she strode across the room and opened the French doors. Ethan walked over to join her and stared out at the clear, shimmering water of the pool. An outdoor kitchen and an elaborate bar made of gray stone sat at the far end of the patio. A table and a dozen lounge chairs were spread out around the rectangle-shaped pool.

Ethan crossed the patio to peer over the edge of the three-foot high rock wall surrounding the pool area. A hundred feet down the small hill beneath them was about thirty feet of sand. Beyond that, the ocean rolled in and out in a steady rhythm. At the bottom of the hill, a hundred-foot wooden dock stretched into the sea. A white Sea Ray Sundancer boat gleamed in the sun as it bobbed in the water at the end of the dock. He didn't know much about boats, but he did know that one looked like a good time.

"This is the life," he muttered.

"I could call it home," Isabelle agreed.

"Whose boat is that?"

"The owner of the house," Stefan answered as he stepped onto the patio and shaded his eyes against the sun. "We can take it out whenever we want though."

"Now?" Ethan asked.

Isabelle laughed as she looped her arm through his again. "It's getting a little late, but we'll take it out soon. We haven't tried it yet either. Come on, I'll show you to your room. We found this great little place on the beach where we can have a couple of drinks if you feel up to it later. You'll love it."

"I'm up for it," he assured her.

He grabbed his bag before she began to walk him down a hallway. "Bathroom," she said and pointed at one of the doors. "I figure these two bedrooms can go to Ian and Aiden." She nodded toward two more closed doors. "They're smaller, and they're young, so they won't mind the lack of space."

He laughed at the mischievous gleam in her eyes. "I knew there was a reason why you're my favorite sibling."

"I won't tell the others if you won't."

"I won't," he assured her as she stopped before another room.

"And this is yours. Ours is at the end of the hall. I'll let you unpack now."

He gave her a brief nod before opening the door on a sun-drenched room. His gaze ran admiringly over the large room as he stepped into it. He placed his bag on the four-poster California King bed draped in translucent white fabric. The room was far larger than his room at home, but it didn't contain as much furniture.

A fifty-two-inch flat screen TV hung on the wall across from the bed; there was a dark mahogany dresser beneath it. The only other pieces of furniture were a baby blue upholstered chair in the corner on the opposite side of the room and two nightstands, one on each side of the bed. The floor beneath his feet was more of the white tiling he'd seen throughout the house. Even though the room was sparse, and the color austere, something was inviting about it.

His gaze drifted to the glass doors and balcony on the other side of the room. He left his bag on the bed as he was drawn toward the doors. Opening them, he stepped onto the balcony and inhaled the ocean-scented air as he savored the view and the sound of the water crashing onto the sand below. Yes, he could definitely get used to this.

CHAPTER TWO

Emma leaned back in her chair to study the ocean rolling against the shore. Lifting her glass, she took a sip of her margarita and watched the die-hard sunbathers still trying to soak up the fading rays of the sun. Calypso music played in the background, and she found herself feeling almost drowsy as she began to lose herself in the music and tequila.

"Emma, woohoo, earth to Emma." She blinked as a hand waved in front of her face, drawing her attention to her friend, Jill. "There you are!" Jill declared with a smile. "What were you thinking about?"

"Nothing," Emma answered honestly. "And it was great."

Jill laughed as she pulled the yellow umbrella from her piña colada. The braids she had put into her mahogany brown hair today clicked together when she moved. Emma found she enjoyed the noise of the dozens of multicolored beads at the bottom of the braids; they sounded almost musical. The chunks of platinum blonde hair Jill recently streaked through her hair stood out amongst the braids. Her sable-colored eyes were warm as she leaned back in her chair and stretched her long, deeply tanned legs before her. A tan she'd earned while growing up in San Francisco and somehow managed to retain even through the endless, Pennsylvania winters at college.

At five-eleven, Jill was one of the tallest females Emma knew. Jill's height came in handy for the volleyball scholarship that had helped put her through college, as had her lean physique and amazing athletic ability. Jill hoped to get a job as a PE teacher or volleyball coach now that she was out of school; Emma knew she would be great at either job.

"We're free girls," Jill said happily and lifted her glass over the center of the table.

Emma leaned forward to clink her glass against Jill and Mandy's. Being free was the best feeling in the world, Emma decided. She was free from college, free from Tristan...

She hastily shut down all thoughts of Tristan. Memories of her ex had no place in this beautiful paradise with her two best friends.

"You two are free," Mandy said. "Some of us will be returning to college in the fall."

"You're the one *insisting* on going to medical school and trying to save the world," Jill teased.

Mandy smiled as she shifted in her chair. The blue bandanna wrapped around her head covered the black hair she'd cut into a bob just below her earlobes. Mandy's mocha-colored skin gleamed in the fading light of the sun setting over her bare shoulder. Her deep brown eyes were thoughtful as she fiddled with the straw in her drink.

"I don't know what else I would do with myself," Mandy admitted. "If I can't become a doctor..."

Her voice trailed off as her gaze turned to the window. The only thing Mandy ever dreamed of being was a doctor, and she'd spent their four years in college studying her ass off to attain that goal. When Mandy was five years old, her parents were killed in a car crash. Mandy was lucky enough to survive the crash, but her right leg was crushed so severely it had to be amputated. She was so adept at using her prosthetic that anyone who didn't know her, would never realize her leg was fake if she were wearing jeans.

After the accident, Mandy spent a lot of time in hospitals and rehab. She'd once told Emma the only thing that got her through those depressing and pain-filled days were the doctors and nurses who saved her life and the unwavering love and support of her grandparents. Mandy swore all those years ago, she would one day become a doctor so she could save children too.

"You will," Emma assured her. "You aced the MCATs."

"Yeah, well, that was just a test; Stanford is going to be a whole different ball game," Mandy said.

"Only you would think the MCAT's are *just* a test," Jill muttered as she stabbed her straw repeatedly into her frozen drink. "I barely passed my finals."

"To be fair, that's because you were out till two every morning of finals week," Mandy reminded her.

"I was simply taking the edge off," Jill said with a laugh.

Emma leaned forward and squeezed Mandy's arm. "You're going to do great, Mandy, believe me."

Mandy forced a smile. "That's still two months away. Right now, I have the whole month to enjoy with you two lovely ladies."

"Damn right!" Jill declared. "And then we *all* have to return to the real world." Jill downed the rest of her drink. She waved at a passing waitress, asked for another one and three shots of tequila.

Emma wasn't entirely sure what the real world was anymore. She'd spent her entire life in school; now she didn't know what to do with it. She had a bachelor's degree in history;

one she'd intended to use to become a history teacher, though she would probably have to get her master's too.

When she'd started her college life, she was certain she would enjoy teaching for the rest of her life.. Halfway through this year, she suddenly realized the last thing she felt like doing was spending the rest of her life inside a school building.

By then, it was too late to change her major or figure out a different plan. She wouldn't mind working in a museum, or some other historically oriented place, but she knew how difficult it was to come by those jobs, and once again she would probably have to get her master's.

Jill had recently suggested she move to California so they could all rent a place together. At first, Emma was unsure if that were something she'd like to do, but the more she thought about it, the more appealing she found the idea. She'd always wanted to see California, she could stay with her two best friends, and if she couldn't find a job she could always wait tables or return home. At least she'd get to try something new.

Her parents wouldn't be happy when she told them about her change of heart, but that was a conversation saved for after this trip. For now, she was determined to relax and enjoy the next month with her friends. The three of them had been saving for this trip since being placed together as roommates their freshman year. One day in passing, Mandy had told them her grandparents owned a home in Bermuda. It had been in their family for generations, and they rented it out to people.

Talk of renting the home was originally just a fun idea they batted around between them. As the semester wore on, and their friendship strengthened, renting the house became something they were determined to do. They busted their asses at crappy jobs, and they'd scrimped and saved until they raised enough money to rent the house for a month. Now it was finally *their* time to celebrate.

"Beach tomorrow for sure," Jill said. "I want to hop in on a couple of volleyball games and scope out some of the guys."

"Sounds like a plan to me," Mandy said.

"Maybe we can even get Emma a date," Jill teased.

Emma gave her a wan smile as she fiddled with the tiny umbrella she'd placed on the table. "I think I'll continue to stay away from men for a little while."

"It's been a year, Emma," Mandy said.

"Not long enough," Emma muttered.

The waitress returned with Jill's drink order and placed it on the table. Jill grabbed her new drink and leaned forward. "You need a good fling to forget about that asshole completely."

Emma stared back at her as her foot began to tap on the floor. She realized they were concerned about her, but she wished they would understand she was content to stay single, and a fling wasn't exactly her thing.

"It will take more than that to forget about Tristan," Emma said.

Jill sighed and pushed one of the shots of tequila toward her. "Let's not say that piece of shit's name again for the rest of this trip. Drink up."

Emma was more than happy to agree to those terms as she picked up the shot glass and downed the tequila. Her face scrunched up as the liquid hit her tongue and burned all the way down her throat; it wasn't overly unpleasant and made her feel warm and fuzzy. She placed the glass on the table and turned to watch the waves roll in and out again as Jill ordered another round.

"That should be illegal," Jill purred.

"Wow," Mandy breathed.

Emma didn't look to see what they were talking about, which annoyed Jill enough that she kicked Emma's shin under the table.

"Ow," Emma said and leaned forward to rub her shin.

She shot Jill a disgruntled look, but Jill smiled annoyingly in return and nodded her head toward whatever had caught her and Mandy's attention. Emma immediately spotted the two men Jill indicated as they were both large and exuded a raw sexuality. They were two of the best-looking men Emma had ever seen in her life. Her jaw almost dropped, but she caught herself in time to stop *that* from happening.

Both men had dark hair framing their faces, broad shoulders, and powerful forms. The similarities ended there between the two of them. The one with black eyes appeared older, he seemed more aloof as he searched the room, and his hair was more the color of coal. The one with the most beautiful emerald eyes she'd ever seen had a more youthful air to him as he leaned against the counter. His hair was a blue-black color that reminded her of a raven and made her itch to run her fingers through it. The muscles in his forearms flexed as he clasped his hands before him.

She couldn't tear her eyes away as she drank in the details of his body. Stubble lined his chiseled, square jaw; she could almost feel it rubbing against her cheek and over her throat. The sensation was so real that everything around her became irrelevant. Her gaze drifted to the full lips curled into an endearing smile that made her heart melt. There was a dimple in his right cheek as his smile grew and he unclasped his hands to gesture around the room. The form-fitting dark blue T-shirt he wore hugged his broad chest and emphasized the sculpted muscles underneath. Her gaze traveled over his waist and the obvious bulge in his jeans before she hurriedly looked away.

She kept her lashes lowered over her eyes as she looked surreptitiously at him again. Her breasts tingled as her mouth watered. Something about this man made her entire body react in a way it never had before. She almost rose from the table to go to him but stopped before she made a complete fool out of herself in the crowded bar.

It was all so strange; she didn't understand her reaction to him, but she welcomed it. Seeming to sense her stare, his head turned toward her. The smile slid from his face as his eyes locked with hers. She felt as if she were hurtled through space, and the stars and cosmos were flying by her as she was lost in the intensity of his gaze.

He continued to stare at her as people moved and flowed around them. A tall, brunette woman with golden highlights flowing through her hair walked over to the men. She was speaking as her hand gestured around the room. Jill and Mandy released a low groan when the other man bent to kiss the woman, but Emma barely heard them. With the kiss broken, the woman grabbed hold of the man Emma was looking at, drawing his attention away from her.

Emma had the strangest urge to cry when the connection between them broke. She took a deep breath and bowed her head as she tried to calm her accelerated pulse. It had been over a year since a man touched her romantically; that was the *only* reason she felt so completely out of control right now.

Turning back around, she grabbed one of the fresh shots Jill ordered and downed it.

"I wonder if the other one is single," Jill said as she played with her straw.

"Looking like that, I doubt it," Mandy replied.

Emma didn't even want to think about it as she gulped her drink down. The last thing she needed was another man in her life, considering the debacle the end of her relationship with Tristan had been. A shudder worked through her; she didn't like to recall the time she'd spent with the only man she'd ever had a serious relationship with. Everything between them had started out well enough; he'd been kind to her, and even if she wasn't head over heels for him, she'd thought it was a good relationship until it all went so horribly wrong. What started out as pleasant took an ugly turn into a threatening world she feared she wouldn't escape.

"Maybe it's time to head back to the house," she suggested.

"Things are just getting interesting here though," Jill protested.

"We shouldn't spend all of our money on our second night," Emma replied, but all she could think about was bolting out of the bar. The bizarre reaction she'd had to the man left her rattled and in need of some fresh air.

"True," Jill said. "Plus, there's alcohol at the house for us to enjoy."

Relief filled her as Jill agreed; sometimes she could be relentless. Emma pulled out some cash and tossed it on the table before rising from her chair. Her gaze involuntarily returned to the trio standing at the bar. The man she'd focused on had his back to them and was leaning on the bar. It was a very fine back too, Emma decided as her gaze settled on his taut ass.

Jesus, she had to get out of here, she decided as she forced herself to turn away from him.

Jill slipped her arm through Emma's and leaned against her side. "There will also be plenty more eye candy for us over the coming weeks."

Emma chuckled, but her thoughts remained on the man standing in the corner. She forced her eyes to remain ahead of her as they left the restaurant.

Ethan sensed the minute the woman left the bar; his head turned, and his nostrils flared as he inhaled her lingering scent. He spotted her standing outside the door with her friends. Ethan's gaze was riveted on her as she laughed and placed both her flip-flops into her right hand. There was something about her, something drawing him forward a step before Isabelle rested her hand on his shoulder to stop him.

"Would you like another drink?" she asked.

"Yeah," he answered absently as he watched the woman disappear.

He shook his head and turned back to his sister when she handed him a beer. The woman was a human, someone he should stay *far* away from, but he found his gaze going back to where she had been standing as he took a sip of beer. Around him, the sound of the beating hearts began to reach out to him. He thought he'd fed well enough on the blood bags from the house, but there was the craving for death again rearing its ugly head. Taking a deep breath, he focused on Isabelle and Stefan; he could control it, just like he always did. Just like he would be forced to do for eternity.

CHAPTER THREE

Ethan stepped onto the sand and glanced around at the people gathered on the beach near the restaurant where they went last night. Isabelle carried a blanket in her arms, but he had possession of the cooler loaded with water and beer. Standing beside Isabelle, Stefan didn't look at all pleased with the idea of being on the beach, but he didn't offer any complaint. He did give a scathing glance at a few men lustfully eyeing Isabelle. The men bowed their heads and scurried away.

"Behave," Isabelle told him.

"They're still alive, aren't they?" Stefan retorted.

Ethan chuckled as they walked through the crowd toward an open piece of the sandy real estate. They could have used the private beach by the house, but he'd suggested coming here. Isabelle had looked as startled as he'd felt when the words left his mouth. He hadn't understood why he had the idea at first either, but as his gaze scanned the crowd, he found himself searching for one particular human. The grunts of a nearby volleyball game drew his attention. He focused on the tall woman with braids in her hair he'd seen with the object of his attention last night.

The woman with the braids dove forward, digging the ball out before it hit the sand. She sent it soaring back over to the other side. A few cheers drew his attention to the crowd gathered by the makeshift volleyball court. He searched for the woman, but although her other friend from last night was standing on the sidelines, the one he sought wasn't there.

The odd sense of disappointment he felt threw him off. It was a sensation he didn't like. He almost told Isabelle and Stefan he would prefer to go somewhere quieter, but Isabelle was already spreading the blanket out and settling onto it.

He'd look like an idiot if he said he wanted to leave now, and she might get suspicious as to his reasons. The last thing he needed was Isabelle becoming nosy. She would never let it go if she thought there was a girl he might be interested in or sensed he wasn't telling her something.

His gaze ran over the crowded beach as he set down the cooler. Grabbing his shirt, he pulled it over his head to let the hot sun beat down on his shoulders. "Whoa Casper, I think you just blinded me," Isabelle said and threw up her hands.

He scowled at her before glancing down at his chest. He spent a fair amount of time outdoors in Oregon, but compared to the deeply tanned bodies surrounding him, he was a little pale. He had no concerns about burning though; his body would heal itself faster than the sun could damage his skin.

"Some of us don't spend our days tanning," he retorted.

She pulled off her white cover-up and shot a pointed look at Stefan. "Believe me, that's not how I spend my days."

"Ugh," Ethan groaned.

Isabelle laughed as she dropped her cover-up on the blanket and stretched out her legs. "Like you haven't said or heard worse over the years from Ian and Aiden."

"I have," he agreed, he didn't want to hear it from *her* though.

Ethan stretched his shoulders as he continued to scan the beach. A glimpse of golden brown hair mixed with tendrils of honey blonde swirling through it caught his attention. The woman from last night had hair that color. She was also shorter than her friends, Ethan recalled, as the head bobbed well below most of the other beachgoers. He strained to see her more clearly, but her face remained hidden by the bodies surrounding her.

The head broke free of the crowd. Ethan's gaze latched onto the face that had intruded upon his dreams last night as she stepped next to her friend. The blonde in her hair gleamed in the sunshine; she'd pulled it into a ponytail, but the tips of it still hung to the middle of her back. A smile lit up her face and caused her eyes to sparkle as she cheered on the girl with the braids. Even from here, he could see the flecks of jade green and brown speckling her hazel eyes.

She wasn't beautiful, but he found the cuteness of her round face and pert nose enchanting. She jumped up and down with reckless abandon and pumped her fist in the air. The leggy brunette jogged over to join them after scoring the winning point in the game. The petite woman handed the brunette a towel, and she dried herself off with it. They exchanged a few words before the brunette returned to the court.

The girl with the mocha-colored skin touched the petite one's arm, said something, and hurried away with a subtle limp that would have gone unnoticed by a human. Ethan didn't know what possessed him, but he dropped his t-shirt on the blanket and stepped off it.

The last thing in the world he liked to do was go near humans, but this girl called him as relentlessly as a siren called forth the ships. He hoped he wouldn't end up crashed against the rocks; or even worse, that she would be the one who ended up shipwrecked.

"I'll be back," he muttered to his sister and Stefan.

Isabelle barely glanced at him as she organized her supplies on the blanket. It was good to see she was still the same neat freak, he thought before his attention returned to the game. He kept his eyes focused on the girl as he circled the people gathered beside the court. The sand beneath his bare feet was warm and grainy as it shifted under his weight.

Turning sideways, he was careful not to touch anyone as he slid past the people and stepped beside her. When she stopped jumping, he realized the top of her head barely made it to the middle of his chest. Though she was small at about five-foot-two or three, there was something entirely alluring and feminine about her hourglass figure. The fit of her bikini top emphasized her handful-sized breasts when she started jumping again.

The smell of her brought to mind honeysuckle in the spring as it tickled his nostrils. Though a smattering of freckles dotted her nose, there were few other marks on her alabaster skin. He could hear her blood as it pulsed through her veins. The odd thing was that even though he wanted to taste her, he felt strangely calm around her. Even the beat of the other hearts surrounding him didn't arouse his ever-present yearning to kill. It was the first time in his life he'd ever felt truly peaceful, and the sensation was more pleasant than the aroma drifting from her skin.

She clapped her delicate hands together as she cheered for her friend.

"It's a good match," he commented.

At first, she didn't seem to notice him as her attention remained riveted on the game. Then her eyes slid to his chest.

Her eyebrows furrowed before her head tilted back so she could take him in. Ethan's gaze ran over her almost fae-like features as he stared at her. Her upper lip was thinner than her full bottom lip, a contrast which added to her cuteness. He was tempted to bend his head and nibble on that bottom lip, but he refrained from terrifying the human by doing so.

Emma's mind spun as she tried to think of a reply instead of standing there like an idiot. But it was *him*. She'd hoped she would get the chance to see him again, but she certainly hadn't expected it to be right now, and she hadn't expected him to speak to her first. It didn't matter though; he was still standing there, watching her, and expecting an answer that proved she wasn't a moron.

"Ah, yes, it is." Her hesitant response wasn't the best in the world but at least she'd finally gotten a few coherent words out.

"Is the girl with the braids your friend?"

This brought a genuine smile to her face.

"She is," Emma said.

It took him a few seconds to gather his thoughts as he was charmed by her smile and the warmth radiating from her. "She's good."

"She is. Do you play?"

Ethan glanced at the court, but he found he much preferred to watch her than the game. "I do."

"You should jump in then."

"Maybe later."

Not even when he was sixteen, and fumbling with his first bra, had he felt this awkward and uncertain as he extended a hand to her. "Ethan Byrne."

"Emma Morgan."

Her skin was cool and felt like satin as she took his hand. A jolt of electricity seemed to sizzle from her hand to his, up to his elbow, and through the rest of his body. Her eyes dilated a little as her breathing hitched and her eyes searched his face in astonishment.

His hand involuntarily constricted upon hers as he stepped even closer to her. The heat of her body slid over his flesh as her bare arm came into contact with his chest. It took all he had not to pull her into his arms and kiss her, but he'd probably end up being slapped in the face if he did; something he'd well deserve for molesting her on the beach.

Emma's whole body still vibrated from being in contact with his. She felt as if she'd grabbed an electric fence, something she'd done once as a kid while visiting her cousin's horse farm. This time it was an entirely pleasant sensation whereas that one brought her to tears and sent her running across the yard to her mother's arms.

Fresh jolts of nervous electricity went through her body when his thumb brushed over her skin, and he moved a step closer to her. For one crazy second, she thought he was going to kiss her as his eyes deepened to a forest green color, and he pressed her knuckles against the firm muscles of his flat stomach. She'd known him for all of two minutes, but she would welcome his kiss and found herself longing for it.

"Here."

Ethan hadn't seen the young woman who had been standing with Emma before he approached, until she spoke and thrust a pink drink between them. Emma's hand slid away from his as she fumbled to take the drink. The woman's deep brown eyes were assessing and stony as she scanned him from head to toe. There was no lust in her gaze; she came across more like a mother bear protecting her cub than anything. Ethan held her stare as her assessing eyes came back to his.

"Hello," she said to him.

"Mandy this is Ethan, Ethan this is my friend, Mandy," Emma introduced. She grabbed her straw and took a sip of her drink. The sweet scent of strawberries drifted up to him, but he didn't detect any alcohol in it.

"Hi," Mandy greeted, but she continued to watch him like a hawk. Under other circumstances, he might have found her protective attitude amusing; now, he found it irritating.

A loud cheer drew his attention back to the game. The brunette with braids was jumping up and down as she high-fived her teammates. She jogged over to them and grabbed her towel from the sand. Words spilled out of her mouth at a million miles an hour as she dried the sweat from her body and grabbed the drink from Emma. She closed her eyes and made a pleased sound in the back of her throat as she sipped it.

"Delicious," she said. Her hand stilled on the towel when she opened her eyes again and finally noticed him standing there. A sly grin curled her lips as she thrust out a hip. "Well, hello," she greeted. "And who might you be?"

Emma and Mandy rolled their eyes, and Emma grabbed her drink back from her friend. Ethan smiled at the woman as she dropped her towel on the ground. "Ethan."

"Nice to meet you, Ethan, I'm Jill, and these are—"

"We've met," Mandy interrupted.

Jill frowned as she glanced between Emma and Mandy and then back at him. "Oh."

"We should probably go; I could stand to get out of this sun for a bit," Mandy said.

The disappointment filling him was a little disturbing, but he wasn't in the mood to examine it.

"Maybe we'll see you later," Jill said.

"I'm sure of it." He didn't even look at Jill but kept his gaze locked on Emma as he spoke. He was as startled by the words as Emma appeared to be. Her eyes flickered, and she bit her bottom lip.

She smiled at him, and Mandy took her arm. Their excited

words and laughter floated back to him as he watched them walk away with their heads bent close together. The further away they got, the more aware he became of the cluster of people around him and the blood flowing through their veins. His teeth ground together as his hands fisted. After the stillness her presence had brought him, the influx of awareness was like sandpaper on his skin.

Turning away, he walked back to Isabelle and Stefan. They were both watching him with questioning expressions, but Isabelle jumped on him first. "Who was that?" she demanded.

Ethan shrugged as he lowered himself to the blanket beside her. "Just some girl," he muttered, but he found his gaze drawn back to Emma as she climbed the dunes with her friends.

CHAPTER FOUR

Emma brushed out her hair and let it fall around her shoulders as she studied herself in the mirror. Turning away, she grabbed the purple and white sundress from the bed and slid it over her head. Jill was adamant they go to the bar again tonight. Emma thought she might have a bit of a crush on Ethan.

That thought didn't sit well with her, but there wasn't anything she could do about it. She didn't blame Jill; he *was* gorgeous. Just recalling the feel of his large hand encircling hers caused her heart to pound a little faster and her mouth to go dry.

There was a rod of strength in him, and he radiated an aura both formidable and appealing. She should probably stay far away from him. She'd already become entangled with a man who seemed perfectly normal, and even a little boring, when she first met him, but over time she'd come to realize she'd seriously misjudged his character. Her mistake had caused her nothing but betrayal, aggravation, and a nightmare she wasn't certain would ever end.

She hadn't known him long, but she got the impression Ethan was anything but boring. Though common sense told her to stay away, she found herself intrigued by him and hoping he would be there again tonight. Even if he was there, that was no guarantee he would talk to her again; today might have been a fluke. He may have just been watching the game and looking to pass the time with some idle conversation.

Her fingers twitched as she smoothed the front of her dress and tried to get her nerves under control. She felt as jumpy as a cricket; she wasn't sure she could stand still long enough to carry on a conversation with him even if she did see him again.

Ugh, she was an idiot, she decided as she brushed her hair over her shoulder and turned away from the mirror. Grabbing her purse from the queen-size bed, she tossed the strap onto her shoulder. The cheerful yellow of the room calmed her nerves and brightened her mood as she made her way to the door and stepped into the narrow hallway.

Jill and Mandy were already in the kitchen. Even over the noise of the blender, she could hear Jill singing Buffalo Soldier at the top of her lungs. All the windows in the house and the sliding patio door were open to allow the ocean breeze to flow inside. It was refreshing as it tickled over her skin and brought with it the smell of the hibiscus growing just outside the doorway. Emma stepped into the small kitchen as Mandy shut the blender off and began to pour the red liquid into three different glasses. Over Mandy's shoulder, she could see the cotton candy pink house next door through the window above the sink.

"What's in it?" she inquired as Mandy handed her a glass of the blended concoction.

"A little bit of everything," Mandy answered.

Emma's nose wrinkled as she sniffed at the drink, but the sip she took tasted delicious.

"Are you ready to go?" Jill inquired.

Her braids clacked as she bounced on her toes and danced around the kitchen. Thankfully, she stopped butchering Bob Marley, but she began to hum some other tune Emma did *not* want to hear.

Emma took a big gulp of her drink to get rid of it before Jill launched into her newest rendition of an unsuspecting reggae song. One drunken night, a guy had told Jill she should be on The Voice to get in her pants. Jill hadn't left with him, but that night was the closest she and Mandy ever came to choking Jill as she continued to sing, loudly and badly, until three in the morning. Thankfully, sobriety brought sanity with it, but Jill still loved to sing her out of tune songs.

The cold rushing to her head caused Emma to wince. She placed the glass down and rubbed at her temples to ease the headache the chill caused. "Ready," she muttered.

Jill looped her arm through Emma's and took Mandy's. "Let's go then!" she said excitedly.

"We're not going to see the wizard, Jill," Mandy said with a laugh as she extricated her arm from Jill's.

"I think someone has a crush." Emma tried to keep her tone airy and teasing, but she knew she failed miserably.

"No, I don't," Jill protested. "I'm just looking to have some fun. I don't," she insisted at Emma's pointed look.

Jill smiled even more as she exchanged a look with Mandy. Emma felt a trickle of foreboding slide down her spine as she got the distinct feeling they were plotting against her. The thought drifted away though as they walked down the hill to the small bar on the beach. She tried not to let excitement get the best of her, but she found herself eagerly hoping he was there.

Her excitement faded when they stepped into the nearly empty building. Jill's face scrunched up; her shoulders slumped as she headed over to a table next to the open windows. The tangy sea breeze picked up strands of her hair as Emma settled next to the window and placed her order.

The waiter turned away when the door opened, and Ethan stepped inside with the couple he'd been with last night. Emma's fingers clenched on the table; she sat straighter in her chair. She didn't want to look in case he caught her staring, but she couldn't tear her gaze away from him. His head turned toward them, his eyes latched onto hers, and a smile tugged at the corners of his mouth.

He was mouthwateringly gorgeous with his tousled hair and endearing smile. Emma shifted in her chair, and heat crept into her cheeks. Her blush wasn't just from her embarrassment over staring but also from the desire she felt growing within her. She'd never experienced anything like this before, but just looking at him made her heart race and her palms sweat. She wiped her hands on her dress as she averted her gaze.

Jill and Mandy grinned annoyingly at her when she picked up her drink and took a sip. She couldn't stop her gaze from going back to him as the couple he was with settled onto stools at the bar. Ethan crossed his legs, rested his elbow on the bar and leaned against it. She felt it when his eyes came to rest on her, but she didn't look in his direction again.

"I think it's *you* who has the crush," Jill teased.

Emma shot her a look, but she didn't say anything as she took another sip of her drink. She was looking for something to cool her off, but it didn't have the effect she'd intended. Taking a deep breath, she placed her glass on the table and focused on the dazzling array of pinks, oranges, and reds the setting sun cast over the ocean.

His approach was so discreet, she wasn't aware he'd left the bar until a chair from the table next to them, settled beside her.

"Do you mind?" he asked when her eyes shot to him.

"Not at all," she managed to get out.

He settled his large frame in the chair and stretched his long legs before him. The muscles in his forearms and biceps rippled when he leaned toward her. Heat seemed to radiate from him; she'd thought her palms were sweaty before, but they were worse now as she was drawn toward him like a magnet to metal.

Jill lifted her glass and chugged it down. "I think I'll get another. Want to come with me, Mandy?"

"Sure," Mandy said and pushed herself to her feet. "You need anything, Emma?"

She reluctantly tore her eyes away from Ethan and shook her head. "No, I'm fine."

Ethan folded his arms over his chest and leaned back in the chair as her not so subtle, but extremely astute friends hurried to the bar. Emma gulped when she spotted Isabelle and Stefan watching them raptly from the bar.

"Just ignore them," Ethan told her, hoping to ease her discomfort. Her eyes came back to him. "My sister is just nosy."

"That's your sister?"

"My younger and highly annoying sister, Isabelle, and her even more annoying husband, Stefan."

He grinned as the couple at the bar scowled at him before turning away. She thought they were too far away to hear his words, but their reaction to what he'd said made her wonder if perhaps they had.

"I don't have any siblings," she said.

"You can take a few of mine."

She laughed as she began to relax a little. "How many do you have?"

"Nine."

"*Nine*?" she blurted.

He chuckled. "Yep, nine. It's quite the brood."

"Sounds like it."

"My brothers Aiden and Ian will be joining us in a couple of weeks. They decided to return home after they finished college before coming here."

"They graduated?"

His hair fell over his forehead as he shook his head. "No, they still have some time left; they're just done for the summer."

"We just graduated," she said and gestured at her friends.

He glanced at where Jill and Mandy were standing by the bar; their heads close together as they kept glancing at them. It was amusing, but he wished he could have some time with her away from the prying eyes of friends and family.

"What are you going to do now that you've graduated?" he asked.

Emma shrugged as she twirled her glass on the table. "That's a good question, and I'm not sure of the answer."

The strange sense of calm she brought to him was back again, and he welcomed it as he watched the setting sun play over her hair and skin. It added a glow to her that made her seem almost angelic in the growing twilight.

"You've got plenty of time to find the answer," he told her.

"I guess. What about you, what do you do?"

"Not college," he said with a laugh.

She was aware it wasn't much of an answer, but she didn't press it further. He lifted the bottle to his mouth and took a long swallow. His skin glistened with a thin sheen of sweat as he lowered the bottle again. Something about his gaze made her stomach feel like a thousand butterflies flitted around in it. Her hand fisted as she fought the urge to run her finger over his chin; she was dying to know what his skin felt like.

His head tilted to the side in a way that made her think he was trying to see inside her, trying to understand her, but she didn't know what he was looking for. Feeling a little self-conscious, she fiddled with a strand of her hair.

"Where are you from, Emma?" he asked.

"Upstate New York, but I went to college in Pennsylvania. What about you?"

"Oregon."

"I've never been there, but I've heard it's beautiful."

"It is."

He moved closer and placed the bottle on the table. He carried the subtle scent of male and something enticing that brought to mind springtime and sex as it tickled her nostrils. Her fingers clenched on her thighs as her body quickened. What was wrong with her? She never felt this way around men; not even Tristan had made her feel this turned on, and she'd stupidly thought she might be in love with the pathetic ass.

Unclenching her fingers, she pushed back a strand of hair and grabbed her drink. She could feel his eyes on her as she took a sip. The door opened, and three men stepped into the bar. Emma barely glanced at them, but Ethan's casual attitude vanished as he straightened in the chair and the smile slid from his face. At the bar, Stefan rose from his stool and moved to stand in front of Isabelle.

Ethan prepared himself to launch to his feet if it became necessary when the three vampires entered. He didn't smell the foul stench of garbage on them that would indicate they were killers. It was something he hadn't realized only he and his siblings could smell on the more murderous vampires until Stefan came into their lives.

Ethan had assumed everyone could detect the stench, but it appeared only purebred vampires could do so. It was a handy ability to know if a vampire was a killer or not, but even if he didn't detect the scent on them, he couldn't relax—not with them being in such proximity to Isabelle and Emma.

Isabelle touched Stefan's arm and shook her head no.

Though he relaxed slightly, he didn't return to his seat. Ethan tried to appear casual, but he couldn't turn his gaze away from the men. Attacking Ethan or any member of his family would be a stupid mistake for these men to make, Stefan was old and powerful, and he and Isabelle weren't anything to mess with either.

Emma frowned as she glanced from the men to Ethan then over to his family. The men didn't seem like much of a threat. One of them was blond and could easily be a horse jockey given his small stature, the other was also blond and maybe weighed a hundred and forty pounds soaking wet, and the third was average height and weight with reddish colored hair. The men looked Ethan and Stefan over before moving to the other end of the bar.

"Where are you staying?" Ethan asked. He was still trying to sound casual, but he heard the strain in his voice.

Emma continued to stare at the men before turning her attention back to him. "We're renting a house down the road," she told him. He nodded, but his eyes remained on the men. The skinny one was talking to Mandy who didn't look at all impressed as she turned away from him. "And you?"

His attention came back to her. "Stefan rented a home at the end of the road for a month."

"Nice," she said, but she was more interested in his reaction to the gang of three trying to chat up her friend. "Do you know those men?"

"No, I don't."

Emma frowned as she studied the contours of Ethan's profile. "You don't seem to like them much for people you don't know."

"No, it's not..." he shook his head before giving her a rakish grin that made her smile in return. "I thought I recognized one of them, but I was wrong."

"Oh," she said as Mandy and Jill turned away from the bar and walked over to join them again.

"We thought we'd check out the bar down the road. You coming with us, Emma?" Mandy asked.

She glanced over at Ethan. She didn't want to leave him, but she didn't feel comfortable staying here with a man she barely knew.

"There will be dancing," Jill coaxed with a smile.

"Dancing sounds like fun," Ethan said to her. "I'm sure Isabelle and Stefan will probably come too."

Emma blinked in surprise as he rose beside her. Did *he* intend to come with them?

She wasn't sure how she felt about that. He affected her in such a strange way, and she would like a minute just to *breathe*. But then, she'd been breathing her whole life, and she would continue to do so for the rest of it, breathing was boring. Maybe it was time to hold her breath and take the plunge. She could always breathe again when she went home.

Jill and Mandy looked like two kids who were just handed a giant bag of candy as they watched Ethan walk over to the bar. "Well?" Jill prodded eagerly.

"Well what?" she asked.

Jill rolled her eyes. "What do you think, of him?"

Emma stood up from the table. "He's nice."

Jill slid her arm into hers. "Nice? Chocolates are *nice*, Emma. That man is delectable, and he's into you. A little fling with him before becoming an adult won't kill you."

"I don't *fling*, Jill."

"I know, but for that guy, I'd fling just about anything."

Emma couldn't help but laugh as Jill squeezed her arm before releasing her. Isabelle and Stefan moved away from the bar and walked over to join them. They were one of the most striking couples Emma had ever seen as they stopped before them. Even Jill, who was never shy, appeared a little nonplussed as she took a step back from the overwhelmingly large man and the stunningly beautiful woman at his side.

It wasn't often Emma felt insecure about her looks. She knew she wasn't the most beautiful woman in the world, knew she was considered cute by most people, but she wasn't ugly. Standing across from this woman though, she felt like a child, small and unbelievably young, but they appeared to be about the same age. Isabelle was a good five inches taller than her and possessed an aura of confidence that made her seem older.

Then Isabelle smiled and extended her hand. "I'm Isabelle, and this is my husband, Stefan," she introduced as Emma shook her hand.

Stefan's black eyes were assessing as he took hold of her hand. "Hello," he greeted.

Emma swallowed nervously and instinctively moved closer to Ethan. She got the feeling Stefan could snap her neck if the mood struck him. In fact, looking at them, she had the distinct impression there was more to them than met the eye.

She shook the thought off as Mandy and Jill finished introducing themselves. They were just a normal family on vacation together. She was only feeling overwhelmed because she was so much shorter than they were. It was bad enough being around Mandy and Jill, but now she felt like a sapling in a grove of Redwoods with the three of them around her too.

"Let's go then," Jill said.

CHAPTER FIVE

Ethan liked going to clubs about as much as he would like having his toenails ripped off. He just wasn't willing to walk away from Emma yet, especially after the three vampires entered the bar. They may not be killers, but they could still use her for blood. He moved protectively closer to Emma as she weaved her way through the crowd. The music wasn't overly obnoxious, but it still aggravated his acute hearing.

A man stepped forward to grab Emma's arm. She shook her head and took a step away. Ethan didn't know what possessed him, but he moved rapidly forward to insert himself in between her and the man. The man opened his mouth to protest, took one look at him, and retreated into the crowd. Ethan stayed by Emma's side as Stefan and Isabelle led the way toward the bar.

They found a gap in the crowd of people at the bar and moved in to order a round of drinks. Emma stepped closer to him to escape a woman who was dancing as if fire ants were attacking her. Ethan eyed the woman, unable to understand what she was trying to accomplish as she danced away from them and moved back toward the main dance floor.

The bare flesh of Emma's shoulder glistened in the lights flashing around the bar. Unable to resist the temptation of her skin, he settled his hand on her shoulder. Her gaze shot to him, and her abrupt intake of breath caused her breasts to rise temptingly in the simple dress she wore. His thumb stroked over her silken shoulder as he stepped closer to her. His chest pressed against her shoulder; through his shirt, he could feel the warmth of her body. Fortunately, she was forced even closer to him when the fire ants dancer returned and bumped against her.

A surge of possessiveness rushed through him. She was so small, so weak—so *human.* That thought did nothing to ease the tension building in his chest as he pulled her closer and further away from the dancing bodies. For the first time, the stress building within him had nothing to do with the numerous people or his craving for blood. Instead, it had everything to do with keeping her out of harm's way.

"This isn't usually my type of place," Emma told him, though she enjoyed being forced so close to him by the worst dancing she'd ever seen. Ethan pulled her back another step as the woman's hands flailed crazily about her head. Emma didn't know if the woman was on drugs or if she thought what she was doing could be considered dancing. Either way, Emma was convinced the woman would knock someone out before the night ended.

"Or mine," he told her. He spotted Isabelle and Stefan again amongst the crowd; they'd managed to get a table. Isabelle stood on her tiptoes to wave at him over the sea of heads. "Do you want to sit?"

"Yes!" she shouted. She gestured to Mandy and Jill to let them know where she was going. Ethan slid his hand away from her shoulder, but he kept it on her elbow as he steered her safely through the crowd.

Stepping next to the table, he pulled a chair out for her and held it while she sat. She couldn't help but smile at him; it was such a sweet gesture, and one she'd never experienced before.

"It's crazy in here!" Isabelle shouted over the music.

Stefan looked about as pleased to be here as he would have been to stick his hand in boiling water. In fact, given a choice between the two, Ethan thought Stefan might choose to stick his hand in boiling water rather than endure this noisy crowd.

"Sit," Emma urged and patted the seat of the empty chair beside her.

Ethan grabbed the back of the chair; he pushed it in again and moved closer to Emma as a couple nearly fell into her chair. He tried to shake off the overprotective urges he was feeling, but he couldn't bring himself to move away and leave her exposed again.

His gaze ran over the people in the building. He didn't sense any other vampires amongst the crowd, but he had a feeling the three from the bar would eventually make their way here. There were more people here; they were drunker, and it was poorly lit. This club was prime feeding ground for vampires. He spotted Mandy and Jill dancing with a couple of guys. A waitress came by to take their order and disappeared into the crush of people.

Ethan leaned closer to Emma as her fingers tapped along to the beat of the music and she began to sway. "Would you like to dance?" he asked.

Dancing wasn't something he did often, or well, but the idea of getting the chance to hold her was too appealing to resist. She frowned for a second before smiling and jumping to her feet. She was small, but she moved with easy grace as she came around the chair to stand beside him.

Her hand was swallowed within his when he took it and led her out to the dance floor. He kept her away from the horde of people as he steered her to a less crowded section. They weren't playing a song meant for slow dancing, but he still wrapped his arm around her waist and pulled her against him. Her body fit snugly against his frame as she moved with him.

He didn't notice any of the other people on the floor as everything within him became focused on her. Her tantalizing scent filled his nostrils as his other hand settled onto her lower back. The feel of her breasts against his chest caused blood to rush into his cock. He adjusted his position so she wouldn't feel the evidence of his obvious arousal.

Overwhelming sensations of safety and protection filled her as she rested her head on his chest. She found herself tuning out the beat of the music and focusing on the solid, reassuring thump of his heart. Maybe it was because he was so much bigger and stronger than her, or maybe it was just the tender way he held her, but she felt incredibly secure in his arms.

Unable to resist, Ethan lifted his hand to her hair and let the soft strands of it slide through his fingers. The bloodlust that had yet to be stirred by the crowd around them now slid through his body as the fruity scent of her shampoo drifted up to him. His canines tingled; he fought to keep them from extending as his gaze drifted to the vein in her neck.

Just a little taste, she didn't even have to know, and he could take the memory from her after. The idea was so enticing, he briefly considered pulling her from the club and out into the night, but even as the impulse crossed his mind, he knew he couldn't do that to her.

Her forehead furrowed as she studied him with assessing eyes he found entirely captivating. He bent and placed a kiss on her forehead. He meant to pull back afterward, but his lips lingered against her warm skin as his fingers slid beneath her chin. His lips moved leisurely down her cheeks before brushing against hers.

Lust crashed through him, the heat of her lips burned against his, and the strawberry taste of her mouth suffused him as his tongue swept inside. It was the first time he'd ever kissed a human, he didn't know what he expected, but it certainly wasn't this urge for more. He had to go easy so he didn't accidentally hurt her.

That thought frightened him, but he couldn't bring himself to pull away from her and put some distance between them. Turning her away from the crowd, he backed her into a wall and pressed her against it as his kiss became more demanding.

Her fingers curled into his forearms, and at first she seemed hesitant, but she gave herself over to him with a small sigh. The music and people around them completely vanished as lust consumed him and he completely focused on her. He was close to lifting her dress and taking her right there to relieve himself of the pressure she created within him.

He was seriously considering doing just that as his hand cupped her handful-sized breast. Her breath sucked in; her teeth nibbled at his lower lip as he swirled his thumb around her hardened nipple through the thin material of her dress. Lifting his head, he met her passion-clouded eyes and savored in the desire playing over her face as he continued to tease and fondle her breast. Ever so slowly, he bent his head to hers again. He seized her swollen lips as he released her breast to slide his hand over her belly and down to her thighs.

Emma gasped as his hands left a trail of fire over her body. Her mind spun as she tried to understand what was happening, but she was so swept away by the feel of him that she couldn't recite the alphabet, let alone form a coherent thought. Her heart hammered as his touch brought her to life in ways she never knew possible.

She'd never lost herself to a man—not even Tristan. She'd never thought it was possible to be so out of control she didn't care what happened, but that's exactly how she felt. She was knowingly and completely out of control. As his fingers brushed against the bottom of her dress and touched her bare thighs, she didn't think to say no because inwardly all she was screaming was, *yes*! Inwardly, all she could think was *finally*. Finally, she understood what it was to be a woman touched with such feverish need that, though she knew it was moving far too fast, it was still the most amazing experience of her life.

The blood pulsing through his ears made it difficult for him to hear anything. His fingers caressed her smooth skin as he moved his hand further up under her dress. He touched her panties, pleased to find they were already damp as he rubbed against her through the satiny material.

His body throbbed with his need to possess her. He forgot about everyone around them; he simply had to be inside of her, to consume her. He was pushing her underwear to the side when she jerked away from him.

Reality was like a slap in the face as it crashed back over her. "Wait! Stop!"

She heaved in heaping gulps of air as she braced her hands against his chest and her gaze latched onto his. Emma remained immobile as she waited to see what he was going to do.

Disappointment crashed through him, but he dropped his hand away when she glanced anxiously around them. Heat flooded her face; her lashes lowered over her eyes as she adjusted her dress.

"Emma..."

She turned her face away when he tried to grasp her chin. She couldn't look at him again; she couldn't stand to see in his eyes what he probably thought of her right now. She didn't know what she thought of *herself*. It was one thing to get swept up in a man; it was an entirely different thing to be about ready to screw him in public. She didn't even *know* him. What was wrong with her? What was she *thinking*?

Ethan moved his other hand away from her hip and rested both his palms on the wall beside her head. He may have released her, but he wasn't ready to let her go anywhere right now. He was nervous she would run and never come back if he did. "You must think...I'm not...this isn't something I do," she muttered.

He stopped her with his hand against her waist when she went to move away from him. "Emma, look at me," he coaxed. She threw her shoulders back, took a deep breath, and finally met his gaze. "We didn't do anything wrong."

"I don't behave like this. I don't almost have sex with people I don't know in public places," she retorted defensively.

The fire in her eyes dared him to disagree with her, to say something different. "I didn't think you did." She was still the color of a Maraschino cherry as her gaze went away from him again. "Really, Emma, I didn't. We both got a little carried away; there's nothing to be ashamed of."

"Yeah." Though she was having a difficult time looking at him, and she wasn't completely convinced.

Ethan leaned forward and kissed her forehead to soothe her a little more. His erection still pressed uncomfortably against his jeans. He shifted as he tried to find a more relaxed position, but he didn't think that would be possible until he was inside her. Something he had every intention of being before he left this island, but it wasn't going to happen tonight. Right now, he needed to ease her embarrassment, not make her feel even more pressured.

"Let's go back to the table," he suggested.

"I think I've had enough for tonight."

"I'll walk you home." She opened her mouth to protest, but

he continued before she could do so. "I'm only going to make sure you get there safely. I'll keep my hands to myself, I promise."

He held his hands up innocently beside his head and smiled at her. She couldn't help but smile back at him as she brushed the hair back from her forehead. Embarrassment over her actions remained, but his tone and demeanor helped to ease it. "Okay."

"Let me tell Issy and Stefan we're leaving."

He took her hand and turned away from the wall. A few people glanced at them as he led her through the crowd, but thankfully most barely noticed them. Mandy and Jill had joined Stefan and Isabelle at the table when they returned. "I'm going to head back to the house," Emma told them.

"I'm ready to go too," Mandy said.

Jill looked at her drink before shrugging; she chugged down the rest of it and put it on the table. "Let's go then."

Emma turned to Ethan, she was still a little unnerved about what had transpired between them, but she wasn't ready to say goodbye to him yet. "You don't have to walk with us," she said.

"I've had enough for the night too," he said. There was no way he was going to let her walk around unprotected at night when there were other vampires on this island.

"I think we all have," Isabelle said and rose to her feet.

Ethan was hoping to have some time alone with Emma, but it didn't look like it would happen. Isabelle's eyes focused on their joined hands; she frowned at them before her gaze shot up to his. He could practically see the questions racing through her mind, but he had no answers for her, and he wasn't ready to search for them either.

CHAPTER SIX

Emma stretched and opened her eyes to the sunlight filtering around the edges of the blue curtains she pulled over the glass patio doors last night. She stared at the material as the events of the night came crashing back. Embarrassment curled through her, her face heated at the memory of the wanton way she had behaved, but fresh excitement also spread through her belly as desire pooled inside of her.

She stopped him last night before it went too far, but if they hadn't been in the club, she would have given herself to him. She shook her head as she sat up in bed and pulled the sheet off her.

Slipping out of bed, she pondered what was going on with her as she gathered towels for a shower. She'd never been sexually aggressive; in fact, she'd been with Tristan for almost six months before they had sex. He'd been her first, and things went so wrong in the end that she'd stayed away from men since their relationship ended last year.

Never once had she experienced the urge to rip Tristan's clothes off and have sex in a public place—or lost control of herself in such a way. At one point, she'd thought she could love Tristan. Now she knew she was simply blinded by his good looks, charm, and the fact he was the first serious boyfriend she had. Her parents weren't overprotective of her, and though she was allowed to date in high school, she'd never really met someone she liked enough to date for any length of time, let alone sleep with them.

Tristan broke down her defenses, wove a spell with his smile, his gifts, and his constant, caring attentiveness. After a year together, she walked in on him having sex with another woman. That slap in the face was bad enough, but his dogged persistence at trying to get her back afterward had spiraled into stalker levels that had frightened her enough she looked into getting a restraining order against him.

Then, one day it all suddenly stopped. She hadn't heard from him in a year; she didn't know if he was dead or alive. Though she wished him no ill will, she was glad to be rid of him.

Looking back, she knew she was never in love with him; she'd just liked the idea of finally having a boyfriend. He beguiled her, but more than that she'd always felt like there was something wrong with her. All her friends dated with ease. She'd never really clicked with a man before, never had a big crush on someone. Then Tristan started asking her out, and worried she might be a freak, she'd agreed to go out with him after a month of his persistent pursuit.

There was never any ease to their relationship, at least not on her end; she'd always felt like she was forcing herself through it so she could be more normal. She wasn't heartbroken when she found him cheating on her; she was angry and felt betrayed, but more than anything, she'd felt relieved.

She *finally* had a reason to end it with him that wouldn't make her seem crazy. Tristan was the whole package on the outside: good looking, pre-law, intelligent, and caring. Despite the package, she always felt a little unhappy while with him. Walking in on him with another woman was so freeing she almost gave the girl a high-five. Instead, she'd simply closed the door and smiled as she walked away.

Yes, she was a freak, she decided as she shut off the water. A man she'd known for two days had more pull over her than a man she'd spent a year of her life with. It was crazy, but she found she was okay with this crazy if it meant she would have a chance to talk to Ethan again, to kiss him and touch him.

Stepping from the shower, she grabbed the towel and dried off before starting to dress. After Tristan, she'd decided to take a break from men. She took some time to salvage her beaten pride and wash away the bad taste of Tristan's endless phone calls, text messages, gifts, emails, random visits to her dorm room and even her classes.

Emma shuddered at the reminder of him sitting in the back of her classes, watching her. The feeling of his eyes on her was so vivid, she glanced at the window to make sure he wasn't standing there watching her all over again.

It had gotten so bad Jill and Mandy wouldn't let her go anywhere alone, and though she resented he'd made it that way, she'd welcomed their presence. His final gift, a dozen black roses on her doorstep, and a note saying he would always love her and she would always be his, convinced her it was time to get the police involved.

The paperwork for the restraining order was in the works when everything stopped, Tristan's room was cleared out, and his roommate said he'd just packed up and left. At first, she was doubtful, but over the months she'd relaxed again, and her life gradually returned to normal.

And now her life seemed to have been thrown into chaos all over again. She'd never met anyone who made her feel as unsettled, excited, and turned on as Ethan did. She'd known Tristan for a while before she discovered his secrets and mental issues. She barely knew Ethan, and she was already acting recklessly. He made her forget about her decision to stay away from men for the time being.

She had to be careful and tread lightly here, but she didn't know how to do that around him. He made her feel as if someone had thrown her into the deep end of the ocean.

Emma stepped out of the room and hurried down the hall to the kitchen, but Mandy and Jill weren't there. Seeing the door to the balcony open, she grabbed a cup of coffee and poked her head out the sliding door. She found Mandy lounging in one of the chairs reading a book.

"Hey," Emma greeted.

Mandy placed her finger in the book and smiled as Emma settled into the chair next to her. Mandy's prosthetic leg leaned against the chair beside her.

"Jill still sleeping?" Emma asked.

"No, she went for a run on the beach."

Emma shook her head. "That girl has *way* too much energy."

"Far more than me," Mandy agreed. "We didn't get a chance to talk last night."

"About what?" Emma asked as she took a sip of her coffee and watched the people strolling the street.

Mandy gave her an, '*oh come on*,' look. "Don't think I didn't see you two steaming up the dance floor."

Emma was beginning to hate her Irish skin as she felt a blush creeping into her cheeks again. She hadn't blushed this much since Kirby Jackson pulled her skirt down in front of everyone during the fifth-grade dance. "Mandy—"

Mandy held up her hand to stop her words. "No judgments. Just want to make sure you're okay."

"I am, I think," she muttered.

"He seems nice enough, but—"

"So did Tristan."

"So did Tristan," Mandy agreed. "You can't spend the rest of your life being afraid of relationships, or having that shithead hanging over you, but I also don't want to see you hurt again."

Emma blew on her coffee and twisted the mug in her hands. "Neither do I."

"Where does he live?"

"Oregon."

"Not even close to you."

"Not even a little," Emma agreed.

"Would you be okay with only having a month? I know we kid you about doing something casual to help shed the memory of Tristan, but you're not that person, Emma."

"I know."

And truth be told, she didn't think a month would be enough time. At the end of the month, she knew she would want more and more. Ugh, *she* would end up becoming like Tristan if she wasn't careful.

She sat forward and placed her coffee on the table before rising and walking over to the balcony railing. Maybe she could hide out in this tropical paradise forever, never return home, and just pretend she knew what she wanted from her life.

She rested her elbow on the railing and propped her chin on her hand as she watched the people strolling the streets. It was peaceful now, but she knew in a few hours music from the bars would be going, and the party would start again. She'd drifted to sleep last night listening to the music, laughter, and shouts from the people still enjoying themselves.

"You could come out to California to live with us. Jill is still considering moving closer to Stanford or trying to find a job in the area," Mandy suggested.

"I've been thinking about it a lot," Emma told her. "And not because of him," she rushed to get out.

"I didn't think it was," Mandy said with a chuckle.

"It might be good to move out to the west coast, at least for a little while. I'd like to do something different."

"You might find a teaching job," Mandy suggested. Emma wrinkled her nose and shook her head. "Or something else. You'd at least have us."

"That I would. For now, I'm not going to overthink everything and just roll with it when it comes to him," Emma said as she watched a child dart in and out of the crowd toward one of the stores. "Maybe it will all end badly again, or it will just end, but I'm willing to take the chance."

Mandy dropped her book on the table. "Well, let's hope that doesn't happen."

"He can't end up being like Tristan, can he? I mean I can't find two stalkers in my lifetime, can I?"

"I don't know, Emma, but I think the odds are against it happening again. Unless you're a psycho magnet."

Emma released a small chuckle. "That wouldn't surprise me."

"Me either," Mandy said with a laugh. "I *can* say I barely know the guy, and I already like him more than I ever liked Tristan."

That was easy enough to believe; neither Mandy nor Jill ever really liked Tristan. They thought he was fake and slimy. They believed he was overbearing *before* he started following her everywhere and leaving creepy gifts on her doorstep, on her desk, and at her work. She should have listened to her friends, but she'd been a moron and determined to prove to herself she could have a normal relationship with a man.

Emma shook her head; she stepped away from the railing as

the front door opened. Jill's excited chatter made her frown as she craned her head to peer around the doorway.

"Who is she talking to?" Mandy inquired in a whisper.

"I have no idea," Emma told her.

"Come on in," Jill called over her shoulder as she skipped down the steps. "Would you like a drink? I'm sure Emma is probably up by now. I'll go get her."

Emma almost fell over when Ethan appeared at the top of the stairs. He ran a hand through his sweat-slicked hair, pushing it back from the broad angles of his face. The loose-fitting shorts he wore hung low on his hips, but it was his broad, well-muscled chest that kept her eyes riveted.

Her mouth watered, literally watered, as her eyes ran over the carved muscles of his abs. He didn't have a six-pack; oh no, it was more like an eighteen case. Muscles she hadn't known existed bunched and flexed as he descended the steps.

"I'll take some water," he answered.

Emma jerked back from the doorway, and her gaze shot to Mandy.

"Who is it?" Mandy asked again.

Emma tried to calm her racing heart as she placed her finger against her lips in a shushing gesture. '*It's him,*' she mouthed.

'*Him who*?' Mandy mouthed back.

'*Him!*' Emma forced herself not to stomp her foot as she jerked her head at the doorway.

Mandy's mouth dropped before she broke into a grin showing all her teeth. Grabbing the arm of the chair, the muscles in her forearms flexed as she lifted herself up. She hopped over to the doorframe and poked her head around it. Emma hated the unreasonable jealousy that filled her when Mandy's mouth dropped open. She didn't like the idea of either of her friends seeing Ethan in this state or lusting after him.

Never, in four years, had any of them ever fought over a guy. Not even when Jill and Mandy disliked Tristan, had they been nasty or catty about their feelings for him. They made their opinions known, but they were never mean, and they'd never said, '*I told you so,*' after. There had only been unwavering support.

Mandy and Jill both had more experience with men than she did. Mandy didn't have much more as she spent most of her time buried in her books, and though Jill liked to bounce through different guys, she would never go after someone Emma or Mandy liked. Jill was a flirt, but she would never hurt her friends. Even still, Emma had to take a deep breath to steady herself and lock the green-eyed monster back in its cage as Mandy's gaze remained riveted upon Ethan.

Mandy leaned back from the door and rested against it as she fanned herself with her hand. '*Holy hotness,*' she mouthed.

Jill reappeared and handed a glass of water to Ethan. "I'll go get Emma."

"You don't have to bother her if she's still sleeping," he said.

Jill waved a hand at him before disappearing down the hall.

"Get in there," Mandy hissed at her.

Emma looked at her helplessly; uncertainty and apprehension paralyzed her. If she stepped out there now, there would be no turning back. She'd barely been capable of separating herself from him last night. It was all moving too fast, yet even as the thought swirled through her mind, she yearned to go in there. Heat coiled in her belly as she recalled his kiss and the feel of him against her.

No, there would be no going back if she walked in there now. She may end up with the broken heart Tristan hadn't inflicted on her, but she so wanted to take the plunge. If only her feet would move.

"Emma!" Jill's voice was tiny as it drifted through the house.

Swallowing, Emma forced herself to step forward. "Out here!" she called.

Ethan lifted his head to look at her as she stepped into the doorway. The fiery gleam in his gaze caused her toes to curl as her hands clenched before her. What was it about him that made her forget everyone else in the room? Even in her cut-off shorts and a loose-fitting tank top, he somehow made her feel like the most desirable woman in the world.

Ethan wasn't at all thrown off to see her stepping through the doorway; he'd smelled her the second he walked through the door and known where she was. He wasn't sure how she would feel about seeing him after last night, but the sight of her made his day better as the morning sun illuminated her from behind. Her thick hair pulled into a loose knot, rested against the nape of her neck. His gaze lingered on the vein in her neck before moving over her body. Even in her baggy clothes, she was the most enticing woman he'd ever seen.

When he'd left the house, he'd been looking to have a good run to work off some of the remaining sexual frustration she aroused in him last night. When he ran into Jill, he'd known the only way he would feel better was to see Emma again. That strange sense of peace worked its way through him again as his eyes returned to hers. She looked a little shy as she folded her hands before her, but the smile she gave him warmed him from the inside out and helped to calm him further.

"There you are!" Jill said as she stepped back in the room. Emma reluctantly tore her attention away from Ethan as Jill hopped down the stairs and strode toward the kitchen. "Ethan and I ran into each other at the end of our morning run."

"I see." *Oh, that was a terrific piece of conversation,* she thought with an inward groan. But her tongue felt glued to the roof of her mouth.

"It's so peaceful out there in the morning," Jill continued.

Ethan's gaze remained riveted on her as he lifted the glass of water to his lips. He didn't require the water to survive, but it was good to wet his throat and helped cool him down. "And I couldn't turn down a drink," he said.

Jill waved her hand at Emma from behind Ethan's back in a gesture for her to come closer. Mandy nudged her shoulder a little as she stepped forward, but Emma's feet were planted more firmly than an oak tree's roots. Ethan's gaze went briefly to Mandy's missing lower leg. To his credit, he didn't become uncomfortable in her presence like Emma had seen other people do, and he didn't stare.

"It's good to see you again," Mandy greeted.

"Yes, yes, it is." Her tongue finally came undone from the roof of her mouth only to sputter that crap out. She was better off remaining mute, Emma realized in disgust.

Ethan didn't seem to care as a smile tugged at the corners of his full mouth. Thoughts of kissing him consumed her as her gaze focused on his lips. He drank the rest of the water and placed the glass on the counter.

"The house Stefan rented came with a boat. We were hoping to go out on it this morning, maybe do some fishing and swimming. Would the three of you like to join us?" Ethan asked.

"That would be great," Jill said eagerly.

"Are you sure they won't mind?" Mandy asked.

"Not at all, there's plenty of room, and the more, the merrier," he responded with ease.

"It sounds like fun," Emma said.

"Good. I'll come back and get you in an hour if that's okay?"

"Plenty of time," Jill assured him.

He smiled at Emma before turning and walking up the stairs. "Wear your bathing suits," he called over his shoulder before slipping out the door.

Emma exchanged a look with Jill and Mandy before Jill let out a little squeal and raced over to her. "He likes you," she said eagerly.

"Don't get carried away, Jill," Emma told her.

"Maybe we should let you go alone." Jill tapped her finger thoughtfully against her chin as she studied Emma.

"She can't go out on a boat by herself with three people we barely know," Mandy said.

"I can take care of myself," Emma reminded them.

"Of course you can," Jill assured her. "But Mandy's right, we don't know them."

Emma's pride made her want to argue with them, but she wasn't stupid. Ethan and his family seemed pleasant enough, she didn't think they would harm her, but she didn't know them, and going somewhere alone with them wasn't the smartest idea. It was better to go with her friends than to argue with them over it because of her pride.

"We have to get ready," Mandy said as she slid her arm through Emma's and led her toward the stairs.

CHAPTER SEVEN

"You invited the humans?" Stefan placed the paper he was reading on the table and fixed Ethan with a look that made him wonder if he'd sprouted horns.

"Sure, why not?" Ethan replied casually.

Stefan exchanged a glance with Isabelle, whose arms were resting on the edge of the pool as she treaded water. "Because they're *human*," Stefan said slowly.

"You once dated humans," Ethan reminded him.

Isabelle shot him a look that could freeze fire as she pulled herself from the pool. Ethan almost chuckled, but he thought she might kick his ass if he did. Stefan looked like he might also laugh. He wisely chose not to.

"Since when do *you* want to hang out with a human?" Isabelle demanded. Water dripped onto the bluestone patio with soft drips as she walked across the patio to retrieve her towel from a chair.

Ethan shrugged, but he knew his casual gesture didn't fool his sister. "Things change."

"Or is it *her*?"

Unreasonable anger filled Ethan as he folded his arms over his chest and leaned back on his heels. He didn't like being questioned about Emma, and he certainly didn't like her referenced in that way. "I don't think that's any of your business."

"Ethan—" Isabelle started.

"If you would like me to un-invite them, I will."

"That's not what I'm saying at all," Isabelle gushed. "It's just unusual to see *you* continuously interacting with humans, much less the *same* human. That's all."

"We all change with age."

"That we do. Lord knows I did," Stefan agreed as he rose from the table.

Stefan strolled over to Isabelle and placed his hand on her shoulder. He squeezed it reassuringly before moving her back a step. Isabelle turned to look at him, and from years of experience with watching his parents, Ethan knew they were having a silent conversation with each other. It frustrated him, he was certain they were discussing him, but he kept his temper under control.

"I'm sure it will be fine," Isabelle said.

"It will be," Ethan assured her. "I'm going to get them."

Before his sister could argue with him further, he turned and walked away. His earlier run had helped burn off some of his excess energy, but he could feel it building within him again. He walked at an increasingly brisk pace down the road to the small house where Emma and her friends were staying.

Emma tried not to ogle Ethan as he took her hand and helped her board the boat. Between the home they were staying in and this boat, she didn't know what to make of Ethan or his family. She knew they were only renting the house, but she imagined the rent on this place was more than some people made in a year. She could tell Jill and Mandy were as impressed and overwhelmed as she was by their gaping mouths when they looked around the glistening white boat.

She was so busy trying to take in all the details she didn't realize Ethan still held her hand until he pulled her toward the back of the boat. Or was it the stern? She wasn't sure, as she'd never been on anything bigger than a rowboat before. He settled her into a seat before turning to help Mandy and Jill get seated.

"I'll be right back," he told her.

Emma admired the fit of his swim trunks on his thighs and ass as she watched him walk away. She was so focused on him that she jumped when Jill leaned closer to her and spoke. "What does his family *do* for a living?"

"I don't know," Emma whispered back.

"Maybe they're in the mob."

"Yeah, the mob is *huge* in Oregon," Emma retorted.

Even Jill had to bite her lip to keep from laughing. "Maybe they've decided to expand."

Emma chuckled as she shook her head, but Jill's question made her recall how Ethan avoided her question when she'd asked him about what he did. There was a lot of money here, but it was his brother-in-law's, not Ethan's. She could understand if Ethan didn't have a plan for his future, she wasn't exactly planning or doing much in life right now. Maybe Ethan felt the same way and didn't like talking about it; she hadn't told him everything about herself either.

The boat engine firing up drew her attention to Stefan standing behind the wheel with Isabelle at his side. Ethan said something to Stefan she couldn't hear over the engine, but Stefan glanced at them before nodding. Emma turned her attention to the water as the boat started to pull away from the dock.

Excitement built within her as the powerful vessel hummed beneath her and the wind began to kick up. The boat picked up speed as Stefan steered it away from shore and into the open water. Her hair blew back from her face; the warm, salty ocean spray kicking up around her was cool as it landed on her cheeks and tickled her face. It was impossible not to smile as the boat skimmed over the ocean and plumes of water shot up around them. She turned her body and rested her arms on the back of her chair to watch the wake coming from the rear of the boat.

Ethan's arm brushed against hers when he returned. She watched him as he settled into the seat beside her. Something about him and this whole moment made her feel as if someone had opened the door on the cage she'd locked herself in since Tristan. She could almost feel her wings spreading as she flew free and unexpected tears of joy burned her eyes.

"Are you okay?" Ethan inquired.

"Just the wind," she said as she wiped at her eyes.

She wasn't expecting it when his hand slid into hers. The tears burned their way up her throat, but she managed to keep these from spilling as she wrapped her hand around his large, strong one. He was so powerful and self-assured, she thought he could take on anything and anyone. He would protect her. She had no reason to believe such a thing, but she couldn't shake the certainty of it as she refocused her attention on the vast sea.

Ethan studied her profile as she focused on the water again. The flowing black cover-up she wore brought out the blonde in her hair and made her eyes appear even darker. He felt like she weaved a spell over him; she entranced him.

The boat decelerated as they approached a secluded cove. Emma took in the amazing lava rock formations around them as the boat came to a stop fifty feet from shore. "This seems like a good place!" Stefan announced. Emma rose to her feet as Stefan went down below and came back with four fishing poles and a tackle box. "We can fish from the front and swim off the back."

Mandy and Jill stood, pulled off their cover-ups, and dropped them onto their chairs. "Are you going to swim, Emma?" Mandy asked.

"I'd prefer to fish." There was something enticing about just sitting there and watching her pole while soaking in the sun. She'd made sure to douse herself in sunblock before leaving the house.

"I'll join you," Ethan said as he rose to his feet and pulled off his shirt.

Emma felt like a cartoon character with its eyes popping out as, once again, she was treated to the delightful image of his bare chest with its sprinkling of hair across the carved surface.

He held his hand out and helped her to her feet when she took it. Her heart pounded with excitement and apprehension as she realized the others were all going swimming. She loved the idea of getting a chance to spend some time alone with him, but she was a conversational idiot around him. Even still, she was practically bouncing on her feet as he grabbed two poles and the tackle box before helping her maneuver to the front of the boat.

He handed her a pole and set the tackle box down. Emma popped the locks on it and began to pick through it in search of a lure. Ethan quirked an eyebrow as he watched her expertly attach the lure to the line. "I take it you've done this before."

"Once or twice," she told him with a grin.

He laughed as he dug into the tackle box and pulled out another lure. "I wouldn't have pegged you as a fisherwoman."

"I'm a little difficult to peg," she teased.

Was she flirting with him? Maybe she was only a complete moron when other people were around them. It was a pleasant thought, and it helped to ease her anxiety.

Her whole body reacted when something hot and hungry flickered through his eyes. She sucked in a breath.

"Let's hope you're not impossible," he said.

Yep, she was simply going to melt into a pile of goo or jump him; she wasn't sure which one right now. She wished she'd chosen to plunge herself into the water instead, but the ocean wouldn't be enough to cool her right now. It took all she had to break eye contact with him and cast her line out. She settled onto the edge of the boat and let her legs dangle over the side.

"Where I'm from in New York, we either fish in the summer, ride our ATV's, or sit around a bonfire," she told him as he settled beside her.

She was acutely aware of the heat of his body as the hair on his arm tickled her skin. "My siblings and I spent our time tormenting and daring each other to do some pretty crazy things," he said.

"That sounds like a lot of fun."

"It was."

Her fishing pole made a clicking noise as she reeled her line back in. "If you don't mind me asking, what does Stefan do for a living?"

He leaned a little more against her side. "Not much." Emma frowned at him before glancing questioningly around the large boat. "Family money," he said.

"So, he's not in the mob then?"

He laughed as he shook back his raven colored hair. "No, he's not in the mob."

"Jill will be relieved to know that."

The sound of his rumbling laughter caused her to smile in return. Emma couldn't remember the last time she'd been this happy as they continued talking. He told her more about his massive family and his home in Oregon. She told him more about her mother, who was a nurse, and her father who was a reporter at the local news station.

They lived a simple life, in a small home. She was loved and had a lot of friends through high school. She saw most of them when she returned home for breaks, and they all shared stories. Most of them were returning to live there when they finished college.

"Is that what you plan to do, return home and stay?" he asked as he cast his line out again.

For some reason, the question made him tense. He didn't like to think of her returning home and being so far away from him. He didn't understand where the sudden feeling came from or why it lodged so firmly inside him. He enjoyed talking to her, and the feeling of peace she brought him, but he barely knew her, and he had no investment in her life.

"I'm not sure. I love it there, I love my parents, but I also really enjoyed being away from home. Mandy and Jill asked me to go to California. Jill is from San Francisco, and Mandy is going to Stanford in the fall. They're hoping to get a place together and asked me to room with them too. I'm considering it; it would be fun, and I'd like to see California. I enjoyed experiencing new things while at school, and I don't think I'm ready for that to end. I'd also like to travel more."

"Then don't let it end."

She gave a small laugh. "It's just a matter of finding a job so I could stay there. I waitressed for a couple of years; maybe I could find work doing that again or a job in a museum. I had planned to teach history, but I think I'd prefer to work in a museum or something similar."

"You like history?"

Ethan couldn't help but smile as her face lit up.

"I love it!" she gushed. "There's so much to learn from it, so many lives once lived, so many people who walked through these places, paved the roads, and built the world before us. They fascinate me, and I love to hear their stories, see the pictures, and touch things those people once touched. I'd love to see and explore as many historical places as I can before I die."

"I never really thought about it that way," he admitted.

"I also really enjoyed meeting different people while at school. Some of them weren't always so great." She refused to let thoughts of Tristan ruin this day. "But most of them were."

He looked at her as if she'd just told him the ocean was purple and the clouds were full of pink giraffes. She glanced over herself but didn't see anything out of the ordinary, and she was pretty sure she didn't have anything hanging out of her nose. When she looked at him again, the strange gleam in his eyes, and the small smile on his face, warmed her heart.

She was so different from him, he realized. She was eager to get out in the world and explore new things. She enjoyed being around other people, the one thing he couldn't stand unless he was with her. When he was with her, he could focus on something other than the blood pulsing through people's veins, and the driving urge to bury himself in the release he knew their deaths would finally give him.

Unable to resist, he brushed back a stray tendril of her silken hair. She watched him with wide eyes as her lower lip trembled slightly. It was good to know he seemed to affect her as much as she affected him as she leaned closer to him. His gaze slid over the swell of her breasts thrust upward in her orange bikini top, and then over her rounded hips and flat belly.

Her skin was in the early stages of a tan and the golden color brought out the dark gold in her hair and eyes. His fingers slid over her shoulder and toward her cheek, her skin was as soft as a flower petal against his, and he couldn't get enough of it. He had to forcefully pull his hand away before he forgot about everyone else and lost himself to her again.

"I'm sure you could find work anywhere, and I think it sounds like a great plan," he told her.

She gave him a half-hearted smile, but she missed the contact with him. "I'm not sure my parents would agree."

"It's not their life, is it?"

"No, it's not, but they expect a lot from me."

"I'm sure they do, but I'm sure they're already proud of you."

Beginning to feel a little self-conscious, she decided to steer the conversation away from her. "So, what about you, you never really said what you do."

He cast his pole out again and began reeling it back in. "School's not my thing, never was, and I'm not much of a traveler. I like to work with my hands and mainly do odds and ends."

"A jack of all trades?"

"I guess you could say that. I helped to build a house last year; I enjoyed doing it. I discovered I also like to carve things out of wood around the same time."

He didn't tell her this newfound love of his was a great way to keep himself distracted from his more disturbing impulses. He could often lose himself for hours amongst the smell and feel of the wood within his hands as he carved intricate designs into it. It was never something he'd ever thought to do, but once he started the hobby, he couldn't stop.

"I built a gazebo for our lake at home, a porch swing,

dining room table, and chairs. My favorite is a children's chest I plan to give to Isabelle and Stefan when they have a baby."

"That's amazing."

It also suited him, she realized as she studied his profile. She couldn't picture him wearing a suit and sitting behind a desk. It was too restricting for him, and though she barely knew him, she knew he would be miserable if he were confined. No, he belonged in a natural element of some kind, on a construction site, or on a fishing boat.

"I'd love to see some of it," she said.

The sun played over his handsome features and lit his eyes when he turned to smile at her. The warmth of the rays caused a thin sheen of sweat to break out on his body and made his skin gleam enticingly.

"Isabelle doesn't know about the chest, but I have some photos on my phone I'll show you. I turned it off and threw it in a drawer when I arrived in Bermuda though, so I don't have it on me."

She laughed as she leaned against his side; she enjoyed how easy it was to be with him and how good he could make her feel. "I did the same. There's no way I'm paying *that* bill."

"Me either," he agreed.

She swung her legs back and forth over the edge of the boat. "How old are you?"

"Twenty-six, you?"

"Twenty-two."

Emma cast her line back out as they fell into an amicable silence. Neither of them even had a bite, but she found she didn't mind as she listened to the water lapping against the boat and the splashing and laughter from the others as they swam. She was getting ready to reel her line back in when he leaned toward her and placed his finger under her chin. He turned her face toward his, and before she knew what he intended, he leaned forward and kissed her tenderly.

A sigh escaped her, but just as she was about to lose herself to him, he pulled away. Her eyes searched his face. "You had a bite," he said.

That grin did funny things to her insides and made her feel like a kid on Christmas morning all over again. "I had a what?"

He gestured toward the pole in her hand. "A bite."

"Oh, *oh*," she said again as she finally felt the tug on her pole. She had completely forgotten about it. She lifted it and began reeling it in again, but whatever was there didn't pursue the lure.

The boat shifted; she looked back to see Stefan and Isabelle climbing on board. Isabelle frowned as she studied the two of them, but she turned away when Stefan put his hand on her elbow. She gave a brief nod before slipping into the lower cabin of the boat. Jill and Mandy climbed on next, Jill grabbed two towels off one of the seats and then handed Mandy her prosthetic leg.

Isabelle reappeared and tossed another towel to Stefan. She toweled her hair off as she made her way toward them. "We're going to head back, Mandy and Jill are hungry."

"Sounds good," Ethan said and began to reel in his line. Emma frowned as Isabelle continued to stand there, staring back and forth between them. She gave Emma a tremulous smile before turning and walking back to Stefan. Though she didn't get the feeling Isabelle disliked her, there was something standoffish about her that Emma didn't understand, and it made her a little uneasy.

Gathering their poles, they walked to the back to join the others. Black clouds began rolling in over the island as they drove back to the dock in silence. The ozone aroma of impending rain hung heavily in the air as the wind started to kick up and blew hair around her face. She brushed it back and kept hold of it as Stefan slid the boat into its spot at the dock.

Emma accepted Ethan's hand, and he helped her to climb off the boat. Their footsteps resonated on the wooden boards beneath their feet as they walked up the dock with her hand in his. Emma studied the people hurriedly gathering their things on the beach. Some die-hard beachgoers looked as if they would stay and ride out the storm, but others were already running for cover.

"Would you like to go to dinner tonight?" Ethan asked. "Just the two of us."

She smiled as she tilted her head back to look at him. "I would."

Taking comfort in his solid presence, she rested her head against his bicep. Emma lifted her head from Ethan's arm when a man separated himself from the crowd on the beach. A shiver ran down her spine as she watched the man stroll down the sand with an easy grace. His broad shoulders were hunched forward against the rising wind, and he had his hands shoved into the pockets of his jeans.

He looked so out of place on a beach full of barely dressed people, but he moved as if he fit in amongst them. The thick clouds, turning day into early night, made his hair appear darker, but she knew it was a light reddish-brown color.

Emma's heart slammed against her ribs, tremors racked her body, and despite the heat of the day, she was suddenly freezing. Closing her eyes, she shook her head and took a deep breath before opening them again. Her gaze ran frantically over the beach, but she didn't see the man amongst the crowd again.

"Are you okay?" Ethan inquired.

Emma reluctantly tore her attention away from the beach and back to him. She realized she must look ridiculous standing there gawking at the beach. He was staring at her with concern as she'd abruptly stopped walking in the middle of the dock.

"I'm fine," she replied. "I thought I saw someone I knew, but I was wrong."

She *had* to be mistaken because there was absolutely no way Tristan could be here. *No* way he could know she was here. He'd been out of her life for a year now. Surely her mind was playing tricks on her, and she'd imagined things. Still, she couldn't shake the icy chill settling into her bones.

CHAPTER EIGHT

Ethan pulled the chair out for Emma and settled in across from her as the waiter placed their menus on the table and filled their water glasses. It was their fifth date this week. They had spent most of the days with his family and her friends, but dinner was just them, and he liked it. They would meet up again with the others for drinks afterward, but these couple of hours alone had become his favorite hours of the day.

Her hazel eyes danced in the candlelight as he settled in across from her. Over the past few days, he'd come to enjoy spending time with her more and more. Her smile could light up a room, and her laugh was so buoyant and carefree, just hearing it made him smile too.

He'd always believed humans were only good for blood, and even then he only used blood bags. Though he knew his brothers and The Stooges had sex with humans, he never trusted himself enough to, just as he'd never trusted himself to feed directly from one. He wasn't sure if the others knew those two things about him, he'd never told them, and he tried to play it off that he was like them. They never asked about his habits, but they knew he didn't go to the clubs as often as they did, and he'd never walked out of the club with a human like they had.

She may be human, but he was eager to have Emma beneath him, even if he was concerned about what might happen. He experienced no driving urge to kill when she was around, but he was afraid he might lose control of himself with her. She was a human; she was weak and vulnerable. There was a chance he could injure her. Even as he thought it he knew it could never happen, he'd kill himself before he ever put a bruise on her.

The idea of drinking her blood without her knowing was repulsive to him. It would be delicious—powerful and filling—but he would never taste her unless she knew about it. For the first time, he wanted to feed on a human without the driving compulsion he always felt to lose himself in their blood as he watched the life slip from their eyes. Without feeling as if he would welcome the eventual death of the person more than the actual blood itself.

She would *never* know about him though. She would run screaming from him if she discovered the truth, like any sane human would, and it was the last thing he wanted to happen. He was determined to enjoy the three weeks they had left together. He wouldn't let the knowledge of what he was push her away, frighten her, or put her in any danger. There were already three other vampires roaming this island, he hadn't seen them again, but they could become a threat to her.

From what Stefan told him, he knew some of his kind liked to hunt and kill other vampires for more power. He hadn't sensed much of a threat from those three, but he wasn't willing to risk Emma's life or the lives of her friends. He would kill them if they even thought about trying to get close enough to harm Emma.

His gaze drifted back to her as she tapped her chin with her index finger and studied the menu. The waiter returned with their drinks, took their order, and left. Emma's hair shimmered in the glow of the candle, appearing more blonde than brown as the firelight danced over it.

"So, Emma, how is it you're still single?" he inquired.

The question startled her enough she sloshed the wine against the side of her glass. They'd had some fun dates over the past few nights. Dates which involved talking about the music they liked, their favorite TV shows, movies, and books. They'd discussed their families and friends, but the conversation had stayed away from past relationships, something she was more than happy about.

She forced a smile and took a sip of her wine before answering. "I guess I'm just lucky."

He laughed as he leaned forward to grab his whiskey. The ice clinked against the side of the glass as he took a sip. "So no relationships for you, ever?"

He was trying to sound teasing and carefree, but he could feel pressure steadily building within him. What if there was someone else in her life? She didn't seem like the type to cheat on someone, but what did he know? She could have a boyfriend back home. Emma shrugged, but for the first time her eyes didn't twinkle. A new tension resonated in her body, one he'd never seen before, as she grew unbelievably still.

"There was someone," she murmured and glanced away from him.

He thought he might break his glass, but he couldn't get his hand to ease up on it. "Was it serious?"

"I'm not sure I ever knew what it was, but it didn't end well."

"Did he hurt you?" Emma's eyebrows rose, and even he was shocked by the growling tone of his voice as he leaned toward her.

"No, well I mean not physically. He kicked the crap out of my pride though. At the time, I thought he broke my heart, but I was never in love with him. I tried to convince myself I was."

"Why would you do that?"

Emma watched him as he sat a little away from her again. He was trying to look casual, but a muscle twitched in his jaw. "To seem normal, I guess."

She felt like such an idiot as she tried to explain it to him. Why had she tried so hard to fit in back then? Her parents loved her no matter what. Jill and Mandy thought she was perfectly fine. She was the only one who had believed something was wrong with her, but until Ethan, she'd never felt an intense attraction to a man. It still seemed a little odd, but she didn't question it anymore, not when he was sitting across from her.

"He was my ah...my first..." her voice trailed off as heat crept into her cheeks. "My first serious boyfriend, my first *everything*, and he was extremely charming. I tried to convince myself he made me happy; he convinced himself it was okay to sleep with other women."

"He was a fool."

She smiled again, but sadness continued to enshroud her. "That he was."

"I'm sorry you were hurt."

A small laugh escaped her. "The funny thing is, I wasn't. I was so relieved I finally had a reason to call it quits with him, I practically did a happy dance all the way down his hall afterward."

"Then why were you trying to convince yourself you were happy with him?"

She took another sip of her wine as she pondered her answer, but the only thing she could think of to say was the truth. Leaning closer to him, she rested her hand on the table as she said the words she'd never said to anyone. "Have you ever felt like you don't belong?" she inquired. "That no matter what you do, no matter how many friends and family you have, something is missing inside of you?"

Ethan felt as if she looked inside him and saw what he felt every day of his life. She couldn't know the worst of it, but for the first time, he'd encountered someone he was certain could understand the emptiness residing within him. "I know exactly what you mean."

Emma searched his face, but he didn't seem to be trying to manipulate her like Tristan used to do. His words were sincere, the bleakness in his eyes touched her in a way nothing ever had before. Without thinking, she took his hand. His fingers slid over hers as he rolled his hand beneath hers and grasped it in return. Unlike with Tristan, a sense of belonging stole through her whenever she was near him, and she felt as if whatever was missing inside her was finally found.

"I thought Tristan could make me feel normal, but I always felt as if I had to force it when with him. It never felt right. And he was a little unstable. I didn't know it while we were dating, but his issues became apparent when I broke up with him."

Ethan took another sip of his drink as he studied her. "What kind of issues?"

Emma frowned as she tried to decide how much to reveal to him. There weren't many people willing to date someone with an emotional basket case for an ex, but he didn't seem like the type to run for the hills, and she didn't see any reason to keep it from him.

"He became extremely possessive after the breakup, started following me, calling me all the time, and leaving me gifts. He appeared in my classes, classes that weren't his. He would sit in the back and watch me. His gifts grew steadily stranger, more disturbing, and more terrifying. The last one was a dozen black roses with a card I swear was written in blood, and it scared the hell out of me. I finally went to the police about him, but he disappeared before they could do anything."

Ethan kept his mouth closed as he fought to retract the fangs that extended while she spoke. He finally regained control of himself enough to talk again. "You haven't heard from him since?"

"Not in a year, and hopefully never again."

Ethan nodded but rage still simmered beneath the surface. That was a human he would gladly kill for frightening her if given the opportunity. He found it odd the strange behavior would abruptly cut off, but that kind of behavior wasn't something he understood. Her ex didn't sound like a very stable person. Maybe he killed himself, or maybe someone else did the deed.

"What about you?" Emma inquired though she wasn't certain she wanted to hear the answer. "Any serious relationships?"

"Nothing serious."

"Not the settling down type?"

He smiled at her over top of his glass. "I just haven't met the right one yet."

"Do you believe there is a *right* one?"

For him, it was a distinct possibility. "I do."

"So is there a string of broken hearts behind you?" It wasn't the subtlest way of asking about how many people there were in his past, but she wasn't exactly skilled at subtlety.

"None of those."

"I'm sure you've had lots of girlfriends."

"Five, and they were all aware it wasn't going anywhere before it started."

Emma frowned at him. He was gorgeous, she was sure a whole lot more than five women had thrown themselves at him over the years, but he spoke of his relationships as if they were business deals.

"You make it sound like they were an arrangement," she remarked.

That's what they were to him, but she wouldn't understand.

"Not really," he replied. "From the beginning, they knew it wouldn't be serious, and when it was time to part, we would do so amicably."

"How could you possibly know that at the beginning of a relationship? What if your feelings changed over time?"

"I just knew they wouldn't." She frowned at him in confusion, but he didn't know how to explain it to her, didn't know how to make her understand without turning her away from him. "You know how you said it always felt forced with Tristan, well that's kind of how I felt with them." It wasn't exactly the truth. Due to the way he'd grown up, he'd always known about the existence of soul mates, and he'd known going in none of those women were his mate. "I was never going to spend the rest of my life with one of them."

"Were they one-night stands? Never mind, you don't have to answer that, it's personal," she blurted after.

"I've never had a one-night stand," he told her. It was something he felt she needed to know, as he had every intention of pursuing something with her. "That's not my thing."

Her head tilted as a playful gleam lit her eyes. "You're just a romantic at heart."

Ethan chuckled as he leaned back in his chair. "I'm not so sure about that."

The waiter arrived with their food. He didn't require it to sustain him; in fact, he'd never eaten human food until very recently, and only when around her. He picked at the contents on his plate to avoid her suspicion. The raw steak wasn't overly bad, but it was the blood he sought as he put it in his mouth.

The bags of blood Isabelle stocked didn't seem to be doing the trick quite as well as they used to. It was Emma's blood he thought about when he consumed the bags now. He could try and find another human to feed from; it might satisfy him a little bit more. The idea of doing that was extremely unappealing to him, and if it wasn't Emma, he was feeding from, he knew there was a chance he might kill them.

Emma glanced surreptitiously up at him as they ate. She'd never met anyone like him. Most of the men she knew were good guys; they didn't purposely set out to hurt people, they weren't all nutball stalkers, but she'd never heard one of them say they entered into their relationships with the clear-cut understanding it was never going to go anywhere. She also didn't know many men who had never had a one-night stand or hooked up before, but there was no reason for him to lie to her about his past.

He was fascinating to her, and the more she learned about him, the more attracted to him she became, which was something she hadn't thought possible. She could barely take her eyes away from him as they ate their dinner, and if they weren't in this restaurant, her hands would be all over him.

He lifted his head and caught her watching him, but she didn't look away, she couldn't. She was pinned by his gaze, swamped with the growing need working its way through her body. She found it increasingly difficult to breathe, let alone eat, so she placed her fork down.

"Would you like anything else?" he inquired.

You, she almost said, but she bit back the word and told him no instead. She couldn't sit in this restaurant with him for a minute longer. She felt like she was going to claw her skin off if she didn't get up and start moving soon. A cold shower would be great, but she didn't think that would help her right now either.

In fact, she thought the only thing that would make her feel any better was to be in his arms again. Their other dates over the week had ended with a sweet kiss, there had been no more instances like the one at the club, but she desperately craved his hands on her flesh again, *now*.

Ethan paid the bill and walked around to help her rise from the chair. He could feel the increased heat of her body and hear the escalated pace of her heart. Recognizing her increasing desire, he couldn't resist touching her and brushed his hands over her shoulders as she rose from the chair. Her breath hitched; her breasts rose against the confining front of her dress. When her honeysuckle scent increased with yearning, he felt it wrapping around him and drawing him irresistibly closer to her.

The last thing he wanted was to meet up with the others, he much preferred taking her back to her house, but that was her decision to make. He kept his hand loosely around her waist; his chest brushed against her arm as he wound his way through the tables and people.

They were almost to the door when the sky opened, and a deluge of rain fell. He went to hold her back, but she was already stepping outside. He followed her out the door and stood beside her beneath the overhang as the rain pelted the ground in a loud crescendo which drowned out the noise of the restaurant.

"It should be over soon," he said. "We can wait inside."

The mischievous look she shot him over her shoulder should have warned him, but he still wasn't expecting it when she asked, "Why?" and stepped into the storm.

Disbelief and amusement filled him as she tilted her head back and lifted her arms to the sky. Laughter trailed from her as the falling rain plastered the deep blue dress to her body. He could only stand and stare as she tilted her head back to the sky.

Something about the picture of her laughing in the rain made his heart clench and caused a strange warmth to spread through him.

He thought he could stand there and watch her forever, but the urge to touch her drove him into the rain. She was still laughing as she dropped her head to look at him. The rain turned her hair darker and caused it to curl as it clung to her face and neck. He barely noticed the drops of water as they pelted against him; the only thing he could focus on was *her*.

"It feels wonderful!" she cried above the noise.

Words failed him. It felt as if he was taken over by something entirely primitive, something that would only be appeased by touching her. Wrapping his arm around her waist, he lifted her up and pressed her flush against his body. Her mouth parted, but before she could speak, his lips descended on hers in a kiss that would have been bruising if the contact of their mouths didn't immediately eased some of the strain within him.

A groan escaped him; his erection was extremely uncomfortable as it pressed against the front of his jeans. Her fingers curled into his shoulders, her mouth opened to his. She tasted of wine as his tongue entwined with hers. He could lose himself in her forever.

If it weren't for the fact he wouldn't allow anyone else to see her naked, he would have taken her here and now without any thought to where they were. If it were any other girl, he wouldn't care if someone else saw her body, but no other woman had ever driven him this crazy before, or pushed him to these kinds of heights. No way was he about to play show and tell with any part of her body.

Her breath came in shallow gasps when he broke the kiss. He needed a moment to regain control of himself, but the vision of her, soaking wet, with her lips swollen from the force of his kiss, did nothing to curb his appetite for her.

"Emma," he groaned.

She rested her forehead against his; the hoarse tone of his voice caused a small shiver to run through her. She inhaled the scent of the rain clinging to him, and took pleasure in the feel of his powerful arms around her. "I think we should get out of the rain," she whispered against his lips.

It took everything he had to put her back on her feet and release her. The smile she gave him was as enticing as Eve with the apple, he decided as she stepped away from him. He almost grabbed her again, but she clasped his hand and started to run. Her laughter trickled through the air as she dashed in and out of the puddles.

Even when he was a kid, he'd never played in the rain, but he found himself laughing as he jumped in and out of the puddles with her. This woman beside him was such a joy; she made him see the world in an entirely different way and made him long to experience things he had never tried before.

Emma couldn't stop laughing as she spun in front of him and danced a few feet further away. He ran at her, but she turned and raced up the hill toward her house. She knew he could catch her, but he didn't until she was at the door. His arms encircled her waist; his warm breath blew against her neck as he bent his head and kissed her. A shiver worked its way through her body; her laughter faded away as her skin caught fire from his touch.

Slow things down, she told herself, but even as she thought it she could feel a wetness between her legs, and her breasts ached. Almost as if he was reading her thoughts, his hand slid around to the front of her dress and cupped her breast. She bit down on her lip to keep from crying out as her nipple hardened beneath his gentle ministrations. Emma forgot all about the keys she had pulled out of her purse as her hands flattened on the door and her head tilted back.

His lips moved over her neck before pressing against her ear. A low moan escaped her; her entire body became engulfed in heat, a heat that would only be extinguished by having him inside her. The rigid length of his erection pressed against her buttocks as his free hand slid down to wrap into the skirt of her dress. She could feel the hemline of it edging upward, but she knew this time she wouldn't stop him. She needed him too badly to have this end now.

So lost in him, she didn't realize the hand pulling her dress up had moved away until it covered her hand holding the keys. She relinquished the keys to him; he held her against him while he unlocked the door. The harshness of his breathing sounded in her ears as he opened the door and carried her inside.

Ethan wanted her with an intensity bordering on obsession. He should leave here; in the state he was in he could be a threat to her, but the thought of leaving made him feel even more unstable. He wouldn't hurt her, he didn't know where the certainty accompanying the thought came from, but he knew it was *true*. He would cut off his hands, tear out his fangs, and kill himself before he ever harmed her.

The dim illumination from the light left on in the kitchen spilled over her face and wet hair. She'd never looked more desirable, he realized as he stepped closer to her. Seeming to sense something within him, she hesitated for a second before sliding her arms around his shoulders. She stood on tiptoe to press a kiss against his lips. His cock jumped in his jeans at the feel of her breasts pressing against his soaked shirt. He forgot all about the water dripping from them as he lifted her off the floor.

Her legs wrapped around his waist, a small breath escaped her as he settled her onto the undeniable evidence of his arousal. They should go to her room, but he couldn't bring himself to take one step away from her to walk down the hall. Desire clamored through his veins; it took everything he had not to rip the dress from her body and leave it shredded on the floor. He would scare her if he did. She was a human; he kept reminding himself as he braced her against the wall. A human with blood he would give anything to have in his mouth, a human who was driving him nearly mad with desire.

And he had never been with a human before. *Easy*, he counseled himself, *just take it slow*.

His last relationship was based on nothing but violence, sexual gratification, and pain. He would never allow Emma to know such depravity, and he didn't want that kind of a relationship with her. She would never know that kind of brutality; she would only know the immense pleasure he planned to give them both.

His hands ran over her smooth thighs as he pushed the dripping dress higher up her waist. Excitement pulsed through his veins as his fingers brushed against the edge of her underwear. He waited for her to pull back, to tell him no again, but she only pressed closer to him. A low groan escaped him as his fingers stroked her clit through her panties. Even through the material, he could feel her heat and a wetness he knew had nothing to do with the rain.

The blood clamoring in his ears made it nearly impossible to think as a muffled cry escaped her, and her fingers curled into his shoulders. He tore his mouth away from hers to leave a trail of kisses across her cheek before taking her earlobe in his mouth and lightly sucking on it.

Emma almost screamed; she was possessed with the wild urge to tear her nails across his flesh as her body begged to be filled by him. She'd never experienced anything like this overwhelming need before as his hands and mouth teased her to even higher levels. A part of her wanted to beg him to end her torment, but the other part hoped it never ended.

Pushing aside the edge of her panties, his fingers brushed against the trimmed hair of her bikini line before finding her moist center and slipping inside of her. Emma jerked as he *finally* filled her in some way, and his fingers began to stroke the blaze within her toward a raging inferno.

A groan of satisfaction escaped him as Emma's cry sounded in his ear. She was so hot and wet just the feel of her muscles around his finger almost caused him to come. He kept her pressed against the wall as he slid his fingers in and out of her at a leisurely pace. Her rapid breaths sounded in his ear as she began to rise and fall with his increasingly demanding movements.

"Ethan."

His name on her lips was his undoing. He slid his fingers from her and grabbed the lacy edge of her panties. The thin material gave with a small tearing sound, her eyes widened, but she didn't tell him to stop, and she didn't appear fearful.

Adjusting his hold on her, he clasped her ass with one hand as he grabbed for the button of his jeans with the other. This was not the way he had planned to do this his first time with her. He'd planned to savor every inch of her body, intended to relish every second he was inside her, but that would have to wait until a later time. He couldn't stop to take the time to do those things; he had to have her *now*.

He felt like a wild animal as he unbuttoned his jeans and pushed them and his underwear down. There wasn't time to take them off completely, but his dick was finally freed from its constraints.

Easy, he told himself, but there was no going easy here, there was no holding back. His skin felt as if it would blister and burn off if he didn't possess her soon. He was throbbing with his need and half-crazed with it.

He was half-afraid she would stop him as he pressed the tip of his throbbing cock against her wet center. She didn't tell him no though; instead, she pushed more firmly against him and thrust her hips toward him. Adjusting his feet, he lifted her up and drove himself into her. A cry of ecstasy escaped her as she pulled him even closer.

The savage urgency driving him vanished the second her tight sheath enveloped him. The burning of his skin eased as a feeling he'd never experienced before enshrouded him. This was where he was supposed to be, inside of her, *with* her. He finally understood what it was like to come home, and though he suspected he knew what it meant for him, the realization didn't frighten him.

Emma couldn't tear her gaze away from his beautiful eyes as he stretched and filled her. Having him deep within her was the most incredible sensation she'd ever experienced. Her fingers slid over the handsome planes of his face as she fought the ridiculous urge to cry from the wonder of it all. She didn't move against him but took this moment to savor in the feel of him within her.

Complete, that was what she felt in a way she never knew she could or ever thought possible. She understood now why everything felt so forced with Tristan; *this* was where she belonged. It made no sense to her, but she couldn't shake the certainty, or the awe, that came with the realization.

Ethan watched her face as he lifted her up and deliberately lowered her onto him again. Her gold-flecked eyes were clouded with passion as they held his, but he also saw the wonder within her gaze. He kept his hands on her hips as he lifted her up and slid himself into her again. He was finding it far easier than he'd expected to be gentle with her as her body somehow managed to cage the beast within him.

"You feel amazing," he whispered against her mouth.

A shiver of contentment slid through her at his words; her hands grasped his cheeks as she kissed him. Bracing her against the wall, he moved one of his hands off her ass. He grabbed the front of her dress and pulled it down to free one of her breasts. It filled his hand as he cupped and kneaded it until her nipple was a hardened bud against his palm. Bending down, he took it into his mouth and sucked before circling it with his tongue. She held him closer as the caress of his tongue drove her even crazier.

Her cries became more fevered as she started to ride him faster. Releasing her breast, he grabbed her waist once more. The calm he'd experienced upon first entering her vanished as he drove himself more forcefully into her body. His eyes fastened on her neck as she tilted her head back, but he was too lost in the feel of her body to think about her blood.

She cried out in delight as her muscles contracted around him. The force of her orgasm pushed him to ever-higher levels as he thrust into her again. With a loud groan, he finally found his much-needed release.

His head dropped into the hollow of her neck and shoulder. The sweet scent of her blood engulfed him, and though it pricked his hunger, he felt her comforting presence calming him once again. She had the most astonishing effect on him, an effect he didn't think he would ever get used to. He wrapped his arms around her back and pulled her closer as she leaned against him.

"You make me forget myself," she whispered in his ear.

A strange sensation pricked in his chest as he cradled her against him. "You do the same to me."

She pulled back to look at him, and her eyes searched his

face. The smile curling her lips did odd things to his heart. Then, the cloud of satisfaction faded away, her mouth parted as reality seemed to crash over her. Ethan found himself unable to breathe as he waited for her to tell him this was a mistake. He didn't think he could take that right now, not after what had transpired between them, not when she was the only one who brought him peace.

She didn't want anything to ruin what they'd shared, but dread crept through her as she realized what she'd done. Unfortunately, she couldn't deny she'd just had unprotected sex with a man that, though she'd spent a lot of time with this week, she still barely knew him. Not to mention, all she could think about was what he'd said earlier about his past relationships. Maybe he hadn't made it clear earlier, but would he now tell her he wasn't looking for anything serious?

She didn't know how she would take that. On one hand, she couldn't expect him to want anything more than a summer fling with her, they were both on vacation, and they lived on opposite sides of the country. On the other, it was the best sex she'd ever had; she was still basking in the afterglow of the ecstasy having him inside her had given her.

She cared for him; she didn't want to hear the words this would end within the next three weeks, that he already knew she wasn't the one. He wasn't into one-night stands but three weeks together wouldn't be considered a one-night stand. And that was if he even *intended* to continue seeing her after this. There'd been no promises between them; there were no guarantees. Emma shook her head to clear it of her rambling thoughts before she became a bumbling, clingy mess who drove him out the door right now.

"We didn't use protection," she muttered.

He almost laughed out loud but managed to stifle it before he upset her. Unfortunately, he couldn't tell her no diseases could survive in his system. "I've been tested, I'm clean," he assured her instead.

"I'm on the pill, but we still should have used something more." She'd considered going off it after Tristan, but it helped with her acne, so she'd chose to stay on it.

He nuzzled the side of her neck and kissed her. "It's okay, Emma."

"Ethan—"

"It's too late to worry about it now, we got carried away, but we will deal with it *if* the time comes."

She leaned back to look apprehensively at him again, but he kissed her nose before she could offer further protest. Though it was the last thing he wanted to do, he lifted her up and reluctantly pulled himself from her. He placed her on her feet and helped adjust the straps on her dress. Clasping her cheeks in his hands, he tilted her face up and kissed her.

"Why don't you get out of these wet clothes," he suggested. "Where are the towels?"

"There's some in the hall closet; I'll get them."

"I'll grab them, clean up out here, and join you in a few minutes." She looked as if she was going to say more, but he turned her toward the hall. "Go on," he urged.

She glanced back at him as she stopped outside her bedroom door, but he waved her onward. She hesitated before slipping through the doorway to her room. Ethan pulled his jeans up and buttoned them before grabbing the towels from the closet and using them to wipe up the water. He grabbed her ruined panties from the floor and hurried down to the room she'd disappeared into.

She was already lying in bed; she watched him as he entered the room. Her damp hair spread out around her, the white t-shirt she wore was baggy on her small frame and made her appear extremely vulnerable. The thought he would enjoy seeing her like this forever hit him, and he stopped to savor the sight of her.

"There's a towel on the chair for you," she informed him.

He stripped out of his wet clothes and toweled off before crawling into bed beside her.

"Ethan, what does this mean?" She hated asking the question, hated the desperation she felt by saying the words, but she couldn't go to sleep tonight without at least some sort of resolution.

"I don't know," he admitted.

"You said with the other girls you told them in the beginning—"

"You're not like them, Emma. This *isn't* like those other times. I don't know what any of this means, not yet, but nothing that has happened between us is anything like what I've experienced with any other woman. I wouldn't be here right now if it were, I would have already walked out of here and gone home."

Emma couldn't help but smile as her finger slid over his chest and entwined in the curly hairs running across the top of it. She wasn't expecting forever, but at least he wasn't telling her there was no hope for them. The chances of this lasting past the end of the month were slim, but she would take those chances if they could have the next three weeks together. She stifled a yawn as she rested her head on his chest.

Taking her into his arms, he held her close against him as he breathed in her scent. Yes, he could spend every night like this, he decided as she relaxed against him. He was aware the thought and the certainty following it could spell doom for them both.

CHAPTER NINE

Emma's eyes were sluggish to open the next morning as sleep clung to her. The powerful body pressed against her back swept away the last dregs of sleep. The rhythmic sound of his breathing caused a smile to curve her mouth before she rolled over to look at him. He was stunning in the early morning sunshine filtering through the blinds. His arm was thrown over his head; his black hair was in disarray as it curled around his forehead and cheeks. Her heart melted at the sight of him and memories of what they had shared flooded her.

She'd never experienced anything like what she experienced with him last night. Sex with Tristan was pleasant, but she'd never really understood what the big deal about sex was. She'd never lost such complete control of herself with him, never known such a feeling of rightness and reckless abandon before. She'd thought she'd had an orgasm before, but she was wrong. The time she'd spent with Ethan was far shorter than her time with Tristan, yet she'd given herself more freely to him than she ever had to Tristan.

From the kitchen, she could smell coffee brewing, and the

scent of bacon frying caused her stomach to rumble. She brushed back a strand of his hair before placing a kiss on his cheek. The stubble lining his jaw tickled her lips, but she found the sensation enjoyable.

His emerald eyes were on her when she pulled back. Heat crept into her cheeks as his eyes ran over her face. "Good morning," he greeted in a tone of voice that caused her stomach to do a strange little flip.

"I didn't mean to wake you."

He chuckled as he wrapped his hand around the back of her head and pulled her toward him. "The rumbling of your stomach woke me," he said against her mouth.

She laughed, but she was already losing herself to him as his lips slid over her mouth and his tongue brushed against hers. A quickening of her pulse spread through her when he pulled away and kissed the tip of her nose.

"Let's get you something to eat before your stomach wakes the dead," he teased.

"Ugh," she groaned in protest.

He grinned at her before rolling away. Propping her head on her hand, she admired his chiseled ass and the carved muscles of his back and thighs as he walked away from her. The tattoo on his arm flexed as he stretched out his shoulders and back. She admired the black flames on his wrist licking upward toward the black phoenix on his upper bicep.

"Does the tattoo mean anything?" she inquired.

Ethan glanced absently down at his arm. He'd gotten it because he'd relished in feeling the pain from the needle. He'd been determined to punish himself for his endless thirst for blood and to drown out the insanity begging to be heard within him. It had taken almost three days to complete, but he'd sat patiently in the chair as the vampire tattoo artist repeatedly went over the lines until his body stopped healing itself and rejecting the ink.

The tattoo artist assured him after a few hours the ink would begin to stay in, but it had taken days longer than the tattooist expected, probably due to his purebred heritage. Even though it had taken much longer than anticipated to be completed, it hadn't been enough pain for him, and it had done nothing to drown his incessant bloodlust.

"Eternal life," he said to her over his shoulder. "Rebirth. A new start."

She frowned at him, and he could understand her confusion, but he didn't know how to explain he'd hoped the pain would somehow cleanse what was inside him. He should have known it would never work. Looking at her, he felt cleansed and free.

He walked over to her, and brushing the hair back from her face, he bent to kiss her. He fought against the blood flowing into his dick. All he wanted was to climb into bed with her and lose himself again, but she was hungry. Anyone within a hundred feet would know that, and her needs came first.

He reluctantly pulled back and walked away before he couldn't anymore. "It was something to do," he said as he pulled on his underwear.

"I like it," she murmured.

He lifted his jeans to examine them before pulling them on. They were still wet but not soaking, and he didn't have another choice unless he was going to walk around in his boxers. He buttoned them before turning and holding his hand out to her. She took his hand and he helped her rise. He drew her against him.

This man could do the most amazing things she'd ever experienced; he could also make her feel like a child, especially since he was so much larger than she was. She had to tilt her head back to look at anything above mid-chest. The spread of his shoulders was almost three times the size of hers. The thought he could kill her in a second hit her, but even with that realization, she felt immeasurably safe in his arms.

His fingers brushed over her neck as he pushed the hair back from her shoulder. She detested her stomach as it grumbled loudly again. He chuckled, took a step back, and grabbed his shirt from the floor. He flicked his shirt at her, hitting her lightly on the butt with the tip of it.

"Get dressed," he said with a grin.

She frowned at him, but still gathered her clothes and stepped into the bathroom her room shared with Jill's. She brushed her teeth and took a fast shower before dressing in her tank top and cutoff jeans. She didn't bother to blow dry her hair, as she was eager to get back to Ethan and eat some breakfast.

He stood by the window, leaning against the wall, and staring outside when she rejoined him. His head turned toward her, and a lazy smile spread across his lips before he stepped away from the wall and strode toward her. Taking her hands, he pulled her toward him and kissed her forehead.

"You look lovely." She shrugged his words off with a little snort, but a thrill went through her at his sweet compliment. "I was thinking about taking a trip today, and exploring some of the island; would you like to come with me?"

"Sounds like fun."

Goosebumps erupted over her skin when his mouth brushed hers again. She *really* didn't have to eat right now; she found her appetite for him was far stronger than for food as her hands encircled his biceps. His eyes were nearly black when he ended the kiss, and she could feel the evidence of his arousal against her belly, but he stepped away from her.

"Food for you, fresh clothes for me," he informed her with a grin.

"Food is overrated," she muttered.

He chuckled as he took her hand and led her toward the door. Pulling it open, he made a sweeping gesture with his arm as he stepped back to let her move into the hallway first. He walked with her toward the kitchen. They stepped into the narrow living room running parallel to the small kitchen beyond. Mandy sat at the breakfast bar dividing the two rooms, eating eggs as Jill continued frying bacon on the stove. When Mandy looked up and spotted them standing in the living room, the fork paused halfway to her mouth. Emma thought she should feel embarrassed, she'd had sex with him against the wall to her left last night after all, but there was no embarrassment as he stood by her side with his shirt in hand.

Jill was chattering on about something and hadn't noticed them yet. She turned with a plate of bacon in hand and approached Mandy. Jill frowned as Mandy ignored her and finally followed Mandy's gaze to where they stood in the entryway. The plate clattered against the granite as she practically dropped it onto the counter.

"Uh, hey," Jill greeted awkwardly, something she never was. "You hungry?"

"Starving," Emma admitted.

"I should get going," Ethan said. "I'll be back in an hour."

She hated the disappointment filling her over him leaving, but she forced herself to smile. "Sounds good."

He kissed her cheek before slipping out the door. Taking a steadying breath, she braced herself before turning to face her friends again. They both stared at her as if she were a piece of meat they couldn't wait to sink their teeth into. Oh hell, she was in for it, she realized with a sigh. Resigning herself to the barrage of questions she knew were about to unfold, she climbed down the steps and walked over to join them.

"I guess we know why *you're* hungry," Jill said as she heaped eggs onto a plate and placed it in the empty spot next to Mandy. "And why you didn't join us last night."

"We got caught in the rain," Emma told her as she bit into a piece of bacon.

"Oh, I bet," Mandy said as Emma settled onto the stool next to her.

She grabbed a handful of bacon and dropped it onto her plate. "We did!" she protested.

"You are going to tell us much more than that!" Jill declared as she danced away to get more eggs. "You better spill."

"Jill—"

"Not the disgusting details but give us *something* here, Emma."

She shook her head at Jill and dove into her eggs. Their eyes bored into her as she ate. She had to tell them something, but she needed to put some food in her belly if she was going to have the strength to deal with them. With her stomach full, and their patience fraying, she finally wiped her mouth with her napkin and lifted her head to meet their inquisitive gazes.

"It was the best night of my life," she told them honestly.

"Well that's definitely something," Mandy said with a laugh.

ETHAN WASN'T SURPRISED to find Isabelle waiting to pounce on him when he returned to the living room after showering and changing. Her arms were crossed firmly over her chest; her foot was tapping on the floor as her eyes locked on his.

"Where were you last night?" she demanded as she followed him to the fridge.

He pulled the door on the refrigerator open and removed a bag of blood from it. "I was out," he answered absently.

"I was concerned about you Ethan."

"I'm a grown man, Isabelle," he said as he tore the top of the bag off with his teeth.

"Damn it, Ethan!" she yelled as she stomped her foot. "You're a grown man, but I'd still like to know you're safe and alive!"

He took a deep breath as he leaned against the island. He hadn't meant to worry her; he simply hadn't thought of her while he was with Emma. Looking at her now though, guilt tugged at him as she rang her hands before her.

"I'm sorry, but I didn't think mom was here." She wasn't at all amused by his teasing words or his playful tug on her hair. "Come on, Issy, you can't stay mad at me. You know it's impossible."

Some of the unease went out of her as she finally smiled at him. "That's true. Were you with *her*?"

Ethan paused in the middle of drinking the blood; he brought his head back down to look at her. The relaxed, good-natured temperament he'd been experiencing vanished as unreasonable hostility took its place. "*She* has a name, and it would be better if you used it."

He was a little perplexed when Isabelle didn't become riled up at his tone. She tilted her head to the side to study him.

"I meant no offense," she told him. "Were you with, Emma?"

Movement drew his attention to the patio doors when Stefan stepped through them. Stefan's gaze searched the two of them as he strode gracefully across the floor toward the kitchen.

Ethan finished off the bag of blood and dumped it into the trashcan, typically one satisfied him, but it wasn't enough today. "I was."

"You like her," Isabelle said.

Isabelle stepped aside when he opened the fridge. He lifted his head to look at her as she started ringing her hands again and shifted from foot to foot. Isabelle wasn't nervous by nature; in fact, she was one of the most steadfast vampires he'd ever known, but something had her extremely agitated right now.

"I do," he admitted as he closed the fridge.

"She's human," she said as if it were some big secret.

"She is," he agreed as he tore the top off the bag.

Stefan stopped behind Isabelle and rested his hands on her shoulders. "I've never seen you spend this much time with a human before. I uh...are you okay?"

He grinned at her, consumed the bag, and tossed it into the trash. "I've never been better, Iss; you have nothing to worry about."

"Ethan—"

"I know what you're thinking, so just stop." Ethan tapped his fingers on the counter as he thought over what Isabelle had been about to say and the reality growing within him. "Truth be told, I've thought it too."

She inhaled sharply, and even Stefan's eyebrows shot up. "You're really calm about this for someone who never wanted to be mated," she muttered.

How did he tell her the idea of being mated was less concerning to him than it had been to her? He was more concerned he would rip a human's throat out and drain every drop of their blood than he was about finding someone to spend eternity with. Isabelle was never going to know what he harbored inside him though. She could never understand, not with her tender heart, but Stefan would.

They'd butted heads more than a few times when things were unraveling between Stefan and Isabelle, but Stefan was the only one who would understand any of what he secretly dealt with day after day. Stefan was far older than the rest of them, wiser, and a killer.

Ethan lifted his gaze from his sister to the man standing behind her. Stefan's brow furrowed as his eyes searched him. Ethan remained unmoving while he waited for Stefan's gaze to come back to his. Those onyx eyes filled with dawning understanding when they latched onto him, and Stefan gave a brief bow of his head.

"I was never as terrified of it as you were, Issy, I just didn't like being around humans," Ethan told her.

She folded her arms over her chest. "But you said you didn't want it."

"And I didn't," he said. "And I'm not sure if she is my mate or not. It's only been a week, I enjoy spending time with her, but you're talking about something that might not be."

"If she is your mate, then her being human adds a whole layer of complication to something already complicated."

He knew she was only looking out for him, but he could feel his patience wearing thin. He wasn't a child; he'd heard the stories of what happened between his parents; he'd seen first-hand what unfolded between her and Stefan. "I know that, Isabelle."

"What are you going to do if she is?" she demanded.

"I'll figure it out when the time comes."

"Ethan—"

"Enough, Isabelle," Stefan interrupted kindly. "Ethan is aware what being mated entails *if* that's even what this is. There's no reason to harp on it until he knows for sure."

Ethan gave Stefan a grateful nod before focusing on his sister again. "See, there's nothing to be concerned about." It wasn't exactly the truth, but her worry wasn't going to do them any good. He stepped forward and squeezed her shoulder. "I'll see you later."

"Where are you going now?" she inquired.

"You do realize you are the *younger* sibling right?" he reminded her.

"Just a question."

"I'm taking Emma away for the day. I've found a place on the island I think she'll enjoy."

"Oh, okay," she muttered, but she didn't look at all appeased.

Ethan slapped Stefan on the arm as he walked out of the kitchen. He grabbed the helmets sitting next to the door and hurried down to the motorcycle parked against the curb. Stefan had told him it was in the garage a couple of days ago, and since traffic was often congested on the island, he'd decided to grab it for today. He hoped Emma didn't have a problem with riding on a bike, but if she did, they could always come back for the Jeep or rent a scooter. The idea of having her hold on to him as he drove around the island was too tempting to refuse though.

CHAPTER TEN

EMMA EYED the motorcycle warily as she stepped out the door with Ethan. She'd never ridden one before, and though it had always looked like fun, she'd never actually pictured herself doing it. However, until she'd met Ethan, there was a lot she'd never imagined herself doing before, but would be willing to try now, including riding a bike.

"Are you going to be alright on this?" he inquired when they stopped beside the bike.

She took the deep blue helmet from his hands and settled it on her head. It was probably going to give her some major helmet head, but it would be worth it to ride behind him. "I've never done it before, but it looks like fun, and it can't be much different than a four-wheeler."

He nudged her hands aside when she fumbled with the strap and buckled it under her chin. "I think your friends are watching us," he told her as he made sure the helmet was on right.

"Oh, I'd bet on it!"

"Are they trying to make sure you're safe?"

"Nope, they're just nosy, but I love them."

He chuckled as he tapped the sides of the helmet. She looked adorable with the large helmet on her head and her hair curling out around the sides of it. He briefly contemplated forgoing the trip and taking her back inside to spend the rest of the day in bed, but he wanted to take her somewhere they could be alone, have some fun, and do something she might like.

"All set," he told her and stepped away. He put on a red helmet before settling onto the seat. He held his hand out to her, and she took it. "Swing your leg over."

Emma was careful not to kick the bike as she swung her leg up and over. It was taller than she expected, but with Ethan's help, she settled herself onto the seat behind him.

"Wrap your arms around me," he instructed.

Emma moved a little closer and slid her arms around his waist. She gasped when he grabbed her arms and tugged her forward until she was snug against his back.

"I'll only bite if you ask me too," he told her with a wink.

That wink, and the images his words conjured in her mind, caused her heart to do a strange little flutter. She realized if she didn't watch herself here she could fall head over heels for this man.

"I'll have to remember that," she told him and forced herself to relax against his back.

"Please do." Ethan heard the hoarseness of his voice, but he couldn't help it. Not when thoughts of biting her and tasting her churned through his mind.

"Where are we going?" she asked him.

"It's a surprise," he told her.

She continued to hold his gaze until he turned away to start the bike. A delicious shiver worked its way through her as her breasts pressed firmly against the muscles of his back. They strained against her as he fired up the bike and pulled away from the curb. He kept his speed under the thirty-five-kilometer speed limit as they drove down the road on the left-hand side. She was glad she wasn't driving as watching him do it was disconcerting to her; she had to fight the urge to jerk him back to the other side of the road when cars and scooters approached.

Even at their relatively slow speed, the wind rushing around her and blowing her hair back gave her a sense of freedom she found enthralling. It took everything she had not to release his waist and throw her arms out to the side as he weaved expertly in and out of traffic. She couldn't stop the laugh escaping her as they hit an open expanse of road and he drove faster.

Over his shoulder, she watched as the world rushed by in a blur that made her eyes water, but she still wished they could go faster. The motorcycle eased back as they came to a highly congested area of traffic. Though she wanted the speed again, she found she wasn't disappointed as she nestled closer to him and rested her cheek against his back. He smelled of Irish Spring soap and the fresh ocean air. Coming to a complete stop behind a line of vehicles, he put his foot down. His hand rested against her joined ones on his waist while he waited for traffic to start moving again.

Yes, she could most certainly lose her heart to him, she thought as a feeling of peace and security stole through her.

It took some time, but eventually, he found a parking spot and stopped the bike. Emma reluctantly slid her arms away from his waist and climbed off the bike to examine the area. She removed her helmet and shook out her hair before trying to finger comb out her helmet hair. It didn't matter; she would take a bad hair day every day for the rest of the year if it meant climbing onto the bike, with him, again.

"Have fun?" he asked as he settled the helmets onto the back of the bike and locked them into place with a chain.

"I could do that every day," she said honestly.

"I'll have to remember that."

She wasn't entirely sure how to take that, but she wasn't going to spend all day trying to puzzle it out. With him, she could simply *be,* and she intended to do that as they walked down the street together.

"Can you tell me where we're going now?" she inquired.

He pointed up the hill to a large house set in the center of an open green field, surrounded by a massive stone wall overlooking the ocean. Large cannons were positioned to face the sea on the hill around the house. It was an old military fort, she realized.

"It's the Bermuda Maritime Museum," he explained. "I thought you'd like to look around it."

Emma couldn't find her voice for a minute as tears suddenly burned her eyes. The urge to cry was silly, but he'd remembered her love of history. It was one of the sweetest and most thoughtful things anyone had ever done for her. She blinked back the tears as she focused on him once more.

"I'd love to," she said honestly.

He clasped her hand as he led her toward the large front gates and the ticket booth tucked within the rock walls. She took a map as he paid for the tickets, and they entered the museum. They explored the grounds and the small waterfall as they made their way toward the old keep at the top of the hill.

The smell of must assailed her as they stepped into the cool and shadowed interior of the massive home. All the windows were open to allow the breeze to drift through the home. The dark wooden floor beneath her feet creaked as they moved through the rooms of the building. She examined all the pictures hanging on the walls and read the plaques beneath them. She ran her fingers over the large tables and chairs filling many of the rooms, examined the coin and book collections, and spent nearly two hours admiring everything within each room of the house.

Ethan remained patiently by her side as she explored every inch of the seemingly endless home. If he'd been with anyone else he would probably be bored out of his mind by now, but he relished in her endless fascination of the things within the house and her enthusiasm as she excitedly told him about the things she was reading on the plaques. She did have a fervor for history, and he was glad he'd learned about this place after their talk on the boat.

Stepping onto the balcony running around the entire upper floor with her, he stared across the glimmering aqua sea to the cruise ship parked at the wharf. People walked about the house below them, but he didn't pay them any attention as he stood behind Emma and slid his arms around her waist. Resting his chin on her head, he watched the boats and jet skis skimming across the water as he savored this moment and this woman.

"This is amazing, thank you for bringing me here," she said.

"Anytime, you actually make history enjoyable."

She laughed as she turned to face him. He kissed her cheek and took her hand as he led her back into the building, downstairs, and outside again into the powerful rays of the sun. They walked a different pathway down to the pool where the dolphins and a sea turtle were kept.

Emma's face filled with delight as she watched the mother and baby dolphins swimming through the water and the sea turtle being fed. After a half an hour they moved on to explore the rest of the fort.

They walked through a couple of side tunnels before climbing up to stand beside the massive cannons. He'd brought his phone to take photos and snapped pictures as she posed and smiled. A passing tourist offered to take their picture together, and he gladly accepted, which was something he'd never done before. No matter what happened, he knew he would always want a picture of the two of them together. They went through another building which told of the wild animals on the island and the numerous shipwrecks around it before exiting the gate.

He held her hand as they explored the shops and peeked in the windows of the stores in the area. There were so many beautiful and unique things she would like to take home with her, but the limited space in her suitcases, and the limited funds in her wallet, kept her from picking up most of it.

Ethan was examining a chess set carved from stone when she stopped before a deep purple dress, swirled through with vivid blues and greens. The sleeves were short, and off the shoulder, the waist cinched and high. She ran the soft material through her fingers before grabbing the price tag. Her eyes widened at the cost, and she dropped it as if it burned her. She cast one last look at the dress before strolling over to join Ethan by the board.

"Do you play?" she inquired.

He shook his head as he straightened away from the board. "My father does though, and I think he'd really like this. I'll come back and buy it for him when we're ready to leave."

"You're really close with your family," she said as they exited the store.

"I am."

It was strange to hear him be so open about it. Tristan had hated to talk about his family. The only time he mentioned them was if she asked a question, and then his answers were terse and uninformative. She'd never met his parents, and she wasn't sure if he had any siblings. He'd mentioned a sister once, but she'd gotten the impression she may have been dead as he'd spoken about her in the past tense.

Emma slid her hand into Ethan's again as they made their way through a few more stores before stopping at a restaurant. "Ready to take a break and get something to eat?" he asked.

"Am I ever," she told him. Her stomach rumbled, and though she was wearing comfortable flip-flops, her feet were tired. It would be nice to sit down and take a break for a little bit.

The restaurant was crowded when they stepped inside. Ethan stopped at the desk to talk with the cute brunette hostess standing behind it. Emma couldn't hear what they said over the noise of the place, but she could see the lustful gleam in the woman's eyes as her gaze ran eagerly over him. Anger simmered through Emma, she wrapped her hand around Ethan's arm and took a step closer to him. The woman didn't even glance at her as she started to shake her head but then began to nod along for some reason.

The woman grabbed two menus and gestured for them to follow her. He had to use his power of persuasion for the woman to give them one of the reserved tables in the packed place. Keeping a grip on Emma's hand, he stayed protectively in front of her as he led her through the crowd to a deck at the rear of the building.

A young man stumbled back and almost bumped into Emma, but Ethan managed to move her out of the way in time. The look Ethan shot the man made him blanch, and he hurried back toward his friends. Emma didn't notice though as she was looking at the photographs of fishermen and boats lining the wall on their left.

She inhaled the fresh salt air as they stepped onto the large deck. The sea breeze drifted over them and blew the hair back from her face. The hostess sat them at a table in the corner, placed the menus down, and cast one last lingering glance at Ethan before she hurried away. Emma had no idea how he managed to get them such fantastic seats so quickly, but she loved it.

"I could get used to this," Emma said. Ethan folded his arms over his chest as she placed her hands on the rail of the banister and leaned over to stare at the water. "There's a lot of fish down there!"

Her eyes sparkled in the sunlight when she turned toward him. Something inside his chest constricted, his hands fisted as he fought the urge to grab her and kiss her. He knew one kiss wouldn't be enough, and he didn't think Emma, or anyone in this restaurant, would appreciate anything more than that. Instead, he enjoyed watching her as she rose and leaned over the banister to look at the water below.

It amazed him how much joy she found in life. He hadn't realized how much he'd taken it all for granted. She danced in the rain and gushed over the fish because, to her, life was finite and every second of it should be savored. History fascinated her because one day she would be one of the human ghosts she read about, and others would walk in her footsteps. He was never careless about life, but since he was old enough to understand, he'd known mortality wasn't a concern for him. He'd never been as enchanted with life as she was.

Until now.

What he found enchanting now was *her*. He admired her backside as she leaned further over the railing and pointed at something that caused the young boy who joined her to smile at her. Ethan understood why the child was drawn to her, she was impossible to resist as her laughter ensnared him, and her smile warmed even the coldest recesses of his soul.

Brought forth by the overwhelming need to touch her, to share in her happiness, he rose from his chair and walked over to join her. He slid his arm around her waist and pressed his chest against her back as he leaned over her to look into the clear water below. Her honeysuckle scent drifted up to him as she turned her head to smile at him. He was unable to resist dropping a kiss on her silken cheek.

It terrified him to think about what would happen if she learned the truth about him. He was a monster, he survived on blood, and the compulsion to kill was always with him. What would she do when she found out?

His arm tightened around her at the thought; something sinister rippled beneath his surface. She might run screaming from him, and he wouldn't blame her if she did, but he didn't know what kind of reaction it would elicit from him.

He couldn't think of that now; if he did, he wasn't sure he could stop himself from dragging her out of here and forcing the change on her. He would despise himself forever if he did. If there ever came a time when he told her the truth about himself, and she ran away screaming, he would let her go. He would set her free to enjoy the rest of her life. There was no way he would ever take from her the pure joy encompassing her, no matter what the consequences for him might be.

He nuzzled her neck and leaned over to look as the boy pointed at a silver fish darting through the water. He held onto her waist as she climbed onto the bottom railing and leaned over the top rail to look beneath the deck. The boy wasn't much smaller than she was as he climbed up to join her.

"Teddy, get down from there!" a woman scolded. She grabbed the boy's hand, shot the two of them a look, and hurried away from them with her child.

Emma had to bite on her inner lip to keep from laughing as she turned toward Ethan. "Are you going to yell at me too?" she whispered.

His hands slid over her waist and up to her belly. "I don't think it would do any good."

She hopped off the railing and grinned at him as she turned in his arms. "It probably wouldn't," she admitted.

He kept his arms locked around her waist as her back rested against the rail. Her legs were stretched out between his; her palms rested on his stomach. If she had the foggiest idea what she did to him, she would move them. Instead, her fingers made small circles over him. Her hands clenched in his shirt as he leaned over her and pressed a kiss against her lips.

Her mouth opened to the questing probe of his tongue. His hands clasped either side of her face. He held her tenderly as he tasted her. The tantalizing dance of his tongue caused her heart rate to skyrocket. He might find some satisfaction in knowing he affected her so much if she didn't do the same exact thing to him.

Her eyes were filled with awe when he pulled away from her. "I think we should probably sit before we give the people here a show," he told her.

Emma didn't particularly care what the people around them thought when he was standing so close to her. "I believe we may have already given them a show," she said with a laugh.

He didn't disagree with her as he stepped away and returned to his seat. The waiter stared at them both before hurriedly taking their order and disappearing again. "Can I see the pictures on your phone of your woodworking?" she asked.

"Oh, yeah," Ethan had forgotten it was on him as he pulled it from his pocket.

He'd shut the data package down so no one could call in or out, but he could still access his pictures. He brought up the photos and flipped past the ones from today and of his siblings, before coming to the ones he'd taken of his work.

Turning the phone, he handed it to her, and she took it from him. He found himself riveted and barely able to breathe as he waited to see her reaction. The smile slid from her face as she flipped through the pictures, and when she looked up at him, the look of astonishment on her features captivated him.

"They're beautiful," she said honestly. "You have an amazing gift."

In fact, they were some of the most breathtaking pieces of furniture she'd ever seen in her life. The intricate flowers and vines carved into the gazebo must have taking hours of endless patience. The rocking horse and blocks on the front of the trunk meant for Isabelle were done with such tender care, she could feel the love he already felt for his future niece or nephew.

There were so many times over the years he'd felt as if he were cursed, to hear her say he had a gift seemed so strange, yet she believed her words. But then she didn't know he was a monster. "Thank you."

She smiled at him as she handed the phone back. "Do you plan to try and sell some of them one day?"

"Maybe one day," he said as he slipped his phone into his pocket, though he had no intention of doing so. They were for him and his family only; he didn't want to deal with the interaction with others he would have to endure to sell his pieces. "I'm glad you like them."

"I love them."

For the first time in his life, he felt a little shy. Thankfully, he was saved from saying anything more as she rose to her feet.

"I have to go to the bathroom; I'll be right back," she said.

Ethan fought the urge to go with her as she wound her way through the crowd to the restrooms next to the bar. He didn't like the idea of her going alone into the bar, but he could see the bathroom from here, and he couldn't be that overprotective of her. She would fight against any restrictions he might try to place on her. She'd already had a bad experience with an overbearing, frightening man; she wouldn't put up with it from him.

With her gone, he became steadily aware of the solid thumps of the hearts surrounding him and the metallic scent of the blood pulsing through the veins so close to him. He hadn't realized just how much she drowned out the human odors and sounds when she was near. Even when he was under control, there was never a time when he was unaware of the walking temptations surrounding him. When she was with him, it was as if the rest of the world ceased to exist. He knew the walking, talking, bodies of warm blood were still around him, but he didn't care about their existence.

But now he could feel the darkness creeping steadily through his system, teasing him with its promised words of release and satisfaction. If he would give in just once, it would all go away, but even as he thought it, he knew he was wrong. It would never go away; it would only claw at his insides until he was out hunting and killing every night to satisfy his insatiable thirst.

It would go on until he became one of the monsters confined to the shadows as every death made the sun more unbearable, crossing water became increasingly difficult, and he reeked of the garbage scent he and his siblings detected on the vampires who tried to kill them.

He could never hide his dirty secret from his family then; they would know what he was, what he had become, and they would never accept him. They would love him for eternity, but they would never condone his actions. He would be on his own, a monster adrift in the world until someone, or something, finally put him out of his misery.

Ethan's hands fisted, he inhaled a deep breath and focused on the ocean as he tried to regain control of himself. Emma shut out the world when she was with him, but it was now louder than before he'd known her. It would be so easy to stand up, talk to the first person he saw, slip away somewhere quiet, and just give in to the bloodlust within him. He may even be able to do it before Emma returned.

Sweat beaded across his brow as his fingernails dug into the flesh of his palms. He could feel the blood welling up from the gouges he created, but even as he pulled the tissue back, it knitted itself closed again. Right *there* was a man who was so close Ethan could have him out of here in seconds. His fangs tingled; his mouth watered as a ringing sounded in his ears. All he could think about was finally giving in to the impulses he'd denied for so long.

He was getting ready to put his feet down and go to the man when a small hand settled on his forearm. In an instant, the world went still again, the pounding beat of his heart eased, and his fangs retracted into his gums. He found himself able to breathe again as calm settled over him and he turned to face Emma.

She smiled at him as she sat on the chair across from him again. She went to remove her hand, but he seized it. After what had happened, he couldn't lose the contact with her so soon. A small trail of his blood smeared the back of her knuckles; he wiped it hastily away with his thumb before she saw it. The fact he left the trail, that he'd sullied her in this small way, made him feel dirty and unworthy, but he still couldn't bring himself to release her. He was terrified of what he would become if he did.

CHAPTER ELEVEN

EMMA WAITED outside the store for Ethan to purchase the chess set for his father. Calypso music drifted from somewhere down the street. She couldn't help but hum and tap her foot as she examined some lovely, hand-painted bottles set up in the window of the store. She lifted her head and spotted Ethan at the cash register; she waved to him when he looked up and caught her staring.

He smiled at her before turning his attention back to the cashier. His gaze kept going surreptitiously to Emma as he waited impatiently for the woman to ring up his items. Knowing Emma was right there helped him keep his cool, but the world was closing in on him again. He wiped away the sweat beading across his forehead and wrapped his hands around the counter.

"Is there anything else you would like?" the woman inquired and touched his arm flirtatiously.

Ethan jerked away from her and glanced at Emma again when she wandered away from the store. *Stay in sight,* he pleaded silently.

"No," he grated at the saleswoman, hoping the tone of his voice would dissuade anymore of her interest and spur her into action. The woman eyed him uncertainly; Ethan took a deep breath as she finally completed his purchase.

As the song ended, Emma turned back toward where the motorcycle was parked. She didn't want this day to end, but she was looking forward to getting back on it with him again. He appeared in the doorway of the store and held his right hand out to her as he shifted the bag into his left hand. She took it and followed him the few steps down the street to the motorcycle.

He put the chess set into the saddlebag and helped her with the helmet again before settling onto the seat. Feeling a little more confident this time, she climbed on behind him and slid her arms around his waist. Heat encompassed her as she pressed her breasts against his back. She flattened her hands on his stomach and felt the ridges of his muscles beneath her hands as he started the bike and pulled away from the curb.

She rested her cheek on his back as she watched the water and scenery go by on the narrow, winding roads. She savored the power beneath her legs and the strength of the man in front of her. Leaning back in the seat, she could no longer resist the urge to throw her arms out to the side as they drove through a less crowded stretch of road.

She laughed as the wind blew over her face, tickled her skin and plastered her clothes to her. It felt as if she were flying, as if she were free of herself and could do anything she wanted in this world. Her head tilted back as a gleeful shout escaped her. The last of the lingering tension and fear she'd been feeling over Tristan vanished like dandelion fluff in a storm. She was moving on, she was living life in a way she never had before, and it was the greatest thing she'd ever experienced.

She was still laughing as she lowered her arms and

wrapped them around him again. "Feel better?" he asked as he briefly turned his head to look at her.

"I feel wonderful!" she cried. She hugged him tighter as they entered an area of the island she recognized as being close to where she was staying.

He turned down a couple of side streets before stopping in front of her house. Emma held onto him for a second before reluctantly releasing him. Sliding off the bike, she reached up to pull the helmet off, but he was already taking hold of the strap.

"I had fun today," she told him.

He smiled at her as he removed the helmet and placed it on the seat. "Good. That means you'll go to dinner with me tonight."

"I don't know; you might get sick of me," she teased as she bumped his hip.

"Never." It was the way he said the word with such conviction, more than the actual word itself, that caught her attention and caused her to flush with pleasure. "But I *would* like to change my clothes first."

"So would I."

He wrapped his arms around her waist as he bent to kiss her and lifted her as he straightened back to his full height. She loved the way he made her feel so small, yet so protected. He bent her back and kissed her deeply before setting her on her feet again.

Still more than a little dazed from his kiss when he released her, she took an unsteady step back. "I'll see you in a couple of hours?" he asked.

"Okay."

Turning on her heel, she shot a smile over her shoulder at him when he lightly slapped her behind. She practically skipped up the steps to the house when she heard the bike fire up and pull away from the curb. Opening the door, she stepped inside to find Mandy reading in the living room and Jill on the computer. They both focused on her as she shut the door.

"Did you have fun?" Jill inquired.

"A blast," she admitted as she hurried down the stairs.

Jill grinned at her as she closed her laptop. "Well, you definitely did something right last night."

Emma froze as she frowned questioningly at her friend. "What are you talking about?"

Jill pointed into the kitchen. Emma leaned around the doorway to see what Jill was talking about. Her mouth dropped open when she spotted the massive bouquet of colorful flowers sitting on the table.

"Those are for me?" she blurted as she approached the flowers.

She recognized half a dozen birds of paradise in the bouquet, but that was where her identification skills ended. There had to be at least three dozen flowers in the blue vase.

"Our names weren't the ones on the card," Mandy said as she approached.

Emma pulled the card from the plastic holder at the edge of the vase. All it had was her name typed on it. "I can't believe he did this," she muttered.

"You deserve flowers, and that boy knows it," Mandy said.

"Or maybe he couldn't believe *you* did something," Jill teased.

Emma rolled her eyes at her friend and shook her head. She smiled though as she leaned forward to inhale the heady scent of the flowers. Yes, she could lose her heart to him, she decided.

"ETHAN." He had known Stefan was in the doorway before he spoke. "Can we talk?"

Ethan glanced at him as he tugged a clean shirt over his head. His hair was still damp from his shower, but it would dry soon enough. "Come in." Stefan glanced behind him before stepping into the room and closing the door. "Where's Isabelle?"

"Outside, on the phone with your mom."

"She'll be busy for a while."

"She will." Stefan agreed as he walked over and sat in the chair in the corner. "So are you ready to tell me what's going on?"

"I thought we'd already had this discussion."

"I'm not talking about Emma being your possible mate. I'm talking about *you.* Isabelle always assumed you were like her and trying to avoid finding your mate, but that's not the case, is it?"

Ethan studied Stefan as he leaned against the bureau. If anyone would have any understanding of what he was going through, what was inside him, it was Stefan.

"No, it's not," he admitted. Stefan's steady gaze was focused on him as he steepled his fingers before his face and waited for Ethan to continue. "It's the blood."

Stefan dropped his hands down. "The blood?"

"The *humans.* Even when I was in high school, I knew I was different from my siblings, my parents, and The Stooges. They could be around humans with far more ease than me, and even enjoyed them more than I did. There was always this hunger for them inside of me, this yearning to *taste* them, even before I reached maturity."

"And when you reached maturity?" Stefan prompted.

"And then, unlike the rest of my family, it became almost unbearable for me to be around humans without wanting to kill every single one of them."

The subtle rise in Stefan's eyebrows was the only reaction to his blunt statement. "Have you talked to your brothers about this? They may not have hit maturity yet, but they might be experiencing the same thing as you without you knowing it."

"No, they're not like me; you know that as well as I do. You've been out with Aiden and Ian; they're more than happy to be in the clubs with humans or at college living among them. They can feed directly from a person; I've never trusted myself to do it. Maybe some of my younger siblings might feel this way, but I've watched them, and I don't think they do."

"You've never fed directly from a human before?" Stefan inquired.

Ethan took a deep breath as he braced himself to reveal something he'd never revealed to anyone before. "Until recently, I'd never done *any*thing with a human before. Blood bags and vampire women were my only experience. Since high school, I've had only minimal contact with people. I've gone to great lengths to keep it hidden from everyone."

"You've done well at it; I never suspected anything like that." Stefan stared at him before he rose to his feet and walked over to the balcony doors. "I've always believed some of us are just more twisted when we're changed," he said thoughtfully. "I most certainly was, and so was Brian. Your father and The Stooges weren't. It would only make sense that certain pure-bred vampires would also have that malevolence within them when they're born. I don't think it makes us evil, but I do believe it makes us more susceptible to becoming murderers who thrive on taking a life. You've dealt with this your whole life, and you haven't given in to it; just because it's in there doesn't mean it rules you."

"The thirst, sometimes..." Ethan broke off as he shook his head. "Sometimes I don't know how I haven't killed *every* human in a room before." There were times when the image of it was so vivid in his mind that even after he shook it off, and looked around to find everyone still alive, it still took him a few minutes to convince himself blood didn't cover him and all their throats were intact.

"I know how you feel."

Ethan lifted his head to look at Stefan. *Yes*, for *once* someone understood how he felt. Stefan had focused his anger and need to kill on other vampires to gain strength, but he'd already changed his ways by the time he met Isabelle.

"And it's not the same with Emma?" Stefan asked.

"Not at all. She even makes it easier for me to be around other humans. It's as if they fade into the background when she's there."

Stefan stepped away from the doors. "You realize that fact only adds to Isabelle's concerns, don't you?"

"I do."

"It seems strange you're not trying to bolt like your sister did," Stefan said with a snort.

"Emma might."

Sadness flickered over Stefan's face before he rapidly covered it. "Yes, humans can be difficult. When do you plan to tell her about this?"

Ethan didn't know the answer. He was terrified of what might happen when he *did* tell Emma, but he was beginning to realize it would be inevitable. If she was his mate, then things were only going to get worse before they got better. For the first time, he felt true panic as he realized there was a good possibility he could lose her. She wasn't a vampire; she wouldn't experience the impossible to break mate connection as a human. The laws of his kind didn't bind her, and he didn't know if he ever wanted them to.

He should back off now, walk away before the bond intensified and he couldn't part from her with his sanity still intact. He was already in over his head, and he was going to take her down with him if things between them continued to grow.

"Fuck!" he hissed as he turned away from Stefan.

"Ethan—"

Ethan lifted his hand to stop Stefan's words as he paced over to the door and back again. "I'm looking to condemn her to a life of blood and death, to this *hunger*."

"She'll control the hunger better with you around, just as you do when she's around," Stefan said. "Just as Isabelle and your mother, and your father and I do. It's more likely she won't experience what it is you battle every day because of you."

"What if I pass it on to her?"

"It doesn't work that way, Ethan."

"Then how does it work?" he demanded.

"I don't know. But if it worked that way your father and The Stooges would have inherited Beth's more homicidal tendencies, but they didn't."

"There's still a chance she could."

"I don't think so, there's no darkness in her, not that I can tell anyway. I really believe it must be inherent in all of us to begin with."

Ethan thought over those words before he turned toward him. "This darkness, this *thirst*, why us?"

"I don't know," Stefan admitted. "I was colder as a human, but I blamed it on the events of my childhood. Looking back, I think it was more than that. There was always a darkness in me, and my change amplified it. But asking that question is like asking why some people are killers and others aren't. Is it birth, circumstances, are they driven to it? You're asking questions there are no answers to; don't get caught up so much in searching for the answers, it will only eat you alive."

"Then what do I search for?" he asked.

"What you want for yourself and for her. What this is between you. If you believe she's your mate, it will make you stronger, or it will destroy you."

Ethan stared at Stefan for a minute before resuming pacing. "I guess being almost three hundred years old makes you able to give such sage advice."

"And tangling with your sister. She was a bit difficult in the beginning if you do recall."

Ethan released a short bark of laughter and turned away from Stefan. "That's putting it mildly, but then I wasn't exactly easy on you either."

"No, you weren't," Stefan agreed. "There is another thing you must remember in all this." Ethan shot a questioning look over his shoulder. "You, Isabelle, and your siblings all exhibit abilities none of the created vampires have. Such as smelling out vampires who kill humans. You and Isabelle are both stronger than any vampire your ages should be. What you feel may be intensified because you *are* stronger. You were born into this, and there are probably things all of you can do that none of us know about—things which may affect each of you differently. Emma may be the one to give you the relief from the demons you fight before your bloodlust drives you to kill."

Ethan started to see Stefan in a new light. He was no longer the egotistical older vampire chasing after his sister. Stefan was his friend, someone he could turn to in a way he couldn't turn to any of his siblings, not even Isabelle.

A knock sounded on the door before Isabelle opened it. She poked her head inside. "I could have been naked," he told her.

She frowned at him. "It's good to know you would get naked in front of my mate."

Ethan scowled at her and shot Stefan a look. "You're a lucky man," he said sarcastically.

"I've never heard that before," Stefan said and gave Isabelle a loving smile in an attempt to placate her.

"We can change things," she replied haughtily.

The smile slid from Stefan's face. "Never."

"I didn't think so," Isabelle said with a grin. "What are you two talking about?"

"Big Macs versus Whoppers, I'm personally a Whopper guy," Ethan told her.

"You're hilarious," Isabelle retorted.

"How is mom?" he asked to distract her from her line of questioning.

"She's good, missing us, and I *did* notice the change of topic."

Ethan grinned at her as he strode forward and rubbed the top of her head. "You always were a quick one," he told her as he slipped past her and out the door.

"Why don't we all go out to dinner together tonight?" She grabbed his arm to stop him before he could escape. "I'd like to get to know Emma better."

"You might scare her off."

She scowled at him. "I am *not* frightening."

"You've obviously never met you." Uneasiness flickered over her features. He realized teasing her wasn't helping her growing apprehension about his relationship with Emma. "Why don't we meet for a drink at the bar later?" he suggested.

She looked as if she would protest, but Stefan stepped forward and rested his hands on her shoulders. "Good idea."

Ethan would like to stay and reassure her more, but he had to get out of here and back to Emma. Even the constant battle he waged to keep himself in check wasn't as consuming as his driving need to make sure she was safe. He squeezed Isabelle's hand, turned away from her, and hurried out the door.

CHAPTER TWELVE

EMMA GLANCED around the crowd gathered inside; Ethan held her hand as he led her through the people toward where Isabelle and Stefan sat at the bar. It took everything she had not to fidget when they both turned and leveled her with curious stares.

"Hi," Isabelle greeted with a smile, but her eyes were assessing.

Emma fought the urge to glance at Ethan for reassurance, but she'd never hid behind someone before, and she wasn't about to start now.

"Hi," she said and forced a smile.

"Sit down," Isabelle said and patted the seat next to her. Emma slid onto the stool next to Ethan's sister. "Ethan told me you just graduated from college, what are you going to do now?"

"I'm not sure," Emma answered and leaned over to place her drink order with the bartender.

"What do you want to do?" Isabelle inquired.

Emma felt like a witness on the stand as she leaned back in

her chair and met the amazingly pure violet eyes of Ethan's sister. "Still haven't figured that out yet."

Isabelle laughed as she picked up her drink and took a sip. "Did you like college?"

"I had a lot of fun there." She was incredibly grateful when her drink finally arrived, and she had something to do with her hands and eyes. She lifted it and took a sip.

"Where do you plan to live now that you're done with school?" Isabelle asked before Emma had a chance to swallow.

"Isabelle, enough," Ethan said as he rested his hands on Emma's shoulders. Isabelle's eyes flickered between the two of them; a muscle twitched in her cheek as her jaw clenched. "It's not the Spanish Inquisition."

"Sorry," Isabelle said to Emma.

"It's okay," Emma assured her.

"It's just that Ethan doesn't bring many girls around; in fact, I've never met a girlfriend of his. We were beginning to wonder if he liked girls."

"Isabelle!" Ethan hissed as Stefan choked on his drink and laughed loudly. Emma didn't know if she was mortified or if she wanted to laugh. She settled for chuckling with Stefan as Isabelle smiled innocently at Ethan and he glared at her in return.

"Ignore my sister; we don't let her out in public very often," Ethan grumbled.

"More often than you," Isabelle replied cheerfully.

Emma started to relax as the banter between the siblings eased the mounting stress. Isabelle focused on her again, but her inquisition seemed to be over as she turned the conversation toward music and television shows. A pleasant hour slid by, and Emma was beginning to realize she enjoyed Isabelle's company when she wasn't trying to pry into her life.

Ethan leaned over her and ordered two more drinks for them. He stiffened suddenly as his head turned toward the front door. Emma frowned as Isabelle and Stefan also became rigid and turned in their stools. She tried to see what had caught their attention, but she could barely see anything beyond Ethan's chest.

"What's the matter?" Emma inquired.

Ethan shook his head and moved even closer to her, overwhelming her with his heat and delicious scent. She didn't know what was going on, but she was unable to stop herself from wrapping her hand around his powerful forearm. He glanced down at her and forced a smile, but it didn't reach his eyes.

"Everything ok?" she asked.

"It's fine," he said and bent to drop a kiss on her forehead. Emma found herself instinctively reacting by pressing against him. She heard his harsh intake of breath seconds before his mouth drifted down to brush against hers. Her toes curled, and her fingers dug into his arm as his lips seared hers and he nibbled her bottom lip. Disappointment filled her when he pulled away, but his hand remained on her shoulder, and his body stayed against hers.

Emma frowned as Stefan slid to his feet beside Isabelle. From around Ethan's chest, she finally spotted the three men who had caught his attention the last time she saw them here. Two of the men glanced over at them, but the third focused on the dance floor.

"Are you sure you don't know them?" she inquired.

"I'm sure." He turned toward her and finished off his beer. "Would you like another drink?"

"No, I think I've had enough."

He took her hand. "How about a walk on the beach?"

Emma looked at the three men who were now on the dance floor. There appeared to be nothing wrong with the men, but no matter what he said, she knew Ethan and his family were reacting strangely to those guys. Whatever it was they didn't like about them, he wasn't going to tell her, and it didn't matter if they were leaving the bar.

"That sounds great," she said and slid off the barstool. She turned to Isabelle and Stefan as Isabelle stood too. "Are you coming with us?"

Isabelle glanced at Ethan before shaking her head. "No, I think we're going to head home."

Ethan was careful to keep Emma away from the three unknown vampires as he led her outside. He walked with Isabelle and Stefan over to the Jeep in the small parking lot, grabbed his backpack from the backseat, and closed the door. He nodded to them and tapped the closed door before turning to Emma. She was studying the bag slung over his shoulder with a raised eyebrow.

"Big plans?" she asked.

He smiled at her as he claimed her hand and pulled her close to his side. "Just a few supplies for tomorrow."

"Awfully sure of yourself, aren't you?"

He laughed and released her hand to slide his arm around her waist. "I'll go home tonight if you want me to."

It was the last thing in the world she wanted as she leaned against him and kicked at the warm, grainy sand beneath her feet. She'd never felt this secure before as her skin tingled where it came in contact with his. The mellow ebb and flow of the ocean soothed as the salty scent of it washed over her. Light from the moon and stars glimmered on the water; she almost felt as if she could walk across the sea and touch the moon as it hung heavily in the clear night sky.

"It's beautiful," she murmured.

"It is," he agreed, but his eyes were focused on her as they walked further down the beach. "I'm sorry Isabelle was so overwhelming."

Emma brushed back a strand of hair blowing across her face. "I enjoyed talking to her once she stopped..."

"Grilling you?" he suggested when her voice trailed off.

"Yeah, I guess that would be the best way to describe it."

"She's overprotective of all her siblings. I think it comes from being the oldest female."

"I think it's what comes from having brothers and sisters; it must be nice. I mean it's not great when you're on the receiving end, but I understand. She loves you and apparently, she was also beginning to question your sexuality," she added with a laugh.

He chuckled as he shook his head. "Sometimes, I'd like to strangle her."

"I think that also comes from having siblings."

He kissed the top of her head. "I think this is where we exit."

She followed his gaze up the hill to the small house where she was staying. "Jill and Mandy are probably still awake."

"Then I promise not to jump you in the entryway again."

Emma couldn't stop a burst of laughter from escaping; she pinched his side before darting away from him and fleeing across the sand. Her feet slipped in the loose sand, but she forced her small legs to move faster. She could hear him steadily gaining on her. She tried to dash to the side but his arms encircled her waist, and he lifted her off the ground. A squeal of delight escaped her as he pressed her back against his chest and spun her around in a circle. Lightness filled her heart as he stopped spinning and walked with her the rest of the way across the beach to the road.

"I don't think carrying me is helping with the not being

jumped in the entry part," she told him when she felt his erection pressing against her spine.

"Maybe not, but I'm not ready to let you go."

Was he trying to make her fall in love with him? If so, she was dangerously close to it as he set her on her feet in the driveway. "Ethan..."

She found words failed her as his emerald eyes met hers in the moonlight. Emotion swelled so vehemently in her chest she almost threw herself into his arms and buried her head in his chest. "What is it, Emma?" he asked worriedly.

She shook her head and turned away from him. She'd sound like a complete moron if she started stuttering on about feelings and whatever other foolishness had been about to spill from her mouth. Pulling the key from her pocket, she slid it into the door and pushed it open. Jill and Mandy were sitting on the couch with drinks in their hands. Classical music, Mandy's favorite, drifted through the room.

"Hey, guys!" Jill greeted. She'd taken all the braids out of her hair yesterday; it tumbled around her shoulders in waves emphasizing her high cheekbones and pretty features. "Did you have fun?"

"We did," Emma answered. "What about you guys?"

"It's a party wherever we are," Jill assured her.

"Very true," Emma agreed as she kicked off her shoes and placed them in the hall closet.

"There's some margarita mix still in the blender, help yourselves," Mandy offered.

"I'm good," Ethan said as he walked over to stand beside her.

"I think I've had enough for tonight," Emma told her and cast a shy glance at Ethan. "I'm ready for some sleep."

Jill and Mandy both smirked as they took another sip of their fruity drinks. "Sleep tight," Mandy said as they turned away.

"I don't think there will be much sleep going on in there," Jill whispered, and they both burst into loud giggles.

Emma shook her head but followed Ethan to her room.

"I HAVE SOMETHING FOR YOU," Ethan said as he ran his index finger in a circle around the small of her back. Her hair tickled against the bottom of his chin, but he didn't move to brush it away.

Emma had to force herself to lift her head to look at him. She was so thoroughly exhausted and satisfied all she wanted to do was lie there and never move again. "You do?" She stifled a yawn as she asked the question.

"I do."

He sat up and swung his legs off the bed with far more energy than she had right now. Emma put her elbow on the bed and plopped her head on her hand as she watched him walk across the room to his backpack. The light from the single candle on the nightstand revealed his skin was still slick with sweat as it played over his taut muscles and firm ass. Much to her surprise, she found herself growing aroused again as he dug into the bag.

He pulled something out and turned back to her. It looked incredibly small in his hands, but the sight of the dress she'd admired in the store earlier caused her to bolt upright in the bed. Her exhaustion vanished as the blanket fell away to reveal her breasts. Her mouth dropped as he walked over and sat on the bed beside her.

"You shouldn't have," she breathed.

"I saw you looking at it today; I hope I got the right size."

She finally tore her attention away from the beautiful dress and focused on his exquisite face. Something in her chest swelled as she met his eyes; she wasn't quite sure what the feeling was as she'd never quite experienced it before, but she knew she never wanted it to end.

"It's...it's beautiful," she stammered. "But it was so expensive and—"

"No ands," he said forcefully. "I wanted to get it for you, and that's that."

She was tempted to argue further with him, but she couldn't when he was smiling at her and holding *that* dress. "Thank you," she whispered.

"Come on, let's see if it fits," he said. He rose to his feet and gestured for her to do the same.

Emma stared at him for a second before tossing the rest of the blanket aside and climbing out of bed to stand in front of him. She tilted her head back and raised her arms for him to slide the dress over her head. The material felt like a feather caressing her skin as it settled over her. It hugged her curves before flowing out at her waist. The bottom of it spun out around her as she twirled in it.

"I love it!" she cried and stopped spinning to throw her arms around him.

Relief filled Ethan as he wrapped his arms around her and pulled her against him. He hadn't been sure how she would react when he gave her the dress, thought maybe she would believe it was too much or he was moving too fast. He knew they needed to talk about everything, but his experience with conversations about relationships consisted of three words, *don't get attached.* Those were the last three words he would ever utter to her.

There was nothing more perfect than her, or the joy she radiated right now, he was certain of it. He was already growing erect again as he slid the dress up her body and pulled it over her head. Her pert breasts, rounded hips, and soft skin were bared to him once more. He draped the dress over the chair and began to edge her toward the bed. He was going to enjoy burying himself inside her for another couple of hours, relish feeling every bit of her all over again.

The sound of her laughter was contagious, and he found himself laughing with her as they tumbled onto the bed together. She had the most radiant smile he'd ever seen. He traced his finger over her lips and across her chin.

"It's a perfect fit," she whispered as she threw her arms around his neck.

"Just like you," he muttered against her lips.

Something flickered through her eyes; her grin turned playful as she wiggled beneath him. "I'll have to give you an extra special thank you for the dress and the flowers," she said as she nibbled his bottom lip.

Ethan was in the process of losing himself to her when her words registered. He propped his hands on either side of her head as he held himself above her. "What flowers?"

Emma frowned as the smile left his face and his eyes became as icy as the tundra. Her hand fell away from his cheek as he stared at her.

"What flowers?" he demanded again.

"The flowers in the kitchen. The ones you sent me this afternoon," she said hesitatingly. An almost lethal air surrounded him as he pushed himself off her.

"I didn't send you flowers," he said.

He turned and walked to the door so fast, she barely registered he was leaving before she was gaping after his naked backside. She scrambled off the bed as he disappeared. Grabbing her robe, she tugged it hastily on as she followed him down the hall, praying with every step Mandy and Jill weren't still awake. He was completely heedless of his nudity as he stalked across the living room to the kitchen. He was either nuts or the most brazen man she'd ever encountered.

Emma caught up with him as he stopped by the island where the flowers sat. He frowned at them before grabbing the card. Scanning it, he returned it and turned to her. "I didn't send these, Emma."

Her forehead furrowed in confusion, then the color drained from her face as she stared at the flowers with a look of abject horror. She snatched the vase off the counter, stalked over to the trashcan, stepped on the foot pedal, and dumped them unceremoniously into the trash. The lid slammed closed with an air of finality as she turned away. Ethan watched her agitated movements as she hurried across the living room and jerked the curtains closed over the glass doors leading to the balcony.

There was a firm set to her shoulders, but he didn't miss the tremble in her hand as she finished closing the curtains. "Emma, do you know who those are from?" She didn't speak as she walked around the room and pulled the rest of the curtains shut. "Emma?"

"I thought I saw him the other day, but I didn't believe it was possible," she muttered as she returned to the kitchen and yanked the curtains over the sink closed.

Ethan clasped her hand before she could walk past him. Hostility grew inside him as he took in the frantic look in her eyes. He hated that look, and with sudden certainty, he knew he would do anything he could to make it go away.

"Who, Emma?" he asked in a deceptively calm voice.

Her eyes zipped wildly around the room before settling on him. "Tristan."

It took him a minute to place the name, but when he did,

rage settled over him. He somehow managed to keep himself composed as her troubled eyes watched him.

"You saw him the other day?" he asked.

"Yes, I mean no!" she cried. "I thought I did, but it *couldn't* be him. What would he be doing *here*? How would he know *I* was here? But who else would have sent them?"

He pulled her against his chest as tears spilled down her cheeks. It wasn't until her tears wet his skin that he realized he was naked. Bending down, he lifted her and swung her into his arms. It amazed him how little she was as he carried her down the hall and placed her tenderly on her bed. He turned back and noiselessly closed the door before settling beside her and pulling her into his lap.

"Tell me what you think you saw," he coaxed.

Finding comfort in his strong arms, Emma curled closer as his presence helped ease some of the instinctual terror sprouting forth with the realization Tristan might be on this island. She told him what she saw the other day on the beach.

"My parents wouldn't send them; I know Jill and Mandy didn't do it. If they weren't from you, that only leaves him," she whispered.

Ethan brushed her glossy hair back from her forehead as he tried to soothe the shivers racking her small frame. "If they are from him, then I will take care of it," he vowed.

"I don't want to see you hurt over this. Tristan is unstable; I don't know what he's capable of doing. I don't understand how he found me."

Ethan's jaw clenched, but he couldn't tell her why he had no fear of any human. "Are you sure it couldn't be someone else?"

She frowned as she searched her mind for anyone else who would send her flowers. She came up with nothing. "I'll call my parents and ask them tomorrow, but I *know* it wasn't them. They would send more of a card with them."

Ethan rested his chin on top of her head and ran his hands up and down her arms. The desire he'd felt for her earlier disappeared. All he wanted now was to keep her protected and ease her worry. He would do everything he could to make sure she stayed safe, even if it meant killing his first human.

CHAPTER THIRTEEN

Jill was about to dump the leftover eggs into the trash when she froze and looked up at Emma with consternation. Emma was tempted to hide behind her coffee mug; unfortunately, it didn't offer her much protection from her friend's probing gaze.

"Why are the flowers in here?" Jill demanded.

Mandy leaned forward on her crutch to see what caught Jill's attention. Her forehead furrowed as she lifted her head to look at Emma. "Did you two have a fight or something?"

"From the sounds I heard last night there is no way they were fighting," Jill said.

It may be useless, but Emma lifted her coffee mug and held it before her face.

"Then what *is* going on?" Mandy's hand pushed the mug back down so she could look Emma in the eye.

"The flowers aren't from Ethan," she admitted.

Mandy frowned at her before glancing at the trashcan. "Then who are they from?"

"Your parents?" Jill asked as she finished scraping the eggs into the trash.

Emma shook her head. "I called them this morning; they didn't send them either."

"Then who would..." Mandy's voice trailed off as her hand slipped away from Emma's mug. "No, that's not possible."

Emma closed her eyes and placed her mug on the counter. "I thought I saw him the other day."

"Are you serious?" Jill blurted and tossed the frying pan into the sink.

Emma winced at the clattering sound and glanced over her shoulder. She'd left Ethan in the shower, but he wouldn't be in there much longer. She didn't want to retell this story in front of him. She knew he wouldn't, but the look in his eyes last night made her think he might kill Tristan if he got his hands on him. Emma didn't want to see that look again now.

Mandy and Jill pulled the stools around to the other side of the breakfast bar and settled across from her as she told them what happened. "Does Ethan know about this?" Jill whispered.

"I told him everything," Emma said.

"What does he think?"

Emma shrugged and took a sip of her coffee. "Probably that he got messed up with a girl with far too much baggage for his liking."

"Emma," Mandy said in a disapproving tone.

"He was really understanding," Emma admitted. "But would you blame him if he did feel that way, especially if Tristan is here? That is *beyond* insane."

"And it sounds like something Tristan would do," Jill said.

Mandy rested her hand on Emma's arm. "And we'll kick his psycho ass if he thinks about coming anywhere near you."

Emma couldn't help but smile at Mandy's ferocious tone. "I know you will."

"Are you okay?" Jill asked.

"I'm scared," she admitted. "If he was on the beach and sent those flowers, that's a whole new level of craziness. If he followed me here then how long has he been following me without my knowledge, and what else is he willing to do?"

Emma didn't want to think about what he might have seen her doing without her being aware. When he'd been harassing her daily, she'd been extremely conscious of her surroundings and what she was doing nearly every second she was awake. A few months without him in her life had loosened her vigilance of her surroundings and actions. As more time passed, she'd returned to a nearly normal life—a life he may have been hiding in the shadows and spying on for a year. The thought almost made her throw up the eggs, but she managed to keep them down.

"You're not going to find out," Ethan said.

The three of them jumped in surprise. They were so intent on their conversation, they hadn't heard Ethan approach until he spoke and rested his hands on her shoulders. He bent down and kissed her cheek before straightening.

"Want some eggs?" Jill asked and swung her legs to the side of the stool.

"No, thank you," Ethan answered. "I need to run home for a bit; I forgot to pack a toothbrush."

"Then you must go," Emma teased him.

"Are you going to be okay here?"

"I'll be fine," she assured him. "Jill knows Karate."

"Hiya!" Jill said and chopped at the counter. "Proud yellow belt right here."

"Isn't that the lowest one?" Ethan asked.

"What color is your belt?" Jill retorted.

Ethan released a low laugh. "You got me there."

"Don't worry," Emma said and rested her hands on his chest. "Flowers aren't really ominous or threatening."

Ethan studied her as she slid off the stool and stood before him. The last thing he wanted to do was leave, but he had to feed, and he needed to do it soon if he was going to remain around her and her friends for the rest of the day.

This morning, he'd woke to the rhythmic pounding of her heart and the almost cinnamon scent of her blood as it pulsed through her veins. It was the first time her blood had ensnared him in such a way. He knew it was an indication their relationship was progressing faster than he'd anticipated, but that would have to wait. She had too much going on in her life right now; he refused to put even more on her.

He would have to keep himself in control and feed better from now on, but upon waking he'd been torn between taking her again and sinking his fangs into her throat. The decision was made for him when she rolled over and cupped his balls with her small hand. He grew aroused again at the thought of her tiny hand running up and down his shaft before her body slid on top of his.

Ethan bent and kissed the top of her head before he decided to pull her back into the bedroom and push the limits of his restraint. "I'll be back in a little bit," he promised.

"You don't have to be concerned about me, really," Emma said as she walked with him to the door. She didn't want him coming around because he felt he had to, or because he felt sorry for her, and she definitely couldn't handle him getting hurt because of her. She hoped their relationship would continue, but she wouldn't blame him if he walked away. "If Tristan is here, you don't want to get wrapped up in the mess he creates."

He took her hand and turned her toward him when they arrived at the door. "If I didn't want to be here anymore, I wouldn't be."

She smiled at him and turned her cheek into his hand. "Thank you."

He bent and kissed the tip of her pert nose. "I'll see you guys soon!" he called to Jill and Mandy.

Jill leaned across the breakfast bar to look at them. "We're going to hit the beach soon, so we'll probably be by the volleyball nets!" she called.

"Maybe you should stay here until I get back," he said quietly to Emma.

Emma shook her head. "Even if it is Tristan, I didn't let him win before, and I won't let him win now. I'm not going to hide from him. We'll be fine."

He didn't look at all appeased, but he kissed her again and stepped out the door. Jill and Mandy had stopped smiling when they entered the living room after she closed the door.

"You really think it's Tristan, don't you?" Mandy inquired.

Emma was tempted to deny it, she didn't want to come across as a drama queen in case she was completely wrong, but she couldn't shake the knot of apprehension in her gut. "I do."

"We'll be on the lookout for him then, and if he comes anywhere near you again, Emma, I swear I'll cut off his nuts," Jill vowed.

Emma bit her inner cheek to keep from laughing at the solemn look on Jill's face.

"Now get your bathing suit on, it's time to catch some rays," Jill commanded.

Emma wasn't much for sitting in the sun and catching rays. Maybe it was because of her Irish heritage, or perhaps it was the fact she found it boring, but today she found herself quite content to lay in a lounge chair under an umbrella. It was probably because she was up with Ethan, talking and making love, until almost four in the morning.

Mandy was beside her with a book propped on her chest and her sunglasses in place as she read. Even with the shade of the umbrella, the warmth of the day, and the thuds and groans of the volleyball game going on nearby, lulled her.

She didn't recall falling asleep, but the sun was higher in the sky when she woke later. Rolling over, she turned to find Mandy with her head tipped sideways and the book she'd been reading laying by her side. An inelegant snore escaped her.

Emma stifled a laugh as she pulled herself up in the chair. Jill was still on the volleyball court, high-fiving her teammates. She didn't think she'd been asleep for long as they were the same teammates Jill was playing with before she fell asleep.

Emma turned, reached for her water bottle, and froze. Sitting beside the water bottle was a single black rose. A note rested on top of it. Emma pulled her hand back as swiftly as if a scorpion sat beside her. She continued to eye the rose, certain it would sprout legs and come after her.

She almost shrieked when a shadow fell across her, but though she suppressed the scream, she couldn't stop herself from recoiling so much she nearly fell out of the chair.

"What's wrong?" Ethan demanded as he knelt by her side.

She blinked at him as she tried to calm the erratic beat of her heart and get herself back under control. Taking a deep breath, she composed herself a little more, but her hand still shook as she pointed at the rose lying beside her chair. A line creased his forehead; he took a step back to look at the rose. Something sinister slid through his eyes, something that unnerved her almost as much as the rose did.

He bent to grab the flower then stood to survey the area. A lethal air vibrated from him as he turned in a circle.

He could kill someone, she didn't know where the thought came from, but it blazed across her mind seconds before he knelt beside her again. The threatening air surrounding him eased as he met her eyes and tenderly touched her arm.

"Are you all right?" She managed a nod in response to his question. "When was this left?"

"I don't know, I just woke up, and it was lying there."

He glanced at Mandy who still slept soundly before focusing on Jill. Pulling the note from the rose, he dropped the flower beneath his foot and stepped on it.

"Do you mind?" he asked as he held up the note.

Emma shook her head; he ripped the envelope open and removed the note. His frown intensified as he read over the words before scanning the beach again. He held the note out to her. Emma almost waved his hand away, but if it was from Tristan, she suspected he was somewhere nearby, watching them. She would not give him the satisfaction of thinking he frightened her.

She took the note from him and unfolded it. *You still belong to me, you always will, T.*

Emma crumpled it in her fist as volatile anger swelled up within her to replace the fright. She climbed to her feet beside Ethan and turned to survey the crowd.

"Do you see him?" he asked.

"No, but he's out there. I know he is."

Ethan wrapped his arm around her waist and pulled her against his side. "Maybe we should get you out of here."

She agreed, but she found her feet frozen in the sand. "No."

Standing on tiptoe, she placed her hands on either side of his face and turned his head toward her. His eyes searched hers for a moment before his mouth descended on hers. Relief coursed through her as the feel of him burned away her dread over the realization Tristan had been so close to her again, that he *was* here. She hadn't escaped his persistent torment.

The world completely faded away as her mouth opened to

the gentle probing of his tongue. Tristan didn't matter; nothing mattered as Ethan's powerful arms enveloped her and he lifted her off her feet. Her body pressed flush against his as he held her. She wanted nothing more than this man and the way he could make her feel as if she were falling apart and coming together all at once.

She was breathless when he pulled away to look at her. There was something almost loving in his eyes as he searched her face before bowing his head to rest his forehead against hers. He was the most amazing man she'd ever met, and she was putting him at risk. Tristan was a ticking time bomb about to go off.

"I might be putting you in danger," she whispered.

"I can take care of myself."

"I'm not sure what he's going to do, or what he's *willing* to do."

"No matter what he does, I'm going to stay by you. Seriously, Emma, don't worry about me. I'm a lot stronger than I look."

"You must be as strong as a horse then."

"Stronger," he said and kissed her temple.

Though his words were supposed to reassure, she couldn't help but fear for him as her hands curled into his shirt and she dropped her head against his chest. Why did Tristan have to come back into her life just when she was moving on from his memory?

"I think I'm ready to go home," she said.

"I can help with that."

She gathered her things before kneeling at Mandy's side. Shaking her friend's shoulder, she woke her to explain what was going on before they left.

CHAPTER FOURTEEN

"THAT DRESS IS BEAUTIFUL," Jill said as she leaned against the doorway of Emma's room.

"Isn't it?" Emma gushed as she smoothed the front of it.

"The man is hooked," Mandy said as she pushed past Jill and walked over to sit on Emma's bed.

"I'm not so sure about that," Emma said with a laugh.

"Oh yes, he is. Men don't buy clothes for women they don't care about."

Emma frowned as she turned to face her friends. She'd never really thought about it that way, and if she *really* thought about it (something she'd tried not to do over the past year), Tristan hadn't bought her anything until after she left him. In fact, they'd rarely gone to dinner, and she could only recall one movie they ever saw together.

What was I doing with him? She wondered for the thousandth time. How had she gotten trapped in such an unhappy relationship and convinced herself it was good?

Her parents were incredibly loving, they rarely fought, had a happy marriage, and her father was one of the most attentive men she'd ever encountered. But somehow, she'd ended up with a manipulative, cruel, unfaithful, and unstable ass who was still trying to ruin her life.

"I suppose they don't," she murmured as she ran her hands over the front of the dress.

"Nope, they don't," Jill agreed.

Emma stepped in front of the mirror; she pulled her hair back and twisted it into a loose knot resting against the nape of her neck. Jill walked over and began to sort through her earrings on the dresser.

"Wear these," she said and held up two dangling butterflies interwoven with the colors of green, purple, and blue. They matched the dress perfectly.

Emma smiled as she took them from Jill's hand. "Perfect," she agreed.

A knock on the door brought up all their heads. "I'll get it, finish getting ready," Jill said and fairly bounced out of the room.

"Where are you going tonight?" Mandy inquired.

"I don't know, Ethan just told me to wear this dress, and that it was a surprise."

"Sounds like it might be fancy," Mandy teased.

Emma enjoyed the feel of the earrings dangling from her ears as she shook her head at her friend. "Let's hope it's not too fancy."

Jill appeared in the doorway again; she was fanning herself with her hand as she walked into the room. "He is so *hot*," she whispered. "From the look of that man I don't think you're going to make it to dinner tonight."

"Jill—" Mandy started.

"No seriously, I almost jumped him when he walked through the door."

Emma tried to stifle her chuckle, but Mandy and Jill's laughter did nothing to help her hold back.

"There's something wrong with you," she told Jill as she slipped her feet into her sandals.

"With me? There's something wrong with you if you make it past the salad," Jill retorted. "Public place or not."

Great, just what she needed, to be tempted by him in a public place again. She'd been able to turn him away last time, but now she knew what it was like to have him on top of her, inside of her...

Ugh, even now her mind was wandering down treacherous pathways, and her body was beginning to heat.

Emma wiped her suddenly damp hands on a towel and took a steadying breath. She was incredibly curious to see what it was making Jill so enthusiastic about his appearance. Mandy climbed to her feet and looped her arm through Emma's.

"Now let's go, I have got to see what has Jill practically drooling like a bulldog," Mandy said.

"Oh, you'll be drooling too, believe me," Jill replied and led the way out the door.

Emma followed them and had to keep her jaw from dropping when she spotted Ethan standing by the door. His hair was brushed back to reveal the broad planes of his face. The black shirt he wore hugged the muscles of his chest; the sleeves were close fitting around his biceps and flexed as he adjusted his position. His black slacks hugged an ass she'd held in her hands before. The hungry gleam in his emerald eyes made her want to retreat to her room with him right then and there.

"You look beautiful," he told her as he strode toward her.

Was she supposed to speak? Apparently, she was as Mandy nudged her in the back. "Thank you," she managed to get out.

He held his arm out to her, and she took it. "Hope you don't mind walking, it's not far."

"Not at all," she assured him with a smile.

She glanced back at Jill and Mandy only to find them both fanning themselves. *'Told you so,'* Jill mouthed, and they both bit their bottom lip to keep from laughing out loud.

Emma had to agree with them as she closed the door behind her. Keeping hold of his arm, she leaned against his side as they walked up the hill.

"Where are we going?" she inquired.

"Patience," he told her.

They were still a couple of hundred feet from his house when she realized that's where they were heading. "Are we meeting Isabelle and Stefan?"

"No."

The fact he didn't elaborate on his answer piqued her curiosity more as he stopped outside the door to his house and unlocked it. He made an elegant sweeping gesture with his arm for her to enter first. A giggle escaped her as she stepped into the foyer and waited for him to close the door. He locked the door, took her arm, and led her across the beautiful living room.

She frowned at him as he stopped her before the French doors leading out to the pool area and pushed the doors open. Her hand flew to her mouth as she spotted the two-person table set up on the patio with a single white candle in the middle of the red tablecloth. Beyond the table and patio walls, the ocean and setting sun provided the perfect backdrop for a dinner scene she only thought existed in romance novels or movies.

A lump formed in her throat as she turned her head to look at him. He may not have known what he was doing when he set up this table, or maybe he had, but he had completely stolen her heart. The smile he gave her didn't help, and it was taking everything she had not to start crying with joy.

She only had two weeks left on the island; she hadn't even *known* him for two weeks. She shouldn't be feeling like this so early in the relationship but she'd never felt like this about *anyone* before, and she never would again. This was a once in a lifetime experience, and it was *hers*. It seemed too good to be true, and though she was terrified of what would happen in two weeks, she was going to enjoy every second of the rest of the time they were together.

The amount of emotion in Emma's eyes robbed him of his breath. The setting sun shimmered in her hair and caused her hazel eyes to turn the color of cat's eyes. Watching her, he no longer held any doubt about what she was to him, and he wanted nothing more than to have her by his side for eternity.

He wasn't sure she would still be standing next to him if she knew half the thoughts running through his mind. And just how was he supposed to break the news to her? His mother almost left his father, and they dated for a good month longer than he and Emma. He wouldn't blame her if she went screaming into the night and never looked back, but tonight wasn't the night to dwell on it.

Tonight was just for them, and hopefully, a good way to help her forget about her asshole ex-boyfriend, who was already as good as dead in his mind.

"This is amazing," Emma whispered. He smiled at her as he took her elbow and walked her over to the table. Pulling out a chair, he waited for her to sit before pushing it in. The heat of his body burned into hers as he leaned forward to light the candle before her.

"I thought a light salad and some chicken would be good," he told her.

"You cooked?"

He chuckled as he bent to kiss her cheek. "There are some things even *I* can't do. I am good at ordering out though."

"So am I," she told him as she unfolded the napkin and

placed it on her lap. He went back inside and came out with two small bowls of salad. "Where are Isabelle and Stefan?"

"Stefan was kind enough to pack up my sister and take her over to St. George's for the night," he answered. "They won't be back until tomorrow night."

Warmth spread through her, the beat of her heart picked up as excitement trickled through her. She was hungry before they sat down, but her appetite vanished at the realization they had this whole place to themselves. Lifting the fork, she forced herself to take a bite of the crisp salad sprinkled with fruits, nuts, and cheese.

They became so engrossed in conversation, she didn't realize she'd finished her salad until he took the bowl away and brought out two plates of chicken. "This is delicious," she told him.

"I'll be sure to pass on your appreciation," he told her as he leaned back in his chair and folded his hands behind his head. He enjoyed watching the rise and fall of her chest against the bodice of her dress. The swell of her breasts was barely visible above the neckline, but even still, he longed to trace his fingers over the bared flesh, to feel it beneath him and to run his tongue over it. He was getting an erection just thinking about it as she ate.

His eyes were almost predatory as he watched her finish off the last of her dinner. She was finding it difficult to breathe as she placed her fork down and folded her hands in her lap. "Would you like some dessert?" he inquired.

Before she could think, a single word popped out of her mouth, "You."

She'd never been so brazen before, but something about this man made her completely forget any inhibitions. His eyes darkened, and his nostrils flared as he rose swiftly from his chair. Emma was uncertain of his intentions as she watched his lithe movements; he grabbed their plates and returned to the house with them. Excitement pulsed through her; her throat was dry as she waited for him to come back.

If she hadn't seen him reemerge from inside, she wouldn't have known he was there as he glided silently over to her. He pulled her chair back and held his hand out to her. Emma slid her hand into his and allowed him to help her to her feet. Leaning over, he blew out the candle before turning back to her. "All you had to do was say so," he murmured.

Those words caused her heart to slam against her chest as he reached for the knot of hair resting against her neck. His eyes burned into hers as his fingers nimbly pulled the pins from her hair. His gaze was admiring as his fingers slid through it and he let it tumble around her shoulders.

His hands slid over her bare shoulders and down over her ribcage. He could feel and hear the rapid beat of her pulse as it rushed through her veins. Both pricked his appetite but not enough to douse the lust pulsing through him. His dick was so fucking hard he thought it might burst right out of his pants if he didn't get them off soon, but he intended to go slow and savor every inch of her body.

His hands slid over her thighs as he began to push her dress upward to bare her lacy black panties, flat stomach, and matching, black strapless bra. Her arms rose so he could tug the dress over her head. The color of the bra and panties emphasized her creamy complexion and round curves. She inhaled sharply when he began to trail a finger teasingly across the top edge of her bra. Her hands came up to his chest when he took a step closer to her and then another.

Grasping her waist, he lifted her and placed her on the table. Emma couldn't tear her gaze away from him as he planted his hands on either side of her and leaned closer. She was already wet and aching for him to fill her, but he seemed determined to go slow, and no matter how badly she wanted the torment to end, she was enjoying every one of his caresses.

"Do you know what I want to do to you tonight?" he inquired as he nibbled on her bottom lip.

"What?" she managed to get out.

"Everything."

His finger dipped down; it trailed leisurely over her stomach to the edge of her underwear. She didn't know what *everything* entailed, but just the thought of it made her want to jump on him then and there. His gaze came back to hers; a smug smile curved his lips as he pressed closer to her and took possession of her mouth. The tempting pressure of his cock rubbing against her through the layers of their clothing almost made her scream and tear the pants clean off his beautiful body.

As she eased her hands down to his zipper, he seized them. "No," he said in a hoarse whisper against her lips. "I'll be the only one doing any touching right now."

Frustration swelled through her, but she forgot about it as his mouth moved over her neck and down to her collarbone. Her head tipped back; a small moan escaped her as he unhooked the front clasp of her bra and freed her breasts. Warm air flowed over her exposed flesh seconds before his mouth enclosed her right nipple and he began to suckle her breast. A jolt ran through her; her fingers dug into her thighs as she fought the overwhelming urge to grab him.

"Ethan!" she gasped when his mouth took her other nipple.

He seized her hands when they jerked in her lap, and she instinctively went to touch him. Releasing her breast, his emerald eyes came up, and his face hovered inches away from hers.

"Don't make me tie you up," he murmured.

Her heart gave an excited lurch the likes of which she'd

never felt before. A thrill went through her, and though she'd never really thought about anything like that, she couldn't help but become more aroused by his words. A small smile curved his mouth while he continued to study her. Emma knew exactly how it felt to be hunted as his hands slid down her arms and his fingers wrapped around her wrists.

"You would like that, wouldn't you?" he asked.

Emma no longer had a voice to respond. He gently clasped her hands behind her back with his right hand. He lifted her bra with his left hand and held it in front of her before moving it behind her back. The lacy material was soft against her skin as he held it to her wrists.

"Wouldn't you, Emma?"

There was a challenging gleam in the eyes as they held hers. It took everything she had to keep breathing as anticipation held her motionless.

"Yes," she finally managed to get out.

A victorious smile curved his mouth as his fingers deftly worked the material into a tight knot around her wrists. His hands clasped her cheeks; he lifted her face and kissed her lips. "I am going to enjoy tormenting you."

She had no doubt as his hands returned to the edge of her panties. His eyes remained on hers as he lifted her ass up to work her underwear down her thighs and drop them on the patio. The night air caressing her exposed flesh did nothing to cool the heat of her skin and the fire sizzling through her veins. He trailed his fingers across her thigh and toward the junction between her legs. Just when she thought he was about to ease some of her misery, he pulled his hand away.

A groan of protest escaped her, but his finger against her lips silenced it. "You're not going to get off that easy."

Emma didn't think she would ever breathe again as his finger slid away from her mouth. Reaching behind her, he dipped his fingers into the glass of water still sitting on the table. His finger slipped away from her lips as he pulled out a piece of ice and moved his hand back toward her body.

Her eyes dilated when he placed the ice against the side of her neck. He loved watching the delight playing across her features as he slid the ice across her collarbone and lower toward her breasts. He held her eyes before bending to lick away the trail of water the ice cube left on her flesh.

A groan escaped her, but it faded when his mouth claimed her hardened nipple. Excitement coiled through her at the exhilarating sensation of the ice sliding over her body and the heat of his mouth as he followed the steady descent of the ice. Her skin was alive with the feel of him, the tension mounting in her body was making it almost impossible for her to stay still; she'd never experienced anything like what he was doing to her.

A moan of protest died on her lips when his mouth left her skin, but then he grabbed her hips and pulled her closer to the edge of the table. His eyes were back on hers; his hands grasped her inner thighs and pushed them apart. She found she couldn't breathe as she waited to see what he would do next. The anticipation growing within her only increased as a mischievous smile curved his mouth before he knelt before her.

The cold of the ice, and the fire of his mouth against her inner thigh, were tortuously exquisite as he moved over her skin. Emma found herself unable to look away as he moved higher up her thigh at a languid pace that almost caused her to fall off the table. A bolt of lightning seemed to go through her as he rubbed the ice over her clit before placing the cube into his mouth.

Then his mouth was on her center, and she forgot about everything else as his tongue slid in and out of her, leaving her boneless and struggling to breathe. Her hands jerked against the bra. The article of clothing was far stronger than she ever suspected it could be as it remained securely wrapped around her wrists. A small gasp escaped her as one of his fingers slid into her, driving deeper as he stroked the blaze of passion growing within her to more epic levels with his hand and tongue.

Ethan savored in her taste as he pulled her firmly against his mouth. Even though the ice had numbed his tongue, he could tell she tasted like honey as he delved deeper into her core. He didn't think he would ever get enough as she moaned and squirmed against him.

He felt the tightening in her muscles and knew she neared release as her breath came faster. Driving in and out of her with his fingers, he pulled slightly back to run his tongue over her clit. A startled cry escaped her, and her muscles contracted fiercely around his fingers as her thighs clenched against him. Satisfaction slid through him; he tasted her climax as tremors continued to rack her body.

He rose to his feet to take in the sight of her. Her eyes were dazed and smoky in color as they met his, she looked sated, but he was far from done with her. He began to unbutton his shirt and slid it off. Her eyes followed his movements; they lingered on his long, thick cock when he finally freed it from the confinement of his pants. His body was pulsing with desire as he stepped closer to her and rubbed the head of his shaft against her wet center.

All his muscles tensed as he watched her lips part and her body arched against his. A smile curved his mouth as she strained against the bra keeping her wrists together. She was completely at his mercy, and yet there was no fear in her gaze as she watched him. Taking her waist, he pressed his head against her center, teasing her with it before driving into her.

"Yes," she breathed as her head dropped against his chest and her legs wrapped around him.

He understood how she felt as a sense of completion stole through his body. The scent of her washed over him, the pulse of her blood caused his fangs to tingle with the urge to taste her, but even as the thought drifted through his mind, it vanished. For now, it was enough to be inside her, feeling her against him, and taking solace in the relief her body gave to him.

He'd enjoyed being in control up to this point, but now he realized he was never in control. She'd always had complete control over him, she just didn't know it, and now all he wanted was to feel her hands on him. Stretching behind her, he released the knot in the bra and pulled it free. Her arms wrapped around his neck, and she pressed her mouth against his throat.

The salt of the sweat slicking his skin was pleasant tasting as she kissed his neck. The storm she thought his mouth and fingers so expertly put out was rapidly growing within her again. He was like a hurricane, powerful and all-consuming. She clung to him and rhythmically rode out the storm his passion created.

Joy and love swelled through her, and she almost cried from the force of the emotions swamping her. Love, she was in love with this powerful man who took possession of her heart and body. She lost herself to the demanding rhythm of his movements as he propelled her to higher and higher levels of pleasure. Her fingers dug into the flesh of his back as another splintering orgasm tore through her. She almost screamed out loud, but his mouth was on hers again as he thrust into her one more time and released a growl of pure satisfaction.

CHAPTER FIFTEEN

Ethan rolled away from the window and stretched out his hand for Emma, but as he was reaching for her, he knew she wasn't there. He shot up in the bed and tossed the blanket aside. Following her scent, he made his way into the living room and then beyond to the patio where he'd made love to her last night. He spotted her lithe body slicing through the pool seconds before her head popped above the surface. A smile curved her mouth when she spotted him standing next to the water.

"Good morning," she greeted as she rested her arms on the edge of the pool and tilted her head to look up at him. "You just like walking around naked, don't you?"

"You're one to talk," he said as he knelt before her. He brushed the wet hair back from her forehead and admired her ass and legs as she treaded water.

She turned her cheek into his hand and kissed his palm. "I was going to make breakfast, but you don't have any food here."

He knew there was no food in the fridge, but he was glad

he'd made sure to take the blood out and store it in the garage before she came over last night. "We're not much for shopping."

"So I discovered."

"Are you hungry?"

She shrugged and ran a hand over his thigh. The muscles bunching beneath her palm made her forget all about the rumbling in her stomach as her hunger turned carnal. "Yes," she murmured.

He grinned at her as he slid into the pool. Emma swam backward, but he caught her quickly and pulled her back by her foot. She let out a little squeal as his hands moved steadily up her leg until he grabbed her waist. Her mouth was wet and tasted of chlorine as he kissed her, but he couldn't get enough of her.

Emma arched her hips against his, but he gripped her waist and spun her around. A gasp escaped her; her hands curled around the concrete side of the pool. One of his arms wrapped around her stomach as the other slid up to fondle her breasts.

The water, and his hand sliding over her flesh, made her skin tingle all over. She cried out as his mouth seared over her neck, and his cock slid into her. The pangs in her stomach were completely forgotten as his body enfolded hers and she lost herself to him.

It was sometime later before she drifted back to earth and the pool water around her. Ethan's arms were still wrapped around her; his breath warmed her neck as he held her close.

"You may be the death of me," she murmured.

His chuckle made her smile as she leaned against him. "I could say the same to you. We should get you some food."

"Aren't you hungry?" she asked.

"Not right now."

He reluctantly withdrew from her warmth. As soon he was out of her body all he wanted was to be back inside of her again. The feeling of possession crashing into him, made it so he was unable to move for a minute. He fought to keep his fangs retracted. She was *his,* and the driving urge to mark her as such caused his vision to blur, and his body shuddered.

"Ethan?"

"Hmm." It was the only sound he could get out as he nuzzled her neck and inhaled her scent. He was playing chicken with the devil right now, but he still couldn't bring himself to pull his mouth away from her neck.

"I've never felt like this about anyone before." She couldn't look at him as she said the words; she couldn't believe she'd uttered them. She felt exposed, vulnerable, and raw as she ducked her head away from him.

"Neither have I." Those words finally brought back his control, finally brought him back to what he wanted to be when he was around her—a good man. A man who didn't think about blood, death, and destruction, but about her and just how happy she made him. His fangs fully retracted when he kissed her neck this time. "Neither have I."

Tears of joy and relief burned her eyes as his hands stroked over her stomach. "Come on, let's get you out of this water. You're starting to resemble a raisin," he teased.

He kept his arm around her as he swam over to the stairs and walked out of the water with her by his side. He retrieved towels from the cabana and gave her one. The massive towel she wrapped around herself nearly encompassed all her small frame.

"I'm leaving in two weeks," she said.

His hands froze on the towel; the strangest sensation shot through him. It took everything he had to suppress the snarl that almost tore from him. He inhaled a shuddery breath as he strained to retain his composure. It wasn't something he wanted to think about, but it had to be addressed, and soon. She didn't know it yet, but he didn't plan to let her go.

"I don't want this to end, Emma."

Her smile lit up her entire face as she looked at him from under spiky, wet lashes. "Neither do I."

He used the towel to pull her close and kissed the tip of her nose. "Then we will figure it out."

Emma grabbed her dress and underwear from where they fell last night and followed him inside. She took a shower and emerged from the bathroom to find him sitting on the bed, also freshly showered. It felt weird to slip the dress back on, but she didn't have any other choice as he rose from the bed and handed her a bag. She tossed her underwear inside.

"A toothbrush would be beautiful," she muttered.

He laughed and looped his arm through hers as they left the house and made their way back to where she was staying. "My brothers are arriving in two days, so my place is going to get a little crowded. Hopefully, Jill and Mandy won't mind my company."

"Jill might be chasing after your brothers."

"I don't think Ian or Aiden would complain."

Emma unlocked the door and pushed it open. The home was unusually silent, but the aroma of maple syrup and bacon wafted from the kitchen. Her stomach grumbled loudly in response to the delicious scents. "They must be at the beach already," she said as she dropped her shoes by the door and hurried to her room.

She changed and joined Ethan in the kitchen where he pushed a note toward her. She recognized Jill's girly handwriting on the piece of paper telling her they were at the beach. Opening the cabinets, she grabbed a box of cereal and two bowls. "I'm not hungry," Ethan told her.

She glanced questioningly at him over her shoulder but put

one of the bowls back. Pouring herself a bowl of cereal, she added some milk and walked over to sit next to him at the breakfast bar. The rumbling in her stomach eased as she eagerly filled it with food.

A loud bang outside froze her with the spoon halfway to her mouth. Ethan's head turned, his jaw clenched, and for a second she thought he sniffed the air. Then, he was rising and hurrying so fast toward the door it would be an average person's jog, but he was still only walking.

Emma was coming around the breakfast bar when he pulled the door open. His muffled curse and the abrupt stiffening of his shoulders should have prepared her, but she wasn't prepared for the spectacle of the dead cat on the stoop.

Emma's stomach turned when she saw the unnatural angle of the poor animal's neck. She couldn't comprehend what she was seeing, or why the cat was there, until Ethan bent to examine it. With his body out of the way, her eyes were drawn to the giant red *slut* scrawled across the blue door.

It felt like her mind waded through quicksand as it tried to process everything she was seeing. Then, she spotted the paper Ethan pulled away from the cat. "Ethan—"

"Stay back, Emma." She barely heard him, but something about the tone of his voice froze her in place.

His upper lip curled into a sneer; he went to crumple the paper, but she stopped him. "I want to read it."

He glanced at her over his shoulder. "I'm not sure you do."

Emma threw her shoulders back and stretched out her hand. "I'm not backing down from anything he does."

Ethan glanced at the paper and the dead cat before reluctantly handing her the note. Emma hated the shaking in her hand, but she couldn't stop it as she took the paper from him and slowly unfolded it. She recognized Tristan's hastily scrawled writing immediately.

You're still mine, no matter who you fuck. Next time it will be his body on your doorstep. I'm watching you.

Emma's stomach twisted, and she almost threw up the meager contents of her breakfast. She knew Tristan wasn't right in the head, that something malevolent dwelled within him, but she'd never expected this—the poor cat.

Tears spilled down her cheeks as she took in the broken body of the innocent animal. At the same time, rage swelled up within her, but she wasn't sure if she was more infuriated, saddened, or terrified right now.

Ethan rose and stepped toward her, but she held up her hand to ward him off. "You should stay away...he's not...he can see..." she choked out as her gaze went over his shoulder to the door beyond.

"I don't care," Ethan said and wrapped his arms around her.

Her hands flattened against his chest as she tried to push him away, but he refused to let her go. Despite her good intentions to keep him away, she found her fingers curling into his shirt and pulling him closer.

"You should be running from here. You should be getting as far from this insanity as you can. You're in danger—"

"No, I'm not," he said forcefully. "And I am not going *anywhere*. No matter what happens, I'm staying by your side, Emma."

"Ethan, he's obviously unstable, look at the cat." She took a shuddery breath as she fought not to fall apart completely. "We should call the police."

His hands flattened on her back. "There's no proof he did any of this, Emma. I know you thought you saw him, but we don't know where he is, or where to start looking for him. The police can't do much."

She frowned at his words. "But they can start looking for

him. With his prior history, if they can find him on the island, they may be able to do something."

Ethan's mind spun as he tried to come up with some way to keep her from going to the police. It was the normal, *human* reaction to something like this, but he didn't want human interference. He was determined to find this man and seek his revenge. He'd tried for years to keep his murderous impulses restrained, but he was willing to let the monster inside him feast on the bastard tormenting her. But if humans were involved, and Tristan went missing, they might look to him.

"If I don't report this, and it escalates, they'll question why I waited," she continued.

None of the reasons running through his head sounded like a plausible excuse for her not to go to the police without sounding suspicious or unsupportive. He'd have to make sure Tristan's body was never found.

"Okay, I'll call them. Why don't you sit down and try to relax," he said as he led her over to the couch. "Do you want me to get you anything?"

Emma shook her head as she sat numbly on the couch. She realized she was still holding the crumpled note and dropped it on the table.

By the time the police left Emma felt completely drained, another shower and a nap sounded like two of the most pleasant options in the world to her. Ethan was in the kitchen when she emerged from the shower, the delicious scent of grilled cheese drifted to her, and though sleep had been her next goal, comfort food seemed preferable right now.

She settled onto a stool at the breakfast bar as he flipped

one of the sandwiches in the pan. "I scrubbed the front door," he told her.

A pang stabbed her heart, and some of her appetite dwindled away. "Thank you."

"The police will find him; it's not that big of an island," he said reassuringly.

Emma hoped so; they seemed concerned about the situation, competent, and promised to keep an eye out for Tristan. Ethan placed a plate with two sandwiches on it before her. Resting his arms on the counter, he bent down to look her in the eye.

"We're going to get through this," he told her. "Now eat."

Emma picked up one of the sandwiches and started peeling the crust from it. "Thank you, for everything. I think most people would run screaming for the hills at a dead cat on a doorstep and the knowledge of a psycho ex."

"I have a lot of crazy things in my life too."

"Like what?"

Ethan took a deep breath and watched as her small fingers deftly peeled the last of the crust from the sandwich. "Like nine overprotective, incredibly nosey siblings, and a crazy house I share with some of them. It's rarely quiet, and they're always into one thing or another. My parents are so in love that, at times it's sickening, and their crazy friends from college also stay on the property with us, along with my brother-in-law, when he and Isabelle aren't traveling."

"Your parent's college friends live with you too?" she asked in disbelief.

Ethan had never found it odd The Stooge's stayed with them over the years, but he could see how it would be strange to an outsider. To a human.

"They never really grew up," he said with a forced smile. "I guess we should call them The Lost Boys instead of The Stooges."

"They never married?"

"The Stooges?" Ethan snorted. "No. Believe me, when you meet them you'll understand why."

Emma paused in the middle of biting into her sandwich to look at him. *When she met them*, a shiver of delight went through her at his words and the unspoken promise behind them.

"Why do you call them The Stooges?" she asked.

He smiled as he rested his elbows on the counter before her. "Yet another thing you'll understand when you meet them."

She grinned back at him and took a bite of her sandwich. Her smile faded as her thoughts returned to the events of the day. "Your life may be chaotic, but no dead things were left on your front porch."

One day she would understand there were plenty of dead things and blood in his life, but she had enough going on without dumping more horror in her lap right now. He would probably have to do it sooner rather than later from what he'd heard about the beginning of his parent's relationship, and what he'd witnessed with Isabelle and Stefan, but right now all he cared about was keeping her safe.

She finished off the first sandwich and began to peel the crust from the next one methodically. "No dead cats at least," he said.

"That's always a bonus."

When she finished the second sandwich, she picked at the crust on her plate. "You pull the crust off just to eat it?" he asked.

Her forehead furrowed as she glanced at the plate. "I never really thought about it, it's just something I've always done. I guess it is kind of weird."

"Not at all," he assured her as he leaned forward to kiss her. "Do you want another one?"

She thought about it for a second before shaking her head. "No, I'm good."

The door opened, and she turned to watch as Jill and Mandy entered the house. "Why is there a bucket of water and a sponge outside?" Jill's eyes were on something Emma couldn't see as she asked the question.

Emma wasn't ready to deal with their concern yet, but she knew she had to. "I forgot about those," Ethan said as he walked around the counter toward them.

Grabbing the plate full of remaining crust, Emma made her way over to the trashcan and dumped the food inside before setting the plate in the sink. She heard Ethan talking with her friends, but she couldn't make out what they were saying. When Mandy and Jill appeared on the other side of the breakfast bar, she knew they'd already received the rundown on what happened. Mandy looked like she was trying not to vomit, and Jill was about three shades paler than yesterday.

"Are you okay?" Jill demanded.

Emma didn't know how to answer that question.

"Of course she's not okay. I swear, Emma, if I see that asshole I'm going to kill him!" Mandy declared as she stormed around the counter and hurried over to her. "Don't worry, hon; we're going to keep you safe. That piece of shit won't dare come around the three of us."

Emma tried not to cry as Mandy and Jill threw their arms around her and huddled close.

Ethan cleared his throat from the doorway. "Okay, four of us," Mandy amended.

The warmth and security of her friend's arms helped to ease her anguish. She wiped her eyes as she stepped away from their embrace.

"Thanks, guys, but I think it would be best if you stayed away from him. He's crazier than he used to be. I don't understand this," she said with a shake of her head.

"They say people like him escalate, Emma. No one knows why, but the police will catch him," Jill brushed the hair back from her face in an attempt to calm her further.

"I hope so. That poor cat." Emma shuddered and hugged herself. "Tristan's completely lost it."

Mandy and Jill were unable to keep their uneasiness hidden from her as they exchanged a look. "We *will* get through this," Mandy promised. "Maybe we should go home early."

Panic shot through her, and her gaze flew to Ethan. His jaw clenched, he folded his arms over his chest, but he didn't say anything. The thought had already crossed her mind that she should leave. Tristan would follow her, she was certain of that, but she would be away from her friends, and they would be safer.

"Maybe *I* should just go," she suggested.

"Absolutely not!" Jill said vehemently. "We're not letting you travel alone with that douchebag running around. If you go, we all go."

"Jill—"

"No arguments," Mandy interrupted. "Jill is right."

"If you would like to go, I will go with you," Ethan said. "I'll make sure you stay safe. No one will harm you, Emma. Not while I'm around."

Jill and Mandy glanced at her in surprise, but their surprise was nothing compared to hers.

"Your brothers are coming, Ethan, your family is here," she said.

"They'll understand. You're my biggest concern right now."

If she hadn't already been falling in love with him, those words would have started the plunge. As it was, she realized he had just pushed her completely over the edge. How was it possible she'd only known him for such a short time, yet he'd taken possession of her heart in a way no other man ever had?

It seemed too good to be true, and she supposed she should be leery, but she couldn't be when he said things like that and stayed by her side when others would bolt.

Tristan had shown her how awful a relationship could be, and he was continuing to show her that now. With Ethan, she saw how fantastic one could be...what it could be like to trust someone and have them raise her up instead of trying to tear her down. Her heart continued to swell with love, and she was beginning to feel like an idiot for standing there staring at him.

"Awww," Jill said so quietly Emma barely heard her.

"I think *I* might be falling in love with the guy," Mandy whispered.

Emma released them and walked over to him. She slid her arms around his waist and rested her head on his chest.

"I'm not going to run," she said. "It will only give him satisfaction, and he'll follow me. We're here to have fun, and we're going to try and have it. The police know, they'll be looking for him, I'll be no safer in the states than here."

Relief filled Ethan as he held her against him. He would have an easier time keeping her safe while they were on this island. He may not know exactly where Tristan was, but he would figure it out while they were here.

CHAPTER SIXTEEN

Emma leaned against Ethan's side as they walked along the beach back to the house. The warm air caressed her skin, and she couldn't rid herself of a goofy smile. It had taken a lot of prodding for them to get her out the house, but she'd finally relented to Ethan, Jill, and Mandy's insistence she had to try and have fun.

She'd had a couple more drinks than she was used to tonight, but she was hoping to ease some of her strain over the awful events of this day. Walking down the beach with Ethan though, feeling his body against hers, she could almost forget everything that had happened and the fact Tristan was somewhere on this island. It was peaceful here. She felt secure with him and her friends so nearby.

Jill and Mandy were ahead of them, giggling together as Jill ran through the sand. She made some strange dancing motion with her hands and legs that made Emma realize *she* was the sober one. Though lights from a couple of bars, and some homes, filtered over the sand, there were few people on the beach. Emma stifled a yawn as Jill twirled in circles that looked more like a spastic marionette than the ballerina Emma thought she was trying to emulate.

"She's not going to try out for a beauty pageant, is she?" Ethan inquired dryly.

Emma chuckled. "I hope not."

The gentle sound of the ocean on her right was almost enough to lull her to sleep on her feet as she stifled another yawn and snuggled closer to Ethan. Jill began to sing, which was the one thing worse than her dancing, as she hopped back to Mandy and slid her arm through hers.

"I think I'm going deaf," Ethan said.

"Can you make me deaf too?"

She'd meant the question to be airy, but he'd become rigid against her and abruptly stopped walking. Emma frowned as she turned toward him. His eyes narrowed; his eyebrows furrowed over the bridge of his nose as he searched the night around them. His nostrils flared, his head began turning slowly back and forth. Apprehension slid down her spine; she'd never seen him look like this before, never seen such a look come over *any*one else before.

"Ethan?" she asked. Jill's singing was growing distant, but Ethan remained unmoving on the sand. "Ethan, what's wrong?"

A shimmer of movement to the left caught her attention seconds before Ethan pushed her forward. "Run!" he spat and turned away from her.

"What?" she cried.

"Run, Emma! Now!" he shouted.

A scream swirled up and choked in her throat. She swore his eyes flashed red when he looked at her over his shoulder. It was impossible, completely impossible, no one's eyes could do that. He was pushing her forward before she could pause to consider what it was she might have seen in his eyes.

"Go!"

The urgency of his voice, and the look on his face, caused her to turn and flee toward Jill and Mandy. Her feet slipped in the sand, her lungs burned from exertion, but she continued to race onward.

Ethan spun to face the threat he sensed in the air. The shimmering on his left caused him to move in that direction. He used the strength flowing freely through him since he was a child, and which only intensified tenfold upon his reaching maturity, to hone in on his prey.

Ethan seized the vamp by the throat. He lifted the man above his head as if he weighed no more than twenty pounds and slammed his two-hundred-pound frame into the sand. The man landed on his back with an explosive exhale that blew the hair back from Ethan's face.

Lips skimmed back to reveal the man's fangs as he hissed and his eyes turned a volatile shade of red. Ethan had never seen the vamp before, but the aroma of a landfill radiated from him and caused Ethan's nose to wrinkle instinctively.

"Who are you?" Ethan growled.

He didn't get an answer though as another flash on his right caught his attention. This one wasn't coming at him though; it was heading for Jill, Mandy, and *Emma*. Ethan twisted the head of the man beneath him sharply to the side. The crack of his neck breaking resonated loudly through the air, it wouldn't kill the vampire, but he wouldn't be following them for a little while.

Launching to his feet, Ethan poured on the speed as he raced across the beach to where the girls were heading toward the road. Mandy's gate was the most awkward he'd ever seen it as she struggled to run through the shifting sand. She stumbled and nearly fell, but Emma and Jill grabbed her arms and held her as they helped her forward.

The other blur was almost to them when Ethan lowered his

shoulder and smashed into it. Years of playing football with his family and The Stooges had trained him on how to take down another vampire, and he did so now with ease. Satisfaction filled him as he heard a couple ribs give way from the impact, and he felt the unhinging of the other vampire's shoulder.

The vampire sprawled across the sand, kicking it up around him and causing Emma and the others to turn at the sound of the commotion.

"Keep going!" Ethan yelled at her, but their eyes were on the other vampire who rolled over and climbed to his feet.

"Tristan!" Jill blurted.

The color drained from Emma's face, and Mandy looked tempted to leap on the man. That would be the biggest mistake she ever made, as Tristan's red eyes gleamed in the night.

"What...what are you *on*?" Jill stammered.

Ethan's heart pounded with excitement and bloodlust as he focused on the man across from him. Tristan was about six foot, a little shorter than he was and appeared to be about twenty pounds lighter. Ethan didn't get the impression he was dealing with an older vampire, like he had the first time he'd encountered Stefan, To him, Tristan smelled as if he'd been rolling through garbage for a week. Tristan may not be older, but he was feeding on humans, killing them, and gaining strength from them.

Ethan didn't care what this vampire fed on, didn't care about the power that came from the murder of innocents; he was going to kill him. The fact Tristan was a vampire only made it better. He wouldn't have to murder a human, and he would enjoy taking down the monstrosity across from him, but he couldn't do it in front of them. This had spiraled into something he hadn't expected, but he couldn't allow Emma to see the brutality residing so strongly within him right now. He moved to the side, placing his body between her and Tristan.

Emma's mind spun as she tried to process what she was seeing. Mandy's hand dug into her arm with enough force to bruise her skin, but she didn't care. Mandy stepped forward. Emma knew her well enough to know her innate curiosity was drawing her closer when she should be running for the hills. They all should be fleeing, but it seemed the sand had turned to concrete around her feet as she found it impossible to move.

Tristan's eyes were the color of a demon's in the night. The flash of red she thought she saw in Ethan's eyes, had it really been there? Was he something like Tristan, and just what *was* Tristan?

Her mind spun as she tried to process everything going on. The two of them looked like they were about to tear into each other like a T-rex on a triceratops. They stared at each other with a predatory look completely out of place for a human.

The realization took its time to come, but once it did, she couldn't shake the certainty she wasn't looking at two people. If she hadn't seen the red in Ethan's eyes maybe, just *maybe*, she could convince herself Tristan was on something or wore contacts. It didn't seem implausible after all, but no, there was far more going on here. She had no idea how it was possible, but there was something entirely inhuman about them.

Her heart raced, her palms were damp, and her throat was dry as Ethan stood before them. His frame partially blocked Tristan from her view, and she had to look around him to see the strange thing Tristan had become. Whatever he was, Ethan wasn't the least bit afraid of him, which made her head spin even more.

"You have to leave," Ethan grated at Tristan from between clenched teeth.

Tristan rocked back on his heels and moved to the side so he could see around Ethan. Emma's skin crawled as his hideously creepy eyes focused on her. She knew they weren't, but she got the sensation those eyes were laser beams burning through her skin to reveal everything inside her.

"I don't think so," Tristan responded.

Ethan took a threatening step toward him. He was larger than Tristan, but Tristan had those freaky eyes and that look on his face. A look which said he would like nothing more than to tear her open and rip her to shreds. This was not about love with Tristan, but it never had been.

She'd realized a long time ago Tristan didn't love her. He hadn't pursued her because he loved her and wanted her back. He'd pursued her for his own perverse reasons, and now those reasons were warped by something far more malicious and sinister than anything he'd been before.

"You weren't expecting me," Tristan continued in a lilting voice far more appropriate for a kindergarten teacher.

"You weren't expecting me either," Ethan sneered.

Ethan took another step toward Tristan. He struggled with the urge to launch himself at Tristan and sink his fangs into his throat. There would be power in his blood; it was how Stefan had gotten so powerful before he stopped killing their kind. He would relish in the power Tristan gave him, delight in feasting on the blood he would spill.

"Emma, I need you to go," he said in a low voice.

"Ethan—"

"You and your friends have to get out of here, Emma, now. Run!"

She was almost as frightened of him as she was of Tristan, but the idea of leaving him here nearly tore her to shreds. There was no way she could do that. If something happened to him, she would never forgive herself.

"I can't leave you here," she whispered.

His shoulders hunched forward a little, the veins in his arms stood out as his hands fisted more forcefully. He turned to look at her. Like a blown tire, all the air rushed out of her lungs as eyes the color of burning coals stared back at her. A startled squeak escaped Jill, and she jumped backward, dragging Mandy with her.

"Go!" he roared.

Emma's legs were wobbly as she took a few more steps back. It was Mandy who recovered the fastest though. She took a hasty step back, tugged on the arms still holding her, and jerked them both forward. Ethan's eyes continued to burn into Emma's; she couldn't tear herself away from the sight of them. This couldn't be real. It simply couldn't be. Yet she knew it was as true as the ocean's continuous ebb and flow.

What is he? She wondered frantically as her gaze searched the fierce contours of his set jaw and cheekbones. He was whatever Tristan was; something lethal and something far beyond the mortal realm she'd always been part of, and always been so certain of. The whole world blurred and shifted before her, but she had no time to wrap her mind around it as Jill and Mandy propelled her across the sand.

Mandy leaned heavily against her side, her extra weight was a strain on Emma's shoulders, but Emma refused to release her. She was having a difficult time trying to run through the sand with her prosthetic leg, but she was keeping up with them. The shock of what they had just witnessed made Emma's legs feel like she was trying to walk with her ankles tied together. She couldn't quite get her feet to work cohesively, but she still managed to get them to move enough to get off the beach and onto the pavement of the road.

Ethan turned his attention back to Tristan; an evil smile twisted his mouth as he finally had a chance to get him alone. He'd seen the look on Emma's face, the revulsion and terror radiating from her eyes. She wasn't supposed to find out like this, there was no easy way to break this news to anyone, but this was a complete disaster. It was something he wasn't sure he could ever fix, but he would make sure this monstrosity never went near her again.

"She really was a good piece of ass," Tristan said in a taunting tone of voice.

Ethan had never experienced such a burst of rage in his life as he did at Tristan's words. With a ferocious snarl, he lunged forward. He almost had his hands on Tristan when a scream reached his ears. The nearby restaurants and bars diminished the sound, but he detected it.

Tristan grinned at him as he danced backward across the sand. "By the way, I have more friends."

Those words weren't like a cold glass of water in the face; they were more like being dunked into Niagara Falls in the middle of January. He didn't hesitate, didn't think twice about Tristan as he spun toward where he last saw Emma and her friends. Thoughts of Emma pushed him over the sand faster than he'd ever moved in his life. It almost felt like he was flying, his feet barely touched the ground as he covered the beach in bounds that would surpass a Cheetah. The world rushed past him in a blur.

The only thing he saw were the three people ahead of him, and the vampire pursuing them. There was no way the three of them could escape the woman honing in on them, even as the thought crossed his mind Mandy stumbled and went down. From the shadows, another vampire emerged.

Emma's shoulder was wrenched when Mandy went down; Jill groaned on the other side of her as they were both almost pulled over with Mandy but they somehow managed to remain on their feet. Emma's lungs were on fire; there wasn't enough oxygen in the air as she panted heavily to get more of it into her body. The woman with red eyes pursuing them was getting closer, and from the shadows of a cropping of palm trees, another man emerged. She bit back a scream and released Mandy's arm to snag a brick sized rock off the ground.

"Get inside!" Ethan's bellow echoed through the night. *"Emma, get in the house!"*

There wasn't enough time for that though as Jill managed to get Mandy onto her feet and the woman jumped at her. Panic for her friends and herself took over. Acting on instinct alone, she held the rock as she swung her arm up and smashed it against the side of the woman's head. The force of the blow jolted her arm and knocked the rock from her hand, but it also sliced the side of the woman's face open. Blood poured from the gash that revealed her cheek all the way to the bone.

Jill had Mandy's arm around her shoulders as they stumbled past her, but the woman was already recovering from the blow and coming back toward her.

"Key! Key! Key!" Jill shouted as Mandy scrambled for the key in her pocket.

Emma stumbled back and fell against the side of the house. Her heart leapt into her throat when the woman's lips peeled back to reveal two lethal-looking fangs hanging over her bottom lip. Emma's mind spun in circles faster than the earth spun on its axis. There was no way to process what was coming at her. Even as every sane part of her screamed this must be some nightmare or alcohol-induced hallucination, the rest of her knew there was no way to deny the events of this night.

"Holy shit," Jill said.

Mandy swung a fist at the man who had emerged from the palm trees and was bearing down on Emma. Emma threw her hands up against the man's chest, he was as solid as a rock and just as unbending as her pushing, and Mandy's fist in his chin did nothing to deter him.

The rattling *ting* of the key falling from Mandy's hand onto the stone walkway was extraordinarily loud, and condemning, in the night.

This is how I'm going to die, Emma realized as she felt the man's breath against her neck and then the cool press of his fangs on her skin.

At first, she thought she was screaming as an echoing bellow tore through the air, but her mouth remained closed while she fought to keep the man off her.

A loud crack reverberated through the air, and the man's head twisted to the side. Ethan appeared behind the man. The unnatural angle would have killed a human; it only caused this monstrosity to stumble around.

Behind Ethan, she spotted the woman, Tristan, and four others coming at them in the night. Ethan grabbed the stumbling vampire and shoved him at the others, knocking them back.

"The door!" he shouted.

"I dropped the key!" Mandy's cry was full of distress as Jill knelt to search for the key.

A frustrated sound escaped Ethan as he spun back around. Jill rose to her feet as he wrapped his arm around Emma's waist, and before she could protest or respond in any way, he lifted her firmly against his side. Pushing through Mandy and Jill, he raised his free hand and smashed it against the door handle. Wood splintered as the handle gave way and he banged his hand on the door. It flew open and crashed against the wall with enough force to crack the plaster.

Jill had been leaning against the doorframe; she fell ungracefully through the open door and sprawled in a heap upon the tile in the entranceway. Ethan grabbed Mandy's arm, pushed her through, and followed swiftly behind with her still pressed against his side.

"The door!" Jill gasped as she tried to scramble back to her feet.

Ethan remained unmoving in the living room with Emma in his arms. He could feel the tension in her body, the way she held herself away from him, and smell the sour scent of her fear. Her hands didn't curl into him but remained flat against his chest. The brisk beat of her heart could be felt against his arm as she tried to catch her breath.

"They can't come in here," he said.

Even as he spoke, Tristan appeared in the doorway with the woman at his side. They were both leering at them as they rested their hands against the frame. Though blood still trickled from the wound Emma inflicted on the woman, she could no longer see the bone. She thought she should be surprised or horrified by that, but after the events of this night, she didn't think anything would surprise her again.

Ethan saw four of Tristan's cohorts, but he sensed at least two more hidden somewhere in the night. A growl escaped Ethan; he stepped forward and slammed the broken door closed just as Tristan blew a kiss at Emma. The only sound in the dark house was the rapid breaths of the women surrounding him.

Emma was uncertain how to react now that they were safe from Tristan. A part of her wanted to cling to Ethan, to curl up against him and cry. The other part wanted to shove off him, grab her friends and flee from here as fast as they could. He may have saved them, but he was one of those *things*.

What was he going to do with them now?

CHAPTER SEVENTEEN

"WHAT WAS THAT? No, never mind, *don't* answer that," Jill muttered.

Emma couldn't see anything in the shadows enshrouding the house. Her heart raced faster than the winning horse of the Kentucky Derby, and there was no way she was ever going to breathe normally again.

The shuffling of feet and a curse from Jill accompanied a thud. As light burst into the room, Emma realized she couldn't live in denial.

Ethan turned toward her; those eyes, which had just been the color of rubies, were back to the emerald she knew so well.

She saw the hesitation in his eyes, the wariness and sadness in the face staring back at her. She'd come to love that face, but how could she love him when she realized now she didn't even know who, or *what,* he was? There was no way to love someone when there was no trust. Her trust in him was stomped beneath the events that just transpired. She didn't know if he would kill her now that she knew there wasn't something entirely human about him.

"Please..." she had to swallow to continue. "Please, put me down."

He winced a little and bowed his head toward her. She refused to flinch away, but even so, he must have sensed something as he lowered her to the ground. Emma remained unyielding against him until he slipped his arm from her waist. She inhaled a shaky breath of relief as she took a hasty step away from him. The anguished look in his eyes pulled at her heart. There was nothing she could do about that; she wasn't the one with the secrets, she wasn't the one who wasn't *human.*

He'd also just let her go, and he wasn't making any attempt to come after her, or her friends. Her mind was spinning, her legs felt weak, but she refused to sit down. She didn't want him to think she was intimidated by him, or afraid of Tristan, she wouldn't give either of them the satisfaction. Though she was more than a little intimidated and frightened of them both, their eyes were freaking *red!* Or at least they had been.

Emma's gaze drifted over to Jill and Mandy. Jill remained standing by the door, her hand on the light switch, her face pale beneath her tan. Mandy managed to get back to her feet, but she looked as if she were debating sitting on the floor again. Mandy's eyes met and held hers, Emma didn't know what to do or say. It didn't matter if she intended to remain standing; her legs weren't going to hold her anymore. She walked over and sat on one of the stools at the breakfast bar.

Ethan turned to watch her, his hair was disheveled, and blood dried in the corner of his eye. Even as she spotted the blood, she realized the cut it came from had healed.

"What are you?" she choked out.

His eyes were unwavering on hers. "I didn't plan on you finding out like this."

"Finding out what?" she demanded.

"Emma—"

"*What are you*?" She hated the nearly hysterical tone of her voice, but she couldn't control it.

Ethan glanced at her friends before focusing on her again. "Now isn't the time."

"Now is the *only* time." He ran a hand through his disheveled hair before walking toward her. She tried to jerk her hands away when he took them, but he refused to release her. "Ethan, tell me."

"Vampire. I am a vampire. *They* were vampires."

The words should have been staggering, they should make her run screaming or laugh in denial, but they were the words she'd expected him to utter, no matter how insane or improbable they were. She also knew they were true.

"Emma, I'm sorry," he said. "It wasn't supposed to be like this. This isn't how you were supposed to find out."

"And how was I supposed to find out?" she croaked.

"I don't know how I was going to tell you," he admitted. "I'm not sure how anyone can be told this sort of thing reasonably."

"But you *were* going to tell me?"

He clasped her cheeks and tilted her head, so she had to look up at him. "Yes."

"Why?"

"Because I care for you."

Some of her disbelief started to wear off. She jerked her face from his hands as a hot poker of anger pierced her. "Lies are not the way to show someone you care for them."

He recoiled before reaching for her again, but she slid off the stool and took a step away from him. She simply couldn't deal with him right now; she just couldn't, not on top of everything else. Her ex had just tried to kill her and her friends, her ex who was *also* a vampire.

She shook her head, was she some freak magnet? First

Tristan and now Ethan. Or perhaps she was a magnet for the undead if they were even undead.

Ethan's shoulders slumped; his eyes followed her as she walked over to join her friends. Jill and Mandy stared at him as if he were a shark who had climbed out of the water and walked onto the shore. They huddled closer to Emma as she stood with them. He hated the look of betrayal and apprehension shadowing Emma's eyes. Earlier she had looked at him with such trust and love; now she stared at him as if he were a monster.

And if he were honest with himself, he would admit that's exactly what he was. He survived on blood, thoughts of murder consumed him, and he had caused her to look at him like *that*.

"What are you going to do with us?" Emma asked.

The question was like a knife through the heart, but he kept his face impassive as he watched her. "Do with you?" he inquired.

"I assume this was something we weren't supposed to know. It's not as if it's public knowledge vampires exist," Emma said with more strength than she felt.

Jill grabbed her arm, and Mandy bent to pick up a small vase on the coffee table. Emma didn't know what they were going to do if he came after them, she didn't know how they were going to defend themselves against him. She'd seen some of his brutality outside, and she had a feeling she'd only caught a glimpse of what he could do.

"I would never hurt you, Emma. *Never*." Though his words were meant to be comforting, she found they weren't. He hadn't mentioned Mandy and Jill either, something not lost on Jill.

"What about us?" Jill demanded.

Emma stepped forward as Ethan's gaze ran over Jill and

Mandy. She would fight him to the death before she ever let him harm her friends.

"I have to call my sister," he said.

"That's not an answer," Emma grated through her clenched teeth.

"No one is going to be hurt, not by my family or me. I will keep you all safe." Though he said the words, she didn't trust him, and she sensed something more beneath his calm exterior. Of course, there was something more beneath his exterior; there was a whole world of secrets and lies she'd never dreamed of discovering.

"I think you should leave," she said around the lump in her throat. She didn't know if she felt like crying or screaming more, but she did know she needed some time away from him to comprehend everything that had happened.

"You can't be alone, Emma, they're out there—"

"And you're in here," she whispered. "I can't...not right now. I just can't."

"Emma," he stepped toward her, but she held up her hand and shook her head.

"Please Ethan, I can't right now. You have to go."

The look on his face was nearly her undoing. He had lied to her and kept secrets, but she had just ripped out his heart. It wasn't something she wanted to do, she took no pleasure in it, but she had to get away from him right now. Tears slipped down her cheeks as he bowed his head and glanced at the broken door.

"They can't come in here, can they?" she asked.

"No, but—"

"Then we're safe if we stay inside."

He looked as if he was going to protest further, but he closed his mouth. The sun was rising into the sky when he pulled open the broken door and stepped into the dawning day.

Emma couldn't stop the tears from flowing as she watched him walk away.

Ethan looked around for the vampires, but they had fled before the rays of the sun touched on the earth. This was not their time to roam free, she would be safe in the house right now, but it still took everything he had to put one foot in front of the other and walk away from her.

"What happened?" Isabelle demanded when he walked through the front door. He pushed her hands aside when she tried to wipe the dried blood away from his eye. "Are you okay?"

"Isabelle, don't," he muttered.

"Ethan, what *happened* to you?"

She was worse than a gnat as she followed him down the stairs. "Back off!" he snapped at her when she pulled on his arm.

Stefan rose and stepped toward them when Ethan jerked his arm away from Isabelle's grasp. "Ethan—"

"Isabelle, come here," Stefan said in a low tone that froze Isabelle in place.

Ethan moved past his sister and to the fridge, he needed something to take the edge off the rage festering within his chest. The urge to tear something apart with his bare hands and sink his fangs into it grew rapidly inside him. He craved blood and death, but all he had right now was the bags of blood in the fridge. He should have stayed to watch over Emma, but if he didn't feed soon, he didn't think he could keep himself restrained for much longer.

Pulling a bag from the fridge, he didn't bother to tear off the top as he sank his fangs into the bottom of it. The blood filled his mouth, but it did nothing to ease the frustration boiling inside him. He tossed the empty bag aside and stood for a few minutes with his hands fisted and his shoulders heaving as he tried to keep his volatile emotions restrained. He'd messed up, he'd screwed up real bad, and he had no idea how to fix it.

There was always mind control. He could make her forget, and he could make her care for him again, but he would hate himself for eternity if he did, and one day he would have to tell her about himself anyway. There was no way to escape the truth. He'd also put her at risk if he took away her memories. She had to know what Tristan was, learn what Tristan's limitations were, and how she could keep herself safe from him. He should have told her more before he left. He would have to tell her more to keep her safe, but he couldn't do it when she was looking at him as if he had just choked her kitten.

"Fuck!" he bellowed and drove his fist into the fridge with enough force to dent the stainless steel door. Isabelle jumped, and Stefan stepped in front of her. Ethan would never harm his sister, but with the way he felt right now, he thought he could tear this house down with his bare hands.

"Ethan, what happened?" Isabelle asked again.

His shoulders heaved as he tried to steady himself, but it was impossible. "She knows."

Isabelle inhaled sharply. "I'm assuming she didn't take it well."

Ethan shook his head and tugged at his hair as he ran his fingers through it. Taking a steadying breath, he told them everything that transpired over the night. He drank two more bags of blood while he spoke, but he barely tasted them, and they did nothing to ease the growing pressure inside him. Emma was the only thing that would make him feel better, and she wanted nothing to do with him right now.

"Are you okay?" she asked when he finished.

"No."

He'd meant to tell her, yes, but she knew he wasn't okay,

that he may never be okay again. She'd gone through something like this with Stefan, maybe not quite this bad, but they were separated, and it had nearly destroyed Isabelle. If the clawing sensation in his chest was any indication, it might destroy him too.

"Does she know what she is to you? Does she know she's your mate?"

"No," he told her flatly. He couldn't tear his gaze away from the massive dent he'd left in the fridge as he strained to retain his composure.

"You have to tell her."

"Isabelle—"

"No!" Isabelle grabbed his arm and pulled him toward her. "No, you *have* to tell her. She can't be allowed to shut you out Ethan, and if she knows the truth, you can work through this together. She *won't* shut you out if you tell her the truth."

"What will we be working out? Her ex-boyfriend tried to kill her last night, she's seen the evilest side of us, of *me*, and I'm going to condemn her to this life? Destroy her?"

"You won't be destroying her, but if you don't tell her she could destroy *you*! Ethan, she has to know, please tell her."

"Isabelle," Stefan said. He took her arm and tried to pull her away from Ethan, but she refused to release him. "Isabelle, step away."

She finally released his arm, but Stefan only succeeded in moving her a few feet back. "Tell her, Ethan, please," she pleaded.

Ethan turned away from the tears brimming in his sister's eyes. "I haven't had any of her blood, and we've only known each other for a couple of weeks. I'll take care of her ex, I'll make sure she's safe, but I can walk away from this, and I *will* walk away from her after. She deserves that much."

"But you won't be able to," Isabelle whispered. "No matter

how strong you are, and no matter what you think, you won't be able to walk away. We couldn't."

"You were both vampires—"

"Dad couldn't and neither could mom!" she cried and stepped toward him. "She cares for you, Ethan, I've seen that. If you talk to her, I think she'll understand, but you have to give her a chance to make a choice."

"This is *my* choice," he growled.

"What about her friends?" Stefan inquired. "What are we going to do about them?"

Ethan shook his head and stepped away from the fridge, his teeth clenched as his eyes turned toward the growing day. "I don't know."

Stefan nudged Isabelle behind him as he stepped forward. "We can't leave them with this knowledge and not know what they will do with it. We can strip their memories, change them."

"I don't know if Emma will allow that," Ethan said.

"She may not have a choice on this one. If you insist on taking this path of leaving her behind then you have to realize she cannot be left behind with the knowledge she has."

He knew Stefan was right, but he couldn't bring himself to do something that might upset her more. "They won't say anything, who would they even tell?"

"There are people out there who would believe whatever they say and would prefer to see us dead. You may not have come across any hunters, but they are out there, and they are lethal. This is as dangerous for all of them as it is for us," Stefan said.

"You're not going to touch her," Ethan warned.

"I won't touch her, but you have to think about this reasonably, Ethan, this has to be taken care of, for all of our good. From what you've told us about this group of vampires, we may require more help to take care of them."

"Ian and Aiden will be here tomorrow," Isabelle reminded him.

"We may need even more help than them. Neither of them has reached maturity yet. They're strong, but if this group is feeding on humans then they're also strong, and there may be even more of them than what Ethan saw tonight. We're going to have to figure out how to take them down. The humans can't be left alone though."

"Those vampires also have human help," Ethan said.

Isabelle did a double take. "What makes you think that?"

"Judging by the smell of those vamps, they're not moving around in the daytime, yet things were left behind for Emma during the day. There's a human helping them, most likely under their control, or they have a vampire with them who hasn't killed as many people as the others have," Ethan explained. "If it's a human then they can go in that house. I'm going to go back, she probably won't let me in, but I can keep an eye on the place and make sure she stays safe."

"You should go with him," Isabelle said to Stefan.

"I'm not leaving you alone," Stefan told her.

"I can take care of a human or another vampire," she retorted. "You should go with him."

"I'll be just fine on my own," Ethan informed her.

Isabelle's expression was resolute as she folded her arms across her chest. "No, you're not going to be out there all alone."

"They can't move about in the daytime, Isabelle."

"Then we're all going." He knew there was no arguing with her when she spun on her heel and disappeared down the hall.

"This could get ugly," Stefan muttered.

Ethan tore his attention away from where his sister had vanished to meet Stefan's gaze. "It already has."

CHAPTER EIGHTEEN

"I STILL DON'T KNOW how to wrap my head around any of this," Jill muttered as Emma put a cup of coffee before her. "I mean, what the *hell* just happened?"

"I don't know," Emma said. "Nothing good."

"I feel like we just walked into a bad sci-fi movie or a hidden camera show. I keep waiting for someone to jump out and shout, 'Gotcha!' at us," Mandy said as she sipped at her coffee. "And Tristan, wow *Tristan*. I bet this is why he disappeared all of a sudden."

"I suppose dying would put a damper on his stalking habits," Emma muttered.

"Do you think they're dead? Do you think Tristan *died*?" Jill asked.

"Isn't that how it's supposed to happen? Or at least that's the way it's always worked in the books and movies, right?"

"Who knew books and movies were right about this. There was no way we ever would expect this to be true, *ever*. What are you going to do, Emma?"

"I don't know," she admitted as she sat on a stool across from them. Her eyes drifted to the broken door. They'd propped it closed. "What *do* I do?"

"I can't begin to answer that question. This is complete insanity," Mandy said. "I would say you should run and catch the first flight off this island, we *all* should, but Ethan saved our lives last night, and the way he looks at you with so much caring; you can't fake that look."

Emma sipped at her coffee as she continued to study the ruined door. "You saw what happened between Tristan and me in the end. Ethan lied to me; he started all this knowing it was built on a lie. What kind of a relationship could we even have? What would become of me, of him? His freaking eyes were *red*, Mandy."

"Yeah, that's an image I won't be forgetting, ever."

"You're going to need Ethan's help to get through this Emma; we don't know how to handle Tristan, not like he does. I understand you feel betrayed, more than a little frightened by this whole thing, but he may be the only one who can protect you right now—protect all of us," Jill said.

"That's just it though," Emma said as she placed her cup of coffee down. "I don't want anyone to protect me. I was finally free of Tristan; I thought I was finally *free*, and yet I'm once again trapped by circumstances completely beyond my control. I don't want to rely on anyone; I want to have control over my life and not be trapped again."

Mandy took her hand and squeezed it tenderly. "It's not fair, but you're not trapped. You have choices here. Just let us know what you want to do, and we'll stand beside you. Would you like to leave?"

"And if Tristan follows?" she murmured.

"I don't know," Mandy said with a sigh. "I don't know anything anymore. We'll have to get more answers from Ethan when you're ready, but for now we'll stay inside, and we'll try to get this straightened out the best we can."

Emma lifted her cup again and blew on the steaming coffee before taking another sip. "Yeah, I guess."

A shadow fell over the window, alerting her to the presence of someone outside before a knock sounded on the door. "Hopefully, that's the guy who's going to fix the door," Jill said as she rose to her feet.

Mandy and Emma moved with her, but when Emma spotted Ethan and Stefan on the other side of the door, she stepped back. Jill cast her an apologetic look before lifting the door a little and pushing it out of the way. Ethan's eyes found her instantly; her traitorous heart did a strange little flip-flop that almost made her melt, but she straightened her shoulders and met his gaze head-on.

"How are you doing?" he asked.

"Fine," she lied.

He glanced at Stefan and then behind him to Isabelle. "I wanted to let you know we'll be outside if you need us for anything."

She opened her mouth to tell him to come inside, to hold her and make the horrible events of the night better but her tongue stuck to the roof of her mouth. "You could come to our place, stay with us. It would be safer there, especially with our younger brothers coming," Isabelle offered eagerly.

Emma's gaze traveled over them. "You're all like them, like him?" she asked though she already knew the answer.

Isabelle glanced at Stefan before nodding. "There is a lot to explain," Ethan said. "When you're ready to talk."

Jill nudged her, but Emma was having trouble finding her voice again. "We have a lot of questions," Jill told him.

"You can never tell anyone about this, ever," Stefan said gruffly as Emma studied them with a fresh set of eyes. The aura of power they exuded was always there; she'd picked up on it before, but now she finally understood the reason why. Isabelle's face was filled with anxiety as she watched Emma. She was ringing her hands before her, a gesture Emma never thought she'd see the usually confident woman make.

"Who would believe us even if we did tell someone?" Mandy asked.

"Some people would," Stefan told her. "People who would like nothing more than to see all of us dead."

Emma's eyes flew to Ethan. No matter how upset and frightened she was right now, the last thing in the world she wanted was to see him hurt, in *any* way, and she especially didn't want to be the cause of it. But then, she'd already caused him to be hurt last night when Tristan and his friends attacked them. She stepped toward him before catching herself and stopping near the stairs.

"No one will know anything," Emma promised.

She forced herself to look away from Ethan before she started to cry and forgot all about him keeping such a *huge* thing from her. But she supposed it wasn't a first date conversation to have. She didn't see how anyone could work the whole, 'hey, by the way, I'm a vampire,' talk in between the, 'what was your major,' and 'what's your favorite color,' conversation topics?

Ethan exchanged a look with Isabelle and Stefan before turning his attention back to the others. He didn't know if it was enough, but for now, it would have to do. He could change Jill and Mandy's memories on his own; he knew he would only alienate Emma even further if he did though. It would also have to be done relatively soon; if it went past a week, he wasn't certain he, or Stefan, could still do it.

He studied Jill and Mandy, two women he barely knew, but they now had his and his family's future, in their hands.

That thought didn't sit well with him, but to be fair, his family was the only protection Jill and Mandy had against Tristan and his friends. They were all going to have to count on each other to get through this.

"Can we come in?" Ethan inquired.

"I don't think we could stop any of you, not after what we witnessed last night," Emma replied.

"Isabelle and Stefan haven't been invited in yet," he reminded her. "You may not own the home, but you're residing here right now, and that's what matters."

Emma's mind flashed back to the first morning Ethan arrived here, and Jill had so cheerfully invited him inside. Jill had no way of knowing then that she was inviting in someone with the ability to kill them. She could feel Jill and Mandy's eyes on her as she studied Ethan, Isabelle, and Stefan. They hadn't known before, but they knew now, and she couldn't allow them into this house until she had a better idea of what was going on.

"No, I'm sorry, but no," she said. "We don't know any of you, not really. Jill and Mandy..." She hated the tears burning her eyes, but she refused to shed them as she unwaveringly met Ethan's troubled gaze. "I just can't."

A pang stabbed through Ethan's chest, but he bowed his head in agreement. "That's fine."

"Wait!" Isabelle cried.

She stepped forward, but Ethan grasped her arm and held her back. They stared defiantly at each other for a minute before Ethan shook his head. Isabelle's shoulders slumped, and she gave Emma a longing look. Stefan pulled her away from her brother; Isabelle glanced back at Emma as she reluctantly allowed herself to be removed from the doorway.

"If you need anything, anything at all, we'll be outside."

Ethan turned around and left the doorway before Emma could respond.

"It's almost like having two stalkers," she muttered.

Jill rested her hand on her shoulder. "At least one of them wants to keep you alive."

Emma released a harsh laugh. "I guess that's the silver lining in all this."

"There should always be one," Jill said.

"I think I'm going to try and get some sleep. Unless you want me to wait for the new door? It's my fault, after all."

"It's not your fault, and I'll handle the door," Mandy offered. "I'm still pretty wired anyway."

Emma turned away from her friends. All she could think about was lying down and getting some sleep, though she had a feeling sleep would be elusive.

CHAPTER NINETEEN

THE ROOM WAS ENSHROUDED in darkness when she woke sometime later. Memories filtered back over her, and it took all she had not to groan and bury her head under her pillow. "Shit."

She stared at the lengthening shadows moving across her walls and tried to decide if she wanted to get out of bed right now. The shock, anger, and horror over what happened last night had faded while she was sleeping, and now all she felt was a deep ache in her chest.

She was falling in love with him. She'd found a freedom with him she'd never known could exist, and now she was left only with the hollow shell of those feelings. In his arms, she didn't feel inadequate and trapped, she felt secure and cherished, but it was all a lie.

Or was it? Everyone had their secrets, she had revealed all of hers to him, but some secrets were harder than others to reveal, and this was a big ass secret.

Emma shook her head and threw back the sheet she'd become entangled in. She was hoping a shower would clear her head and ease the growing anguish in her chest, but she doubted it. Stepping beneath the stinging spray of the shower, she stayed under the warm water for a good half an hour before finally turning it off.

Emerging from the shower, she wrapped a towel around her hair and another around herself. She returned to the room and was grasping for the lamp on the bureau when a small noise caught her attention. Her hand froze, her gaze darted around the room, but she couldn't see much through the dark. Even still, her breath was trapped in her lungs as she continued to search the room.

Then she heard it again. Grabbing the lamp, she spun to her right as something came at her from the shadows. Whatever it was, it crouched low and moved with far more speed than she'd thought possible for something so small. And then it was rising, growing taller as it continued to come at her.

A strangled cry escaped her; the plug ripped from the wall as she swung the lamp up with all of her might. The force of it wrenched her wrist in its joint as the lamp cracked in half and part of it toppled to the floor. Her attacker was knocked off balance by the force of the blow, but even still their hands entangled with the towel and nearly ripped it away from her. She lifted what remained of the lamp and crashed it down onto the person's back. The second blow sent the light tumbling from her numbed fingers as the air rushed out of her attacker.

The person had fallen in the direction of the other door to her room; there was no way she could reach it without being caught. She grabbed the top of the towel as she turned toward the French doors opening onto the balcony.

The towel in her hair tumbled away as she dashed around the rocking chair in the corner. She picked the chair up and heaved it blindly behind her to dissuade her pursuer. Her hands fumbled over the latches on the French doors, but she realized too late the locks she'd set earlier weren't in place. She just managed to fling the door open when a hand tangled in her hair, and her head was jerked cruelly back.

Involuntary tears filled her eyes as her neck twisted to the side and agony lanced through her brutalized muscles.

"Tristan wants to talk," a man hissed in her ear.

Panic tore through her to push away the pain. Fighting like a wildcat, she kicked backward at the person holding her, and her fingers tore at the hand in her hair. An arm wrapped around her waist; she was lifted off her feet and pressed against a burly chest. The man holding her wasn't tall; his head was right behind hers now, but he was strong. Without thinking, she swung her head back and smashed her skull off the man's face.

A sickening crack accompanied his startled yelp. That cry and the hot wash of liquid dripping down her back was her reward for breaking his nose. With the man thrown off by her attack, she pulled her arm forward and drove her elbow roughly into his ribs. A grunt escaped him, and his grip on her eased.

Emma threw herself forward with enough force to tear herself free of the man's grasp. Off balance, she stumbled and crashed into the glass of the French doors. Thankfully, the glass held up, but she bounced off the doors like a manic rubber ball. Behind her, she could hear the heavy breathing of the man coming at her. There wasn't going to be enough time for her to get away from him.

A scream rose and died in her throat when the balcony doors burst open, and a shadow rushed into the room. Emma fell back, and even though she couldn't see him, she instinctively knew it was Ethan with them. A startled scream filled the air as Ethan lifted the smaller man and smashed him into the wall with enough force to crack the plaster.

The loud snarl that tore from Ethan made the hair on Emma's arms and neck rise. She'd been about to go and help him with the man, but she found her feet frozen in place. The man squealed at the same time a strange sucking sound filled the room. She tried to deny it, but she knew what the sound was, what it meant.

Nausea twisted her stomach; a dull thud filled the room as the body hit the floor. Her hand shook as she searched for the switch in the bathroom and turned the light back on. Ethan's head swiveled toward her; his eyes were burning coals in the dark caressing his body.

His gaze relentlessly held hers; he seemed almost to be daring her not to run away screaming from him as he wiped away the blood staining his mouth with the back of his hand. Though her brain was screaming at her to flee, she found she couldn't. He killed for her, and as repulsed and petrified as she was, she couldn't turn her back on him, he deserved better than that.

"Did he hurt you?" he demanded.

"No." She barely heard the word, but she knew he had when his eyes closed and he took a deep breath.

"Emma!" Mandy shouted.

The door to her bedroom burst open, and the light turned on. Emma blinked against the glare.

"What happened?" Jill cried.

The crumpled body on the floor drew Emma's eyes. Ethan moved swiftly to the side and grabbed the blanket off the bed. He tossed it over the man lying on the floor, but not before Emma caught a glimpse of the blood trailing from the puncture wounds in the side of the man's twisted neck. Whatever thoughts she had of the man possibly still being alive were doused by his unseeing eyes.

"Who is that?" Jill demanded.

"The gardener," Mandy said in a flat voice. "I saw him pruning the hibiscus the other day. What is he doing here?"

"He attacked me." Emma hugged the towel tighter around her as she recalled it was all she wore. "He said Tristan wanted to talk with me."

"Why would he do that, and how does he know Tristan?" Mandy demanded.

"Tristan must have gotten to him," Ethan said as he studied the blanket on the floor.

"Gotten to him and done *what*?" Emma asked.

"Taken control of his mind."

Emma's head spun, but before she could think of anything to say, a new noise drew her attention to the French doors as Isabelle and Stefan appeared on the balcony. She tugged the towel closer around her. Ethan stepped to the side, yanked the sheet from her bed, and wrapped it firmly around her.

"You can do that?" she inquired as she tilted her head to look up at him. His eyes were still red as they met hers; a muscle twitched in his cheek, and she could almost hear his teeth grinding together.

He fought the urge to crush her against him and never let her go. Instead, he forced himself to release her and drop his hands back to his sides. He had killed a man. He'd thought it would have eased some of his primal urges to destroy, but it didn't. It only showed him what he was missing as the life force of the man pulsed through his veins, and the taste of the warm blood lingered on his lips. He wanted *more*. Touching her, if only for those brief seconds, had helped bring him some serenity though.

She had to let him into her life again; she had to forgive him and start trusting him once more. As much as he didn't like to admit it, Isabelle was right; he needed Emma in his life if he was going to stop killing. He wouldn't have her in his life unless she were willing to be there though, and unless she loved him too.

"Do what?" he asked as he'd forgotten what it was they'd been discussing.

"Take control of people's minds?" she inquired.

"Yes." He started to turn away, but her brisk inhalation brought his attention back to her. His eyes narrowed on her paler face and now trembling lower lip. "No, Emma, I've never done it to you."

"How do *I* know that?" she inquired.

"Because I wouldn't be lurking in the shadows outside your house, I'd be in your bed where I *belong*." He hadn't meant to be short with her, but the hideous events of the past two nights were pushing him toward a breaking point he wasn't sure he could survive. "And they," he thrust his finger at her friends. "Wouldn't remember any of this. Everything I've done is for *you*, and I will not violate your mind or the mind of anyone else. Believe whatever else you want about me, but *know* that much."

He turned away from her, but her tiny hand on his arm stopped him again. "Thank you," she breathed.

"Anything for you, Emma."

Her mouth dropped open, but she didn't try to stop him again as he turned away from her. She didn't understand any of this, but his words left her speechless and her heart aching more than it had when she first woke.

"What are we going to do about him?" Isabelle nodded toward the body.

"I don't know," Ethan answered. "Weigh him down and drop him into the sea."

The prospect didn't please him. The man had injured Emma, he would have taken her to *Tristan,* but he was an innocent in this, one probably corrupted against his will.

Emma turned toward Stefan and Isabelle. "You can both come in."

Ethan's head shot up at Emma's words; hope filled him as she seemed to have decided to give them at least a little more of her trust. Isabelle and Stefan exchanged a glance before stepping into her bedroom.

Isabelle gave Emma a small smile before hurrying to Ethan's side. "You didn't have a choice," she murmured. "Even if he was under someone else's control, you didn't have a choice."

He knew she believed her words, but this was something he had always wanted. Guilt was beginning to eat at him as he stared at the motionless body on the floor. Emma started to walk toward her friends, and without thinking, he reached out and grasped her hand. He needed the connection with her and the tranquility she brought to the tumultuous seas coursing through him. He expected her to recoil, but her eyes shot to his, and her fingers brushed over his. More of the bloodlust and strain eased from him as his flesh remained in contact with hers.

"Stay close," he told her.

She bowed her head and pulled her hand away to wrap it within the sheet. Her eyes were darker due to the shadows under them. The lines around her mouth hadn't been there yesterday, but she was alive, and that was what mattered. He watched as she walked over to join her friends, they enveloped her in a hug and hovered around her.

"He wasn't so innocent." Ethan's attention was drawn away from Emma by Stefan's words.

"What makes you say that?" Ethan inquired.

Stefan held up the man's arm to reveal a trail of faded bite marks from his wrist to his elbow. "There are enough here to make me think he allowed at least some of the vampires to feed on him daily. I don't think he was under anyone's control; he came here of his own free will to ingratiate himself further with them."

"Why would he do that?" Emma asked.

"Some people in this world will do anything to be closer to a vampire, will allow themselves to be used as food if there is the slightest hope they could one day become a vampire. We call them Feeders," Stefan answered.

"Why would anyone allow that?" Jill looked as if she'd been told to suck on someone's toes as she asked the question.

"The promise of immortality is incredibly enticing to a lot of people." Stefan dropped the gardener's arm away in disgust, wiped his hands on his jeans, and rose. He pulled Isabelle away from the man and moved her over toward the bed.

This revelation helped to ease some of his guilt over killing the man. He no longer disliked the idea of tossing his body into the sea.

"At least we know who was leaving you presents during the day," he said. "Though there could be others." The color faded further from Emma's face, her eyes shot to the open French doors and then the hall behind her. "We will keep all of you safe."

She bowed her head but the anxiety etched onto her features didn't ease.

"We have to get rid of him, now," Stefan said stridently.

"The sun has set, Tristan and his friends will be out again," Isabelle said nervously. "We can't move him now."

Ethan studied the darkening sky before turning his attention to Emma. Her eyes were riveted to the body beneath the sheet. "He has to stay here tonight, doesn't he?" she asked.

In answer to her question, laughter drifted in from outside, and something clattered across the balcony. Ethan leapt to his feet and hurried toward the doors.

"Ethan, don't!" Isabelle cried and scurried over the top of the bed toward him.

Without thinking, and driven by concern for Ethan's safety, Emma left her friends behind and ran toward him. Stefan made a move to grab her, but when Ethan turned toward him with a low growl, he dropped his hand down and stepped aside. Emma glanced between the two of them as confusion rolled through her, and she stopped a few feet away from Ethan. She would like nothing more than to throw herself into his arms to keep him from stepping outside, but if she threw herself into his arms now, she knew she would never look back.

She could forgive him one day though, she realized, not everything was black and white in this world. Sometimes the colors were the most frightening part of it. She realized that now, but it still didn't mean they could be together. There was too much she didn't understand...was scared of; he was part of a world she'd never known existed until yesterday. He belonged to a world she wasn't part of.

When he looked at her like he was now, she found herself not caring about any of those things. He'd risked his life for her, had killed for her, and he was staring at her as if she were the only thing in the world he could see. *No* one had ever looked at her like that; it made her feel loved in a way she never had before.

Then a new sound resonated from outside and he was turning away from her as more laughter echoed through the night. "He'll call the police to try and set us up, I know he will," Emma whispered.

"We can take care of the police," Stefan said. "They'll never remember they were here when we're done with them. He won't call them though; he's here to torment you and to taunt Ethan into responding. They have to be taken care of before anyone else dies."

Isabelle grabbed Stefan's arm, stopping him before he could leave the house. "There's more of them than you think," she hissed. "I can smell them."

That was the oddest statement Emma ever heard, but she wasn't about to question them on it. For now, there were some things she would prefer not to have elaborated.

"How many are there?" Stefan asked.

"More than last night," Ethan murmured. "At least eight, maybe more."

Stefan's forehead furrowed as he frowned and looked toward the doors. "Eight? Why are there eight of them together?"

Emma pulled the sheet closer around her when Ethan stepped in front of her and pushed her back a step. "Is that unusual?" she inquired.

"That many together, yes. What they're doing, and why, is something I don't understand," Stefan answered.

"The ones last night were young, and judging by the smell, and the way they're moving, these are young too." Ethan's nostrils flared as he scented the night. "Tristan created them."

"What?" Emma blurted out.

"These vampires are Tristan's creations."

"Of course they are," Stefan said with a note of realization in his voice. "Young, impetuous, and eager to please their creator."

"But where is *his* creator?" Isabelle asked.

"Not all of those created are willing to stay with their creator, I certainly wasn't," Stefan said bitterly.

Isabelle wrapped her hand around his arm and stepped closer to him. Emma glanced at Isabelle and Ethan as a new thought occurred to her, how were they both vampires? Had the same person changed them at the same time, or around the same time? But he'd talked about his parents and his numerous siblings; were they all vampires too? It was just more questions to add to the growing heap of them, but the heap would have to wait until later as laughter drifted in from outside again.

"We need to think about this before engaging with them," Isabelle said and stepped forward to close the doors. "But neither of you are going out there without me."

"You're not going out there," Stefan said briskly.

"So it's settled that we're not engaging with them tonight," she said with a falsely sweet smile.

Emma's gaze drifted back to the man lying next to the bureau. Her stomach twisted, she looked away before she spilled what little contents were in her belly as the eerie laughter continued to drift in from outside. "They'll stay out there all night," she whispered.

Ethan stepped closer to her; he went to rest his hands on her shoulders but dropped them down before he could. "I think you should get dressed." She frowned at him and then at the sheet wrapped around her. "Please, Emma."

She gathered the clothes she'd set out on the bureau before getting into the shower and stepped into the bathroom to change. When she came out of the bathroom, she immediately noticed the room was straightened, and the body removed. Emma frowned at the bare spot where the man had lain. Life had been lost there, yet not even a drop of blood marked it.

"Where is he?" she asked.

Ethan turned away from the doors and folded his hands behind his back as he studied her. Even with clothes on, she was still the most enticing female he'd ever laid eyes on, and she was the only one who could save him. She was also the only one who could drive him over the edge.

"Stefan moved him into the bathroom down the hall," he told her.

"How are we going to get a body out of here in the daylight?"

"We'll figure out a way to take care of it, don't worry about that."

Emma fiddled with the frayed edges of her cut-off shorts. "I feel like there's far too much for me to worry about lately."

"I'm sorry Emma, I—"

"Don't apologize, Ethan, please. Nothing can be done to change it, and I'm not sure I'd want to."

"Really?"

She hated the hope in his eyes. "I'm not ready to sit and talk about us. I'm not ready to continue this relationship. We've known each other for two weeks, and you've already met my crazy ex and killed someone. It might just be me, but I'm pretty sure that's a bad omen. Like even worse than the groom seeing the bride in her wedding dress before the ceremony, or a black cat crossing your path kind of bad omen. I'm not one for superstition, but this goes *beyond* that."

He moved away from the doors. "I'll kill anyone who tries to come after you again. *Any*one."

Emma swallowed at his words, and her gaze drifted to the curtains he'd pulled over the doors. She could hear the other vampires out there, still running around and laughing like a group of patients who had escaped the asylum. He stepped closer to her, and despite all the words she'd just uttered, she found herself instinctively swaying toward him. Her skin came alive at the prospect of touching him again.

What was this influence this man had on her? She fisted her hands at her sides to resist touching him. "I can't stay in this room, not anymore," she said to distract herself.

A jolt of electricity shot through her as he rested his hand on her elbow. "Understandable. The others are in the living room."

She couldn't help but move closer to him as he led her from the room and down the hall. "He was human when I knew him. Tristan was," she clarified at his questioning look. Ethan frowned as he thought over her words. "I mean, I realize I didn't know what you were, I assumed you were human too, but he *had* to have been human."

"I'm sure he was," Ethan assured her.

"If he wasn't," she stopped abruptly and tugged on his arm. "Do you think he twisted my mind or changed my memories in some way?"

Ethan pulled her a step closer to him. "I believe he *was* human when you knew him, Emma. If he wasn't I don't think you would be here. When you first walked out of his life, there was nothing he could do to get you back but harass you. He would have changed your mind *then* if he'd been a vampire. I think he disappeared from your life because he was changed, and he was with the creature who made him. He's returned now because he's stronger, and he has a way he *can* get you back by bending your mind to his will."

Cold horror spread through her at his words. She couldn't think of anything worse than what Ethan described. "That *is* why he's here, isn't it? To change my memories and make me do what he wants."

"Emma." He took her hands and held them loosely before him. "I'm not going to let him get to you, I promise you. Whatever happens between us, you must know I will never let anyone hurt you. Not him, not me, *no* one."

She found she couldn't breathe as his fevered gaze burned into hers. There was so much between them, but as she searched his eyes, she couldn't think of one reason why she wasn't kissing him right now. Then again, he had just killed someone and probably still had the taste of their blood in his mouth. That was reason enough, or at least it should be for any sane person, but she still found herself longing to taste him.

Instead, she forced herself to take a step back to keep some distance between them. No matter what her heart and body desired, her mind was screaming at her to maintain her distance.

For a moment, Ethan had thought she would finally come to him, but it wasn't to be. He sighed as he thought over their conversation. "Did Tristan go out in the daytime when you were together?"

He fought the urge to drive his fist into the wall at the mere thought of that man touching her, holding her. If he lost his temper in front of her now, he would officially drive the final nail into what would become the coffin of their relationship.

She frowned as her gaze ran over him. "He did, but so do you."

"I can because I'm not a killer, or I wasn't," he said as his gaze drifted toward the bathroom at the end of the hall. "The sun will be tougher for me to handle now, but I haven't killed so much I won't be able to withstand its rays. It's when murder becomes a part of you, a constant daily thing that the sun's rays become impossible for us to endure. For some of our kind, killing someone is something they partake in daily. The more a vampire kills, the stronger it becomes, yet the weaker it also becomes. The vampires with Tristan are to a point they can't tolerate the sunlight. That much was made clear this morning when they fled as soon as the sun came up. If they continue this way, it will become increasingly difficult for them to cross bodies of water too."

"You mean to tell me they could become trapped on this island, terrorizing these people?" She'd go to Tristan before she ever let innocent people suffer because of her.

Ethan couldn't stop himself from grabbing her shoulders at

the panicked and appalled look on her face. "No, they'll leave before that's possible. Tristan was sick and twisted before all this began, but I doubt every human he changed was the same way. Self-preservation is key for almost everyone; it's even stronger in our species. Once immortality is gained, it's not something willingly given up. Keeping themselves trapped on an island with a growing pile of bodies and missing people reports will arouse suspicions amongst the humans. It's almost a sure way to guarantee their immortality comes to an end. They'll leave before they're trapped here."

"Even Tristan?"

Ethan thought over her question before shaking his head. "No, I don't think Tristan will go with them if they leave and you are still here. What he's become has done nothing to ease the madness residing in his mind before he changed. His safety isn't his number one concern, his obsession is."

"And I'm his obsession."

"You are," he confirmed.

"And what am I to you?"

Words tumbled through his mind so fast he didn't know what to say. There was so much he had to explain to her, so much he had to tell her, but he wasn't sure where to begin or how to start to make her understand what she was to him. In the end, he settled for the simple truth. "You're my everything."

His words melted her heart. "Ethan—"

"I didn't say that because I expect a response from you, or because I expect it to make everything better. I said it because it's the truth, and you have to know that."

How could she possibly stay mad at him when he was saying things like that to her? She didn't have time to process the question or how to answer it before Isabelle appeared in the hallway.

"Are you two going to join us?" Ethan tore his attention

away from her to focus on his sister. "I think it's time for us to answer some questions."

"So do I," Ethan agreed. He reluctantly removed his hands from Emma's shoulders. "Come on."

Emma almost grabbed his hand, but though his words had melted a good chunk of her resolve, she thought it was better to have some of her questions answered before she made any rash decisions.

CHAPTER TWENTY

EMMA SETTLED onto the couch between Jill and Mandy; she folded her hands before her as she studied the three vampires across from her. She'd just said that to herself, three *vampires*, but that was exactly what they were, what *Ethan* was. She watched them as they moved with the fluidity of liquid mercury around the room. It was impossible not to see them as predators now that she knew what they were, but she didn't feel the urge to get up and run away like she'd experienced last night.

She wasn't frightened of them anymore, she supposed she should be, but she couldn't seem to summon the emotion. Maybe she was as batty as Tristan, but she didn't think so. These three had done nothing to warrant her fear; Ethan had saved her and her friends' lives multiple times over the past twelve hours. Even if there was never anything between them again, she would always remember him with love, and she would think of him daily.

Her heart shriveled a little at the thought of never being with him again, but her mind, full of its annoying practicalities, reared back to life. She had a family and friends; she didn't know what Ethan expected from her if she were to stay with him. What would she lose or gain, what was she *willing* to lose or gain?

"What is it you want to know?" Stefan inquired from his position by the sliding doors leading to the balcony.

"Who changed you?" Emma asked, her gaze focused upon Ethan.

"No one changed Isabelle or me, or any of our siblings. We were born this way," Ethan answered.

"That's possible?" Mandy asked as she wiggled forward on the couch. Emma could almost see the scientist wheels spinning in her head as she practically salivated over Ethan's words.

"It is," Ethan confirmed.

"So you're not the living dead?" Emma inquired.

"Well, considering Isabelle and I never died, no, we are not the living dead."

"But to be changed, you have to die?" Jill's eyes were focused on Stefan as she asked the question.

"Yes," Stefan slid his arm around Isabelle's waist and pulled her against him. A twinge of longing coiled through Emma's chest as she watched them, she found she couldn't look at Ethan.

"Your heart still beats?" Mandy asked.

"And we still breathe. Think of the change as similar to being brought back to life after a heart attack, like being hit with a defibrillator. The heart briefly stops beating, breathing ceases, but you're still aware of what is going on around you. Then the influx of vampire blood shocks the heart back to life. We become something more afterward, but we also retain our ability to do human things such as reproduce, eat, breathe, and have a heartbeat."

"Amazing," Mandy breathed. "What exactly *are* you? I

mean where did vampires originally come from? Was Dracula the first?"

Stefan and Ethan both chuckled as Isabelle shook her head no. "Vampires go much farther back than Dracula, or so the legends go," Isabelle said. "It's said they go back to a time when demons used to roam the earth freely. They were forced to retreat when humans began to hunt them and sealed themselves away in what the legends claim to be Hell."

"And these demons gave their blood to humans before they were forced into Hell?" Emma inquired.

"No, they mated with humans. The first vampires were *born*. They discovered later that by sharing their blood they could create more of their kind, but we were born of this world," Stefan explained.

Emma could feel her eyebrows in her hairline, but she couldn't seem to get them to go back down as she examined the three of them.

"Because they were born of two vampires, Isabelle and Ethan, as well as their siblings, exhibit stronger abilities, especially for their young ages," Stefan continued.

"Amazing, just amazing," Mandy said again. "And you are immortal?"

"Yes," Ethan confirmed.

"Your blood, does it have healing capabilities?"

"It does," Isabelle said.

"Just imagine the possibilities," Mandy murmured.

"There are no possibilities," Stefan said gruffly. The malevolent look in his eyes made Emma's skin crawl and caused her to slide a little further back on the couch.

"Back off, Stefan," Ethan said in a low rumble that did nothing to lessen the unease growing inside her.

Isabelle rested her hand on Stefan's arm and pulled him back a step. Stefan relaxed visibly, but his eyes remained fixed on them. Isabelle shot a pointed look at Mandy. "*No* one is going to say anything, Stefan," Isabelle assured him.

"No, of course not," Mandy gushed. "It's just the scientist in me, the future doctor talking about the possibilities. I would never say or do anything about it though, I swear. It's just fascinating."

Emma stared defiantly at the three of them as she rested her hand on Mandy's arm and squeezed it reassuringly. "Of course you wouldn't say anything," she said soothingly. "The three of you don't kill, but do you feed on humans?"

"Some of us feed on them but don't hurt them," Ethan answered. "I prefer to use blood bags."

"Before Stefan, that was what I did too," Isabelle said.

"I feed on humans when it's necessary, but they're never aware of it," Stefan informed them.

"You're safe with us," Isabelle said reassuringly.

"You told me you could control people's minds and alter their memories. We've seen how fast you can be, is there anything else you can do?" Jill asked.

"Our hearing and eyesight are exceptional, better than a human's, and we're stronger than any human," Ethan told her.

"We've seen," Emma muttered. "Is the stake through the heart thing real?"

"It is, but to be fair, a stake through the heart would kill anything. Beheading and fire too. For some, sunlight is another way to go," Ethan continued.

"Good to know," Emma said as she curled a strand of hair around her finger and tried to digest this information. This world she'd never imagined could exist was all so strangely fascinating and bizarre.

"I don't like the idea of staying in the place where someone died, especially with that body still in here," Jill said.

"We'll take care of it first thing tomorrow morning," Stefan promised. "But going out there right now is not an option."

"You can come stay at our place. There's more room, and with Aiden and Ian arriving tomorrow, there will be more protection," Isabelle offered. "Ian and Aiden can share a room, that won't be new to them."

Mandy and Jill looked at her, but Emma didn't know what to think about the idea of sleeping in a home with five beings who could kill them with ease. However, she was sitting in *this* house with three creatures who could kill them and a dead body. She had to admit she preferred the five lethal beings and no dead guy over the three of them in a home where someone had been killed, and where everything had gone to shit in less than twenty-four hours.

But she didn't know about sharing a home with Ethan either. She didn't know if she could maintain her restraint and distance if they were put so closely together.

Her eyes drifted back to Ethan.

"I'll leave you be, Emma," he promised, as he seemed to sense where her thoughts were going.

Isabelle spun toward him, she opened her mouth to speak, but Ethan gave her a censuring look and shook his head. She closed her mouth. Her face remained scrunched in disapproval as she stared at her brother. Stefan squeezed Isabelle's shoulder.

"What is it?" Emma inquired. "What's wrong?"

"It's nothing," Ethan assured her with a forced smile, but Emma didn't believe him. There was something he wasn't telling her, something upsetting Isabelle as she continued to stare helplessly at him. "I think it would be better if you came to our house, but that is entirely your decision to make."

Emma clasped Mandy and Jill's hands. "Can we have some time to talk?" she asked.

The three vampires exchanged a look before nodding.

"We'll be in your room, scream if anything happens," Ethan told her.

She waited until she heard the click of the door closing before she turned to her friends. "What do you want to do?" she asked quietly.

"I think we should stay with them, Emma, look what happened tonight. There's no guarantee a human won't try something there too, but I've lost all interest in staying in this place," Jill said and shivered in disgust.

"Your whole trip is ruined because of me," Emma muttered.

"It was ruined because Tristan is a freaking psycho. Besides, judging by the looks of Ethan, I'm immensely curious about meeting these brothers of his," Jill said with a wink.

Emma laughed as Jill succeeded in easing some of her anxiety. "They're younger than him."

"Even better, fresh meat."

Emma couldn't stop laughing as she leaned against her friend's side. "Can you honestly believe this is our lives right now?"

"Not even a little bit," Mandy said. "Things will never be the same again."

Emma couldn't help but agree as she glanced at the hallway. She was curious about what else it was Isabelle and Ethan were keeping from her, but she didn't mention it to Jill and Mandy. They didn't like the idea of being here anymore, and they would be safer at the other house. Emma was far more concerned about their safety than whatever it was Ethan still wasn't telling her. She had a feeling she would find out eventually anyway, and nothing could be more astounding than what she'd already learned.

~

EMMA DROPPED her bags on the floor by the bed she'd once shared with Ethan. She turned away from it as memories of that fantastic night trickled through her mind. Even though she couldn't see him, she could feel him within the room; his presence was as commanding as the waves crashing against the shore.

Taking a deep breath, she turned to face him as he leaned against the frame of the door. His lips were pinched, lines etched the corners of his mouth, and his eyes had taken on a reddish hue that wasn't quite the red she'd seen the other night, but they most certainly weren't the pure emerald of his eyes.

"Are you okay?" she asked nervously.

"Yes." He was anything but okay though. What felt like a panther clawing at his chest, and the tightening in his gut, had increased overnight. Now he was certain he could drain *five* more people and still not satisfy his thirst. Watching her now was the only thing making him feel even a little better. He had to feed, but needed to make sure she was settled in before he could retreat to the world of blood feverishly beckoning him.

"I can stay with Jill and Mandy. Maybe we can find a cot to put in their room or an air mattress, so you don't have to sleep on the couch," she offered.

"I'll be fine," he assured her. "I'd like for you to stay in here." He didn't add he hoped she would welcome him back into her arms or that it would be easier to protect her if her friends weren't in the way.

"Ethan," she said when he turned away from her. "Thank you."

His shoulders hunched up, but he didn't say anything as he left the room and made his way to the kitchen. They'd taken the body of the man out on the boat this morning and tossed his weighted remains into the ocean. Thankfully, the police never arrived. He and Stefan moved the body so quickly through the early morning hours, he doubted anyone had seen them. If they were spotted, the humans probably hadn't had the time to process what they had seen.

Isabelle took a step away from him when he walked over to the dented fridge. It creaked as he opened it, and for a second he thought the hinges might give out, but the door held.

"I'll have to buy another one of these before we leave," he said as he removed three bags from inside.

"That's not an issue right now. Are you going to be able to do this?" she asked.

"Of course."

She hovered near his elbow as she leaned against the counter. "Look at me." He grabbed a bag and tore the top from it with his teeth before looking at her. "Have you seen your eyes?"

"Haven't had the pleasure of a mirror lately."

"That much is obvious," she retorted. "You look like you've been up for a week straight."

He frowned at her before downing the contents of the bag. "I feel like I have. I take it my eyes are red."

"No, they're some weird combination of your green and red. I've never seen anything like it before Ethan."

"Well, isn't that interesting." He ripped the top off another bag and consumed the contents. "Don't you have to get to the airport?"

Isabelle sighed and shook her head. "You're a stubborn fool."

"It takes one to know one."

A footstep in the hall caused him to drop everything into the trash. The last thing he wanted was for Emma to see him feeding; she was freaked out enough as it was. When he saw it was only Stefan, he retrieved the bag of blood from the trash and nodded to him before retreating to the pool area. He settled in the shade of an umbrella as the sun now made his skin itch in a way it never had before. He listened as the two of them left the house, but his attention remained focused on the sun shining off the clear pool water. It was the last place he'd made love to her, the last place he'd been inside her and known complete calm.

There wasn't enough blood in the world, he decided as he tossed the empty bag into the trash and went to get more.

ISABELLE EAGERLY SEARCHED the crowd of passengers getting off the plane as they walked around her. She spotted Ian easily amongst the crowd. At six-four he was the tallest of her siblings, and taller than most of the people around him. His golden hair was disheveled and curled at the corners of his sky blue eyes. Not only was he the tallest of her siblings, but he was also the most built with his broad shoulders and chest. His heavily muscled arms were emphasized by the black wife beater tank top he wore.

Aiden was at his side; at six two he was shorter than Ian but still tall. He also had a more lean, whipcord build than Ian and Ethan. His black hair was shorter than the last time she'd seen him, and his eyes were darker than Ethan and her father's; they were more of a leaf green than an emerald.

Ian reached out and pushed Aiden's shoulder, knocking him slightly off balance. Aiden lowered his shoulder and shoved into Ian's chest in response. They both laughed and smiled as they continued to jostle each other through the crowd. For a minute, her heart soared as she savored in the sight of them. It had been almost a year since she'd seen them, and she'd missed them so much. It had been an amazing experience to explore the world with Stefan, but she was ready to get home to her family. This was supposed to be a happy reunion, yet all she felt was stressed out.

Rising on her tiptoes, she waved above the crowd to get their attention. They stopped shoving each other long enough to look at her and Stefan.

"There she is!" Aiden broke into a broad grin when he finally saw her. He barely acknowledged the people around him as he rushed forward.

Isabelle released a little squeal when he wrapped his arms around her, lifted her off the ground, and spun her around. Ian claimed her as soon as Aiden released her. Isabelle clung to him while he twirled her around before placing her on her feet. He grinned at her as he held her shoulders and leaned back to inspect her.

"It's good to see you, sis," he said and slapped her on her shoulders.

"You too," she told him.

He stepped away from her and turned toward Stefan. "Stefan," he greeted and extended his hand.

Stefan clasped his hand and shook it. "Where's Ethan?" Aiden inquired as he scanned the crowd of people moving around them.

Isabelle felt her smile slip away when they both turned questioning looks on her. "We have a problem," she told them.

CHAPTER TWENTY-ONE

ETHAN LIFTED his head from his hands when the front door opened. He didn't have to see them to know his brothers had arrived; he could hear and smell them. He lifted the glass of whiskey sitting on the table before him. It probably wasn't the best idea to be drinking right now, but it seemed to be the only thing helping to curb the edge of the growing insanity within him.

He took a sip of the liquid and braced himself for the invasion of his family. Solitude was best for him right now, but there was no way his family would give him the opportunity. Ian poked his head out of the house first, but Aiden was right behind him. Isabelle shoved them both out the door and stepped onto the patio behind them.

"Look at you, drinking all by yourself, in the middle of the day; somebody's wallowing in self-pity." Though Ian smiled, his voice held no humor, and his eyes were troubled as he studied Ethan.

"If you join me, I won't be by myself," Ethan said.

Ian's eyes widened as he approached, he hesitated as his

gaze locked on Ethan's. He knew what his eyes looked like now, knew what his brother was seeing, and if Ian looked like this, he would hesitate before approaching him too. Ethan lifted his drink and saluted his brother with it before downing the rest of the contents. He'd drank so many of them, he didn't feel the burn anymore. He didn't feel a buzz either. There was only a softening of the razors slicing his stomach and chest apart.

"Here's to afternoon drinking," he muttered and refilled his drink.

"Ethan—"

"Don't talk, just drink," he interrupted Ian.

He lifted his glass and swirled the amber liquid around.

"Those are my kind of words," Aiden said as he dropped into the seat across from him. He already had a beer in hand. His brows were drawn together as he studied Ethan, but he took a swig of his drink. "Though they're usually uttered during more festive times, but here's to moping."

"I'm not moping!" Ethan snapped at him.

Aiden snorted. "Could have fooled me. Anyway, where is the little human?"

"She's in her room, and you're to stay away from her," Ethan warned.

"I think it's only right I meet my future sister-in-law."

"That most likely won't happen."

Aiden stared at him before leaning forward and resting his elbows on his knees. "When you're not such an obstinate ass, you'll realize not only *will* it happen, but it *has* to happen."

Ethan glowered at him as he took another sip of whiskey. "Not if she doesn't want it to."

"Ethan—"

"No!" he barked. "Like I've told Isabelle, back *off* on this."

Aiden's cheerful demeanor vanished, his forest green eyes were steely as he relentlessly held Ethan's gaze. Ian slid into the chair next to him, grabbed a glass, and poured himself some whiskey.

"You smell different," Ian commented.

"I killed a man," he admitted. "And I'll do it again if it means keeping her safe."

"So Isabelle said," Aiden replied.

"Do I smell like a landfill?" he inquired.

"No, nothing that bad, but it's different...maybe like over-ripe fruit," Isabelle answered. "It's nowhere near as repugnant as the smell coming off the vampires with Tristan."

"Good to know," he murmured.

"What about her friends?" Ian asked.

"What about them?" Ethan asked.

"Are we going to allow them to keep their memories?"

"She'll hate me if I take them away," Ethan told him. "I won't mess with her mind, and I won't allow any of you to either. She has to know the truth if she's going to stay safe."

"At this point, they all do," Stefan said. "We can't warp their thoughts to our bidding to keep them here. I don't think they'll be a threat to us, they care for Emma, and will help to keep her safe."

"If they become a threat to us?" Aiden asked.

"I'll kill them myself," Stefan said flatly.

Ethan remained silent as he thought over those words. "Even if she hates me after, if they somehow become a threat to her I'll kill them too, but I *do* believe they'll keep our secret and do whatever it takes to keep her alive."

"If you two are confident of that then I'll trust your judgment," Ian said. "Have you talked to dad yet?"

"No, why?" Ethan asked.

"Because if anyone knows what you're going through, it's him."

"Yeah, I guess, but I don't want to involve him or mom.

They're thousands of miles away; worrying them isn't going to do anyone any good."

"They would be on the first plane here if they knew," Isabelle said as she and Stefan settled into the other chairs.

"And that's the last thing I want to happen. There's danger here; the two of you shouldn't even be here," he said to Aiden and Ian. "You haven't even hit maturity yet."

"Well, one of us hasn't," Ian said and shoved Aiden's shoulder. Aiden scowled back at him and flipped him the finger.

"You did?" Isabelle demanded of Ian. "When?"

"Last month," Ian answered. "I figured I'd wait until summer break to tell everyone."

"Well, congratulations," Isabelle said and squeezed his hand.

"I guess that would be the term for it," Ian said with a smile before turning his attention back to Ethan. "But we're more help than you think, and we're not going anywhere, so get that thought out of your head. You know we're stronger than young vampires, even before we reach maturity."

"If something happens to you—"

"Mom will kick your ass, so it's a win-win for us all," Aiden broke in with a laugh.

"We may need more help than just you two though," Stefan said. "There are quite a few of them, and although they are young and less powerful, they're also driven by their thirst for blood and their need for death. They'll be volatile and unpredictable."

"My parents won't be brought into this; I won't take the chance of them being hurt," Ethan said. "And we can't tell The Stooges without my parents somehow finding out about it. They're not exactly good at keeping secrets."

"That they're not," Aiden agreed.

"I wasn't talking about your parents," Stefan said.

"Who then?" Isabelle asked.

"Brian."

Even Ethan felt his eyebrows shoot up. "Didn't you tell him you'd kill him if you saw him again?" Aiden inquired.

"I told him if *he* found *me* again I'd kill him, but this time I'll be finding him," Stefan replied.

"Potato, Potahto," Ian said.

Stefan leaned back in his chair. "He's one of the strongest vampires I know, other than myself." His gaze slid over Ethan and Ian before turning to Isabelle and taking her hand. "Though I do believe there's more power inside all of you than we've yet to see, I'm not willing to put any of you in harm's way on a belief."

"What makes you think that?" Aiden inquired.

"The fact you can identify a killing vampire by their smell even before you hit maturity. The fact you are far stronger than any turned vamp of your years would be. The first vampire was born, but there's no record of what they could do. There are also only about a hundred born vampires in existence. We have no idea what you might be capable of under extreme duress, but I can tell you having your mate threatened will bring it out of you. We also don't know what it might do to one of you after if you're able to tap reserves of power we've never seen before. Would you be able to let it go, or would it destroy you?"

Ethan appreciated Stefan didn't look at him as he spoke, but he knew his words were directed at him. "I'd say Ethan's eyes lend some credibility to your theory," Ian said.

Ethan scowled at him and drank the rest of his whiskey again. "You're all a little too obsessed with my fucking eyes."

"And you're a little too nonchalant about it," Stefan said. "There's power in you, in all of you, and if you allow it to get out of control, we could all be in peril."

Ethan simply held Stefan's unwavering gaze. There was

nothing he could say to that; he knew it was the truth, knew he was walking a fine line between man and monster right now. He had no words for Stefan, so he refilled his drink and leaned back in the chair.

"Can you get in touch with Brian?" Isabelle inquired.

"Yes."

"You've kept in touch since we last saw him?"

Stefan shook his head. "No, but I'll be able to track him down."

"I thought you didn't trust him," Ian said.

"I don't, but—"

"I do," Isabelle interrupted. "He's lethal, don't get me wrong, but I don't believe he's a threat to us."

"I have to agree with her," Ethan said and finished off his drink. "He's not going to team up with them against us."

"How do you know that?" Aiden asked.

"Because he doesn't kill indiscriminately. He kills to gain power but not because it's what he thrives on, and he only kills those who have killed humans."

"We're not the kind of vampires he goes after," Stefan said. "He's trying to punish the ones who destroyed his life by murdering vampires who kill. It's not simply to gain power."

Aiden stared at all of them before finishing off his beer and dropping the bottle on the table. "Yeah, okay," he muttered. "And he is powerful."

"Do you think he'll come?" Isabelle asked.

"Brian's never turned down a fight before, but I don't know, maybe he's changed," Stefan said.

"Get in touch with him," Ethan said. His gaze drifted toward the doorway of the house as he sensed Emma's approach. "But if he arrives here and it turns out he is different, and he *is* a threat, especially to Emma, you won't have to worry about killing him, Stefan, because I'll do it myself. She's coming."

Ethan rose as Emma appeared in the open doorway. She froze when she spotted them; her eyes scanned his family before landing on him. He heard the increased beat of her heart as her forehead furrowed and she frowned at him. He despised she had to see him in such a state, but though he tried to get them back to normal, he'd lost all control over the color of his eyes. He was slipping, but he would do whatever it took to keep her safe, even from himself.

Emma couldn't tear her eyes away from Ethan's strangely colored ones as he moved around his brothers to approach her. She could smell the whiskey on him even before he stopped in front of her. There was something about him, other than being one of the living non-dead, that frightened her. It had nothing to do with the eerie color of his eyes, or that she'd never seen him drink so early in the day, and everything to do with the desperate air she sensed around him. An air that eased when he took her hands.

His eyes turned back to their beautiful emerald color so fast it stole the breath from her. A smile tugged at the corner of his mouth, and yet such desolation and loneliness surrounded him that it tugged at her heart.

"Are you okay?" she whispered.

"I'm fine," he assured her.

"Ethan—"

"Come meet my brothers."

He tugged lightly on her hand, drawing her forward when all she wanted was to talk with him and make sure something wasn't wrong. Her eyes were drawn to the two large men sitting in the chairs near Isabelle and Stefan. Jill would be tripping over herself when she saw these two, Emma decided as they rose to their impressive heights.

"This is Aiden and Ian," Ethan introduced.

"Nice to meet you," Emma said.

They were both sporting crooked grins as they stared at her before exchanging a glance with each other. "Nice to meet you too," Aiden said and extended his hand to her.

Emma hesitated before taking it. Beside her, Ethan stiffened, his body pressed closer against hers, and Aiden hastily released her hand. Ian nodded toward her, but he didn't offer his hand, and his eyes never left Ethan. Emma frowned as she glanced at the group of large, imposing men gathered around her. Men who could tear her head off and use it as a volleyball if they so chose.

Trepidation trickled down her spine, and though she knew he was no different than them, she instinctively moved closer to Ethan. He rested his hand on the small of her back.

"We were just talking about Tristan," Ethan informed her.

"I'm sorry. I know this wasn't the vacation you were planning," Emma apologized to Aiden and Ian.

Aiden laughed and ran a hand through his black hair. It was impossible not to know the three of them were brothers, she realized as she looked at them. They were similar in appearance and possessed the same almost carefree air, or at least they all had before things with Tristan started. Her gaze slid up to Ethan standing rigidly by her side. There was nothing carefree about him anymore, not like there was when she first met him. Stress radiated from him, even when he looked down at her and smiled.

"We've experienced worse, and we're more than willing to help. Our siblings are always trying to get us into trouble," Ian said. "But we usually end up saving their asses."

"Like hell," Isabelle muttered as Ethan frowned at him. Ian grinned at them in return.

"I don't want to see anyone get hurt," Emma said as she glanced at everyone gathered around her.

"*No* one is going to get hurt," Ethan promised. "And believe me, these two can handle themselves."

"As I said, we'll be pulling their asses out of the fire," Ian insisted.

"I'm going to kick your ass if you keep it up," Isabelle told him.

Aiden and Ian laughed, but Emma remained uneasy as her gaze traveled over them. How could she possibly ask them to risk their lives, for her?

"I uh...I have to take a shower," she said.

Ethan almost grabbed her when she stepped away from him. The change in her demeanor made her seem more distant than she'd been since discovering what he was. He forced himself to let her go. Being overbearing wasn't the way to get her to come back to him, if she *ever* came back to him.

He fisted his hands at his sides; he could feel the hunger within him blazing back to life as his attention returned to his siblings. Ian tilted his head to the side to study him; Aiden shook his head and turned away.

"You know what really sucks," Aiden said as he twisted the top off another beer.

"What?" Isabelle asked.

Aiden flipped the cap away as he turned to face them. "When the two of you finally do get laid, you turn into raving lunatics."

Isabelle stuck her tongue out at him while Ethan glowered. He stormed around the table, slid back into the chair, and poured himself another whiskey.

Emma turned away from the window when she heard the door open. The sun had begun to set, its rays spread across the sky in a colorful array which had held her captive for the past five minutes. Ethan stood in the doorway; his eyes still had a strange red hue to them.

"Is there anything you need?" he inquired.

You, the thought blazed through her mind, but she clamped her mouth shut before she could blurt it out.

"I'm good," she said instead. "Jill and Mandy?"

"They're playing cards with everyone else."

"Oh."

"Would you like to join them?"

There were a thousand things she would like to do right now, but joining the others for a game of cards wasn't one of them. She couldn't tear her eyes away from him as he remained standing in her doorway. He looked torn between walking away and coming to her. "Not right now."

He bowed his head and stepped away. The broken air surrounding him was more than she could stand. "Ethan." He stopped and turned back to face her. The hope in his eyes caused tears to burn in hers. "Are you okay?"

He forced a smile to his face. "I'm fine."

She couldn't shake the feeling he was lying to her. "Would you tell me if something was wrong, something more than the obvious? You've already kept something from me, and I can understand why, but please don't do it again, and don't lie to me. I don't know if I could take it."

His eyes searched her face as he stared at her; finally, he stepped into the room and closed the door behind him. "I won't keep anything from you anymore, Emma, but there are some things I would prefer not to burden you with."

A small snort of laughter escaped her. "Look at everything

I've burdened you with. Your life is in jeopardy because of me. *Please* tell me what is going on with you."

"You could never be a burden, not to me, and I *will* kill Tristan."

She flinched at the straightforward way he said he would kill Tristan. The idea of it seemed not to affect him in any way. What had she gotten herself into with all of this? Walking over to the bed, she slumped onto it. She lifted her head to look at him as he leaned against the door.

"And you're okay with that?" she whispered.

"I'm okay with anything that keeps you safe."

"This is all so much. My best friends are playing cards with vampire siblings; the man I thought I was falling in love with is talking about killing my ex as if it's the same thing as ordering fast food."

Ethan did a double take as those words spilled from her lips. "You thought you were falling in love with me?"

She frowned as she lifted her head to look up at him. He stepped away from the door; his eyes were back to their normal green hue. The look on his face made her feel as if she were the most cherished and priceless jewel in the world. She'd never thought a man could look at her with so much hope and...love?

Yes, that was what radiated from his eyes. "I did," she breathed, unable to tear her gaze away from him.

"And now?"

"And now, where do I fit into all this? Your world isn't mine, Ethan. Your world is something I can't even begin to understand. How could I possibly allow myself to love you when I'm not sure what would become of me?" He rapidly moved across the room and knelt before her. Taking her hands in his, he held them against his chest as he looked into her tear-filled eyes. "I don't belong—"

"You belong with *me*," he said vehemently. "My world is not a dismal one; there is love and laughter in it. My family—"

"What about *my* family?"

He released her hands and slid his fingers across her face to her hair. He brushed it back as he moved closer to her; he needed to touch her. It was the only thing that made the monster growing within him subside.

"There are things we will figure out, if you become like me, you can keep seeing them for at least a few years without question. After, we can work on changing memories—"

"They're my parents," she interrupted. "I can't mess with their minds like that."

"Emma," he groaned.

It was all right there, right before him. The hope she could love him and agree to be with him grew within him. He didn't know what he would do if it were ripped away from him again.

"I love you," he said. Her mouth parted as she gazed at him in awe. "I will love you for eternity. If you tell me to leave, I will, but if there's any chance you will allow me to stay, there is something else you must know about me, about my kind."

She searched his face as he continued to kneel before her. Something in his demeanor made her think she wasn't going to like what he had to say. But she was the one insisting on full disclosure.

"What is it?" she asked.

The bed dented as he sat beside her. The heat his body emitted warmed her to the tips of her toes. Her skin tingled when his arm brushed against hers. It was the strangest sensation to be afraid of someone and so unbelievably attracted to them at the same time. No, she wasn't afraid of him, that wasn't the right word. She was wary of him, unnerved by what he was and the world he existed in, but she knew he would never harm her in any way.

"There's something about vampires that is unique only to us," he told her.

"Something more than drinking blood?"

He chuckled as he took hold of her hand and held it in his lap. "Yes, something more."

"Please don't tell me you can turn into a bat or something. I'm not so sure I can handle having slept with someone who can fly."

"We stay entirely human in shape," he assured her.

"That's good to know. So, what is this uniqueness?"

His thumb stroked the back of her hand. "When we meet the person or vampire we're meant to spend the rest of our lives with, we form an intense bond with them. One that cannot be severed. One that can drive us mad if we happen to lose our mate or if the bond isn't completed."

Emma didn't know where he was going with all of this. It seemed so strange, but then again, there was nothing normal about him or his family. "And how is this bond completed?"

"Sex and the exchange of blood, if one is a human then it's necessary they become a vampire too."

An unsettling feeling was beginning to form in the pit of her stomach. Her hand tightened around his as she struggled to breathe normally, she knew he could hear the increased beat of her heart, and her palm was becoming sweaty. "I see," she murmured.

"My mother and father are mated, so are Isabelle and Stefan. My father nearly lost control of himself before completing the bond with my mom, Stefan and Isabelle tried to stay apart but it almost killed her, and it nearly drove him insane. I've never seen anything like what Isabelle went through while they were separated, she was in such agony, and there was nothing I could do to help her."

"That must have been awful," she murmured.

His gaze was haunted when it came back to her. "It was. I didn't understand it at the time, not completely, but I understand it now."

Though she tried her hardest to keep it from happening, her bottom lip began to tremble. "Ethan—"

"This is your choice, Emma; I won't force you into anything, ever. If you decide this is not the life for you, I will respect your wishes. I'll make sure you're safe, and I will go away."

"It can't be me," she whispered. "How could you possibly think I'm your mate in such a short amount of time?"

"It *is* you, Emma; I have no doubt."

Her head spun as she tried to grasp what he was telling her. She felt the impulse to pace, almost jumped up from the bed, but she didn't think her legs would support her, and she didn't feel like falling flat on her face. She remained where she was.

"The bond between mates is so strong they can read each other's thoughts and communicate with one another telepathically. The pathway between the minds opens when the bond is completed," he continued. "I don't expect a decision from you now, but if you choose to come back to me, you have to know what you're getting into. If you come back to me, there is no going back, not for me. This is forever."

The urge to grab a paper bag and breathe into it filled her. She felt as if a tornado had just picked her up and dumped her in the middle of a bunch of munchkins.

"Oh, crap." Those two words did absolutely nothing to describe how she felt right now, but they just popped out. "Why do you believe so strongly I'm your mate?"

He'd tried so hard to keep his more volatile side hidden from her, but now he may have to expose it. She stared at him as he sought to think of a way to explain it to her without frightening her even more. "Don't lie to me, Ethan, if there is even a small chance all this could work out, you can't keep anything else from me. I'll never forgive you if you do."

He leaned forward to press a kiss against her forehead. "I won't lie to you, and I'll never keep anything from you again, but I don't want you to be frightened of me."

"You could kill me before I blink. There's nothing you could say that would be any more frightening."

"I'm not so sure about that."

Those words were about the least reassuring thing she'd ever heard. "Not telling me is scaring me more."

He leaned against her side. "This connection, just the touch of you, it calms me in ways I never thought possible. I'm not like my siblings. They're easy going in ways I've never been before."

"But you've always seemed happy to me." Emma's tone revealed her confusion.

"Because of *you*, and I was happy with my life even if it was stressful at times, but I'm different than they are. There's always been something inside of me, something deadlier, something crueler than what they are. I've fought for as long as I can remember to keep my thirst and my impulse to kill under control."

He waited for her to recoil from him, to jump up and run away, but she remained where she was, and she didn't look at all horrified by what he was telling her. For some reason that made him feel he had to elaborate on his words, he *had* to make her understand what a monster he was. She would get up and walk away when he finished anyway; he might as well make it sooner rather than later.

"Killing is all I've *ever* desired, and once I reached maturity, and stopped aging, the urge to drive my fangs into someone's neck and bathe in their blood has been a nearly constant battle for me."

Emma took a deep breath as she tried to process his words. "But you've never done it before that man last night?"

"No, he was my first, but I've kept myself away from humans because of that constant fear. You're the only human I've ever been with Emma, the only one I've had extended contact with in years. I didn't think it was possible for me to be around a human for any length of time until I met you."

"Then maybe you're more like your siblings than you thought."

Ethan lurched up from the bed and paced away from her. "I'm not like them, they're good, and I'm twisted. There's something *wrong* with me."

"There's nothing wrong with you Ethan," she whispered.

"If you knew some of the things I've done to try and escape what is inside of me, you wouldn't think so," he growled.

"But you've never killed anyone before yesterday, and you don't hurt people."

"Not anyone who didn't ask me to." The widening of her eyes and her recoil from him was what he'd been looking for. "I've inflicted pain on vampires who asked me to, and I've asked them to do the same to me, in bed."

Emma's breath caught in her throat as his words sank in. She leaned back as he returned to her and rested his hands on either side of her. "You would cringe if you learned the things I've done to try to make what is inside me go away. It would make even the most diehard sadist cringe, or perhaps it would make them proud. We don't die, Emma; we can go far beyond what any human could to gain pleasure from the pain."

Emma gulped as she searched his face. He was attempting to push her away, she knew, but no matter how much he tried to convince her he was unredeemable, she saw the longing in his eyes. He expected her to run, expected her to turn away from him and call him a monster just like he believed he was, but no matter what he said he could never be a monster in her eyes.

"I have been whipped so severely the skin on my back was completely gone. It took me hours to heal from it, and you know what I did? I got off on it, Emma. I've been chained for hours, burned, branded and beaten to the point I've had broken bones, and I got *off* on it because I *enjoyed* it. I did the same to the woman who asked me for it, and I got enjoyment from *that* too."

"Stop," she whispered.

"Stop what?" he snarled as his eyes turned red.

Emma thought a reasonable human would cringe away from him; she tilted her chin and glared up at him. "Stop trying to push me away!"

"Would you like to know what else I've done?"

"No."

"But you want to know it all."

"That isn't you, Ethan," she whispered.

"You don't know who I am."

"Don't I?" she retorted with defiance. Some of his antagonism deflated as he studied her. Yes, she did know who he was, more than anyone else she knew who he was, and she was still sitting before him. "Whatever you did, or whatever was done to you, wasn't something you deserved no matter how much you believe it was. If I know anything, it's you can't be trapped by your past, you'll only be buried within it if you are, and if you allow that to happen, you *will* be lost."

"You're too good for me."

"I'm not perfect, Ethan!" she snapped, her patience fraying. "I don't understand what you're trying to do here? Shock me into walking away, bring me closer, or prove some point. Why are you telling me this?"

He stared at her as he tried to figure out the answer to her question. She had asked to know everything, but that wasn't why he was telling her this. He was telling her because for once he could tell *some*one every awful detail he'd tried to deny, been too ashamed to face, and fighting to keep buried about himself. He could finally unburden himself, and though he was going about it in a bad way, he found he *had* to get it out.

"Because I can," he admitted as some of his anger faded away. "Because I can tell you things I've never told anyone because I *have* to tell you. Because I've lived with this and fought it for so long, but I was so certain one day I would lose the battle, and be consumed by the power of death. Last night, with that man, the voice inside promised his death would bring me release, it only made it so I crave *more*. Then, you touch me. The driving bloodlust, the burning urge to kill, it all just fades away, and for the first time in my life, I have peace. You are my angel, Emma, but I'm a monster."

She was trying to let her mind rule over her heart, but those words drove her to her feet and over to him before she could stop herself. She wrapped her arms around his waist and rested her head against his chest.

"You're not a monster; you're my hero. I'm so unbelievably confused and uncertain right now; I do know you're a better man than you give yourself credit for. You *are* a good man, Ethan, that's the whole reason you've never harmed anyone who didn't deserve it or didn't ask you for it."

Ethan couldn't believe she was willing to touch him after what he revealed. He stared at the top of her head before coming to his senses and slipping his arms around her shoulders. It felt so unbelievably good to be holding her again, and though he believed she was wrong when she told him he was a good man, he couldn't let her go.

"You shut the world out," he whispered into her hair.

"You can't lock the world out, that's not living."

"You make it possible for me to live in the world then."

He would be her complete undoing, she realized. It was so difficult to keep her distance when he was saying things like that to her.

"I'm not entirely sure what this world is anymore," she said with a small laugh.

"These past couple of days have been a lot for you, I know. I'll give you time to decide what it is you want."

She forced herself to release him and take a step back. His hands lingered on her shoulders before slipping away. The minute the contact with him was lost, his eyes took on that reddish color. Emma shuddered as she searched his face.

"I don't understand. You said your father was nearly driven mad, that Isabelle almost died, yet you would let me go?"

He rested his hand against her cheek. "The only thing I care about is your safety and happiness. If that means I have to walk away, then I will."

"And what will happen to you?"

"Don't worry about me."

Emma frowned as he turned away from her and walked toward the door. "But I *do* worry about you. What will happen to you Ethan, will you go mad; would you die?"

His shoulders hunched forward as he grabbed hold of the door handle. "I will stay away from you."

It wasn't an answer to her question, but she didn't have time to press him on it as he opened the door and left the room. Emma took a step after him. Tears formed in her eyes when the door shut with a click of finality. Everything inside her screamed to go after him. She remained unmoving as his words continued to swirl through her mind.

An eternity with a man she was certain she was in love with, but what about *her* life? How could she give up everything she'd always known? Would she have to give it all up?

Her heart felt like it was shattering; tears slid down her face as her thoughts turned to her parents. She couldn't stand the idea of messing with their minds in any way. Then there was everything he revealed about his sexual history. She didn't know how to assimilate the man who touched her with such tenderness and care, with the one who enjoyed inflicting and having pain inflicted on him so much.

CHAPTER TWENTY-TWO

IT WAS nightfall when she emerged from her room. She hadn't meant to fall asleep, but exhaustion had taken hold after Ethan's revelations, and now she was wide awake. There was a light on in the kitchen. The rest of the house was still as she made her way down the hall. A small squeak escaped her when Ethan lifted his arm from his eyes as she stepped into the living room; she hadn't seen him lying on the couch until he moved. She clutched the edges of her robe together and let out a nervous laugh as a small smile tugged at the corners of his mouth.

"Everything okay?" he asked.

"I fell asleep. Is everyone else already in bed?"

"They are."

There were sundaes topped with whip cream and cherries that didn't look as enticing as he did when he sat up and put his feet on the floor. The muscles in his back flexed when he dropped his head into his hands and ran his fingers through his disheveled hair. She'd never seen a man as chiseled as he was, and her mouth began to water.

"Are you hungry?" he asked.

"Just getting some water."

"I'll get it for you."

"You don't have to..."

He was already rising to his feet and heading toward the kitchen. The shorts he wore hung low on his waist, revealing the v-shape of muscles at his hips and the trail of hair leading to an enticing place she yearned to touch again. Her heart raced as she followed a few feet behind him. He pulled a bottle of water from the fridge and handed it to her.

"Thank you. Has Tristan done anything tonight?" she asked.

"Not so far."

"Do you plan to stay awake all night?"

"I can't sleep anyway." He leaned against the counter to study her from those strangely red and green eyes.

Emma took a sip of water as she studied him. Her fingers twitched as she fought the urge to touch his smooth skin. She would give anything to ease the tension in his shoulders. Anything to turn the color of his eyes back to the vibrant green she loved so much. Unable to hold his gaze, her eyes darted to the fridge. She frowned at the massive dent in it.

"What happened?" she inquired.

He barely glanced at it. "I lost my temper the other night after what happened with Tristan and punched it."

Emma's eyebrows shot up as she stared at the massive dent in the middle of the heavy-duty appliance. The amount of force behind the punch must have been about the same as a charging bull. "Remind me not to piss you off."

"I'd cut my hands off before I ever touched you in anger."

Her eyes flew back to his; her heart melted at the absolute conviction behind his words. "Ethan, I don't want to hurt you."

"You're not, Emma."

"Your eyes—"

"I'm all right."

"My family—"

"I know how important family is. You've met some of the crazies who are a part of mine."

She chuckled as she took another sip of water. "They're not so bad."

Her body heated and tingled as his stare burned over her skin. She took another drink to wet her parched throat as she prepared herself to ask her next question. "Did you want to do to me what you did with those other women?"

She could feel the color creeping into her face at the question. She barely heard her own words, but he inhaled harshly, and his hands clenched on the counter.

"No," he hissed. Her eyes flew up to his. "Not once did I ever think about doing such a thing to you, or having you do anything like that to me."

"Did you..." she broke off and swallowed heavily, she was pretty sure if she touched her face right now she might burn her palms. "Did you miss it? Was what happened between us lacking in some way for you?"

He clasped her chin as she ducked her head and nudged it upward. "Look at me, Emma." He didn't speak again until her lashes reluctantly fluttered upward and she hesitatingly met his gaze. "Nothing was lacking between us, *nothing*. What *is* between us is something pure and wonderful. What I did with those women was lacking, and I never want to experience it again. I've never been as fulfilled as I have since meeting you."

"Ethan," she breathed as tears filled her eyes. She didn't think she'd ever heard such amazing and beautiful words before in her life

"But you're still not ready for me, are you?"

"It's not that."

"You're not ready for my world. If you were, you wouldn't be asking me questions."

"What would I be doing?" she whispered.

"You'd be taking me to bed."

She smiled tremulously at him. "I don't think that's a good idea right now."

His hand slid away from her chin. "Maybe you should try and get some more sleep."

She was thrown off by the change of topic, but his eyes started turning a deeper shade of red as he watched her. "You're right," she mumbled. "Thank you for the water."

A trickle of apprehension slid through Emma as she noticed his hands clenched around the edge of the granite countertop and the corded muscles standing out in his arms. A bead of sweat formed on his forehead. She did this to him; she was *doing* this to him.

"Ethan." She stepped closer to him to try and comfort him. She had to do something to ease the awful look on his face other than just walking away.

"Eternity, Emma—blood, death, *your* death." His eyes pinned her to the spot as they became the color of a stop sign and seemed to convey the same message. "You remember those things when you come near me; you remember those things when you think you might want to touch me again."

Her hand lifted toward him before dropping back to her side. "I want to touch you *all* the time," she whispered. "I'm scared. I've just found out something I thought was only a legend is real, and my ex is trying to kill me. Even through all of that, I want to touch you. I'd like nothing more than to have you hold me because I think it would make it all better, but I can't hide behind you. I have to face this, but no matter what happens you have to know, I will *always* want to touch you. No one has ever made me feel like you do, you're like a drug to me, and if I'm not careful, I'm afraid you're going to burn me out and destroy me just like a drug would."

She didn't realize she was crying until the first fat drop fell onto her hand. She hastily wiped it away and then wiped her cheeks. Ethan stared at her with a mixed look of awe and horror. The red faded from his eyes, and this time it was him who took a step toward her.

It felt as if a ripple of static electricity slid over her skin as he came closer to her. Oh yes, she wanted to touch him, just as badly as a heroin addict craves their next hit, and with as much knowledge the next hit might kill her.

"I have to go," she gushed out and turned and bolted from the room.

She felt like a child as she fled into her bedroom and quietly closed the door. Her hands shook as fresh tears streamed down her face. What an awful mess all of this was, what an awful, *heartbreaking* mess.

And yes, as she stood there leaning against the door and weeping uncontrollably, she realized that was exactly what this was. For the first time in her life, her heart was shattering.

Emma let her hair drop back down before plopping onto the bed beside Jill and Mandy. She couldn't do anything with it anyway, and right now she didn't care. Her eyes were still bloodshot, and felt as if someone had thrown sand into them. She'd barely slept last night, she didn't look much better than she felt, and her hair was not cooperating with her at all.

She turned back to her friends, it was on the tip of her tongue to tell them what Ethan revealed to her yesterday about mates, but she held back. Though she didn't understand it, she knew his revelation was something extremely private. He'd spoken of a bond that went even deeper than human love, and he wouldn't appreciate it being shared with others.

"I'd like to get out of this house if only for an hour," she muttered.

"I don't see why we can't, there are still plenty of daylight hours left for us to enjoy," Jill said cheerfully.

Emma stared at the balcony doors as she thought over those words. "The humans they control can move about in the daytime though."

"I'm not saying we go out there alone, I'd like to keep you alive, but our vampires are completely capable of moving about in the sunlight."

"*Our* vampires?" Mandy asked.

Jill tossed back her hair as she flashed a smile. "I wouldn't mind making one of them mine for at least a night or two."

"You're incorrigible," Emma told her.

"Have you *seen* his brothers, I'm only human after all."

Emma shook her head. "Yes, you are, and you're annoyingly accepting of the fact they could eat you in the middle of the night."

Jill waved her hand dismissively. "You're still alive, so I'm sure I'll survive."

Emma couldn't help but laugh at Jill's cavalier attitude as her friend fairly bounced on the bed.

"But we have to get out of this house before we all start to go stir crazy and try to kill each other," Jill said.

Emma agreed as she walked over to the mirror and tugged her hair into a loose knot against the nape of her neck. There was nothing she could do about her eyes, so she grabbed a pair of tinted aviator sunglasses and slipped them on. It wasn't much of an improvement, but at least she didn't look like she'd just been on a weeklong bender anymore.

"Let's go see if we can get an escort out of this place," Mandy said and climbed to her feet.

Emma took a deep breath and braced herself before opening the door. She felt like a kid trying to catch Santa, but after the events of last night, she wasn't sure how well she was going to be received by Ethan. She wasn't surprised to find all of them gathered on the patio. Ethan was leaning back in his chair, legs out before him, and his arms crossed over his chest. A pair of black sunglasses covered his eyes, and though she couldn't see them, she felt it the instant they landed on her.

Any words she'd been about to utter died. Thankfully, Jill wasn't as easily overwhelmed by a man as she was. "We were hoping to get out of this house for a bit," Jill said.

Ethan remained silent as his gaze stayed locked on Emma. It was taking everything he had not to fall apart, not to give in to the spiraling pit of madness he felt opening just beneath his feet. The sight of her helped take away the edge of his impending insanity. But like the whiskey, it was only a temporary fix, one that would only dull the agony until his mind splintered apart and he would finally have to be put down. It was a conversation he planned to have with Stefan and Brian when Brian finally arrived; it was time to face the reality he may have to be destroyed when all this was over.

If not beforehand...

No, he would keep his sanity until he ensured her safety. He could keep control of himself long enough for that to happen, or at least he hoped he could. Even now he could feel the monster within him slithering through his mind, urging him to take her, to change her, to ease his misery and screw the consequences. She would forgive him over time; she would have no other choice if he completed the bond. He would *never* forgive himself though, and he loved her too much to violate her in such a way.

"I think that might be a good idea. I wouldn't mind checking out some things," Aiden said.

He loved his siblings, but there were times when he would really like to choke them. His jaw locked as his gaze slid toward Aiden. "So would I," Ian said.

"It's too dangerous," Ethan grated out from between his teeth.

"No more dangerous than in here. You said yourself they can't move around in the daylight," Ian reminded him.

"There are more humans out there; any one of them could be under Tristan's influence."

"And any one of them could try and get in here," Jill pointed out. "As long as we stay together, we'll be fine."

Ethan's teeth ground together; his fingers dug into his biceps as he took a deep breath and tried to calm himself. They couldn't possibly know every part of him hurt, even his hair. They didn't understand all he wanted was to tear the throat out of someone, feast on their blood, and give in to the relief he knew the insanity would offer him.

"It would be good to get out," Emma agreed.

Ethan could feel their gazes burning into him as they all turned toward him. He felt the force of the *no* burning in his throat, but the hope in her voice kept his tongue nailed to the roof of his mouth. The only thing she'd asked from him since all this started was time. She didn't hate him for keeping this from her; she hadn't run screaming from him even when he'd tried to get her to do so. How could he deny her something so simple?

"I don't think it's a good idea," Isabelle said.

His arms dropped down to his side as he sat up in his chair and focused on Emma. "If you agree to stay by my side, I'll take you wherever you want to go."

"I'm not sure about that, Ethan," Stefan cautioned.

Ethan rose to his feet and stepped closer to Emma, and the

closer he got to her the less the bloodlust building within him tore at his insides. Unable to stop himself, he rested his hand against her elbow. A breath of relief escaped him as the feel of her skin soothed him even more. It took all he had not to crush her against him and ease the burning, but her words from last night still echoed in his mind, and he'd be damned if he was the one who destroyed her.

Her head tipped back to look up at him. Through the shaded lenses of her glasses, he could see the beauty of her bloodshot and swollen eyes. The sound of her crying had drifted to him last night and torn at his soul. There was nothing he could do to make it better for her though, not while she was still trying to figure out what path she was going to take.

"You *have* to stay by me though, Emma," he reiterated.

His words probably should remind her of Tristan's overbearing demeanor, maybe they should be a warning, but she didn't take them as such. Tristan would never walk away from her. No matter what this did to him though, Ethan *would* let her go.

"I will," she promised.

He forced a smile as he bowed his head in acknowledgment of her words. The last thing he wanted was to be out around other humans, to have *her* out around other humans, but she'd already been caged by someone else, he wasn't about to cage her too.

"Where do you want to go?" he asked.

She looked to Mandy and Jill who shrugged in response. "The beach," Mandy suggested.

"Volleyball," Jill said with a grin.

"Is that okay?" Emma whispered to him.

He squeezed her elbow. "It's fine. We just have to change."

"So do we." Emma turned and hurried away with her friends.

Stefan waited until Isabelle, and his brothers went inside before stepping next to him. "Are you sure about this?"

Ethan barely glanced at him before nodding. "It's what she wants."

"And what about you? Can you control yourself?"

"I'm going to have to."

He said the words, but he wasn't entirely sure what he was capable of when they got around all of those people, and all of those blood-pumping, painfully tempting heartbeats.

CHAPTER TWENTY-THREE

EMMA SETTLED onto one of the lounge chairs and dropped her feet down on either side of it. Ethan sat beside her; he was holding himself as carefully as someone holding the most priceless vase, on a ship, in the middle of the Bering Sea. Watching his almost mechanical movements was excruciating.

This was an incredibly bad idea, she realized as she studied his rigid profile. He'd barely said two words since they left the house, and now his nostrils were flaring as if he'd just run a marathon. Unable to resist touching him, she rested her hand on his arm.

Emma marveled when he visibly relaxed at her touch. He was the strongest man she'd ever met, yet she had this incredible effect on him. She was weak and small, and he needed her. A lump formed in her throat, and her hand curled around his forearm as she tried to give him more comfort.

"We can leave," she offered.

He didn't even turn his head to look at her. "No."

Emma frowned at him before turning to search the crowd around them. Isabelle was sitting in the lounge chair beside her, but strangely enough, Stefan settled beside Ethan. It was the first time she'd ever seen the two of them sit separately. Aiden and Ian joined Jill over by the volleyball game, and Mandy sat on the other side of Isabelle. The dull thud of the volleyball bouncing back and forth, and the grunts of the people playing, filled the air.

Ian looked up and frowned when he spotted Stefan sitting beside Ethan. He elbowed his brother and said something before breaking away from the game and coming over to join them. Yes, this most definitely was a mistake, if Ethan's actions weren't a big indication of that, the reactions of his family members were.

"I'm fine." Emma stared at Ethan as his head finally swiveled toward her. His eyes remained covered, but she knew they weren't green. "Relax."

She couldn't relax though, not when he looked as if he were going to fracture at any second. Emma squeezed his arm again and released him. A shudder went through him, but when she went to touch him again, he shook his head. "Don't, Emma."

Her hand hovered in the space between them; frustration filled her before she dropped it to her side. She folded her hands before her as Aiden and Jill jumped into the game and started playing. Though she enjoyed watching them, she couldn't get herself to sit back in the chair, not when Ethan was in such obvious discomfort. Ethan stiffened suddenly; his head turned as he seemed to catch sight or smell of something.

Emma almost jumped to her feet when she spotted the three men in the bar walking toward them from across the beach. Ethan was already up and moving. His hand went in front of her like her mother's used to when she was forced to hit the brakes too hard in the car. A low growl escaped him as he stepped in front of her.

"Grab him!" Isabelle hissed at her.

Emma glanced at Isabelle as Ethan's sister rose to her feet. Her eyes were intense on Emma as she gestured toward Ethan's extended hand. His rigid posture made her realize he was about to launch himself at the men, something that couldn't happen in public. She didn't understand why these men set Ethan and Stefan off so bad, but Ian also rose to his feet as they continued to approach.

He'd just told her not to touch him, but the instinct to keep him safe caused her to grab his hand. It clenched around hers as he visibly relaxed a little again, but she could feel the hostility still running through his body. The men's eyes were wary as they stopped before the group gathered around her.

"Can we talk to you?" the shortest one asked Stefan.

"You can say whatever it is you have to say, here," Stefan told him.

Ethan stepped further in front of Emma as the red head's eyes landed on her. Ethan glanced at Emma and then back at the men. They couldn't know they could speak freely in front of her. They couldn't have any idea she knew about their species while she was still human.

"Stefan, go and speak with them," he said gruffly.

"Ethan—"

"It's fine," Stefan interrupted Isabelle. "I'll be right back."

"I'm coming with you," Isabelle said.

Stefan shook his head at her as he stepped away from the crowd. "Nothing is going to happen," he assured her.

Isabelle stood uneasily in front of the chairs, but when Emma went to rise, Ethan shook his head. "Stay here," he said.

Ethan kept his eyes on Stefan as he made his way across the sand and toward the ocean with the others. "Why would you let him go alone?" Isabelle demanded.

"They're not killers, Isabelle, but they can't know Emma has any knowledge of our existence," Ethan answered. "Even if they're not killers, they will still do whatever is necessary to protect themselves, and our kind, from being exposed. Besides, nothing is going to happen in broad daylight."

"They're vampires," Emma breathed.

"They are," Ethan confirmed.

How many of them were there? She wondered as she finally understood why they had always acted so strange around those men. Isabelle moved closer as Stefan turned away. The trio watched as Stefan walked back toward them before they disappeared into the crowd. "What did they want?" Isabelle asked when Stefan was close to them.

"They're leaving the island," Stefan answered. "They're catching their plane in a few hours."

Ian frowned as he folded his arms over his chest. "And they had to tell us this why?"

"Because they saw us sitting here and thought they should warn us there's another group of vampires on the island. Apparently, they had a run in with some of them last night, and it didn't go well. They're leaving before the heat of the local authorities is felt, or hunters are alerted due to the increase in murders and disappearances on the island."

"And you believe them?" Ethan asked.

"I do," Stefan confirmed. "They're frightened, and they plan to escape while they still can."

"That's wise of them," Isabelle muttered. "Maybe we should consider it too."

"Where would we go?" Ethan inquired. "Tristan *will* follow Emma, and I'm not luring a group of volatile vampires near our family."

"He might not be able to find her if we take her to our house, and if he does find her I can guarantee he'll rethink his actions when he encounters all of us," Ian said.

"Or he'll make even more vampires to come at us with, and we will be putting *everyone* at risk," Ethan countered.

"What about my family?" Emma inquired. "He's never been to my house, but he knows where I'm from, and he knows my parents' names. He could find them without a problem. I'm not going anywhere without them, or my friends, if we leave this island."

"No one is leaving the island," Stefan said. "Not yet anyway. For now, we are all still safe here, and it's only a matter of time before they slip up and we're able to get them. If it becomes too dangerous, we'll leave and figure out what we're going to do afterward. Brian is coming, we'll have a better chance of taking them down then, and we can think of a plan when he arrives."

"Who's Brian?" Emma inquired.

"Someone we know," Ethan answered.

From the tone of his voice, she didn't think it was someone he liked or was excited about seeing. "We should stay until he arrives," Isabelle reluctantly agreed.

Emma was so focused on the conversation, she didn't notice the rain clouds rolling in until the sun was completely blacked out. Her head tilted back just in time for a raindrop to fall onto her nose. A small laugh escaped her but judging by the look of the clouds, there would be more to follow.

"We should probably—"

Isabelle's words were drowned out by the deluge of rain suddenly unleashing upon them. The force of the rain stung her skin, Emma threw her arms over her head, but it did nothing to block the water pelting against her. Ethan's arms encircled her and lifted her against him.

"Go to the mall!" Isabelle shouted.

"Make sure Jill and Mandy are safe!" Ethan yelled at her over the rain and the people squealing around them as they scrambled for cover. "I have to get Emma out of here!"

Terror trickled through her as she realized more than rain may have come in with the clouds. Ethan kept one arm around her waist and one over her head to keep her sheltered as he ran with her toward the road and the group of buildings across the way. She was soaked through by the time they made it to the street.

"The clouds," she panted as they raced across the steaming asphalt. "It was cloudy when I saw Tristan the first time."

"They'll part soon," he said, but his head moved constantly about as he searched the darkened day. They made it to the overhang in the doorway of the mall and took shelter from the rain with a group of at least ten other people. Ethan turned her into a corner and pressed himself against her. Her body instantly began to heat as she rested her hands against his chest.

His head dropped down a little, and she found herself staring into the reflective black lenses of his glasses. Her breath froze in her lungs as she stared up at him; her nipples tingled as his chest brushed against hers. Her mouth went dry as her fingers involuntarily curled into his shirt. It was impossible to control her body, impossible not to react to him when they were in such proximity to each other. Her gaze drifted to his full mouth and the raindrops lingering there like drops of dew.

Laughter and excited chatter filled the little alcove as more people crowded in around them, she didn't notice any of them though as she remained riveted on him. She longed so badly to taste his lips, to kiss the water from them. It was taking everything she had to keep herself restrained. Death Emma, he'd told her. That's what her life with him would entail, *her* death, but there would also be so much love and joy for more years than she'd ever imagined having. Her mind spun at the realization; her fingers pressed more firmly against him as she savored in the heat coming off his body.

A muscle in his jaw twitched as a vein in his forehead stood out and sweat beaded across his upper lip. "Ethan—"

"Too much," he grated out as he moved closer to her to avoid the people pressing against them. Even with her there, he was having a difficult time shutting them out. All he could think about was placing his lips against her throat, and tasting the blood flowing through her veins. "It's all too much."

People jostled and pushed against them as even more tried to take shelter under the overhang. Her back was brought up firmly against the brick wall. She glanced rapidly around as she sensed a pending meltdown within the man standing against her. Grabbing his hand, she edged along the wall to the doorway of the mall. A growl escaped him as someone bumped into his back and shoved him forward. Emma's eyes widened as she glimpsed the tip of a deadly fang when his upper lip curled into a sneer.

Concern for him blazed to the forefront, if she didn't get him out of here soon, something horrible would happen. He would hate himself if he lost control and killed someone, and there would be no way for her to cover it up and keep him safe if something bad happened. She knew it was because of her he was so unstable, and she had to do something to help him, *now*.

Forgetting about trying to be polite about their escape from the alcove, she threw an elbow into the back of a girl too busy moaning about her wet bathing suit to notice her. Apparently, this ridiculous complaint was the worst thing in the world, if her bitching was to be believed, but right now Emma was willing to rip the thing off her if it got the girl out of her way.

Emma elbowed her more vehemently again before lowering her shoulder and shoving the girl aside. The girl cursed at her, but Emma didn't pause to apologize as she grabbed the door and pulled it open.

Cold air blasted against her. Her wet skin immediately

broke out in goosebumps as she stepped into the entryway of the small mall. Normally, in her soaked condition, she wouldn't enter the building, but it was the only way to escape the crowd.

A few people passing by shot them dirty looks as water dripped from them in soft plops on the stone floor. She didn't pay them any attention though as she searched for somewhere they could hide and regroup for a few minutes. There was no way anyone would let them into one of the stores, and it was probably best to get Ethan completely away from people.

Her feet squished on the floor as she moved further into the building. Before they made it into the main hallway, she spotted a solid wood door with a *Do Not Enter* sign on it. Grabbing the handle, she pushed it open and stepped into the small closet crowded with mops, brooms, some feather dusters, and shelves of bottles filled with cleaning supplies. Shutting the door of the janitor's closet, she flicked on the light switch next to it and pushed in the lock on the handle.

Ethan kept his back to her, his head was down and his shoulders hunched forward. He flinched away from her when she rested her fingers on his back. "Don't," he snarled.

Feeling as if she'd been slapped, Emma's hand fell back to her side. A sense of helplessness encased her as she leaned against the door to watch him. She should be scared after what she'd seen outside, she could sense the instability within him, but even though he'd been on the verge of destroying those people out there, she felt no concern over her safety when it came to him.

"This is because of me, isn't it?" she inquired.

"This is because of me, of what I am, even before you I was a monster," Ethan told her.

She was taken aback by his words. "No, you weren't."

He turned on her so quickly, she didn't see him move before his hands were beside her head on the door. Though she wasn't scared of him, her breath still hitched as he lowered his face to the same height as hers. At some point in time, he had taken his glasses off to reveal the burning red eyes hidden beneath them all day. Eyes that showed his continued spiral out of control.

"You don't know what I am, Emma, what I'm capable of, or the *thoughts* I have." He leaned closer to her, his nose and mouth practically touched her neck as he inhaled deeply. "The things I want to do to you, if you knew what they were, you would run screaming."

Perhaps she would, but she couldn't help but feel oddly titillated by his words and his breath as it tickled her neck and ear. She was a train wreck, but it was because of him, she'd gone off the rails. Her palms pressed against the door as he pulled away to look at her.

"I stayed away from humans because I knew their blood and life force was a temptation I might not be able to resist one day, and then I met you. You made it all better. With you, the incessant clamoring for blood wasn't as loud, and I found I could face the world again."

"Thoughts don't make you a monster, Ethan, actions do."

"If you knew my thoughts right now, Emma, you wouldn't be so certain of that."

"And what are they?" she whispered.

He leaned so close their noses nearly touched. "What I wouldn't give for just a taste of *you*."

Her breath caught in her chest, she bit her bottom lip as her heart raced with excitement and apprehension. She was trapped in this tiny closet-sized room, with a man who was talking about drinking her blood, and instead of fleeing she found herself saying words she'd never expected to say, "Taste me, then."

His eyes became a more vivid shade of red; she knew if

there had been actual flames within his eyes, she would have been burned by them. It wasn't his eyes that would hurt her but the fangs extending over his bottom lip at her words.

"If I'm what you need to help you be stable and to face the world, then do it," she said.

Ethan's jaw clenched; the scent of rain on her skin, mixed with the honeysuckle scent of her intensified as she unwaveringly held his gaze. Those scents were even more enticing than her words. His hand brushed the wet tendrils of hair away from her neck to expose the vein running through there, pulsing with life and begging for him to taste it. It was the vein he wanted the most, the one that would ease and satisfy him, but it would also be the beginning of the end. If he did this, there would never be any turning back for him.

"You don't know what you're asking for," he said from between his clenched teeth. "I can't."

"It will help you—"

"It will *intensify* what I feel for you. If I ever taste you, that will be the end of me. It could only be *us* afterward."

Those words echoed in her mind, and the sane part of her was saying this was all moving too fast. A commitment such as this took years of getting to know each other, of dating, meeting the parents, and fights. Then, if *all* those things were withstood, and there was still love, a ring and the promise of another fifty or so years were exchanged. There wasn't a bonding ritual that would end her life and last for eternity.

The insane part of her was screaming, *just do it.*

The prospect of spending forever with him wasn't as frightening anymore. It was intriguing and exciting; it was something she wanted as badly as he seemed to want her blood right now. This magnificent, powerful man standing before her loved her, and he was offering to share his life with her.

He had no doubts about *her*; he was willing to do anything

for her, even die. When she asked for space, he stepped aside and risked himself to make her happy. Before everything was revealed to her, she'd been falling in love with him, and now, after all this, she realized she *was* in love with him.

Emma's heart raced, even with the cold air caressing her skin, her body was on fire as the heat of him burned against her. Weren't vampires supposed to be cold? Instead, he had the same effect on her as the summer sun on an August day.

"Then let it be us," she whispered.

"Emma," he groaned, and for the first time, some of his anger and stress eased as his head bowed. "You don't know what you're asking for."

"You said I can still see my parents."

"Yes, but it's your *death*."

She rested her hand against his cheek; the stubble lining his jaw was rough against her palm as she leaned forward to press a brief kiss against his lips. "And it's a whole new life. I'm not thrilled about the prospect of having my heart stop beating, but I am thrilled about *you*. You've given me time to figure all this out, and what I've realized is I want *you*; I want to help you and to be a part of your life. I thought you would be happy."

The look in his eyes made her realize it was too much for him to hope for right now, and he didn't know how to handle her words. Taking his cheeks with her hands, she stared at him for a few seconds before pulling him closer and kissing him again. At first, he didn't respond to her, but then his lips eased against hers and his body relaxed.

A feeling of contentment slid through her as she pressed closer to him. His hands slipped away from the door and settled on her hips. The thin, wet material of her purple cover-up pressed against her skin, but all she felt was the heat of his hands burning into her flesh. There was no fear here; there was only love and trust as his tongue slid over hers. She had handed herself over to this man, and all she felt was a soul-deep certainty it had been the truest decision of her life.

Ethan's heart raced, it took everything he had not to tear the clothes from her body and bury himself inside her, but he found touching her helped to ease the raging monster shredding his insides. She was everything to him, and she was finally agreeing to be *his*. His hands slid over her silken thighs as he pushed up the hem of her wet cover-up. His fingers brushed against the edge of the bikini bottom hanging low on her hips.

His body vibrated with need, but he was aware of everything he desired from her, he couldn't do within this small room, he didn't even want to try. She deserved better than this, and he was going to make sure she had it.

A small mewl of protest escaped her when he pulled his mouth away from hers. He caught her hands pressing against his chest, lifted them above her head, and flattened them against the door. Her breath came in rapid pants that caused her breasts to push temptingly against him. A seductive smile curved her mouth as she pressed her hips invitingly against his.

She would be the death of him, but he would welcome that death if she smiled at him. Unable to resist her, he brought his mouth back to hers and kissed her with a deliberate slowness which allowed him to savor the honeyed taste of her. Her hands jerked in his grasp but he didn't release her, and she didn't try to pull away as he left a trail of kisses across her neck and down to her collarbone. His tongue swirled over her rain-dampened skin as he tasted her. He could hear and feel the rapid beat of her heart, but he stayed away from the tempting vein beckoning to him.

"Ethan," she gasped when she felt the press of his fangs against her flesh. The sensation of his fangs scraping over her skin caused her to quiver with anticipation. It was then she knew she'd completely lost her mind, and she didn't care. His eyes were burning embers when they came back to hers, his fangs visible as he stared at her. "I want this."

He released her hands and seized her face between his palms; he stared at her as he waited for her to change her mind, but she had no intention of doing that. When she didn't tell him to stop, he kissed her so ardently he stole the breath from her completely. She jerked a little when one of his fangs pricked her lower lip but it wasn't an entirely unpleasant sensation, and he kissed away the sting of the bite.

A rumble of satisfaction escaped him as he licked away the trickle of blood his bite created. Blood as deliciously sweet and magnificent as he'd known it would be. Even that small bit of blood caused strength to seep through his system as it filled him in ways no other's blood could. He almost bit on her lip to get more, but he knew it would hurt her, and though he would cause her future pain, he was going to do everything he could to minimize it now.

Her fingers curled into his back when he broke the kiss, but before she could protest his heated mouth was on her neck, and his fangs were pressing against her skin. The breath she'd just managed to take rushed out of her again when his fangs sank deep into her flesh. Her body jerked against him when he pierced her vein. The sensation of his teeth piercing her skin was like a pinprick. It was gone almost as soon as she felt it, and once it was gone, there were only endless waves of delight as he held her more firmly against him.

At first, she thought it was only her pleasure from sustaining him, by being in his arms again, she was feeling. Then, she realized she was also experiencing *his* emotions. Her mind was growing overwhelmed with joy and a feeling of becoming one with each other. She'd never realized she was searching for something in her life, but she knew now this was what she'd always been waiting for.

She belonged here, with him, and as he fed from her, she realized he felt it as strongly as she did. Tears of happiness burned her eyes and spilled down her cheeks. The passion she'd been experiencing was dampened by the sensation of completion swelling within her. She couldn't stop crying as her fingers slid through his hair, and her head fell back against the door to offer him better access to her vein.

Ethan clung to her as the monster inside him retreated, and everything within him became centered on this woman in his arms and the gift she was giving him. The rest of the world faded away as her blissful emotions took possession of him. He'd grown up with his parents' close relationship, witnessed what unraveled between Isabelle and Stefan, but nothing could have prepared him for the feelings unfurling within him now. It took everything he had to pull away from her before he took too much, not because he wanted more of her blood but because he never wanted the connection to end.

Disappointment filled her when he pulled away but then his fingers were gently wiping away her tears. His kiss was nowhere near as demanding this time as his mouth slanted over hers. She could taste her blood on his lips, but it wasn't as unpleasant, or repulsive, as she'd thought it would be. Her heart swelled with love as he pulled back to look at her.

There was such affection in his green eyes, she found herself unable to breathe as she searched a gaze she hadn't seen in days. "It will be *us*," he said in a hoarse voice.

She nodded her agreement as she rested her head on his chest and held him against her. "It will be," she vowed.

CHAPTER TWENTY-FOUR

"There you are!" Isabelle cried when they emerged from the mall. The rain had stopped, and the sky was cleared. The air seemed cleaner, though it was more humid. Emma blinked against the sunlight and spotted Isabelle across the street from them with Stefan at her side. "Where have you been?" she demanded as she stalked across the street toward them.

"Getting out of the rain," Ethan replied.

Isabelle's brow furrowed as her gaze slid back and forth between them. Ethan's glasses were back in place, but Emma could feel the more relaxed posture of his body as he stood beside her.

"We've been looking all over for you," Isabelle said.

Though the only place Isabelle was looking right now was at her neck, but Emma knew her dampened hair covered Ethan's bite mark on her.

"You've found us," Ethan said.

"Are Jill and Mandy ok?" Emma asked anxiously.

"Mandy's fine; we were separated from Jill. Aiden and Ian are looking for her now."

Emma took an abrupt step forward. "Separated, how?"

"There were a lot of people on the beach," Isabelle said. "Everyone started running at once. Aiden lost her when she hopped on one of the buses."

"I'm sure she's fine," Ethan assured her. "It was a quick storm. Come on; let's get you back to the house."

"Not until we find Jill," she insisted.

Ethan's jaw clenched, he was about to start arguing with her when he spotted Aiden jogging toward them from the beach. His brother was barely breathing hard when he reached them. "We found her; she just got off the bus again. It took her a little while to get back to here on the bus. Ian's taking her to the house now."

"Good," Emma breathed.

"Come on, let's go," Ethan said and clasped her elbow.

Emma carefully studied the people walking so casually past them. She was half-afraid one of them might turn around and stab her at any second, though she doubted Tristan's plan was for her to be dead. No, she was certain he had something far more sinister in mind for her. She stayed close to Ethan's side, and by the time they returned to the house, she felt jittery and uncertain. The sound of the door closing behind her and the lock clicking into place was music to her ears.

Mandy and Jill poked their heads around the corner of the door from the pool area before they'd even stepped into the living room. "There you are!" Jill hurried across the room and threw her arms around Emma.

"There *you* are!" Emma said and embraced her friend.

"I got a short tour of the area," Jill said with a laugh. "But I stayed dry."

"You okay?" Emma asked Mandy.

"I'm fine," she said and squeezed her arm.

"Who knew rain could be so damn inconvenient," Jill said as she bounced out to the patio again. "But the sky is clear, there's a pool here, and I forgot to leave the volleyball on thc beach so we can always play in the pool."

It sounded like fun, but Emma found herself leaning closer to Ethan as thoughts of retreating to his bedroom filled her. She'd never thought she'd be the type to stay in bed with a guy all day, but right now the prospect of spending all week with him there sounded like a little bit of heaven to her. She was about to give Jill some excuse to leave when the doorbell rang.

Despite her best efforts not to show her distress, not to let everyone know just how rattled Tristan and his band of psycho groupies had made her, she jumped at the sound and spun around. Ethan rested his hand reassuringly on the small of her back.

"I'll get it," Stefan said.

Ethan stepped in front of Emma as he braced himself to launch at whatever might come through the door. Stefan glanced back at Isabelle to make sure she was safe before pulling the door open. There was no death threat on the other side of that door, but Ethan felt his anger rise almost as much as if there had been when he saw who was standing there.

Brian leaned insolently against the doorframe with his arms crossed over his chest and a pair of dark sunglasses covering his eyes. Ethan had almost forgotten how much he disliked the smug asshole until seeing him again.

"You rang," Brian drawled and flashed a smile. "Or I suppose *I* just did."

"Holy shit," Jill whispered behind him. "Is that guy *real*?"

Emma wondered the same thing as her gaze was riveted on the man in the doorway, exuding raw sexuality and an air of superiority the likes of which she'd never encountered before.

Hair, so blond it was nearly white, was cut short to enhance his high cheekbones and pointed chin. Lips the color of blood were a stark contrast to the paleness of his flawless skin. His full upper lip curled into a smile that revealed his extended fangs.

"Brian," Stefan greeted.

"Stefan," he said with a bow of his head. "Are you going to invite me in, or am I going to hang out here all day working on my tan?"

Stefan looked as if he was tempted to drive his fist into Brian's face, but he still managed to step aside as he spoke. "Come in, Brian."

Brian uncrossed his legs as he rose away from the frame. "How nice of you, Stefan, considering the last time we were together you were threatening to rip my head off."

"It's still a very tempting idea," Stefan murmured.

Brian gave him a dazzling smile that caused Jill to start fanning herself. He grabbed a duffle bag from the ground beside him and walked into the house. "Well, if it isn't the pure-breds," he said with a nod to Isabelle and Ethan. Emma glanced questioningly up at Ethan, but his gaze remained focused on Brian, and his posture was rigid. "I'm sorry, I didn't see the young pups back there. I didn't mean to exclude you, what's up boys?"

"Fuck you," Aiden shot back.

"Such hostility from one so young." Brian lifted his glasses to reveal eyes the color of arctic ice as they focused on Ian. "Someone's not a puppy anymore."

"Easy, Brian," Stefan warned.

Ethan frowned as he tried to figure out how Brian would know that when none of them had realized Ian had reached maturity. His attention was drawn away from Brian though by Ian's growled response, "We don't need this asshole's help."

"Apparently, you must, because I can guarantee it almost killed this one to call me," Brian said and slapped Stefan on the back. "Don't worry; I tend to grow on people."

"So do warts," Isabelle muttered.

Brian laughed as he dropped his bag on the floor. "Good to see you too, Isabelle."

Emma's head spun as she tried to get a grasp on Brian when his eyes locked on hers. His expression changed from antagonistic, to one she swore might have been genuine concern, so fast Emma would have thought he had PMS if he wasn't so obviously male.

"Is this her?" Brian asked.

A growl rumbled from Ethan as he stepped in front of Emma and pushed her back a little. Emma rested her hands on his back and poked her head out to look around him. "Don't even *think* about coming near her."

Brian held his hands up and settled his large frame onto one of the stools by the bar. He folded his hands as he rested an elbow on the counter and studied them. "I know better. Now, what is going on here?"

Ethan kept Emma behind him as he moved her toward the couch. The subtle scent of garbage coming off Brian wasn't as potent as the last time they'd seen him; he could barely detect the odor anymore. His scent was probably stronger than Brian's now and more like Brian's was the first time they met.

The difference in smells didn't mean Brian wasn't still a killer, but he hadn't killed a human since they'd last seen him. Maybe he hadn't killed *any*one recently. It eased some of the tension in him, but he still wasn't thrilled about having Brian in the house with Emma and her friends.

Stefan must have felt the same way as he kept Isabelle by his side while he filled Brian in on what was happening.

~

Emma was exhausted by the time she finally retreated to Ethan's room. Ethan closed the door behind him and turned on the light. "He's so strange," Emma murmured as she sat on the bed to pull off her now dry but extremely wrinkled cover up.

"He's a dick," Ethan said as he pulled the curtains on the windows closed.

Emma chuckled and kicked off her flip-flops. "Then why is he here?"

"Because he's an incredibly powerful dick, and as much as I'd like to drive my fist into his face, he'll help us."

"Why?"

"He has a history with Stefan, and we all saved his ass last year."

"So he owes you."

Ethan frowned as he turned to face her. "He does, but I think it's more than that."

"What do you mean?"

He shook his head as he walked away from the windows. "I don't know. The last time we saw him there was a wildness to him; a savagery I thought would one day lead him down the same exact path as Tristan. He's still an arrogant prick, but he's not..." His forehead furrowed as his voice trailed off.

"Not what?" she prodded.

"Not a brutal killer, at least not of humans."

Well, that was *not* what she'd expected to hear, not even a little bit. "Was he once a killer of humans?"

"He was in the past. Though, it was a kill or be killed situation for him."

"That's good to know," she muttered.

He smiled as he walked over to sit beside her. "He's not a

threat to you, or Mandy and Jill. He wasn't that kind of a killer. He has a deadly past, but so does Stefan. Brian's less of a threat than I'd expected him to be."

Emma rested her hand on his arm when he rubbed at the bridge of his nose. "You look tired."

"I don't like being around people." He slid his arm around her shoulders and pulled her against his side. "Except for you, I love you."

Her heart warmed as she wrapped her arms around his waist. "I love you too." Just moments ago she'd been ready to pass out from exhaustion, but she felt her pulse quickening as her skin reacted to his. "When will I become like you, Ethan?"

He dropped his head to brush his lips against her hair. "Are you sure about this?"

"Do I have a choice anymore?" she asked with a laugh.

"I'd like to give you one—"

"But you can't, I made a choice earlier, and I'm going to stand by it. I'd like to do it soon, tonight maybe; I don't think it will be good for me to think about my impending death for too long."

He stiffened against her, his hand stilled on her arm. "It's going to be excruciating for you, Emma."

"Something else I'd prefer not to dwell on."

He lifted her up and pulled her into his lap, holding her against his chest, and cradling her as he rocked. "I'll make it as easy on you as possible," he promised. "But first I have to feed, a lot."

Now that his secret was out, Emma was aware of the blood bags residing on the shelf below the yogurt, apples, and milk bought for them when they'd moved in. It had been more than a little disturbing to see them there in the beginning, but she'd gotten used to it now.

Emma frowned as a new thought occurred to her. "How do you get the blood bags?"

"Stefan has a nurse under his control who works the blood drives and gives him some of the blood after. He also has an orderly at the local hospital who supplies him with blood. We use both sources, so the missing blood isn't picked up on. I'll need fresh, human blood to get you through the transition though."

Fear trickled through her; she tilted her head back to look up at him. "Can you handle feeding from someone other than me?"

Ethan's hands tightened on her at the thought. "Yes, as long as I know it's for you, I'll be all right with it," he assured her. He hoped those words were true, but it didn't matter, it had to be done.

She rested her hand on his chest. "It won't hurt them, will it?"

"No more than it hurt you, and they won't even remember it afterward."

"Will I be able to change people's memories and control them after I'm changed?"

"It will take some time, but you'll eventually be able to do those things. You'll also be able to cloak your presence from others when your powers mature enough. The older we get, the more powerful we become and the better we can deal with our abilities. Your hearing, vision, and speed will also be greatly enhanced. That will take some time for you to get used to, but we'll do it together. You'll also be immortal, and you'll be *safer*."

He said the word safer with such reverence it made her heart ache as his fingers stroked her hair. She had no words for him as she cuddled closer. The steady beat of his heart, and the heat of his skin, warmed her and lulled her into sleep. Her eyes drifted open when he lifted her and carried her around the bed.

She didn't know when it happened, but he'd stripped her bathing suit.

Pulling the sheets back, he laid her on the bed and climbed in beside her. A blissful sigh of contentment escaped when his arms encircled her, and he molded his body around hers.

CHAPTER TWENTY-FIVE

"I'll be back in a couple of hours," Ethan said and kissed her on the forehead. The clean aroma of cucumber-scented shampoo adhered to the curling tendrils of her damp hair, but beneath the shampoo he detected her honeysuckle scent.

Emma clutched his forearms as she stared up at his strained face. "What's wrong?" she demanded.

He shook his head and dropped his forehead to hers. She remembered his words from before about how tough it was for him to be around people, and she suddenly understood the pinched look on his face.

"I can go with you if it will help you," Emma offered.

"I don't want you to see anything that will happen," he said in a strained voice.

"But you said I make it easier for you to be around people."

"You do, and I won't hurt anyone, but I can't have you around this. I'll be fine, Brian and Ian will be with me. Nothing will go wrong."

He was trying to reassure her, but he had no idea how all this would go down. He was counting on the knowledge of her being here, waiting so she could join him, to keep him sane and rational, and to keep him from killing anyone. If something went wrong, he didn't want her there to see it.

She held onto his arms when he went to pull away from her. "Ethan, there's nothing you can do to make me change my mind about any of this or *you*."

He cupped her cheeks and pressed a tender kiss on her lips. "I know, but there are some things I'd prefer you not to have to deal with, and this is one of those things. I'll only be gone for a few hours."

Releasing his arms, she hastily brushed the hair back from her neck. "Drink from me before you go, it will help to take the edge off."

"It's too soon for you."

A small chuckle escaped her. "You'll be taking it all tonight, Ethan; I don't think this will make much of a difference. Even if you only take a little it will help, and don't deny it."

There was no way he could deny that. Not when she was right. His gaze latched onto the bite marks still marring her skin, he could have made them fade with the healing agent in his saliva, but he liked seeing them there and having the knowledge they were his. Seeing them now caused his fangs to tingle as the driving urge to taste her washed over him. Her breasts pressed against his chest as she stepped into him. They'd made love upon waking this morning, but he could feel more than his fangs lengthening right now.

He kissed her as she slid her arms around his neck; lifting her, he pressed her flush against his body. A gasp escaped her, her fingers threaded through his hair as he ran his teeth over the tender flesh of her neck. Her bathrobe fell open to expose her breasts as she wrapped her legs around his waist. Feeling her body moving over his, he knew there was no way he would only be satisfied with taking her blood right now.

Adjusting his hold on her, he grabbed the tie on her robe and tugged it open. The rest of the material fell open to reveal her small, curvy body. Her dusky nipples were already hard as he took one in his mouth and sucked on it. A low moan escaped her; she arched her back as he leaned her against the wall and grabbed her ass with both his hands. Without thinking, he nipped at her breast, drawing blood from it. Certain he'd hurt her, he pulled away almost immediately, but he saw no discomfort in her eyes when they met his. Instead, he saw only desire.

"It felt good," she whispered in response to the concern in his eyes.

She wasn't lying either, though there had been pain, she found she enjoyed it, and it excited her more. A small smile curved his mouth before he bent his head to her breast again. Emma braced herself as his teeth scraped over her; she bit back a scream of delight as his fangs sank in again just above her nipple.

"Ethan!" she cried.

The sensation of her blood being drawn from her in deep waves caused her to tremble as his tongue continued to caress her nipple. He wasn't even inside her, and she was going to lose control. And then he pressed her closer against the wall and released her ass. His hand ran over her thigh and dipped to her already wet center. He slid two of his fingers into her body, filling and stretching her as he began to move his fingers steadily back and forth. His palm rubbed against her clit as he stroked her deeper and more forcefully.

Emma bit down on her bottom lip to keep from screaming. She could feel blood from the bite trickling down her chin, but she didn't care. She was swept away by the feel of him, consumed by the tidal wave of pleasure coursing through her. He spun her away from the wall and took four steps toward the bed. A groan of disapproval escaped her as his fangs withdrew from her breast and his hand slid away from her as he placed her on the bed. She didn't have much time to be unhappy though as he hurriedly shed his clothing and climbed on top of her.

"Would you like to taste me?" he asked in a grating voice.

At first, Emma was confused by his words but then he took a finger and wiped away the blood trickling down her breast. She watched in fascination as he slid the finger into his mouth and licked the blood from it.

"My blood?" he asked.

Her mind spun as she tried to think of a reply. Wasn't she supposed to be repulsed by his suggestion? She was anything but repulsed though as the thought brought forth erotic images which caused her fingers to curl into the sheets beneath her.

"Yes," she whispered as her heart raced with excitement and her belly quivered.

His eyes burned into hers as he bit down on his finger and held it out to her. Two drops of blood quivered on it and slid down as she watched. He lowered the finger and traced her lower lip with it.

Her tongue flickered out to taste the blood sliding over his skin before drawing his finger into her mouth. The blood was metallic but unexpectedly pleasant as she ran her tongue over it and sucked on his finger. Passion blazed hotly in his eyes as he slid his finger away and bent his head to run his tongue over her lips.

Emma's heart beat rapidly against her ribs as she opened her legs to him and he braced his hands on either side of her head. His large body encompassed hers before he entered her in one powerful thrust. His mouth muffled her next cry as he took possession of her body. She grabbed his ass as she wrapped her legs around his waist and drew him more firmly against her.

"Harder," she breathed against his mouth.

He was holding back, afraid to hurt her, but that one word was all he needed to push him into a near frenzy. He bit her bottom lip as he drove himself into her. Blood pooled into his mouth, but she didn't seem to feel it as her hips eagerly rose and fell to meet his ardent movements and her tongue continued to entwine with his.

Her muscles contracted around his cock, her nails raked the skin of his back, drawing blood as her orgasm tore through her. He didn't stop though; he couldn't possibly stop as he continued to thrust in and out of her. His body demanded release, yet he held back as he relished the feel of being inside her and tasting her. He was completely lost to her as she continued to moan and arch against him.

Another cry tore from her as her muscles contracted powerfully around him again. He finally gave himself over to the release he'd been denying as his orgasm was pulled from him by the undeniable gratification her body gave him. A low groan escaped as his release seemed to go on in unending waves.

Rolling to the side, he pulled her along with him and settled her on top of him as he tried to catch his breath. The tantalizing scents of sex and blood drifted over him; he couldn't help but smile as she clutched his shoulders and fought to catch her breath.

"I think I'll be too tired to be a threat to anyone now," he told her as he nuzzled her hair.

She laughed as she lifted her head to look down at him. "I know I am."

His saliva had already healed the wound on her lip, but there was still some dry blood on her chin. He wiped it away with his thumb before bringing her chin down to kiss her. He could already feel the desire for her blood creeping through him again, and he knew he was getting close to a dangerous precipice. If he didn't complete their bond soon, he would become the threat Stefan and his father were at one point.

He lifted her hand and kissed her knuckles before reluctantly withdrawing himself from her and rolling away. "I have to go."

Emma propped her head on her hand as she watched him walk across the room. The scratches she had left on his back were already gone, but dry flecks of blood clung to his skin. He disappeared into the bathroom and showered before reappearing in the doorway. Her gaze raked over his chiseled pecs, carved abs, still partially erect shaft, lean hips, and powerful thighs.

Mine, the thought rose out of nowhere. It was so overpowering, she was certain it was true.

"You heal fast," she whispered.

He gave her a lopsided smile as he pulled on a pair of boxers. "You will soon as well. Our saliva also has a healing agent in it, that's why your lip is fine now. It's also why you'll never have to worry about diseases again."

Emma frowned at him as she sat up and pulled the sheet against her. "Really?"

"Yes. None of that will be a concern for you."

"It's all so strange," she mumbled as she ran a tremulous hand across her now healed lip. There wasn't even a bump from where his teeth had pierced her skin. She couldn't tear her gaze away from his sculpted physique as he pawed through a drawer and came up with a black t-shirt.

"Ethan?" There was a questioning expression on his face when he turned toward her. "You're mine, right?"

He broke into a grin and strode across the room toward her. Emma stared at him as he placed his hands on either side of her on the bed.

"I am yours for eternity, Emma; I will be your rock, your

best friend, your lover, and the father of your children. I am going to be by your side for thousands of years, and I'm going to love you every second of every *one* of those years. When this bond is complete, you will *never* doubt that again."

"I don't doubt it now," she whispered as she leaned forward to kiss him. "I just want to make sure *you* know."

He laughed as he pulled away. "Oh, I know."

She watched him as he finished dressing before rising to her feet and pulling her robe on again. "Maybe you should take Stefan and Aiden with you too, just in case," she said nervously.

"I'll be okay, and I prefer to have more vampires here, with you."

A knock on the door brought both of their heads toward it. "Let's go, purebred, some of us are hungry!" Brian called from the other side.

"Maybe that guy won't be safe," Ethan muttered.

"Why don't you take Stefan instead?"

He shook his head. "There's no way he'll leave Isabelle behind, and neither of us want Isabelle around this. Are you going to join the others?"

"I'm just going to hop in the shower again, and then I'll go out."

"Okay, just don't go outside, at all."

"I won't," she promised.

"I'll see you soon. I love you."

"Love you too." He gave her a swift kiss and left the room. Emma sighed and headed into the bathroom.

Jill and Mandy were waiting for her when she emerged from the bathroom. "You're really going to do this?" Mandy asked nervously.

Emma dropped the towel she'd used for her hair on the bed before grabbing the shorts and tank top she set out earlier. She already missed Ethan, it was the strangest sensation, one that almost made her feel like a stalker, but she wanted him *here.* It made no sense to her, but she couldn't shake it. She disappeared into the bathroom again and dressed before rejoining them.

"I am," she told them.

"Are you sure about this?" Mandy's chocolate eyes were troubled as she studied Emma.

"I've never been more certain about anything in my life," she said honestly.

"So is this kind of like getting married?" Jill asked.

Emma laughed as she picked up her hairbrush and ran it through the thick mass of her hair. "I think binding yourself to someone for eternity is kind of like marriage," she said with a smile.

"I don't even like to bind myself to someone for a month," Jill said as she sat on the edge of the bed. "Ethan's hot and all, and this is about the biggest understatement of the century, but that's a *really* long time, Emma."

"It is, and I can't wait."

Jill shook her head. "This is crazy; you're going to *die.*"

Emma shuddered at the reminder and dropped the brush. She walked over and sat on the bed beside Jill. "It's going to be okay, I promise, and I *do* want this."

"You barely know him."

"But I feel like I know him better than I've ever known anyone else. I know it sounds crazy, and I know you don't understand, but please trust me on this. Please stand by me. I've stood by all your decisions."

"My decisions didn't result in my death," Jill retorted.

"Well, some of them almost resulted in me killing you if

that means anything," Mandy said. "Especially the night you drove home drunk from the club, in your underwear, and hanging your head out the window like a dog because you were convinced it would sober you up. I wanted to choke you when you passed me on my way back from the library."

"Not my finest moment," Jill admitted. "But I survived."

"And so will I. You heard what Stefan said. My heart will only stop for a second, and then I'll be alive again. I'll be stronger, and I'll be with Ethan, forever. Ugh, I sound like a six-year-old dreaming of a fairytale, and if you were saying these things to me, I'd lock you away until you came down off whatever drugs you were on."

"I'm considering it," Jill said with a laugh.

Emma squeezed her hand before wandering back into the bathroom. "Believe me this is one hundred percent a natural high," she said as she turned the water on and brushed her teeth. She spit in the sink and rinsed it before returning to the bedroom. "And it's a good..."

Her voice trailed off when she spotted Mandy lying prone on the floor, with one hand beneath her and the other stretched out above her head. Blood was already beginning to pool on the tile beneath her head. Fearing she'd fallen, Emma broke free of her paralysis.

She only made it three steps out of the bathroom when something heavy hit her on the back of the head. She was unable to get her hands underneath her in time to stop herself from face planting onto the floor.

Blood burst free of her broken nose. Tears blurred eyes, but even as she was trying to figure out what had happened, hands were grabbing her arms and hauling her to her feet. She opened her mouth to scream, but a rag was shoved into it. Choking on the cloth, and the blood trickling from her nose, she found it difficult to see or breathe as she was pulled forward. She tried to fight against the cruel hands holding her, but everything was blurring into twos and threes, and she was pretty sure her brain jiggled like Jell-O in her skull.

Her toes scraped across the ground as her head lulled forward and she was dragged toward the balcony.

CHAPTER TWENTY-SIX

Ethan lifted his head from the young woman he'd been feeding from. After tasting Emma's blood, the woman's seemed flat, bland. It wasn't awful, but more like water compared to champagne. Looking around the small bathroom, he scented the air as he sensed a strange disturbance in it. The woman swayed on her feet when he released her and took a step away; her glassy eyes were focused on the curtained window in the corner of the room. The bite mark on her neck had already healed when he ordered her out of the room.

He'd fed from four women and one man since leaving the house, and with Emma's blood coursing through him, he felt almost lightheaded from the power pulsing within his veins. The acrid scent of sweat and sulfur drifted to him, he recognized the combination as fear, but the laughter and music from the bar continued to flow into this backroom. He realized the scent wasn't coming from anyone out there.

Unreasonable foreboding gripped him. He took another step forward and inhaled deeply. Where was it coming from?

Grabbing the handle, the door to the bathroom slammed

against the wall as he flung it open and strode purposely from the restroom. Ian and Brian were standing by the pool tables, they each held cues in their hands as they talked with a group of young girls who were eagerly hanging on their every word.

One of the women started to come toward him, but he paid her little attention as he walked toward the door of the bar. His gaze ran across the beach as the sun dipped over the horizon.

"What are you doing?" Ian asked as he placed his cue against the wall and hurried to his side.

"Do you smell that?" Ethan inquired.

"I don't smell anything, are you all set for the night?"

"Yes," he answered absently. "How do you not smell it?"

"Maybe you've had too much," Brian suggested as he approached. "How many humans have you fed from at one time before?"

"Only Emma," Ethan answered absently.

"Wait, what?" Ian blurted as he did a double take.

A strange, knowing gleam came into Brian's eyes as his gaze ran over him from head to toe. "I see," Brian murmured, and Ethan got the distinct feeling he really *did* see. That Brian knew the dirty secret, Ethan hid all these years. That the man he least wanted to understand him, was the one who did.

"You've had human blood before," Ian insisted.

"Only in bags."

"Ethan—"

"Enough, Ian!" Ethan interrupted brusquely.

"But I thought—"

"There's a lot you thought you knew that you don't. Now drop it," he snarled as he stepped out the front door. His head turned as he searched for the scent, but there was a hollow feeling growing within his stomach.

"What does it smell like?" Brian inquired.

"Fear." And then it hit him *who* the smell was coming from. "It's Emma."

He broke into a run as he fled the bar. It felt as if his feet weren't even hitting the ground as he raced up the road toward the house. He'd never moved so fast in his life, he was nothing more than a blur, one barely perceptible to the human eye and could easily be written off as a fleeting shadow.

The doorknob never came into play as he smashed into the door, tearing it clean off its hinges and flinging it across the room. Isabelle let out a startled shout, Stefan and Aiden leapt up from the couch. It took him only a second to ascertain Emma wasn't with them. He fled down the hall and burst through the bedroom door with the same recklessness as the first, but this one stayed on its hinges as it crashed into the wall.

The scent of blood hung heavily in the room; he detected the aroma of Emma's blood immediately before the smell of someone else's filled his nose. His head turned, his nostrils flared as he spotted Mandy lying on the floor.

"What happened?" Isabelle cried as she ran into the room behind him.

Ethan turned and ran for the bathroom, but even before he made it to the doorway, he knew Emma wasn't there. Isabelle was kneeling at Mandy's side when he returned; she was carefully holding her head as she turned Mandy over.

"She's alive," Isabelle whispered as Aiden knelt by her side. "I don't understand; we sensed no one else in the house, no other presence. How is this possible?"

"Aiden give her some of your blood," Stefan commanded.

Aiden bit into his wrist and pressed it against Mandy's mouth to help her heal faster. Ethan was drawn by a small puddle of blood on the floor just outside of the bathroom. He knew even before he knelt beside it that it was Emma's. A bellow of fury tore from him, his back hunched up as his muscles constricted. Stefan grabbed Isabelle and pulled her backward; he pushed her toward the wall and positioned himself in front of her.

Red suffused Ethan's vision; madness crept through his system and twisted within his mind. His body pulsed with the power of the blood he'd consumed today and the rage tearing through him. Something strange was happening to him, his hands fisted at his sides causing the veins in his arms to stand out.

At first, he thought the red hue of fury clouded his eyes, but as he looked closer, he realized his veins were standing starkly out from his body and turning red. The blood pulsing through them was visible, or maybe it was the blood of those he had drunk from today. Either way, it didn't matter as the red color suffused him with more power while it spread through his body. His hearing was more acute as he picked up on conversations going on outside; the room was etched into vivid detail as he pinpointed every particle of dust floating through the air.

"Ethan!" Isabelle yelped.

Aiden pushed a groggy Mandy toward where Stefan had Isabelle pinned in the corner. Stefan's eyes were a fiery red color as he kept his body firmly in front of Isabelle's, but he made no move to come after Ethan. Ian and Brian burst into the room, both sweating and breathing heavily as they scanned the room.

"Holy shit!" Ian blurted when his eyes landed on Ethan.

Brian grabbed Ian's arm and shoved him toward where the others gathered. "Ethan you have to calm down," Stefan said quietly.

"You were supposed to be watching her!" he snarled as he took a step toward him.

"What is wrong with you?" Isabelle gasped as her eyes raked Ethan from head to toe.

Ian tried to get past Brian to get at him, but Brian shoved him back again. "You don't want to tangle with him right now," Brian said in a whisper that drew Ethan's gaze to him. Brian held his hands up and stepped back. "Easy."

The blood roared in Ethan's ears; the madness was taking over as he moved closer to them. The red in his veins seeped out into his skin, turning him the shade of dark molten lava. He'd never seen anything like it, but it meant nothing to him as his thoughts remained centered on Emma.

"What happened here?" he demanded. Mandy's eyes were wide on him, her mouth hanging open as she gaped at him. She grabbed Aiden's arm as she took an unsteady step back. "What happened here?"

She began to shake her head, but then her hand flew to her forehead as she winced. "I don't know. I was sitting on the bed, and the next thing I knew you were all here. Where is Jill?" she asked and lifted her head to look around the room with squinted eyes.

"Not here," Ethan grated.

"You can find Emma," Stefan said in a reasonable tone that only irritated him more. "If you just calm down and think, you can find her, Ethan."

The scent of her blood filled his nose, causing his rage to escalate even higher. The veins in his arms stood out even more; the red suffusing his body deepened as the entire room began to look like blood covered it. Blood. He wanted it so badly right now he could taste it. He could feel it sliding down his throat, and he *would* have it. He would rip off Tristan's head and gorge himself on his blood.

The people standing across from him all shrank away.

"Ethan," Isabelle breathed.

He turned away from them and raced over to throw open the doors to the balcony; he didn't look back as he grabbed the railing and leapt into the night. Though it was a good fifty-foot drop, he landed silently on his feet.

"What *was* that?" Aiden whispered.

"That was one very pissed off purebred," Brian said as he stepped away from the others.

"That was like the fucking Hulk," Ian said.

"We have to go after him. In the mood he's in, he'll kill anything in his way." Brian strode away from them to look out over the balcony.

"Are we even going to be able to stop him?" Ian inquired.

"Probably not, but we have to try." Brian jumped off the balcony and followed the blur of Ethan he saw far ahead of him.

THE SCENT of her blood drew Ethan onward, pushing him faster and faster as he ran up the hillside and past the homes lining it. He didn't know if the others were following him, and he didn't care as he weaved his way through the neighborhoods until he came to a large home nestled in the hillside. His heart raced, anger and frustration warred through him as he stood outside the two-story, robin's egg blue home with three balconies on the front.

Emma was in there, and she was suffering, he was certain of it as the scent of her blood was even more potent here. He circled the home, but he had no idea how he was going to get to her. The front door was wide open when he completed his circle of the house. He could feel his family and Brian coming, but he wasn't going to wait for them as he approached the door.

He spotted Emma immediately, sitting in a chair in the middle of the room. His gaze searched the house. He saw no vampires amid the shadows descending and spreading over the home as night fell. His attention turned back to Emma, her hands were tied behind her back, and her ankles were bound to the front legs of the chair. Her head bent forward, so her thick hair fell to shield her face.

The sight of the blood trickling from her nose rapidly drove him onward. He leapt toward the house only to be knocked back by an invisible wall blocking him from entering the house. Frustration swirled through him, he lifted his hands to press them against the transparent wall, but it was impenetrable. The color permeating his body became such a dark red it was nearly black as the power swirled and pulsed through his body.

On the couch to the right of Emma's chair, Jill sat as rigidly as a board. Her hands were folded in her lap as she stared at the wall across from her. Ethan had seen that dazed look on the faces of anyone who didn't have control over their minds and were now under the command of a vampire.

They'd gotten to her on the bus ride, he realized. She was the reason the others hadn't sensed a different presence in the house. No one else entered the home to take Emma out; Jill had done it on her own. Emma was small and light enough that Jill could carry her to the balcony. The others had sensed no one else within the house, but there had been at least one outside, waiting to take Emma and Jill away.

Ethan's gaze was drawn to the left as Tristan stepped into view.

"There you are," Tristan said in a taunting voice that set Ethan's teeth on edge and caused his upper lip to curl into a sneer.

Tristan's eyes ran over Ethan, and though he tried to hide it, Ethan sensed his steadily increasing fear.

"We've been waiting." Tristan continued as he walked over and rested his hands on the back of the chair. "Haven't we, Emma?"

A snarl escaped Ethan as Tristan's hands settled on her shoulders. The world seemed to lurch out from underneath him as Tristan shook her roughly. Emma's head lulled for a second before she slowly lifted it. Her eyes were dazed and unseeing for a second, but when she finally focused on him she jerked in the chair, and a strangled cry escaped her. Her right eye was nearly swollen shut and already a dark purple color. Her lips were split open, and a line of dried blood ran from her broken nose to her chin. The world around him lost its reddish hue as everything cleared once more. All his rage centered on one thing...murder, and Tristan was the target.

Emma had never seen anything like the man standing in the doorway. She wasn't even entirely certain he could be considered a man anymore. Everything about him reminded her of the pictures she'd seen of Satan in countless paintings and books over the years. A reddish black color covered Ethan's entire body.

Looking at him, she understood where the legend of the devil originated from. Even the whites of his eyes had red veins connecting to the blood red irises. Terror trickled down her spine; a chill slid over her body as her heart seemed to stop beating for a second.

Would he come back from this? He had fought his entire life to keep himself under control, but he'd let it all go. He couldn't lose himself, not now, not because of her. If she was going to die today, she didn't want him to go with her.

"Yes, we have been waiting for you," Tristan continued as he ran his hands over her shoulders and down her arms. Emma shivered and tried to shrink away from his touch, but she couldn't escape his disgusting hands. "This is when the fun can begin. When you can stand there and watch helplessly as I get to enjoy what you stole from me."

"Don't!" Emma snapped when his hands circled her waist and dropped down toward her lap.

Ethan growled and leapt forward only to be thrown back again by the barrier. Tears of helplessness burned her eyes, but she refused to give Tristan the satisfaction of seeing her shed them.

"But then, I did get here first," Tristan taunted.

A shiver of revulsion shook her as Tristan's lips brushed against her ear and his hand slid between her legs. He chuckled as she clamped her legs together, and he squeezed her thigh so roughly the skin broke and blood seeped out.

"I haven't tasted something I want even more though," he whispered in her ear. "You smell delicious."

Emma tried to turn her head away as his hand wrapped around her head and seized her chin. Vomit surged up her throat as his lips pressed against her neck and he inhaled deeply.

"Scrumptious," he said in a tone that made her think he was going to have some fava beans and Chianti when he finished with her.

Brian and Stefan appeared in the doorway behind Ethan; their eyes settled briefly on her before shooting up to Tristan. Brian's breath exploded out of him as Stefan placed a hand against the barrier keeping them from entering the house. Emma tried not to think about the fact they would all be forced to stand by and watch as Tristan did whatever he planned to do to her. Behind them, Isabelle, Aiden, and Ian appeared and spread out across the porch.

"Imagine my surprise when I finally tracked you down, only to discover you were spreading those pretty little thighs," Tristan said.

Emma jerked when he squeezed her thigh again, drawing more blood from her. He ran his hands over her skin, rubbing the blood over her leg before his hand slid down the bottom of her shorts.

"For another *vampire*. I told you, Emma, you are mine, and you will *always* be mine," Tristan murmured.

She stared into his reddened eyes as he lowered his face before her and licked the blood from his fingers.

"What happened to you?" Emma blurted to try and buy herself more time. She suspected her attempt at distraction was useless. "How did you become like this?"

Tristan laughed as his blood dampened fingers stroked over her face. She turned her head away, but he jerked it back and held her chin. He placed his cheek against hers and held her so she had to look at Ethan.

"I caught the fancy of a young girl who admired my unique *ways*," Tristan murmured.

She had admired his insanity, Ethan thought as Brian pressed closer against his side and rested his hand on the barrier. Tristan's twisted mind was incredibly enticing to some of their kind, they would have loved to see what perverted creation Tristan would become, and they were probably proud of this monster standing across from him.

"You're stronger than you think, pureblood," Brian whispered. "You're capable of more than all of us."

Ethan shot him a look, but he didn't respond as his attention was drawn back to Emma and Tristan. His fingers had left streaks of her blood across her face. Frustration filled him. He had no idea how he was going to get to her, how he was going to save her from this monster.

"What happened to her?" Emma croaked in a strangled voice when Tristan's hand wrapped around her throat and his thumb stroked up to caress the underneath of her chin.

"You *are* and always will be my only love, Emma; no one was ever going to come between us. I was the only one who had been within you, and I *will* make you pay for allowing another to take my place, but you are still *mine*. My creator gifted me with immortality and the ability to do as I please. She taught me everything she knew, taught me the joys of our ways. And one day, while she was sleeping, I put a stake through her heart," Tristan said.

Unwillingly she flinched away from him as he pressed a kiss to her cheek. "And just think, she didn't betray me like you have, with this man."

She inhaled sharply as his fingers dug into her chin and he held her so she had to look at Ethan. The fire rose in Ethan's eyes as his gaze burned into hers. She flinched away when Tristan's tongue ran from her chin to her temple, leaving a trail of saliva behind.

"Fuck you!" she spat, unable to keep her temper anymore as exasperation and helplessness tore through her.

Tristan laughed and turned her face to his. "Oh, believe me, Emma; you will be doing that again too."

Nausea and horror twisted within her at the thought. Without thinking about the consequences, she leaned back and spat in his face. His eyes turned red almost instantly, and before she knew what he intended, he raised his arm and backhanded her across the face with enough force the chair toppled over.

Pain exploded through her head, her vision blurred as a roar filled her ears. It felt like a shovel hit her instead of a hand as blood spilled from the corner of her eye. She was still trying to gather her wits when a hand wrapped in her hair. Her skull screamed in protest, strands of hair ripped free as she was lifted off the ground and the chair returned to a seated position. Though it felt like her head would explode, she realized it was Ethan's bellow vibrating through the room.

"It sucks you can't get in here, believe me, I know. I had a door slammed in my face recently too, but this time I'm going to leave it open just so you can watch," Tristan taunted Ethan.

Emma didn't have a chance to react before he sank his fangs into her neck. A scream boiled up in her throat and clogged there as he drained the blood from her body. Her hands and legs strained against the ropes binding her, sweat broke out on her forehead, but though she tried to get away from him, it was useless as the pain made it almost impossible for her to move.

The scent of her blood lured Tristan's cronies from the shadows; she saw the eager gleam in their eyes as they narrowed in on her. Panic tore through her; she somehow managed to get her fingers to spasm as she partially broke free of the paralysis gripping her. A cruel smile curled the lips of the woman she'd hit with the rock as she knelt by her side. Emma's heart raced as she realized her intent, and there was absolutely nothing anyone could do to stop her.

Tristan broke away from her and shoved the woman away. "This one is mine; you can have the other one."

The woman hissed in protest but turned away from her to approach Jill's immobile form. Jill hadn't moved from that spot since Tristan told her to sit and stay as if she were nothing more than a dog. Emma's pulse raced as the woman knelt before Jill and rested her hands on Jill's thighs. Ten more of Tristan's cohorts emerged from the shadows and moved toward her friend.

"No," Emma croaked.

The word was barely out of her mouth before Tristan sank his teeth into her neck again. It was the strangest feeling to go from moving to completely immobile in less than a second, but her body felt as if cement encased it while he fed on her. There was a deafening, almost static sound in her ears due to the rapid pulse of her blood in her ears.

She could barely get her eyes to move toward the doorway. When she did, she couldn't believe what she was seeing. It seemed like there was a clear wall of rubber pushing inward as Ethan put his shoulder down and pushed against whatever blocked the doorway.

Sweat coated his brow as he moved one excruciatingly deliberate inch at a time into the house. What he was doing should be impossible, and she thought perhaps she had taken a few too many blows to the head today, but when she closed her eyes and looked again, he appeared even closer.

He was almost two feet inside the living room when the wall gave. With a roar rivaling the largest of lions, he raced at them in a blur of motion so fast she didn't see him again until he snatched Tristan up by the throat and heaved him across the room. Plaster cracked and shattered as Tristan crashed loudly into the wall. The painting on the wall slid to the ground and broke.

Emma gasped in a breath as her lungs were finally released from their paralysis enough for her to inhale again. Her head lulled down; her chin bumped against her chest as weakness crept through her now mobile body. Her heart felt like lead in her chest as it labored to pump what blood remained through her system.

Ethan grabbed the ropes binding Emma's wrist to the chair and shredded them before seizing the ropes around her ankles. Her limp body slumped to the side, but he caught her before she fell to the ground. He spun her around and hunched protectively over her as Tristan launched himself at them.

A grunt escaped him as something sliced down his shoulder and ripped open his flesh. He realized he'd been stabbed when he felt the air blowing against his exposed skin and the blood spilling down his back.

"Ethan!" Isabelle screamed from the doorway.

He didn't bother to look at her though as he kept Emma pressed against his chest with one arm and swung back at Tristan with the other. The knife, still embedded in his shoulder, hindered his movement but he was still faster than Tristan and managed to catch him across the cheek. Blood spilled as he sliced the right side of Tristan's face open from ear to chin with his claws. The blow exposed the white of his cheekbone and his lower teeth.

Shifting Emma, he bent and placed her carefully on the floor before turning to face Tristan as he came back at him with five of his companions. Reaching back, he wrapped his hand around the handle of the knife and tore it free of the muscle. Fresh blood spilled free, but he paid it no mind as he shoved Tristan back and smashed his hand into the chest of another vampire. Bone gave way beneath the crushing impact as he drove his fist straight into the man's chest cavity. His hand wrapped around the man's beating heart, a victorious smile curving his mouth as the man's eyes widened in horror a second before Ethan tore the heart from his chest and crushed it in his hand.

One of the other vampires fell back, but the other three launched at him while Tristan made a move to get around him toward Emma. Thrusting upward, Ethan's lips pulled back to reveal his teeth as he drove the blade of the knife to the hilt into the sternum of one of his attackers. The man's eyes bulged, his hands clawed at the offending weapon as he staggered back. Ethan seized another man by the throat, lifted him, and threw him into two vampires. Darting to the side, he grabbed Tristan's arm and flung him back before he could reach Emma. Someone grabbed his arm. Ethan jerked it free and spun to face his attacker. His fist caved in the right side of the man's face, shattering his teeth and nose.

Behind him, Emma was struggling to her feet, but he could

hear the sluggish, erratic beat of her heart. If there was any chance she was going to survive, he had to get her out of here, *now*. The rage within him continued to grow as two more vampires came at him. A bellow ripped from him as he tore the throat from one and thrust his fist into the stomach of the other one. He was outnumbered, but his concern for Emma, his fury, and the power surging through him made him realize it didn't matter. He could and *would* kill every single vampire in this house.

Two of them fell back when he drove his fist into the chest of another and tore out his heart. The woman who knelt by Emma's side before turning her attention to Jill fled from the room and down the hallway.

"Mine!" Brian declared and disappeared from the doorway in pursuit of the woman.

Ethan leapt forward as Tristan spun away; he grabbed him by the collar of his shirt and jerked him back before swinging an uppercut at another man who lunged at him. The man's head shot back; blood spilled down his chin as his fangs were driven into his lower lip.

Claws raked over his side, slashing his skin open to the ribs as Tristan spun on him. Ethan barely felt it though as he pulled Tristan toward him and buried his fangs into his neck. He didn't taste the blood spilling into his mouth, didn't swallow it as he tore a chunk of flesh from Tristan's throat and spat it out. Grabbing Tristan's head with both hands, he jerked it brutally to the side. A resounding crack echoed through the room and scared another vampire into fleeing down the hall.

Emma tried once more to get to her feet, but though she willed them to move, they had stopped listening to her. It was getting to the point she could barely feel them anymore. She thought she should be terrified. Instead, she found herself oddly detached from her body and the weakness creeping through it. She wanted desperately to help Ethan, to fight with him, but there was nothing she could do as her body refused the commands of her mind.

She was pretty sure she was dying, it certainly felt that way as her heart did a strange stuttering thing again. Before her, Ethan moved to the side and grabbed Tristan. She'd never seen anything like the bloodbath going on in the room, but she still felt no fear of Ethan as he crushed another heart in his hand. A cry of alarm lodged in her throat when Tristan sliced Ethan's side open, tearing his clothing and skin apart.

"No," she managed to croak when she spotted Ethan's ribs beneath the blood oozing from the lethal looking wounds.

She'd never seen such ruthlessness before, never expected to see it in her life, and yet the sight of the blood and body parts splattered around the room and covering Ethan, didn't make her stomach turn. She was too concerned about the number of vampires still coming at him and the blood seeping out to cover his shirt and jeans.

Emma tried to lift her fingers, but they were as numb as the rest of her. Ethan shoved Tristan away from him and grabbed the arm of another vampire. Blood and bone erupted from the man's elbow as Ethan snapped it in half. Emma winced as the man let out a howl loud enough to rival an ambulance siren. Ethan shoved the man away and grabbed another one. Her eyes felt heavier, she could barely keep them open, but she had to know Ethan would survive this.

Tristan held his hand against his mutilated throat as he stumbled back and turned to try and make an escape. Ethan grabbed the man's arm that he'd broken, lifted him up, and threw him at Tristan. He flew into Tristan's back, driving Tristan to his knees as Ethan hit him with the force of a battering ram. She'd known Ethan was powerful, but she doubted he realized he'd had this much power within him.

Please come back after this, she pleaded silently.

Ethan jumped onto the man he'd thrown and placed his foot on the back of his head. He drove it into the floor and twisted his toe into it, caving in the front of the man's skull. Grabbing Tristan, he seized his head with both hands. Tristan howled, his hands flailed at him as skin and bone gave way. Ethan didn't stop as he continued to turn Tristan's head completely around before ripping it from his body.

His shoulders heaved, bloodlust pulsed through him, and he tossed the head away as if it were no more than a bowling ball. He lifted his head to take in the remaining three vampires in the room. They stared at him in disbelief and horror before turning and fleeing down the hall. Though all he wanted was to tear into something else, to feel more life slipping away in his bare hands, he didn't bother following them; they wouldn't get past the others—especially not Brian.

There was something far more important than blood and death right now. He spun away and fled back to Emma's side. Her eyes were mere slits as she watched him approach, her heart had slowed to an alarming rate, and he knew there was almost no time left for her. He ran into the kitchen and grabbed a towel and knife from it. Wetting the towel, he wiped away the blood covering his forearm as he returned to her side. His knees hit the ground beside her; her body felt almost lifeless, her head flopped against his chest as he gathered her in his arms.

The minute his arms wrapped around her, he felt more of his murderous impulses fading away as his body reeled back in the power and brutality it just unleashed. It was impossible to feel the urge to kill when all he cared about now was saving her.

"Emma?" Jill croaked from behind him.

Ethan didn't look back at the girl, but he could feel her steady approach. The mind control she'd been under broke when whoever had taken possession of her mind was killed. Just as the barrier preventing the others from entering the house fell.

"What happened?" Jill whispered.

"Stay back," Isabelle commanded.

"But what happened?" Jill whimpered.

"We'll explain later," Isabelle promised. "But you have to stay back."

Emma's eyes were only slits and dull as they came up to his. "I love you," she whispered.

"You're going to be fine," he told her, even if he wasn't so sure.

Panic tore through him as he tilted her head back and drew the knife deftly across his wrist. He didn't feel the pain of the blade as his blood poured forth. It was far more blood than his bite would provide, blood she desperately needed. Her eyes fell on his wrist as he held it up to her.

"Do it," she breathed before her eyes drifted closed.

"Drink, Emma," he pleaded as he pressed his wrist to her mouth. "Please." He could feel his blood seeping into her body, but there was no response from her. His lips dropped to her head; he cradled her closer as terror tore through him. "Drink, baby."

She remained unmoving in his arms, her head against his shoulder. The strange red filling his body faded away as his blood slipped into her. He hated to touch her while covered in the blood of the massacre he just unleashed, but he couldn't let her go. Tears burned his eyes as he kissed her forehead and pressed her closer against his chest.

"I can't lose you," he moaned.

A footstep on his right drew his attention to Isabelle as she knelt by his side. Her eyes were troubled as she stared at Emma. "Ethan—"

"She's going to be fine," he growled.

Stefan rested his hands on Isabelle's shoulders and pulled her away. "Don't," she started to protest.

"Stay away," Stefan warned. He pushed her behind him and placed his body in between them.

Ethan turned his attention away from them as he focused everything on willing Emma to live, willing her to stay with him. Emma's closed eyes suddenly flickered up to him, her body stiffened, her fingers jerked on the floor before going completely still as her heart stopped. He felt like a mirror dropped on the ground as everything within him fractured and fell apart. The only thing left of him was a black hole sucking out everything he was. There was no soul, no humanity, as he stared into her unseeing eyes.

And then her heart kicked violently against her ribs, she gasped in a breath as suffering twisted her face and a harsh cry escaped her. Her fingers clenched, her teeth clamped involuntarily down on his arm as her body jerked in his embrace. Though he hated her suffering, and would do anything to take it from her, he was also filled with ecstasy as her heart pounded out a far steadier beat than before. Alive, she was *alive,* and she was going to stay that way.

He rocked her as more spasms racked her body, and her fingernails tore into his skin. Her teeth finally unclamped from his wrist, and he pulled it away from her as the transformation continued within her body. Small mewls escaped her; tears spilled down her cheeks as her feet kicked spastically against the floor.

"I'm sorry, but it will be okay," he whispered in her ear. "This is the worst part."

Emma felt as if she were drowning in agony. Her skin was as raw as when she'd gotten a second-degree sunburn while visiting Florida when she was thirteen. She'd been blistered everywhere her bathing suit didn't cover, but she'd give anything for that sunburn now. Then there had been aloe to relieve the pain, and she'd known her discomfort would eventually ease. Right now, it felt as if this would never stop.

She tried to keep her eyes on Ethan, tried to remind herself why she was doing this, but everything around her blurred. She swore someone was using a jackhammer against the inside of her skull as her head felt like it was going to explode. Her now beating heart felt like it was twisting and changing within her ribcage as if it were tearing free of her arteries and becoming something else. A scream built within her, but she was unable to unclench her teeth to release it.

Her body jerked with so much force a bone in her foot broke with a loud crack when it slammed against the floor. Ethan had never felt so helpless in his life, but he had no idea what to do to make it any better.

"It won't last much longer, and she will get through it," Stefan assured him as he knelt by Ethan's side.

Brian, Ian, and Aiden appeared in the doorway of the house. Blood streaked their faces and splattered their clothes, but they appeared unharmed as they stepped over two of the bodies lying on the floor. Jill had retreated to the couch; tears streamed down her face as she took in the carnage around her. He wanted to hate the girl, but he knew none of this was her fault, and she looked completely heartbroken as she gazed helplessly at Emma.

Brian bent down, seized Tristan's hair, and lifted his head from the floor. His eyebrow rose as he stared at the bulging eyes and twisted mouth. "We have to get this cleaned up."

Aiden looked around the house. "I don't think there is *any* way to clean this up."

Ethan glanced at the red-stained walls, furniture, and carpet; there was little of the original color to be found beneath the blood splattered everywhere. It looked like a macabre funhouse.

"Burn it," he said flatly and turned away when Emma whimpered and dug into his arm with her nails again.

"That will make this job a lot easier," Brian said and dropped Tristan's head dismissively back on the floor. It landed with a dull thud, but Ethan was the only one who heard as Brian was already walking away from it.

Emma's back arched off the ground; her teeth clenched together as the muscles in her throat and jaw stood out. Sweat beaded across her forehead and ran down her face; her face became florid as a scream tore from her throat. Ethan held her in a way that ensured she wouldn't injure herself when her body collapsed again. She went completely still, but her heart continued to beat a solid rhythm in her chest.

"The worst is over," Stefan said. "We have to get her out of here, now."

Ethan was careful with Emma's broken foot, a foot that would most likely heal by the time she woke again as he gathered her into his arms and lifted her. Her head fell against his shoulder; her glazed eyes fluttered open to meet his before drifting closed again. He had to get her somewhere safe, somewhere not covered in blood and remains. Moving as swiftly as possible, he fled the house and left the others behind to deal with the cleanup.

CHAPTER TWENTY-SEVEN

Emma didn't move as she stared around the room, a room far brighter and clearer than she recalled it ever being. A room which held scents she never would have noticed before. The sweet smell of hibiscus was almost overwhelming as it drifted in through the open doors. There was a faint coppery scent she eventually identified as blood, and the enticing aroma of sex beneath it all.

It was all so amazing and overwhelming; she could barely breathe. There was so much to this world she'd never realized before, but she could see, hear, and smell it all now. It was the strangest gift she'd ever been given, and it was a gift that was hers, forever. Her gaze riveted on the colorful lamp by the bedside. She never imagined there were so many different shades of red, blue, and green in the world. She marveled at all of them.

"You're awake."

"I'm awake," she murmured in response to Ethan's words from behind her.

"How do you feel?"

She frowned as she contemplated the answer. "Different. *Alive*," she breathed. "If that makes any sense, considering I died."

His hand on her arm pulled her attention away from the lamp. She rolled over and smiled at him. He sat in the chair beside the bed, leaning toward her with his elbows on his knees. The awful, reddish black color had vanished from him; the blood covering him after the massacre was washed from his body.

There were lines around his eyes and mouth that hadn't been there yesterday. Stubble lined his jaw; his bloodshot eyes made it seem like he hadn't slept in a week but they were back to their normal green hue. She realized now that, though his eyes were mostly emerald in color, there were also flecks of forest green with a little bit of a lime color blended in.

Ethan rose from the chair and sat on the bed beside her when she pushed herself into a seated position. The swelling was already gone from her eyes and nose, her nose had realigned, and there was only a shadow of a bruise beneath her right eye. She still looked exhausted and a little battered, but she was moving, talking, *breathing* as she sat before him. He brushed her thick hair over her shoulder, but Tristan's bite marks had vanished during the change.

"Is Jill okay?" she asked anxiously.

"She's fine," he assured her as his thumb stroked over her cheek.

The love radiating from his eyes was almost more than she could stand as she leaned closer to him. He smelled of the ocean and allspice, or maybe it was cinnamon? She couldn't quite place the scent, but she now recognized it as power, even more power than either of them ever realized he possessed.

"What happened? *How* did it happen?" she asked.

"Jill must have been grabbed on the bus by Tristan or one of his helpers. When they died, whatever hold they had over her was broken. She doesn't remember anything that happened."

"Coming out of her daze, to *that* house, must have been a shock to her," she muttered.

"I imagine it was," he said as he took her hand.

The sensation of his skin sliding over hers caused her to blink in surprise. He'd always been able to warm her and give her a thrill before, but now it made her skin come alive in ways she'd never known possible. It felt like she had ten thousand more nerve endings in her body than before, and *every* one of them was begging for more from him.

"Amazing," she breathed. The smile he gave her eased some of the stress from his face. Finally seeing him relax a little was even better than the feel of his skin against hers. She leaned toward him, becoming more aroused as her breasts brushed against his chest. "This is something I don't think I'll ever get used to."

He smiled as he continued to run his fingers through her hair. "It's one of many new things you'll experience."

"And I'm looking forward to every one of them," she murmured. "Ethan, what happened at the house, what you looked like, has it ever happened before? Does that happen to vampires?"

He shook his head as his hand stilled on her hair. "It's never happened to me before, but I know it would happen again if you're threatened. It won't happen to you though."

"Because I wasn't born into this?"

"Yes."

She couldn't get enough of the feel of him as she ran her hands over his arms. "I'm worried about you."

"Don't be," he said as he leaned forward to kiss her. "I was in control of myself in there, I'm okay with everything that happened in the house, and I would do it all over again. None of us have ever seen anything like it before though. Stefan has always said no one knows what a pureblood might be capable of doing."

"Like walking into a house you weren't first invited into."

"Like that," he said with a smile. "But there's *nothing* I wouldn't do for you."

She lifted his hand and kissed his knuckles. "I know," she whispered. "What is going to happen with the house? With all of those bodies?"

"Brian, Aiden, and Ian disposed of the bodies and set the house on fire. There was no hiding what happened in there."

"No kidding," she muttered. "How is your side?"

He pulled away from her and lifted his shirt to reveal the smooth, unblemished skin beneath. "All healed."

Emma stared at him in disbelief as he lowered his shirt back into place. "And I'll be able to do something like that now?"

"Not as quickly, but yes. Your eye is already better; your nose is healed, the bite marks Tristan left on you are gone, and I bet the broken bone in your foot has set, or it will as soon as you feed."

"Feed," she whispered and poked at the tips of her canines with her tongue. Her hand flew to her mouth when they lengthened at her prodding. "Oh."

He smiled as he took her hand. "It's okay; it's something you'll learn to control, given time. I'll teach you, and I'll help you get through it all. You must feed though, Emma, you don't ever have to feed on a human or a blood bag, but you must feed from me on a regular basis if you're going to stay in control. We also have to complete the bond between us."

Involuntarily, she felt her gaze slide to his neck. Her teeth tingled; saliva filled her mouth as she saw the pulse of blood through his veins. "I can hear your heartbeat," she whispered.

"I'm told you will get used to that too, over time. I imagine it will all be overwhelming at first, but my parents adapted, Stefan and Brian adapted, and somehow so did The Stooges." Emma nodded, but she found it disconcerting that with every beat of his heart, her hunger rose. She was growing increasingly consumed by the craving to feed from him. "Come here."

He wrapped his hand around the back of her neck and pulled her close. His breath was warm against her lips as his mouth moved over hers and his tongue entwined with hers. She became so lost in him she almost forgot the thirst growing within her until he moved her head to his neck.

The potent scent of his blood hit her, causing her fangs to elongate instantly. She could feel his excitement in the quickening of his breath and the hands pressing against her back. Fear at the thought of hurting him slithered through her and caused her to hesitate.

"You have to do this if we're going to complete the bond," he urged. "And we have to do that, Emma. We *have* to."

She knew the words were true; she could feel the necessity of them in her soul. Her entire being was begging her to join with him. Instinct took over, and Emma found she *knew* what to do. She took a deep breath before sinking her newfound fangs into his vein. Happiness slid through her as his warm blood filled her mouth and immediately eased the ache growing within her.

It was more than her hunger his blood fulfilled; it was also completing the bond she hadn't realized she was missing while human. She could almost feel the steel bands of their growing bond wrapping around them to join them for life. No, it was joining them for eternity, she realized as her fingers dug into his back.

Thoughts filled her mind, *his* thoughts. She was swept up in the love radiating from him as his thoughts urged her to bite deeper, and she obeyed. Emma felt his breath on her shoulder seconds before his fangs sank into her flesh. A groan of contentment escaped her as he took her blood. A sense of coming home encompassed her, and she knew joining with this man was the best decision of her life.

Ethan wrapped his arm around her waist and pulled her into his lap as another desire surged to life within him. Shoving his boxers down, he freed his swollen cock. The nightgown she wore had bunched around her thighs; he hastily pushed it upward and settled her onto him. He was pleased to find her already wet with wanting for him as he rubbed his cock teasingly against her opening. She let him know her disapproval of his teasing by biting deeper and blasting her need into his mind.

He chuckled at her impatience and slid himself into her. He was whole now; it was the only thought he had as he buried himself within her. Her bliss slammed into him when she wrapped her legs around his waist and clung to him as she rode up and down.

Ethan withdrew from her shoulder and licked away the last drops of blood on her flesh. Her fangs retracted from his neck; her eyes were smoky and dazed as they met his. Needing to see and feel all of her, he tugged the nightgown the rest of the way up her body and tossed it aside.

A seductive smile curled her lips as she tugged his shirt over his head. Her fingers slid over his chest as she marveled over his chiseled masculine beauty. Bending her head, she nipped at his skin, drawing blood as she moved over his body. She relished in the sweet and salty taste of his skin mixed with the alluring taste of his blood.

Ethan's hands curled into her hair. Her mouth continued its trail of pleasure and pain across his chest. His head fell back as her body continued to move smoothly up and down his throbbing dick. He kept his hands firmly in her back when she retracted her fangs and lifted her head to kiss him. The taste of his blood on her lips only pushed him to higher and higher levels as the bond between them swelled and solidified. The monster within him, the one struggling for years to break free, wasn't completely caged, but it was tamed and subdued by the woman within his arms. He'd never thought such a thing could happen in his life, but she was the greatest gift he'd ever been given, and she was *his*.

Ethan gave himself over to the pleasure engulfing him as she rode them both to completion.

CHAPTER TWENTY-EIGHT

"I'M SO SORRY, EMMA," Jill said for about the hundredth time over the past couple of weeks.

"Jill, stop apologizing, it's not your fault. I'm sorry I got you into this whole mess."

"But I nearly got both of my best friends killed."

"And yourself in the process, don't forget that," Mandy said as she sat on the bed. "It wasn't your fault; let it go before *I* kill you. I think both of you have apologized enough."

Emma laughed as she dropped her last pair of shorts into the suitcase and pulled the zipper shut.

"Do you think you'll get married?" Jill inquired.

"I'm sure it would make my parents happy if we did," Emma said. "But we're already more linked than any marriage license could make us."

"It would be a fun party though."

"Yeah it would," Emma agreed.

"What are you going to tell your parents?" Mandy inquired.

"For now, only that I met the man of my dreams while on vacation. I'm sure that will go over about as well as a lead balloon, and they'll probably think I'm crazy, but they have to meet Ethan. It will still be a few years before they become curious about anything. I'll have to decide then if I'm going to tell them the truth or if it would be best to change their memories. I don't think I could play with my parents' minds in such a way, but I can't inadvertently place them in danger either. It's bad enough you two were almost killed because of this, and you still could be one day."

"No, we won't. No one is ever going to know we have this knowledge," Mandy assured her. "I'd like to keep my head, and you know we would never do anything to put you at risk."

"I know," Emma said, but she was still worried about them.

"Don't worry about your parents now. You have a few years to decide."

"You're right," she agreed. She wasn't ready to let the reality of those thoughts intrude on the happiness she'd just found right now anyway.

"I can't believe our vacation is already over," Jill moaned.

"Neither can I," Mandy said.

Emma dropped her suitcase on the ground and sat on the bed beside Mandy. "It's going to be so strange not to be with you guys every day."

"We'll see each other all the time," Jill said cheerfully.

Emma hoped Jill was right, but she also knew how life could go. Though, now that she would be living in Oregon, they would at least all be on the same coast.

"Are you nervous about meeting the rest of his family?" Mandy asked.

"Terrified," she admitted. "It's going to take me forever to learn all their names. I just hope they like me."

"Well it's usually normal to meet the family before forming an eternal bond with someone, but you were never much for normal," Jill said. "And they'll love you."

Emma laughed as she leaned against Jill's side and savored in the warmth of her friend. She could hear the steady beat of Jill's heart, but it didn't spark her hunger. Over the last two weeks, she'd grown accustomed to the flow of human's blood and the enticing aroma they emitted. It didn't mean they didn't tempt her still, but Ethan kept her fed well enough she could keep it under control.

She was anxious about being on a plane, enclosed with so many people around her, but Ethan assured her she would get through it. To prepare, they'd gone into crowded areas over the past week to help her adjust to the influx of people. Last night she was able to stay in a packed bar all night, and she'd been fine. Ethan made sure she fed well this morning, and she was still rather stuffed.

"Are you ready?" Ethan asked.

She was so lost in her thoughts, she hadn't heard him approach, something that hadn't happened since the change. She knew where he was all the time now, could sense him as easily as she sensed her fingertips. His mind brushed against hers constantly. The open stream of consciousness now connecting them was something she was getting used to, but it was so comforting and intense, she relished in the security and love enveloping her because of it.

"We are." Emma rose and grabbed her suitcase from the floor. She didn't make it to the door before Ethan took it from her. He kissed her cheek and took a step away.

She turned back to her friends as they gathered their bags and walked over to join her. Though they'd taken most of their things over to the other house, they'd still had a few things in Mandy's grandparents' house they'd gathered before leaving. All the damage to both homes was repaired over the past couple of weeks by some handymen who would never remember they'd even been to either house.

She wasn't looking forward to separating from her friends, but at least they would all be flying into Atlanta together. From there their journey together would end. She and Ethan would continue to New York to spend a couple of weeks with her family before going to meet his.

Mandy was returning home to Boston until it was time for her to leave for Stanford, and Jill would return to San Francisco. Ethan's family planned to go back to Oregon and Brian had left the day after Tristan was killed. Even though Brian left without saying goodbye, Emma had a feeling he would be popping into their lives again.

Emma followed Ethan to the front door and paused to take in the home where she'd started this incredible journey. Her eyes lingered on the spot where she and Ethan first made love. There were some bad memories here, but most of them were good, and she wouldn't have changed one thing about this trip.

What started as a simple, fun-filled vacation had brought so many changes to her life and given her the greatest gift ever in Ethan's love. She didn't like leaving the place where it all started, but she was looking forward to starting the next journey of their lives together.

She didn't look back as Mandy closed and locked the door.

EPILOGUE

Three months later,

Emma laughed as Ethan spun her in a circle around the newly assembled dance floor. The flowing skirt of her wedding dress billowed around her before he pulled her back against his chest. A radiant smile lit his face and caused his eyes to twinkle in a way that warmed and melted her heart. She rested her hand against his chest and leaned closer to him as the music switched from upbeat to slow.

She inhaled his enticing scent as he slid his arms around her waist. Emma turned her head to take in the small crowd gathered around them. It had taken her a good week to get the names of all of Ethan's siblings straight, but they had all welcomed her with open arms. Their exuberance was a little overwhelming at first, but they'd also made her feel at home in a world that was still a bit strange to her.

She glanced over as Sera and Liam danced into view. It was amazing how much Ethan looked like his father and just how young his parents appeared. Thanks to Stefan's abilities, her parents saw Ethan's like a middle-aged couple.

Even still, her parents had thought she was marrying into some cult when they first saw all the homes on the property. After meeting everyone though, they decided Ethan's family weren't religious fanatics, doomsday preppers, or trying to kidnap her.

"Can I step in?"

Emma broke into a radiant smile as Ethan handed her over to her father and stepped away. She watched her husband as he weaved his way through the small crowd to where Ian and Mandy stood next to the dance floor. Mandy wore a pretty, yellow bridesmaid dress that emphasized her dark coloring and brought out her brown eyes. She sipped on a drink as she watched the dancing.

It was the first time Mandy was able to visit them, but Emma spoke to her every day through Skype or texting. Plus, she'd made it down to visit Mandy a couple of times when she was too swamped with classes and studying to travel.

Emma was also fortunate enough to have found a job at the historical society in town. The pay wasn't much, but she loved diving into the old documents, homes, and events they worked to preserve. Even if she didn't like lying to her family, and her job wouldn't last forever, she was the happiest she'd ever been in her life.

Ethan sipped at his champagne and smiled as he watched Emma and her father dance around the floor he'd built with Ian and Aiden last week. "It is beautiful up here," Mandy said.

"It is," Ethan agreed as he turned away to look over the lake.

The setting sun shimmered across the surface of the water and reflected the oranges and reds of the changing leaves in the trees surrounding it. The gazebo he'd built was ten feet away from the shore, and they were married beneath it. This place was his home, and by the middle of next month, the house they were building for him and Emma would be completed. Stefan and Isabelle's new home was being built next to theirs; Aiden and Ian were thrilled to finally have the house they built last year to themselves, even if they weren't there for most of the year.

"So are you planning to have the same kind of brood as your parents?" Jack asked as he stopped before them.

"Not right away," Ethan told him. "And I think we'd both be okay with only two or three."

"Thank God, I'm tired of building houses," Jack told him.

Mandy laughed and turned back to her conversation with Ian. His family had been a little hesitant about the fact they'd allowed Mandy and Jill to keep their memories, but as the months slipped by, and nothing went wrong, they accepted the decision. They also liked Jill, a lot, especially The Stooges as she fit in well with their carefree and party going demeanor. She'd been to visit numerous times since they'd returned home.

His focus returned to Emma. She looked stunning in her off the shoulder, white dress, with that smile on her face and a vibrant light shimmering in her eyes. Love warmed his heart, and he couldn't tear his gaze away from her as she moved elegantly around the floor with her father.

Across the way, he spotted Jill in her bridesmaid dress with Mike and Doug. They were gathered around the bar set up on the patio, talking with each other as they waited for the bartender to refill their drinks. His younger siblings squealed as they darted in and out of the dancing people. David yelled at them to stop running, but they'd already disappeared around the side of the house toward the woods.

"It was a beautiful ceremony." Ethan turned at the sound of his mother's voice and smiled at her. Tears shimmered in her eyes when she hugged him. "You're so grown."

"We'll still be here, mom. Your birds keep returning to the nest," he told her.

She laughed and stepped away from him. "That's just fine by me, but you're all starting to find your way, and it's wonderful."

He smiled at her and turned away as his father approached. "Congratulations, son," he said as he shook Ethan's hand. "She's a great addition to the family."

"She is," Ethan agreed as he turned back to where Emma and her father were stepping away from each other. "Now, if you don't mind, I'm going to reclaim my bride."

"Ugh, I give them three more months before they're adding onto this already *extremely* extended family," Jack muttered.

Ethan laughed, but he wasn't about to disagree with Jack as he walked away to reclaim his bride. She grinned up at him and returned eagerly to his arms. Tilting her chin up, he kissed her tenderly as the comfort she always gave to him stole through his soul. Her love had helped tame the savage monster residing within him his whole life and brought him a peace he'd never dreamed of experiencing. She'd given him a gift he'd never expected to receive, and because of that, he would spend an eternity showing her how loved and cherished she was.

Read on for a sneak peek from *Enraptured,* Book 4 in the series. Or purchase now and continue reading: brendakdavies.com/Enwb

Visit the Erica Stevens/Brenda K. Davies Book Club on Facebook for exclusive giveaways and all

things book related. Come join the fun:
brendakdavies.com/ESBKDBookClub

Stay in touch on updates and new releases from the author by joining the mailing list!
Mailing list for Brenda K. Davies Updates:
brendakdavies.com/ESBKDNews

SNEAK PEEK

ENRAPTURED, VAMPIRE AWAKENINGS BOOK 4

Ian opened his eyes and blinked against the sun filtering through the blinds. He glanced at the woman lying next to him in the bed; her blond hair splayed out across the pillow tickled his arm. He frowned as he searched his mind for her name, but his memory failed him. That wasn't unusual, he couldn't recall most of the women before her. It didn't matter anyway, she'd known what she was in for when she left the bar with him last night. He never made promises he couldn't keep.

Throwing the blankets aside, he swung his feet to the floor and ran a hand through his disheveled hair before glancing back at her again. Even though he couldn't recall her name, he wasn't so callous he would wake her up and kick her out of his room, no matter how much he wanted to do just that. She'd given him what he needed most; now she'd become an insignificant detail taking up space in his bedroom.

Over the years, the women he'd slept with had all blurred together to become an endless one-night stand he couldn't escape. At the reminder of the unnatural appetite plaguing him since reaching maturity, Ian shoved himself to his feet. He'd always enjoyed women, had made no secret about that, but since reaching the point where he no longer aged, that enjoyment had turned into something more, something almost uncontrollable.

His need for a woman, and sometimes more than one woman at a time in his bed, had increased. He could barely go more than two days without sex, and when he did he felt like tearing his skin off. It was a bonus to be able to feed off of the women he had sex with, but the blood alone wasn't what drove him to seek out a new companion every night. He didn't know what it was inside of him now, what drove him from woman to woman, but it was relentless and the only thing that satisfied his inner beast was sex. It was a good thing he couldn't get STD's, though he still used condoms to avoid an unwanted pregnancy. The last thing he needed was to explain to a woman he barely knew that her child would be part vampire.

Gathering his clothes, he glanced at the woman again before exiting his room and walking down the hall to the bathroom. Laughter drifted up from below; he smiled when the thudding sound of a football hitting open palms drifted to him from outside. Showering quickly, he toweled off before tugging on his clothes, brushing his teeth, and returning to his room.

The woman was finally awake, laying in wait on his bed. Her arm stretched over her head. A lazy, satisfied smile curved her lips when he entered the room. Her eyes slid over him, before she patted the empty space he'd vacated. "I'd thought we could go for round two," she purred.

"Told you, one night."

"We can pretend it's a *really* long night." She let the blanket fall back to expose her ample breasts and rounded hips. What had been so appealing last night made his upper lip curl in disgust now.

"I don't pretend." He tossed his towel into the hamper in

the corner. He didn't like being short with her, but he made it clear to every woman who came to his bed there would only be one night. He didn't intend to lead anyone on, or get anyone's hopes up by pretending there could be more. It irritated him when they tried to break clearly established boundaries or believed they could somehow change him.

No one would change him, not unless he somehow stumbled across his mate, and he wasn't sure that would even be enough to change his ways. He'd seen the intensity of the bond between his parents and his siblings with their mates, but his internal insatiable hunger tore fiercely at him when it kicked in. He'd never been able to maintain a monogamous relationship before. He'd given up trying in high school when he'd broken his first heart and realized he would break many more if he continued to try to be a one woman man, especially since none of those women had been the one he was meant to spend eternity with. He'd never expected to walk this path in life, never thought he'd bounce from one woman to another this way, but then the future was a complete unknown, even to immortals like himself.

Her fingers slid over her hip and up toward her breast. "I'm sure this once..."

"No. I'm sorry, but it's time for you to go." Bending, he gathered her discarded clothes and handed them to her. "I've got things to do."

Her smile slipped away, her thin lips pressed into a pout that set his teeth on edge. "Didn't you have fun?"

"I did, but it's over." Turning on his heel, he walked over to the door and looked back at her. "You don't have to bother to lock the door on your way out."

Her face fell as she tugged her shirt over her head. Ian hurried down the hall of the frat house he'd been living in since freshman year. The distinct sounds of music, video games, and sex could be heard from the rooms he passed as he made his way toward the front door. The familiar noises and smells of alcohol, sweat, and clean linen Glade air fresheners had become home to him over the past four years. It could be a jungle, sometimes the privacy was nil, but he was accustomed to that after growing up surrounded by fifteen other people. He'd miss this large house and the friends he'd made here when he graduated in a couple of months.

Pounding down the stairs, he walked through the main living room toward the front door. A few guys were picking up the trash from the party last night. A party he'd missed due to his overwhelming need for female companionship. After four years, and his rabid increase in pickups this year, the pickings had become rather slim at the frat house parties. Last night must have been relatively calm as there weren't as many discarded plastic cups lying around as usual.

"Hey Ian," a couple of the guys greeted him.

"Hey, fun night?" he inquired.

"Always," one of them replied with a laugh.

He wasn't so sure about that, but he didn't argue with the kid. Opening the front door, he walked across the porch and down the steps. He walked around the house toward the two guys tossing the football in the backyard. He'd just rounded the corner when the ball flew at him with a ferocity most would have considered hard and fast. The kind of throw that would have knocked a human back a step.

Ian faked a grunt as he caught the ball against his stomach. "Nice throw," he said before tossing the ball back to his friend Milo.

"Nice catch." Milo threw the ball to their friend Oscar. Milo and Oscar were the other members of the frat who had been on the football team with him. The team hadn't made it far into the playoffs this year, or any other year, but he'd had a great time playing with these guys, and they'd become his best friends during his time here. They didn't know he was a vampire, but they knew everything else about him. They'd been good friends, but he doubted he'd see much of them again after graduation. The whole not aging thing tended to put a damper on extended relationships with humans.

"We going out again tonight?" Oscar asked as he passed the ball to Milo.

"Not staying in," Milo replied with a laugh.

Ian caught the ball and tossed it away again. The door to the house opened and closed. Ian leaned back to watch the woman he'd been with last night walk down the sidewalk and make a right at the corner. He really wished he could remember her name; he wouldn't feel like such an ass about what had passed between them if he could. He didn't think of himself as a bad guy. He knew how he was behaving wasn't entirely sane or normal, but he couldn't stop himself.

He didn't know how to stop, and whenever he tried, the clawing sensation in his chest and gut made it nearly impossible to think, let alone control himself. Lack of control in a vampire could spell death for any human within reach if he were to slip even a little bit. Control was imperative and not something he'd given much thought about, until last year when his life had abruptly changed.

Milo glanced back at the girl and shook his head. "I don't know how you do it man."

"The ladies love me," Ian replied with a laugh. "It must be my good looks, something you wouldn't know anything about."

Milo flipped him the finger and threw the ball at him in a perfect spiral. Ian leapt up to catch the ball as Milo charged across the ground at him. Short and spry, Milo had been difficult to catch while playing quarterback, but he'd never been able to tackle anyone. He lowered his shoulder and plowed into

Ian; they both knew Milo would never be able to take him down, but Ian faked being knocked off balance before Milo ran away again.

"Asshole!" Milo jogged backwards with his hands in the air for the ball.

Ian threw the ball back to him. Some of the other guys from the frat began to emerge, and a pickup game of two-hand touch started to unfold. Someone broke out the beer, laughter drifted through the air to mix with the smell of hamburgers and hot dogs cooking on the grill. Girlfriends gathered on the sidelines to cheer on their boyfriends as people from neighboring houses were drawn outside by the loud noise and the luring smell of the cooking food.

During these times, when he'd recently satisfied his more carnal urges and was back amongst his friends, he could almost remember what life had been like before he'd stopped aging. Almost remember the laughter and carefree moments that had made up most of his days. Everything had been so easy then. He'd been an athlete, he'd done well in school, he'd had a set plan for after graduation, and he had a loving family. Now, things were completely different.

He longed for his old life back, to be able to sleep undisturbed through the night without being plagued with the urge for sex. Even now as he joked with his friends, he could feel the urge building within him to go on the prowl for the next warm, willing body.

He refused to acknowledge this might be what the rest of his life was like. He might go completely insane if he had to face this every day. Never had he believed the idea of endless women and sex would become boring and tiresome, but it had started to border on complete monotony a few months ago. The only problem was there was no end in sight, not for him.

~

Paige sat in the hotel bedroom, idly flipping through the channels on the TV as she stared at the changing screens. The daytime was always the worst for her. She had no idea what to do with herself during certain times of the day. She'd already been to the gym and worked out for an hour, already spent another hour having a sparring match with Nabel. Her muscles were still sore from their session. He hadn't taken it easy on her, and she didn't want him to.

The daylight hours weren't so bad when she was at home and had work to fill her days, but she'd taken this week off to follow the latest lead with Nabel. She would have quit her job if she'd had to in order to be here; she'd spent the last four years of her life searching and waiting for this kind of a break.

Tossing the remote aside, she rose to her feet and strode over to the window. She pulled back the heavy curtains to peer out at the bright day. All she lived for now was the night, and it was still too far away for her liking. The night was when she could hunt the monsters plaguing their world, especially the monster that had been plaguing her.

With a sigh, she dropped the curtain into place and turned to face the room. She'd spent far too many of her years living in and out of hotel rooms just like this one. Over the years, they'd all blurred into one endless array of landscape paintings, industrial carpets, and threadbare comforters. They were all some form of beige or white with crappy fluorescent lighting in what was normally a pink or yellow bathroom. This one had thrown a curveball by sporting a blue bathroom with recessed lighting, but the rest of the tiny space was like all the rest.

Paige looked helplessly around the room; she could go back to the gym, but she didn't want to tire herself out before nightfall. She should be napping, but she was far too wired and excited to go to sleep. Grabbing some change and her room key, she stepped into the hall and headed down to the small vending machine area. She punched in the number for a bottle of water. She watched as it fell down and clanked against the machine when it hit bottom. Walking over to the next machine, she debated for a minute before settling on a bag of peanuts.

Heading back to her room, she paused outside of Nabel's door where she contemplated whether or not she should knock. They spent a fair amount of time together, but she wouldn't consider him her friend or someone she would normally pass the time with. She'd bet he felt the same way about her and wouldn't exactly appreciate having her perched on the end of his bed talking about the weather.

Four years ago, she would have just picked up her sketch pad and pencils in order to keep herself occupied, but it had been years since she'd sketched anything. She found herself pining for her old, artistic love as she headed back toward her lonely room. She didn't think she'd ever draw again, that obsession had been replaced with a new one, but at least it would have helped her kill the time.

Opening the bag of peanuts, she popped a couple in her mouth as she moved past his room and back toward hers. The TV was still going and Divorce Court was in session when she settled onto the bed again. She absently began to flip through the channels once more before turning back to look at the sun filtering around the edges of the thick curtains.

Only a few more hours, she told herself. Only a few more hours and she would be back on the hunt for the vampires ravaging their world.

Download *Enraptured* and continue reading:

brendakdavies.com/Enwb

Stay in touch on updates, sales, and new releases by joining to the mailing list:
brendakdavies.com/ESBKDNews

Visit the Erica Stevens/Brenda K. Davies Book Club on Facebook for exclusive giveaways and all things book related. Come join the fun:
brendakdavies.com/ESBKDBookClub

FIND THE AUTHOR

Brenda K. Davies Mailing List:
brendakdavies.com/News

Facebook: brendakdavies.com/BKDfb

Brenda K. Davies Book Club:
brendakdavies.com/BKDBooks

Instagram: brendakdavies.com/BKDInsta
Twitter: brendakdavies.com/BKDTweet
Website: www.brendakdavies.com

ALSO FROM THE AUTHOR

Books written under the pen name

Brenda K. Davies

<u>The Vampire Awakenings Series</u>

Awakened (Book 1)

Destined (Book 2)

Untamed (Book 3)

Enraptured (Book 4)

Undone (Book 5)

Fractured (Book 6)

Ravaged (Book 7)

Consumed (Book 8)

Unforeseen (Book 9)

Forsaken (Book 10)

Relentless (Book 11)

Legacy (Book 12)

<u>The Alliance Series</u>

Eternally Bound (Book 1)

Bound by Vengeance (Book 2)

Bound by Darkness (Book 3)

Bound by Passion (Book 4)

Bound by Torment (Book 5)

Bound by Danger (Book 6)

Bound by Deception (Book 7)

Bound by Fate (Book 8)

Bound by Blood (Book 9)

Bound by Love (Book 10)

The Road to Hell Series

Good Intentions (Book 1)

Carved (Book 2)

The Road (Book 3)

Into Hell (Book 4)

Hell on Earth Series

Hell on Earth (Book 1)

Into the Abyss (Book 2)

Kiss of Death (Book 3)

Edge of the Darkness (Book 4)

The Shadow Realms

Shadows of Fire (Book 1)

Shadows of Discovery (Book 2)

Shadows of Betrayal (Book 3)

Shadows of Fury (Book 4)

Shadows of Destiny (Book 5)

Shadows of Light (Book 6)

Wicked Curses (Book 7)

Sinful Curses (Book 8)

Gilded Curses (Book 9)

Whispers of Ruin (Book 10)

Coming Winter 2023/2024

Historical Romance

A Stolen Heart

Books written under the pen name

Erica Stevens

The Coven Series

Nightmares (Book 1)

The Maze (Book 2)

Dream Walker (Book 3)

The Captive Series

Captured (Book 1)

Renegade (Book 2)

Refugee (Book 3)

Salvation (Book 4)

Redemption (Book 5)

Vengeance (Book 6)

Unbound (Book 7)

Broken (Book 8 - Prequel)

The Kindred Series

Kindred (Book 1)

Ashes (Book 2)

Kindled (Book 3)

Inferno (Book 4)

Phoenix Rising (Book 5)

The Fire & Ice Series

Frost Burn (Book 1)

Arctic Fire (Book 2)

Scorched Ice (Book 3)

The Ravening Series

The Ravening (Book 1)

Taken Over (Book 2)

Reclamation (Book 3)

The Survivor Chronicles

The Upheaval (Book 1)

The Divide (Book 2)

The Forsaken (Book 3)

The Risen (Book 4)

ABOUT THE AUTHOR

Brenda K. Davies is the USA Today Bestselling author of the Vampire Awakening Series, Alliance Series, Road to Hell Series, Hell on Earth Series, and historical romantic fiction. She also writes under the pen name, Erica Stevens. When not out with friends and family, she can be found at home with her husband, son, dogs, cat, and horse.

Made in United States
Troutdale, OR
11/19/2024

25043985R00197